Susan Barker was born in 1978 to an English father and a Chinese-Malaysian mother. Her first novel, *Sayonara Bar*, was shortlisted for the Authors' Club First Novel Award, and both *Sayonara Bar* and *The Orientalist and the Ghost* were longlisted for the Dylan Thomas Award. She lives in London.

Acclaim for *Sayonara Bar*:

'A beautifully written and far-reaching exploration of Japanese culture' Rebecca Pearson, *Independent on Sunday*, Books of the Year

'Funny, crisply written and engaging, *Sayonora Bar* offers sharp insights into some of the less palatable realities of life in 21st century Japan' *The Times*

'With dry humour and crisp observation . . . Japan has not, for a long time, been made to seem so accessible, or so remote' *Literary Review*

'A stunningly eclectic début. Original, often perplexing, always intriguing, *Sayonara Bar* is a showpiece of breathtaking new talent' *Daily Record*

'Highly original . . . A major achievement by an exciting new author' *Independent on Sunday*

'Reminiscent of Haruki Murakami . . . Barker's descriptions are spot on' *JapanVisitor.com*

www.rbooks.co.uk

Also by Susan Barker

SAYONARA BAR

and published by Black Swan

The
ORIENTALIST
and the
GHOST

Susan Barker

BLACK SWAN

Transworld Publishers
61–63 Uxbridge Road, London W5 5SA
A Random House Group Company
www.rbooks.co.uk

THE ORIENTALIST AND THE GHOST
A BLACK SWAN BOOK: 9780552772419

First published in Great Britain
in 2008 by Doubleday
a division of Transworld Publishers
Black Swan edition published 2009

Addresses for Random House Group Ltd companies outside the UK
can be found at: www.randomhouse.co.uk
The Random House Group Ltd Reg. No. 954009

The Random House Group Limited supports The Forest Stewardship
Council (FSC), the leading international forest certification organisation.
All our titles that are printed on Greenpeace approved FSC certified paper
carry the FSC logo. Our paper procurement policy can be found at
www.rbooks.co.uk/environment

Typeset in 11/15pt Giovanni Book by
Falcon Oast Graphic Art Ltd.
Printed in the UK by CPI Cox & Wyman, Reading, RG1 8EX.

2 4 6 8 10 9 7 5 3 1

The
ORIENTALIST
and the
GHOST

Susan Barker

I

I

I am a man who lives in the company of ghosts. They have me under constant surveillance. They watch me cook my bachelor suppers of processed peas and boil-in-the-bag cod. They watch me take out my dentures and drop them in the tumbler fizzing with Steradent. They watch me undo my fly and tinkle in the lavatory. Some ghosts I loathe and some I fear with horripilation and cardiac strife. Others I quite look forward to seeing. The silent ghosts are preferable to the noisy, garrulous ones. *Aren't you a lonely old so-and-so?* said Marina Tolbin, the hawk-visaged missionary (who elected to remain sanctimoniously mute in life, but is strangely loquacious in death). *If only that were true*, I sighed, *but you lot never leave me alone*. Charles Dulwich, who drank the hemlock at the age of forty-six (romantically inspired, it seems, by the death of Socrates), crows of his eternal youth and my irreversible decline. *Where have all your teeth gone, old boy?* He chuckles. *Be careful now! That cup of tea might overstrain your bladder!* I can only sigh and say: *Do you think I can help this decrepitude? Not all of us have been blessed with an inclination for suicide, you know.*

Such merciless scrutiny! Worse still is when the ghosts relive the last anguished moments before dying (Why? Heaven knows! Perhaps to break up the monotony of being deceased). Nothing is more harrowing than watching Mrs Ho fall to her knees on my bedroom carpet, beating her chest in a masochistic frenzy (*Save my baby! Save my baby!* she screams as the flames devour her). Charles tends to lie quietly on my bed as the poison hastens his departure from the world. It is hardly the most riveting of performances, but if I ignore him he gets upset and goes about slamming cupboard doors and clattering my ironing board.

Sometimes I wonder how all the ghosts came here from Asia. Did they fly across together, soaring over continents and oceans like a diamond formation of migratory geese? Did they book flights on some airline of the paranormal? They complain about the factory greyness of the council estate, the many flights of stairs up to my flat, and of the syringe-strewn public urinal of a lift. *Oh, quit your moaning!* I tell them. *I never invited you here to invade my privacy!*

Three weeks ago Adam and Julia came to stay. They are not ghosts, but grandchildren. When they came, flooding my flat with energy and juvenescence, I was not sure if they and the ghosts would see eye to eye.

I thought the defiant youth of the children would frighten the ghosts away (or that the ghosts would frighten away the defiant youth – which would prove tricky to explain to social services). Fortunately neither child seems to have noticed all the phantoms flitting about. Not Julia with her shy, orthodontic smile and the handstands that flaunt her belly. Nor Adam, a teenager monstrous with acne, who locks himself away in the bathroom for hours on end to mourn his dead mother. However, in a flat as small as mine, it is impossible to keep hidden my dealings with the world of the dead. The children overhear me sometimes, talking in Cantonese or Hokkien or English as I converse with Ah Wing or Lieutenant Spencer. They have learnt not to interrupt, and quietly retreat to the bedroom they share. Julia saw me once, tearful in the kitchen as my beloved Evangeline threw crockery and flayed me with her tongue. Julia came and put her hand on my arm (for at twelve she has not yet learnt the selfish ways of a teenager). The poor child believed the tears were for her mother.

They are hard to decipher, these orphans. They are mysterious in their grief. Julia has hysterical fits of giggling, seemingly over nothing at all, and Adam is enamoured of the locked door and avocado-tiled interior of the bathroom. Sometimes they talk in a language I do not understand, like sparrows twittering in Latin. Adam wants me to buy a television and Julia trains to be an Olympic gymnast in the hallway. When they fight it seems as though they want to murder each other, though hours later I open their bedroom door to find the siblings in bed together, weeping in their underclothes (I fear there have been omissions in their upbringing; serious moral omissions). They both wrinkle their noses at the food I cook and they hate boil-in-the-bag cod. I cannot quite believe that they will stay here until they are old enough to leave. That seems like so many years from now . . .

And what of Frances, the daughter for whom I do not mourn?

Frances has yet to join the band of spirits that haunt my flat. But I know she is coming. Some nights I hear her, as spry flames leap in the hearth and her children sleep in the bedroom next door. I hear her as the residents in the block go up and down, up and down, troubling the lift cables into a rhapsody of creaking. I hear her over the wind, going berserk, like a mad dog let loose at the windowpane. I hear her over the howls of Lieutenant Spencer, his slimy intestines surging from his stomach in a re-enactment of the bayonet attack.

Frances Milnar, go away! I whisper. *Leave me alone!*

For heaven help me, the girl must be bent on revenge.

2

Let us go backwards. Quickly backwards. Let us reverse the decline of this ageing body. Let my liver spots fade, my follicles regenerate and my hairline unrecede. Let my skin tauten and tug my wrinkles out of sight. Let my teeth once more submerge themselves in my gums. Let the enamel calcify and fortify. Let my molar abscesses – the evil downfall of my dentition – heal and cast out decay. Let us reverse the crumbling of bones and correct my sinuosity of spine, so I stand tall and erect once more. Let my dying cells heal. Let my dormant member reawaken, and let Eros back in to torment me with libidinous throbs and urges. Let all that is grisly and slack revert to the aesthetics of wondrous youth. Oh, let there be youth! Let us keep going backwards; anticlockwise fifty years. I am a young man again. Do you see me? Gallant, broad and six feet tall. Fine sandy hair and handsome in the conventional, matinée-idol way. I am the one in the panama and linen suit, limp and undone in the Turkish-bath heat. The lone Caucasian, lost in the chaos of Kuala Lumpur airport. It is July 1951 and all around me Tamils, Chinese and Javanese are bustling; heaving weather-beaten suitcases and carrying parcels on heads; a sweltering hubbub of exotic noise. Malaya is three years into the Communist Emergency and seven long years from Independence. I am twenty-five – such abominable youth! – and an infatuated scholar of Chinese; an infatuation that led to the learning of three Chinese dialects before venturing beyond European soil. An infatuation that led me to the Crown Agencies for the Colonies, and to the Far East.

The airline had lost my trunk, and a Sumatran in a *songkok* and turquoise pyjamas informed me it had been left in Dubai. He scribbled down the telephone number to call, should I desire to reclaim it, and sent me on my way. All I had were the clothes on my back, my travel-bag (containing flannel, toothbrush and a well-thumbed copy of *The Handbook to the Emergency*) and a heinous throb in the Romanesque cartilage of my nose. The throb was ten days old and was acquired in Richmond-upon-Thames, when I broke off my engagement to the feisty Marion Forte-Cannon. *Oh, Christopher, you are a bore!* Marion had sighed, before launching her small fist into my face. I deserved it. Disgraceful of me to have kept up the whole engagement façade when I knew I was just waiting for the chance to escape. But what's a chap to do? Fate had

14

more excitement up its sleeve than a life of domesticity and high-tea at Forte-Cannon Hall.

I'd been sent to Malaya to help in the Emergency, a Communist insurrection started by the Chinese, who wanted a Red Malaya under their control. That was out of the question, of course. The British were still there and would never let them. Not because the British wanted to preserve their rule (indeed, I had entered a colonial service in terminal decline), but to get every-thing nice and orderly for Independence. As Charles used to say, *Englishmen never like to leave a mess*. But defeating the Communists was not as easy as everyone thought. They hid in jungle camps, surfacing only in guerrilla warfare. Because of these terror tactics the Emergency went on for over a decade, the Communists running amok, murdering and pillaging and tearing the country apart.

Disencumbered of trunk and possessions, I hailed a taxi for Yong Peng, or The Village of Everlasting Peace. In that old rattletrap of a cab I saw the rainforest for the first time; miles and miles of it, colossal and brilliant green. Great craggy limestone cliffs and rubber plan-tations of tyrannous uniformity. The taxi gasped and sputtered through a valley township, a government building at its hub, with a terrace of bougainvillaea and troops in string vests, playing cricket on the *padang*. We plunged back into dense jungle for a treacherous mile or two, and as we neared The Village of Everlasting

15

Peace we passed fields where Chinese farmers crouched, tending to sweet potato and tapioca crop, babies dangling in slings around their necks. The re-settlement camp was seven months old when I got there and had one thousand and fifty villagers. The perimeter fence was seven feet high and looped with barbed wire. Beyond the fence I saw slattern huts, bare-foot children and a sickly clump of banana trees. The village stretched for a quarter of a mile, ending at the ascent of a steep jungly hill on the far side.

The Village of Everlasting Peace was one of thousands of resettlement camps built to quarantine the Chinese squatters from the Communists. The government wanted to cut the terrorists off from the supporters who supplied them with money and food. So they rounded up the Chinese squatters in army trucks, burnt down their jungle settlements and brought them to live under government supervision in New Villages. It was a frightfully sad business. None of the squatters wanted to leave their homes and they cried and made a fuss. But the War against Communism was no ordinary war and could not be fought in an ordinary way. We had to hit them where it hurt.

The taxi halted at the village gates and the driver, a Tamil gentleman, asked me for the fare. We had attracted the attention of a Sikh guard, standing at the gate with a rifle slung over his shoulder. The guard wore a turban, a khaki jacket and shorts, and long woollen socks pulled up to his knees. He had tremendous, unkempt sideburns and his face was unctuous with sweat. Slamming the taxi door behind me, I went up to him and introduced myself as the new Assistant Resettlement Officer. I asked him if he'd be kind enough to show me to the office of Resettlement Officer Charles Dulwich. The Sikh guard adjusted his rifle, suspicious and taciturn. Sun-dizzy and unsteady on my feet, I repeated my introduction, taking care to speak very slowly. I was interrupted, however, by a great cockerel scurrying, shrieking, down the track towards us and thrashing its feathers in terror. Two Chinese boys scampered after the bird, beating the air with sticks and making war sounds. They halted when they saw me, and I said hello in three dialects. They stared and whispered and the cockerel scuttled and squawked to freedom. The boys then shouted a few words of Malay to the Sikh guard, who laughed and showed off his fine-looking teeth as he waved them away with the butt of his rifle.

Gesturing that I should follow, the guard led me through the gates. And as we journeyed deeper into the resettlement camp my stomach began to weigh more than a stomach ought. During my training for Colonial service I'd seen slide shows of the prototype New Village. The standard was basic, but the huts clean and functional, the villagers camera-shy but good-natured. The Village of Everlasting Peace fell atrociously short of this ideal. It were as though I'd passed through a looking-glass, held up to the prototype to reflect back poverty and filth: a shantyland of cheap huts knocked up from plywood, corrugated iron and palm leaves – huts likely to collapse if the occupants so much as sneezed. Rubbish was heaped in stinking piles as though monuments to the spirit of squalor. Poultry strutted on the hard-trodden earth, indiscriminate about where they pecked and defecated. I heard the dying squeals of a pig as it was slaughtered. The village, I thought, was ripe for disease.

Rubber tapping had finished for the day, but most villagers had gone to work in the vegetable gardens, leaving only the elderly and children behind. The elderly shuffled about, wattles quivering, toothless and sunken-cheeked. Urchins sweeping with brooms taller than they were themselves stared at me out of solemn moonchild eyes. A lame man spat betel-nut juice. An old crone with the wicked glint of dementia crouched in a doorway, throwing scraps to her ducklings. On the door frame hung lucky charms of red and gold, blessing her hovel with sons and prosperity.

'Are you a government spy sent to find out which of us are Communists?' she called out in Cantonese.

'No,' I said. 'I work for the government but I am not here to spy.'

'Hah!' said the woman, 'that is what all the government agents say.'

The Sikh guard had moved on and to catch him up I dashed across a perilously wobbly plank bridging a ditch. On the other side of the ditch a girl was bent by a standpipe, washing potatoes dug out of the soil. The girl was pretty and wore her hair in plaits. When she saw me she blushed and a potato leapt from her hand, as though petrified by her strength of attraction to me. *Gosh!* I thought as the girl scrabbled about after the leaping potato. *They aren't bad, these Chinese girls.* And I felt the unhappy throbbing in my nose subside.

The Sikh guard led me to a wooden bungalow, the only building in the village fit for human habitation. He went up on the veranda and shouted: '*Tuan, Tuan!*'

'No need to shout,' came a voice. 'I'm right behind you.'

I turned round and saw Charles Dulwich for the first time. Good old Charles; pink and steaming with perspiration, and built like a grizzly bear. He beamed and shambled towards us as though the heat had him in shackles. He took my hand in his huge damp paw and shook it.

'Resettlement Officer Charles Dulwich. You must be my new assistant. Splendid.'

Charles had the physiognomy of a dissolute aristocrat. He had a magnificent, meandering nose (broken twice while he was a POW in Singapore) and an alcoholic's complexion, jaundiced and spidery of capillary. When he smiled, the skin around his eyes gathered into deltas of a thousand and one tributaries. He was forty-four when I met him and at the time I thought he was terrifically old.

Charles showed me inside the bungalow, to the rudimentary office with desks and chairs, concrete floor and chicken-wire windows. We each sat down in a rattan chair, or, rather, Charles sat and I *collapsed*. Two days of air travel and the trauma of separation from my trunk had left me fatigued. Furthermore I was depressed by conditions in the village and had to summon the best of my acting skills to hide this. In a bright, inquisitive manner I asked about the villagers and the day-to-day running of the resettlement camp. Charles confessed he was more of an administrator than a 'friend of the people' and attributed this failure to language barriers.

'That's why you're here, old chap,' he said, 'to build bridges between us Foreign Devils and the Chinese.'

Charles dabbed his brow with his handkerchief and told me frankly that my predecessor, the late Ah Wing, hadn't been much of a bridge-builder – in fact, his cold imperious manner had infested the waters with crocodiles.

'Is that why he was murdered?' I asked.

Charles said it may have been a factor.

'Well, I shall do my best to avoid the same fate!' I joked, fatigue robbing me of taste.

Charles apologized for the mess on my desk, cluttered with the late Ah Wing's unfinished paperwork, a green Olivetti and a portrait of a fierce little Chinese lady. The table legs stood in china cups of kerosene and water, ant death traps full of their little black carcasses. It was late in the afternoon and the villagers were returning from the vegetable gardens, jangling bicycle bells and calling to one another, voices rising and falling in colloquial scales. I heard a woman shouting: 'Second daughter! Where are you? Tell third brother to fetch water from the well!' I heard notes faltering from a bamboo flute and the bleating of a goat in its pen.

Let me stop here and confess: my memory is not what it used to be. The events of this morning are already lost in the mists of vagueness. Did I return my library books? Did I go to the town hall and register Adam and Julia for free school dinners? Other resources have to be consulted. So how can it be that the dull, plaintive, half-century-old bleats of a goat are sharper in my memory than a news bulletin heard on the radio not twenty minutes ago? The ether amasses into a finger of blame and points to all the ghosts, the spectral émigrés of my days in Malaya. I often wonder why I've only acquired ghosts from the bandit-ridden end of the Colonial era, and not from any other time in my life. I can't puzzle it out. Old Smythe across the hall died of natural causes in February (God rest his soul) and I've not seen hide nor hair of him since. Resettlement Officer Charles Dulwich, on the other hand, committed suicide forty-eight years ago, but was in my kitchen only last night, smoking opium and reminiscing about the evening we sat on the veranda drinking whisky *stengahs*, as the gramophone trumpeted out 'Ride of the Valkyries' and the villagers cooked Humphrey the Saint Bernard on a great fire. *Do you remember the smell of roast dog?* Charles said. *I drool at the memory*. I'd been terribly fond of Humphrey and didn't care to remember. But *eau de* charred canine filled my nostrils anyway. Just as Charles, the beast, wished it to.

Not all the ghosts are as bothersome as Charles (thank God). Most of the visitations are silent, isolated fragments of the past, recurring in the here and now, before dissolving into nothingness. Sometimes the Sikh guard stands sentinel outside the hallway cupboard, rifle slung over his shoulder, his skin slick with equatorial humidity. Sometimes the pretty girl with the plaits bends in front of the fireplace, washing potatoes as the gas valves hiss. The girl, absorbed in rinsing mud off a potato, then looks up, startled, and the potato once again makes that eternal leap of lust, as though I were a handsome young man of twenty-five, and not the rheumy-eyed old devil lying in ambush in the bath-room mirror. Every day dozens of the not-so-dearly departed come to my living quarters, whatever non-corporeal substance they are made of transfiguring into ephemeral scenes of the past. Every single God-forsaken day. Pity this old man, for they will never let me forget.

The bicycle bells trilled and the bamboo flautist performed his folk-song, and Charles clapped his hands and shouted, *Boy!* and a sulky-mouthed Malay presented himself in the doorway. Charles barked an order to the youth, who disappeared, then reappeared with two glasses on a teakwood tray; all sensual hip movement and demurely lowered camel lashes. He had the prettiest eyes I'd ever seen, and had obviously been destined to be a seductress of the highest order, though some unhappy quirk of fate made him a boy instead, which was of no good to anyone (or so I naively thought at the time). He served us our drinks and lemon-barley water spilt everywhere.

'That vain creature is incapable of putting anything down without sloshing it,' Charles said crossly.

He barked again to the boy, who sulked out on to the veranda. Seconds later there was a flutter above Charles's head as a fan of fluted paper wafted the air, disturbing his pale Byronic curls. The fan was attached to the ceiling and was moved back and forth by a length of string. The string descended to the veranda, where it ended in a loop secured around the big toe of the servant boy. The servant boy sat on a chair, swinging his foot and simmering with humiliation. I thought the contraption vulgar and decadent and very clever. Under the fluted paper breeze Charles tippled on gin and lemon barley and enlightened me about my future duties as Assistant Resettlement Officer.

Evening came and consumed Malaya with a rich and sultry darkness. As Charles lit an oil lamp a powerful siren tore through the village.

'Seven p.m. curfew,' Charles said. 'All the villagers are confined to their huts from now till five a.m.'

'Does the curfew apply to us as well?' I asked.

'No. Though to stray beyond the fence after dark might be damaging to your life expectancy.' Charles gave a rueful chuckle, like a host regretting the north-facing aspect of the guestroom.

We dined on the veranda, the kerosene lamp bringing in moths from far and wide. How the winged fiends rejoiced, pirouetting and colliding midair, their shadowy doppelgängers looming on the walls. We dined on quail-egg soup, duck in ginger and *hoi sin* sauce, jasmine rice and a dessert of lychees and rambutans, served to us by Winston Lau, the cook. Once he'd put the plates on the table Winston retreated to the shadows, hungering for leftovers and resenting what mouthfuls we ate.

Much of the village could be seen from the veranda. One could see as far as the perimeter fence, where armed guards strolled by on night patrol. Tilly lamps illuminated the outermost foliage of the jungle; threshold to the land of scorpions, flying reptiles and orang-utan (and other beasts of razor teeth and poison stings in my wildlife encyclopaedia of South East Asia). The jungle was nature at its most terrible and prolific. Beneath the tranquil surface of leaves it lay in wait, claws protracted.

Candle- and lamp-light leaked from hut doorways and the ventilation gaps under the roofs. Charles told me how the Chinese families lived in those huts in the hours of curfew; how they piddled in buckets and slept back-to-back on thin reed mats, always breathing the breath of others. The look on my face betrayed my disquiet, and Charles quickly reassured me that the squatter culture is very different from ours, and the Chinese are less desirous of privacy.

No sooner had we laid down our forks than Winston Lau swiped our plates and substituted them with tall warm bottles of Tiger beer. The presence of the beer, or perhaps the hiss of liberated carbonates as bottle opener detached cap, soon enticed a gang of Malay Special Constables. They had a slow, languid walk and carefree laughter, as if the rifles they wore were for hunting squirrels. They laughed to hear who I was – as though I were the incarnation of some joke they'd heard about Englishmen – and introduced themselves melodiously; a barbershop quartet of Abdullahs and Mohammeds. They bantered with Charles in Malay and accepted his offer of beer – anticipation of this offer having brought them over in the first place. They drank with drowsy smiles and I found it hard to imagine them chasing bandits or shooting guns or being anything other than good-natured and lazy.

After they had gone I began to yawn – mad, despotic yawns that wrenched my mouth into a fathomless cave. The night was syrupy with heat and the mosquitoes had savaged me, leaving my skin a hideously itchy, bumpy terrain. I scratched, irresponsible as a dog with fleas, until my arms became swollen and bled rubies of blood.

On my hundredth yawn Charles stood up and announced he would put some music on. 'Jolly good,' I murmured.

In his absence the throb of my pulse, made loud and authoritative by alcohol, came into the foreground. The night shuddered with it, the pulsations so forceful I imagined that they were external to me, emanating from the creatures in the jungle undergrowth. 'Violons dans la nuit' started up on the gramophone and the veranda swam in an adagio of strings. Charles returned and, standing before me, made a speech welcoming me to Malaya, a fiendish halo of moths fluttering about his choirboy curls. The speech touched and saddened me and as we clinked together our warm bottles of Tiger beer I was oddly stricken. I told Charles I was going to bed soon after that. The gramophone hissed as we said goodnight, the needle bumping over the empty vinyl at the end of the record.

Later that night I lay in the dark of my hut, on a camp-bed mattress that bore the stains of my predecessor like some lesser Turin shroud. (I flipped the mattress but on the other side found stains of a more sinister and ambiguous nature.) Mosquitoes droned beyond the net, the minute bristling of insect legs and antennae seeming to reside inside my ears. The mattress was slack and weak-sprung and I made a thousand revolutions in my sleeplessness, a human tombola trying to outwit the heat. As I lay there, sweat pooling in the hollows of my flesh, I pined for England; for a temperate climate and Greenwich Mean Time. I thought of Marion Forte-Cannon and hoped her hatred of me would not last, and that she would find another man to marry (old Marion did, thrice over, each husband wealthier than the last). I thought of Charles and his platypus nose, the broken veins in his face like contour lines on a map for alcoholics. I thought of my predecessor Ah Wing, murdered by the Communists, his throat slit so deeply he was near beheaded. They threw his corpse across a path at the Bishop's Head plantation and though four hundred tappers had filed past it on their way home from work not one of them reported the crime back at the village. (Kip Phillips, the plantation manager, discovered poor old Ah Wing that evening, fire ants crawling over him, his spilt blood as thick as treacle.) I thought of my trunk and possessions, my books of Chinese calligraphy and folk-tales, being hawked in a marketplace somewhere in Dubai. I thought of the busy day ahead of me and the necessity of sleep. But dawn came and the sky lightened. And that first night in Malaya I never slept at all.

3

Last night I dreamt I was a wild hog, careering through the jungle. Squealing and galloping as fast as my trotters would carry me, rattan vines lashing me and tree roots snaking across the trail. Behind me came the stampeding of jungle boots and the shouts of huntsmen in Malay and Cantonese, upper-class English and cockney slang, united in the waving of axes and bamboo spears. My heart was an organ of impossible loudness, louder even than my abattoir squeals, and through sow eyes I saw my snout, whiskers of grey and the rounded tusks of my savage underbite. I ran and ran, and made piggy retching sounds as the jungle breathed its primordial breath. The trail widened into a small clearing, the canopy soaring up into a cathedral of leaves. My stumpy legs buckled there and I belly-flopped upon the springy moss. I squeezed my eyes shut. *What a way to go*, I thought, as the jungle boots stomped into the clearing, the shouts became cheers, and the first sharpened stick of bamboo pierced my flesh.

The imaginary pain woke me, sent me flailing upright on the brink of cardiac arrest. As I wheezed and clutched at my chest, Charles Dulwich sat on the end of my fold-out bed, guffawing and dabbing at spectral tears of mirth.

'That was hilarious!' he said. 'That was the funniest nightmare you've had in a long time! Not even safe in the arms of Morpheus, are you, now?'

Charles brandished an opium pipe and was blowing mauvish smoke about the living room. I was too breathless to reply, my pyjamas clammy with the sweat of my subconscious trauma. The mantelpiece clock said it was five past three. Somewhere on the estate a police siren whooped. I ignored Charles and clambered out of bed.

Light shone beneath the door of my old bedroom (now taken over by the orphan siblings) and I heard the rustle of a swiftly turned page. The boy was up reading again. I ought to have told him, as his legal guardian, to get some rest for school. But Adam hasn't been to school in weeks. Julia is out of the door at eight fifteen every morning (odd socks on, buttered toast in her mouth, the knot of her school tie dangling halfway down her shirt) but her lazy brother stays in bed till noon. When he eventually wakes he'll go to the bathroom and meddle with his acne in the mirror for twenty minutes or so. Then he'll sit by the gas fire for the rest of the day, reading his library books. For, though a truant, Adam is a bibliophile truant, an omnivorous reader of D. H. Lawrence, *Basic Plumbing Skills Parts I and II*, Harlequin romances and lurid horrors with blood-splattered jacket designs. As much as I admire his autodidactic streak, he really ought to be in school. 'An O level or two won't do you any harm, Adam,' I tell him. But I don't go on. The boy is old enough to make up his own mind. Besides, one must be grateful he's not a yob. Every child on this estate seems predestined for a life of thuggery – even the most angelic youngsters growing up into thieves and drug addicts and racialists who persecute the Somalis and the Kapoors who live above the shop.

I wasn't keen on the boy loafing about the flat at first. But I've grown used to Adam and his strange antisocial habits – just as he has grown used to mine. He has seen how I rage at the Chinese Detective Pang, how I weep and cower when Evangeline batters me about the head with the frying skillet. When the harassment gets a bit much I go to the kitchen, or climb inside the hallway cupboard. Or Adam might take his book and read on the lavatory. Poor Adam. The school has sent me letters, but what am I to do? I can hardly drag a fifteen-year-old there by the ear, now, can I?

Fortunately Julia (or Jules, as she prefers to be called) never misses a day of school. She likes it there so much she won't get home until eight thirty most nights. 'Homework club,' she tells me. 'Smoking club, more like!' I say. Her navy blazer and grubby mitts reek of nicotine. I told her there'd be no more homework club for her with that carry-on, so now she comes home smelling of spray-on deodorant and spearmint gum. Julia is a mucky little miss. There's always dirt under her nails and tide-marks on her neck. Run her a bath and she'll splash about for two minutes, then yank out the plug and put her nightie on. And don't get me started on her teeth. Whatever must her teachers think?

Seeing as the boy never goes to school anyway, I left Adam to his nocturnal reading and went to the lavatory. I assumed the position and waited a good long while, but there wasn't a drop to be had from the old codger. My bladder is always sending me false alarms, and in the meantime I stand about shivering and risking hypothermia.

When I returned to the living room Charles said, 'Looks like the old plumbing's gone kaput. I dare say you have a kidney infection. You stink of wee-wee!'

I ignored him and huddled under my blankets. Charles began humming some jaunty swing tune, an old favourite on Radio Malaya. I could hear the click of the opium pipe against his teeth, the suck and blissful exhalation. He was wearing that ghoulish smile of his, green and sickly with opiates.

'Tell me, Christopher,' he said, the timbre of his hum carrying over to the spoken word, 'do you have an un-conditional love of life?'

'I don't have an unconditional love of anything,' I said.

The springs of the fold-out bed creaked as Charles made himself nice and comfy.

'Really? Not even for that Jezebel, that sly fornicatress and common harlot Evangeline Lim?' He chuckled. 'You never knew the pain was going to last this long, did you? How long have you been suffering for now? My gosh! Half a century or more! You thought you would get over it, in six months, a year. But here you are, an old man, and the pain is still with you, just as sharp and sweet and excruciating.'

I sighed and pulled the blanket over my head. The old dope fiend does get on my nerves.

'Tell me honestly, if you knew fifty years ago, on the day you nearly died, that you were never going to be happy again, that the rest of your life would be lived in the shadow of your pain, wouldn't you have wished yourself dead? Wouldn't you have slashed your wrists with a razor in the officers' bathing hut? Or leapt from the watchtower with a noose round your neck . . .'

Ever since he drank the hemlock in 1953, Charles has rather fancied himself as something of a dark prince. I refuse to flatter this delusion.

'Suicide is childish,' I said. 'It's pathetic and cowardly and vain. I may not have an unconditional *love* of life, but I do have an unconditional adherence to it.'

'Hah!' Charles laughed. 'That's just the kind of Goody Two-Shoes answer I'd expect from you. Well, let me share with you the good news: your days of adherence will soon be over!'

Charles began humming that jaunty swing tune

again, but it faded away after a few bars. He stayed at the end of the bed, smoking quietly for the remainder of the night. I knew this because I was unable to sleep until the sky went grey. I lay shivering under my blankets, the icy slivers in my marrow refusing to thaw. I blamed Charles for my insomnia and wished him gone. *You aren't my boss any more, Charles Dulwich!* I thought crossly. *You are long dust and bones, buried in the ground.* I'm not sure if he heard me or not, but, as I said, he did not go away.

My first days in The Village of Everlasting Peace were miserable. I'd always been a happy-go-lucky chap, but the filth and squalor and bouquet of human sewage gave rise to an uncommon feeling of despair. I was homesick, puffy and itchy with mosquito venom. The Malay policemen called me 'Mistah Ingerris!' and made fun of my sunburnt skin, which peeled away in leprous shreds. The villagers laughed at me too. They tittered to hear my Cantonese, swinging like a wrecking ball between pidgin dialect and keen grammatical preciseness. I set out on a quest to speak more colloquially, unlearning the rules learnt at university and appointing every villager as my teacher. I consulted rubber tappers about verb usage while probing their socks for smuggled rice at the village check-point. I had children correct my pronunciation as we tore about, chasing geese for shuttlecock feathers. Here and there I made a friend, and it made all the difference to village life. Before long the plywood shacks assumed the guise of normality and the barbed wire looping the village seemed as natural as the rattan vines choking the rain-forest, and less of a man-made means of segregation.

Each day in The Village of Everlasting Peace began with the four a.m. trill of my alarm clock. I'd yawn and stretch and pull a cord so the gauzy layers of the mosquito net lifted to the ceiling. Then, after tethering the cord to the frame of the camp-bed, in my under-pants I'd pad in the dark to the officers' bathing hut (the village was still under curfew, making an encounter with any young lady unlikely). The bathing hut contained a large barrel from which I would scoop water to rinse away the night's stickiness. I always bathed in the light of a battery-operated torch hang-ing from the ceiling, and never alone, for as soon as I started ladling water over myself a family of ribbiting toads would pitter-patter out from behind the barrel to accompany me in a good splashing. (Over the months I became rather fond of my amphibian friends and was aghast when one day at tiffin Winston Lau brought out a plate of tiny roast cadavers, proudly telling me of the trap he'd rigged up behind the barrel.) Goose-pimply from my bath, I'd shave with the aid of a communal cut-throat razor and rusty mirror, the sky lightening to reveal the eerie mists hanging over the jungly hills. Back in my hut I'd open a tin of peaches, spearing up the pieces with my penknife and drinking the syrupy juice. I've always been a lover of the early dawn. My mind is sharpest before the sun has risen. Seated at my slanting desk I'd study Mandarin, or translate the propaganda leaflets of the Malayan Races Liberation Party, until the klaxon wail announcing the end of curfew. Then I'd leap into my shirt and trousers, looping the braces over my shoulders, and hurry on down to the check-point.

Every morning hundreds of Chinese tappers queued in the pre-dawn gloom, rattling latex-collecting tins, jouncing babies and leaning impatiently on bicycle handlebars. Though the siren had howled, the east gate was often shut when I arrived, the guards – visible through the police-hut window – eating samosas and drinking sweet tea. The plantation was a two-mile trek away and the tappers had to collect as much rubber as they could before it congealed in the noonday heat. *Hurry up, hurry up, it's five o'clock already! We have to go to work*, they'd grumble, glaring at the guards and cursing their ancestors. *Good! Here comes the big-nosed devil!* they'd say when they saw me. *Hey, tell those lazy Malays to hurry up and let us out! Drink tea, drink tea! That's all they ever do* ... My predecessor, the late Assistant Resettlement Officer Ah Wing, would not have tolerated such cheek. Ah Wing was a disciplinarian who sent bolshie tappers to the back of the queue. But I would rap on the police-hut door on their behalf, calling the guards away from their dawn banquet of Darjeeling and dahl.

Check-point duty was managed by four guards, a policeman up in the lookout tower (manning a machine gun that rotated to counter both a jungle attack and a village insurrection) and myself, acting as translator. The tappers were inspected two by two. First we had to check that the face on the identity card corresponded to that of the tapper (to ensure that he or she was a legitimate villager and not some Communist impostor). This was no easy feat, as to the untrained eye the Chinese are a very homogenous race. Also, most of the Chinese squatters, having never been photographed before, were wide-eyed in the snapshots (as if being violently goosed), petrified the camera might steal something of their souls. Once identity had been veri-fied we moved on to the body search. Ponytails were undone and hair combed loose. Torches were shone into ears, mouths, nostrils and belly-buttons. Suspicious bulges were prodded and tappers ordered to disrobe to clear up ambiguities. The men resented us frisking their wives. The women resented laying their squalling babies on the ground so we could check inside their nappies. The cyclists resented dismantling their bicycles to let us peer inside the hollow frames. Even water bottles had to be unscrewed and tasted to check for sugar.

It was very strict and time-consuming and tedious. The policemen operated on a guilty-until-proven-innocent principle, manhandling the villagers in a way that initially shocked me. Yet as the days wore on, and I learnt more about the villagers' smuggling techniques, the guards' draconian measures began to seem appro-priate. Any tapper caught violating Emergency Regulation 4C (concerning the movement of provisions into restricted areas) was taken to the police hut for questioning. Once the villagers had been packed off to detention camp I would reread their statements in bewilderment.

Name: Mr Tan
Contraband: Antibiotic tablet, inserted in left nostril.
Statement: *I am old and senile. I often misplace things.*

Name: Miss Yok Lan Ong
Contraband: Encoded message on cigarette paper, rolled and inserted in skirt hem.
Statement: *I do not know how that got there. Someone must have put it in my skirt when it was out on the washing line.*

Name: Miss Tammy Lai
Contraband: Vial of morphine and syringe, placed in her baby's nappy.
Statement: *I am a busy mother of five children. I cannot be expected to keep an eye on them all of the time.*

It was very depressing when a villager was sent to detention camp. I doubt many of them were genuine supporters of the Malayan Races Liberation Army. They smuggled because they'd been blackmailed into it by terrorists who stole up on them while they were tapping and pressed knives to their throats. Or because they had fathers and sons among the jungle bandits and they didn't want them to starve. Far more was smuggled beyond the check-point than we detected. Sergeant Abdullah had a theory that most contraband was smuggled in the lower-body cavities. *A woman of child-bearing age could take up to half a katis of rice,* he told me, *and the men never waddle like that on the journey home.*

The unfortunates at the end of the queue had to wait an hour or two to get beyond the check-point. Every inch the sun edged over the horizon was several *ringgit* lost. (*I won't make enough to feed my family this week!* the last in the queue complained.) I was always relieved to flee the east gate at eight, not least because that was the hour the market gardeners set off for work, presenting the guards with buckets of pig excrement to inspect.

Every morning I took my second breakfast on the veranda with Charles. It was never the most pleasant of meals, for Charles possessed a dichotomy of character and the morning saw him at his worst.

In the hours of moonlight Charles was Bacchus, roaring his heart out as Wagner trumpeted from the gramophone. He'd raise his glass of whisky (or gin or rum or *crème de menthe*) and make magniloquent toasts to the future independence of Malaya, to the victory of the Allied Forces or to the afternoon his Japanese jailers huddled around hand grenades and blew themselves to smithereens. Then he'd get a bit silly and raise a glass to Winston Lau's spicy *laska*, or the piebald mongrel trotting by the officers' hut. In the evening time, assisted by his old friends Johnny Walker and Jack Daniels, Charles was in buoyant spirits.

But in the cruel morning light he was crapulent and bestial, as if he'd descended a few rungs of the evolutionary ladder. He'd scowl in his rattan chair, his shirt buttoned up incorrectly beneath his red braces, his sparse curls wet from the bathing hut. I'd eat my condensed-milk sandwiches and try to ignore Charles as he took wincing sips of his coffee (twice-brewed to tarry potency), Radio Malaya playing tunes of breezy *joie de vivre*, in mockery of our grim repast.

I think it was a misguided sense of duty that made me endure Charles's gargoylesque turn of mouth and yellow-tinctured skin every morning. The hungover Charles seemed to exist in demonstration of some universal principle concerning the conservation of pleasure: *he who inducts the fire of whisky into his veins so the warmth spreads throughout in mimicry of joy shall awaken to a bolt of pain in the skull* . . . I had no sympathy for Charles's self-inflicted misery. While I'd been up since before daybreak, inspecting trouser waistbands for hidden glucose tablets as part of 'Operation Starvation', Charles had been in his bed, snoring those deafening snores of his, infamous throughout the village.

Once sufficiently caffeinated by his special twice-brewed coffee, Resettlement Officer Dulwich would put on his seersucker suit and we'd go to the office to attend to the administrative business of The Village of Everlasting Peace. First I'd read aloud the incident reports filed by the night patrol; of sniper fire from the hills, or villagers arrested for hurling boots over the perimeter fence for the bandits. Then Charles would dictate letters to the District War Committee and the Malayan Chinese Association, requesting funding for more barbed wire and guards, which I clattered out on the Olivetti. Shielded by our panama hats, we'd tour the village in the mid-morning heat, noting what facilities had fallen into disrepair and areas where the *lalang* grass had overgrown (providing cover for the Reds to slither up on their bellies and ambush us). I must confess that as we walked among the ramshackle fly-blown shacks, the popularity of Resettlement Officer Dulwich was rather eclipsed by that of his young assistant. Bare-gummed old ladies would cry out honorific greetings to me and mudlark children would fly lovingly at my shins. The neglected Charles seemed undismayed – or simply too hungover to care – and as we strolled would tut-tut and say: 'Order must be imposed on this mess.' Though only one tenth of the villagers were literate Charles penned civic-minded messages which I translated into Mandarin and posted about The Village of Everlasting Peace.

Villagers! Please think of your neighbours. Do not let piglets and children wander into other people's huts.

In the interests of hygiene please refrain from urinating in areas other than the latrines. Anyone caught doing so will be put on fence-mending duty for seven days.

Anyone caught gambling/eating opium/offering or soliciting the services of prostitution will be arrested, and/or have their rice ration halved.

The Emergency Information Services sent us posters of Surrendered Enemy Personnel to display as part of the anti-Communist campaign. The posters were designed by a team of government propagandists, who were so-called experts in psychological warfare and the mechanics of the Chinese mind. I recall a poster of one pot-bellied defector named Meng. Beneath his smiling photograph was the government's rallying cry for mass surrender:

Sick and tired of seeing loved ones starve and risk their lives fighting a hopeless cause in the jungle? Why not persuade them to turn themselves in? Meng walked out of the jungle three months ago and hasn't looked back since. See how healthy and well-fed he is! And soon he will be reunited with his wife. We understand that Communists make mistakes and are human too . . .

I dare say Meng looked the type to defect from his own mother for a pork dumpling or two, and I had my misgivings as I stapled up that poster. Sure enough, hours later Meng had been rebranded in red ink as an 'Imperialist Running Dog Traitor' and had to be retired from public view.

After tiffin, when the sun was at its zenith and scorched the earth so fiercely even one's shadow went into hiding, Resettlement Officer Dulwich typed up progress reports, or met with Sergeant Abdullah to discuss village security and drink tea with a splash of brandy (or gin or whisky or Amaretto), leaving me free to muck in where I pleased. On Wednesday afternoons the First Battalion Worcestershire Regiment came to help with the construction of the school building, and I often lent a hand there, whistling and hammering planks with the British Tommies. Or I'd troop in the sunshine with the Malay guards patrolling the perimeter fence. When I'd had enough of the security forces I roamed the market gardens, chatting to the toiling villagers and lending an ear to complaints about the over-strict curfew, poor irrigation and a cantankerous spirit that drifted from hut to hut at night, slapping awake first-born sons.

My favourite weekday afternoons were on Tuesday and Thursday, for those were the days the Australian Red Cross nurses came. As their armoured van rumbled into the village, ailing market-gardeners would throw down their hoes and spades and hurry to queue by the medical hut. It never failed to put the brighteners on everyone. I don't see very much of the Aussie nurses Madeleine and Josie these days. I bumped into Maddy in the kitchen of my flat about a month ago, looking heartbreakingly young in a blouse and nurses' pinafore, a Red Cross cap atop her bouncy curls. She had a scouring pad in one hand and a bottle of Cif cleanser in the other, and was scrubbing month-old frying-pan splatters from around the cooker hob.

'There's no need for that, Maddy,' I said.

'Oh, yes, there is!' replied my domineering lovely, scrubbing vigorously. 'If you cleaned up your messes you wouldn't have this impossible build-up of grease. Scrub-a-dub-dub, Christopher, every day! And did you know there's a legion of fossilized peas under the fridge? Disgraceful!'

Then she vanished, leaving the kitchen suffused with a lovely lemony fragrance.

Due to the infrequency of their spectral visits Madeleine and Josie are the most difficult of my Malaya-era acquaintances to remember. I can only conjure up the creamy essence of them: the warm biscuity perfume of their sun-freckled limbs, the tawny wisps loosened from their efficient nurses' buns, the rubber-band twang of their Aussie accents. I went to see them in my very first week in The Village of Everlasting Peace, to get ointment for my mosquito bites (I had twenty-seven itchy bumps the size of tuppenny bits). As I pointed out the worst of them, the nurses' lips twitched with mirth. (*Jeez, Maddy! Check out the Pom and his mozzie bites! There, there, now. We'll put a little calamine on them for you. Hold still and be a big boy!*) As Nurse Josie bent over to remove the calamine from the medical case, the hem of her pinafore lifted to show off her plump calves, the freshly laundered cotton hugging her ample behind. A memory flashed in my mind, of Marion Forte-Cannon flaunting herself in a similar manner over the chaise-longue, but *sans* nurses' uniform (or any kind of meaningful attire), a radiant *you-have-my-consent-to-ravish-me* smile tossed over her shoulder. In the later, unhappier stages of our relationship the smile deteriorated into an *oh-for-God's-sake-be-a-man-and-ravish-me* scowl, but romantic nostalgia inspired me none the less to politely clear my throat and say: 'You know, you two girls really ought to have someone to translate Cantonese for you. Help you understand the villagers' symptoms.'

I nodded to a dour Chinese lady, whom I assumed was waiting to be seen. Nurse Josie also gestured to the old crab-apple.

'Awww . . . that's sweet of you, Christopher,' she said, 'but we've already got the best interpreter in the village, haven't we, Evangeline?'

I gave the Chinese lady a puzzled glance, without the faintest intuition she was to be my future beloved and the source of fifty years of mental anguish. Evangeline was no beauty, and certainly not the stuff of erotic daydreams. Cupid's desire-tipped arrow did not prick my heart.

In 1951 Evangeline Lim was thirty-eight years old, though the hardships endured during the Occupation had aged her by a decade. Her eyes were wrinkle-shrouded, her nose battered out of shape, and her lips miserly and thin. And as if further to ruin her looks, her hair was cropped like a man's. Evangeline did possess one exquisite feature, though. Her eyes, I was to discover, were the colour of smoke (a sure sign of misbehaving

44

colonial forefathers) and as one gazed into them the irises gently spiralled and evanesced. On the afternoon we first met, however, her eyes performed none of their magic. They were cold and suspicious and dark as stones.

'How do you do, Evangeline,' I said. 'You speak English, do you? Terrific. Perhaps we could translate together.'

That solemn creature did not smile back. She responded in a queer-rhythmed English; strangled, with none of the usual Malay-accented warmth.

'Thank you, but your assistance is not necessary. I taught English for eight years at Kajang High School, so I am more than proficient. Also I don't think the villagers will want you here. They are very shy of their diseases, and it is hard enough already for them to come here without some white man staring at them too.'

It hadn't occurred to me that the Chinese peasants might be 'shy of their diseases'. This more than justified my banishment from the medical hut. *Ah well*, I thought sadly, *farewell, lovely nurses! Back to the company of stinky, grunty, khaki-clad men* . . .

'Forgive me,' I said. 'I so wanted to lend a hand . . .'

I thought the nurses would agree with Evangeline, but Nurse Maddy, staring determinedly at the loose strip of muslin bandage she was rolling up, said: 'If Christopher wants to help I don't see why not. We can ask the villagers if it's OK. Most won't mind, I'm sure. And if they do then the Pom can step outside during their examination.'

Good old Nurse Maddy! I thought. Evangeline went a thunderous shade, but said nothing. Only later was I to discover how proud she was of her role as medical-hut translator, and how she wanted it to remain hers and hers alone.

And so began the war of the interpreters.

I embarked upon my career as co-translator a gentleman – politely nodding and smiling when Evangeline saw fit to correct and contradict me. But like most young men I had a lively competitive spirit (it wasn't my impeccable p's and q's that got me promoted to captain of the St Andrews University fencing team!) and my gentlemanly powers could only hold out for so long. The sick villagers became pawns in our quest for one-upmanship; the medical hut, the arena for our grammatical duels and jousts. Together we'd peer at bunions and tonsils swollen to the size of ping-pong balls and listen to descriptions of their physical woes. Then we'd relay what we'd heard to the Red Cross nurses, making sly digs at each other. Our attempts at stealth were laughable. The Red Cross nurses were constantly sighing, eyes lifted to heaven, or exchanging knowing smiles. (To this day I don't know why they didn't chuck me out. Perhaps our quarrelling was an amusing diversion.)

More often than not Evangeline was right to correct me. *Your crazy understanding of Cantonese!* she'd hiss. *To you a rash is a headache and a pain an itch . . .* Our rivalry sometimes took us beyond the bounds of propriety. I remember the afternoon Old Lady Wu sat, wheezing, in the examination chair, her lungs drowning in bilious fluids. Her voice like a rattlesnake in her throat, Old Lady Wu described the chronic symptoms that forced her to sleep sitting upright and made her every waking moment a fight for breath.

When she ran out of puff and could no longer speak, I turned to Nurse Josie and confidently said: 'Old Lady Wu says she coughs up bloody phlegm in the mornings.'

'Old Lady Wu says her phlegm is bloody all the time. Not just in the morning,' Evangeline objected.

'She said her phlegm is bloodiest in the mornings.'

'No, she did not.'

'Yes, she did. She said her coughing is worse then too.'

'Old Lady Wu says her coughing is terrible all the time. See how she is coughing now.'

Old Lady Wu was indeed hacking away as though her lungs were at that very moment disintegrating. I frowned at her for conspiring to give my enemy the upper hand.

'You wicked children!' Old Lady Wu wheezed. 'I am a dying old woman! Stop quarrelling and tell the Foreign She-Devils I want some medicine for my chest!'

I ought to have left the medical hut alone. But I'd caught the fever of competition, and to allow Evangeline such a victory was unthinkable. What made our petty spats even more distasteful was that they were played out against a backdrop of poverty and life-threatening illnesses. The urchins that scampered about The Village of Everlasting Peace suffered from rickets and smallpox, their infant tummies a lair of parasitic worms. Chinese squatter women reached old age at thirty-nine with prolapsed wombs, arthritis-stiffened joints and ulcerated legs the gadflies bothered from dawn until dusk. A weeping girl came with a handkerchief bundle containing a dozen teeth that had fallen out, begging the nurses to put them back in her diseased gums. A mother brought us her baby, howling its little head off because his chest, scalded in an accident with a boiling kettle, had had a stinging con-coction of mandrake and ginger root massaged on it by a Chinese herbalist (who convinced the mother that fire must be fought with fire, then charged her three *ringgit* for his stupidity).

Most Chinese squatter men distrusted Western medicine and thought it harmful to masculinity. So apart from the odd occasion when a hen-pecked husband was dragged to the medical hut by his wife, my afternoons there were spent largely in the company of women, which was not as tantalizing a prospect as it at first might seem, as, done-in by poverty, the stress of multiple childbearing and lack of access to dental care, the fairer sex of The Village of Everlasting Peace were not that fair. Occasionally there'd be a young girl whose beauty triumphed over the scabs and malnutrition, and though my admiration of these lovelies was innocent enough, Evangeline's acid-tongued comments made it seem less so. *Interpret with your ears, not your eyes*, she once muttered, as though my wistful glances were a molestation. Evangeline was one of those prickly over-sensitive types, offended by the male gaze. Had a fortune teller prophesied, in those quarrelsome days, that Evangeline was to be my future beloved, I'd have laughed and demanded my money back. How poorly I knew myself. I used to lie awake on my camp-bed at night, seething over some slight she'd made. (*How dare she belittle me in front of the patients! Arrogant bitch. She never smiles. I bet she hasn't smiled once in her thirty-eight years! I shall get up early tomorrow and learn more vocabulary. That'll teach her . . .*)

The prettiness and Antipodean curves of the nurses were forgotten. Many times the nurses had, in the act of leaning over, afforded me glimpses of the ivory mounds of their breasts, hoisted in no-frills brassières. But this erotic imagery went unexploited as night after night I was consumed by angry thoughts of Evangeline. *I think you're sweet on Evangeline*, Nurse Josie once whispered, when my rival was out of earshot. *Certainly not!* I spluttered, though the vehemence of my denial didn't stop my cheeks turning red.

The other night I woke to find Evangeline sitting beside me on the fold-out bed, wonderment in her eyes as she tenderly stroked my brow. *Whatever must she think of me now?* I thought as I lay beneath her watchful gaze. During our love affair Evangeline was the older woman (I used to joke and call her 'my darling spinster', 'my dear old maid'). But time ceased for her at the stroke of death, and Evangeline is for ever forty years old. An age I have long surpassed. I glimpsed myself through her eyes – denture-less and sunken-mouthed, my skin like a mottled withered peach – and ridiculous vanity and self-pity flared within. How could she bear to touch me? Her tranquil mood was rare indeed. Evangeline is the most violent and destructive of my ghostly acquaint-ances – bursting into my council flat like a vengeful hurricane, whipping up apples and satsumas from the fruit bowl and pelting them at me. *What a miracle to have her sitting so calmly beside me*, I thought. Then our amnesty came to an end.

'I haven't forgiven you,' she said.

And not to be outdone, I said, 'Nor I you.'

Hatred contorted my beloved's face and she spat viciously in my eye. Then she vanished.

It amuses me now to recall our bickering in the medical hut. The simmering dislike of lust in its infancy. We were unaware of it at the time, but those were our halcyon days.

4

Police Lieutenant Spencer came to my flat yesterday, the bloody hole in his khaki jacket torn by the Communist bayonet that eviscerated him in 1953. When he was alive Lieutenant Spencer was a man of arrogance and violence, but in death he is the epitome of dejection.

'Where's me cup o' tea, Goldilocks?' he asked.

'Sorry, Lieutenant,' I said, 'I wasn't expecting you.'

The policeman christened me Goldilocks on the evening we first met in The Village of Everlasting Peace. The nickname is long invalid – for there is nothing golden about my locks any more – but this does not discourage use of the misnomer. Spencer always demands a cuppa when he comes, but even when there's enough left in the teapot I never give him any. He lacks the visceral means to retain beverages, and every sip would seep out of his belly wound and on to my sofa.

I lifted my mug and swallowed some strongly brewed tea, grateful the lieutenant had left his intestines behind. Spencer likes to decorate my flat with garlands of entrails. He dangles them from the light fixtures, or lets them slither across the carpet, like grotesque B-movie snakes. I once saw his guts slinking behind the washing machine, masquerading as one of the water hoses. I once saw them leap from his stomach to the ceiling, like a jumbo-sized umbilical cord connecting the lieutenant to the tiled womb of the kitchen.

We sat quietly together, listening to shifting frequencies of static as my truanting grandson adjusted the radio dial in the bedroom. When he's not reading library books or meddling with his acne, Adam listens to long-wave stations in Arabic and French and other languages he doesn't know. Rather queer as far as hobbies go, but I don't interfere.

'How are you keeping these days, Lieutenant Spencer?' I asked.

Spencer began effing and blinding like a cockney barrow boy, which I took to mean 'Not very well'. Poor old Spencer. His dignity has never recovered since the day his bowels were whipped out by a Communist revolutionary who went by the party name 'Little Mosquito'. Lieutenant Spencer survived four years in Palestine and two years bandit-shooting in the Malayan jungle (with a decapitated-enemy head count of thirty-seven). He was very proud of his murderous prowess and would sooner have ripped out his own guts than let a Communist get his filthy Maoist paws on them. And to rub salt in his already substantial wound, the assassin 'Little Mosquito' was a mere fourteen years old; only just graduated from slaying imaginary imperialist pigs in the schoolyard to being kitted out with his own gun and red star beret. It was a rather humiliating end to Lieutenant Spencer's brutally accomplished career.

Spencer was murdered at the age of twenty-five. When he was alive he was known as a bit of a psychopath (a reputation of which he was very proud, and sustained by routinely capturing geckos in his fist and biting off their tongue-flickering heads). But in his spirit incarnation Spencer's self-esteem is at a low ebb and he is unthreatening, to say the least. There's a strained, comic quality to his angst, like the misery of Stan Laurel.

'You seen Resettlement Officer Dulwich?' he asked. 'Posh fatso with whisky blood clots in his eyes. You see 'im, you tell 'im Spencer's looking for 'im. I ain't no pederast now. I've got me missus down at the Frangipani Club, and what floats Charles's boat, that's his business. He's just me mate. But if you see 'im, you tell 'im Spencer wants a word.'

The true nature of Charles Dulwich's relationship with Spencer was revealed to me the afternoon I caught them making love in the officers' bathing hut (oh, how the afterimages of their ugly naked grunty bestiality haunt me!). The love affair was stormy and passionate, and for Spencer one of utter subjugation. In any relationship he who cares least has the most power, and

Charles didn't care a fig. When I tell Charles his ex-lover is looking for him, he cackles and says: *What? Old Percival? That little bandit gave him quite a bellyache, didn't he?* Or he laughs and buzzes like a mosquito.

Lieutenant Spencer pesters me when he visits. *I ain't heard from Charlie . . . You tell 'im I'm looking for 'im or what?* I deliver every one of Spencer's messages to Charles. I am not to blame if he ignores them. I hate acting as go-between for the dead. Surely there's a more efficient means for the deceased to contact one another – perhaps some directory enquiries of the spirit realm. If Lieutenant Spencer has the metaphysical know-how to disappear and reappear at whim, then he ought to be able to track down Resettlement Officer Dulwich himself without harassing a pensioner drinking his morning cup of tea.

'Charles was here not twenty minutes ago,' I told Spencer. 'He watched me fry some mushrooms and bacon for my breakfast, then left. It's astonishing that you always miss him. He is here a dozen times a day.'

'You tell 'im Percy wants a word.'

'I always do. Why don't you wait here? He's bound to turn up before long.'

But Lieutenant Percy Spencer, heartbroken and mutilated, was gone.

In my early days in the village, I'd often have after-dinner drinks on the veranda with Charles. I enjoyed these boozy soirées, for Charles was a first-rate raconteur, brimful of scandalous tales of expat society;

of *mems* and *tuans* and sin and adultery at the Royal Selangor Club. He gave horrific accounts of his years of wartime jail in Singapore, resurrecting Jap guards from the dead to shout at him in fierce Nipponese accents and twice break his nose. He was also very funny, making extravagant toasts in praise of our dessert of juicy mangosteen, or the song of the mynah bird, or the cyanide capsules gobbled by his jailers upon news of the motherland's defeat. But Charles's jollity was short-lived as a few weeks into our acquaintance his miserablist streak asserted itself. To Charles the Chinese squatters were barefaced liars, the government corrupt buffoons and the departure of the British a Sino-Malay massacre in waiting. He ranted on about the failure of Emergency regulations, but had no alternatives to suggest. Dark ravens flew from his soul and shook their ugly malignant feathers over everything. Loath to be infected by his sneery cynicism, I retreated earlier and earlier to my hut. My after-dinner getaway offended Charles. Affecting high spirits, he'd badger me to stay longer. But I'd flee none the less, safe in the knowledge that Charles could not force me to listen. I was wrong of course, for Charles avenges me in the afterlife, making his ghostly appearances day and night, his bleak monologues depriving me of sleep. Hell hath no fury, it seems, like a Resettlement Officer scorned.

Charles and I were playing backgammon in the bungalow on the evening I first met Lieutenant Spencer. The policeman barged in, stomped over to the gramophone and shunted the needle off the Puccini opera that Charles had selected.

'Enough of that poncey shit,' said Spencer. 'Let's 'ave some proper music off the radio.'

'What am I to do with you, Percival?' Charles sighed. 'I know you lack taste, but there's no need to take it out on my record collection.'

Lieutenant Spencer was five foot seven in jungle boots, stocky, with a criminal photofit face. He joined us at the table, pushing aside a bottle of vermouth and some carved knick-knacks from Borneo to make room for his rolling papers and tobacco pouch. In the bilious shine of the kerosene lamp Spencer reminded me of a muscular, dangerous breed of dog. A pit-bull, perhaps, or mastiff. The music silenced, we could hear the distant rattle of gunfire as the Communists began their nightly jitter campaign against Kip Phillips at the Bishop's Head plantation.

'Bloody Reds,' Spencer said, licking the gummed edge of a cigarette paper. 'They want expatriating. Send 'em back on the boat.'

'Poor Kip,' Charles said. 'The bandits have put so many bullet holes in his roof the man says he's living in a colander . . . I say, Spencer, have you met my assistant, Christopher Milnar?'

It was the first time man and beast had laid eyes on each other, but Spencer quipped: 'Oh yeah, I know old Goldilocks 'ere from when we was at Eton together. Gave you a good flogging when I was head boy, din't I?'

We had a good chuckle at this.

'You written home to Mummy yet?' Spencer sneered.

I laughed again and said that, yes, I'd written to Mummy thrice weekly. The lieutenant glowered, making it clear that he had the monopoly on my ridicule, and that I was not to poke fun at myself again.

After the ban of Puccini from the gramophone, the remote hail of bullets and delirious shrill of cicada became the music for our drinking party. Charles passed the story-telling reins over to Spencer, who was every bit as engaging as the Resettlement Officer. Chain-smoking and gin-swigging and punctuating every sentence with swear words, Spencer described his six-month stint in an isolated outpost in northern Terengganu, where he went on jungle missions, surviving on tinned stew and edible plants and equipped with nothing more than 'me tommy cooker, me knife and Bren gun'. After three months of jungle patrol and not one dead Communist to show for it, the District Officer summoned Spencer to his office for a 'right proper bollocking'.

Spencer was sent back into the jungle, warned that he was on his last chance. He was under orders to report back in ten days, but on his final Terengganu mission he disappeared for two months. After a half-hearted search party returned from the rainforest with one of his boots, everyone assumed Lieutenant Spencer was dead, killed by the Communists or eaten by carnivorous baboons. So when the missing policeman one day walked into the District Office, his uniform in tatters, cheeks smeared with tribal markings, and a bamboo spike through his septum, the District Officer was rather surprised. Spencer told him that he'd been living with a tribe of Orang Asli and learning their indigenous ways.

'Golly! What a marvellous adventure!' said the District Officer. 'But seeing as we're not paying you to go and live with the natives, it's high time we booked you a one-way ticket back to old Blighty.'

Spencer said nothing and gave a piercing two-fingered whistle. An Orang Asli tribesman trotted into the office, barefoot and naked save for a loincloth, a large canvas sack slung over his shoulder. The tribesman opened the sack over the D.O.'s desk and out plopped eleven severed heads. The decomposing heads thudded and bounced, leaving vile splodges of blood on the D.O.'s paperwork, before tumbling to the floor. Each face wore a death mask of terror and outrage, and one or two, loyal to the end, the beret of the Malayan Races Liberation Army. Lieutenant Spencer grinned as he recounted this moment of triumph.

'You should 'ave seen his face when them 'eads landed on his desk! He nearly went as yellow as them noggins was! They were like stinky rotten cabbages, and some of them still had their slitty eyes open. I went off and left the D.O. to count 'em up. Took me Orang Asli mate for a slap-up supper.'

The mass-murderer laughed and Charles hooted and thumped a fist on the table. I smiled feebly. For weeks afterwards I had nightmares in which I too was a decapitated skull, rolling about and head-butting my neighbours in the darkness of the canvas sack. Nowadays I'm not so squeamish. The souls of the dead leave so many grisly body parts about my flat (chopped limbs and gouged-out eyeballs, and let us not forget the lieutenant's magnificent flying intestines!) I scarcely lift an eyebrow at dismemberment any more.

On the night of our first meeting Lieutenant Spencer made no attempt to hide his dislike of me. Daggers flew across the table from his piggy eyes and his nostrils flared like a bull hoofing the ground, ready to charge. I had no idea what I'd done to enrage the policeman (only later would I realize that he considered me a love rival for the affections of Charles), and his hostility unsettled me so much that, at the grand old age of twenty-five, I took up smoking. I filched one of Charles's Lambert and Butler's and lit up, coughing and spluttering on my first drag. The hell-fire in my lungs was worth it, though, for it erected a literal smoke-screen between me and Spencer's animosity – the cigarette an excellent, if incrementally lethal, prop.

The hours passed and we three Englishmen got drunker and drunker. The instrumentalists changed in the night orchestra, as the gunfire at the Bishop's Head plantation ceased, and was replaced by the high jinks of the village home guard hurling hats over the perimeter fence. Beneath the guards' laughter the jungle kept up its creaturely hum.

'More whisky, Goldilocks?' asked Charles.

I hiccuped, obfuscated by booze, and wondered how

many years Charles had been making the nightly sacrifice to Bacchus.

'Don't mind if I do,' I replied, lifting my glass and imploring the powers-that-be that my new nickname not catch on.

The mood of the bungalow became smutty and depraved as Spencer moved from tales of bandit-slaying to a torrent of anecdotes about the whores of the Frangipani Club. Gleeful and unabashed, the policeman described each of his intimate encounters with the Frangipani Club prostitutes, naming personal favourites with a heterosexual zeal that smacks to me, in retrospect, as a denial of his feelings for Charles Dulwich (who laughed raucously, not in the least bit put out). I found Spencer's lewd tales tedious and repetitive. Annoyed by my lack of mirth, Spencer decided I was a virgin.

'Time you got rid o' that cherry, Goldilocks,' said Spencer. 'Get yerself down to the Frangipani Club, get yerself seen to. They've got Malays, Chinks, Indonesians . . . Whores of every colour of mud.'

'Godspeed!' cried Charles. 'There's nothing sadder than a twenty-five-year-old virgin.'

They were baiting the new boy and I was naive enough to bite. The assumption that I was innocent of the fairer sex offended me, as did the proposal I remedy this in a house of ill repute. Not once in my life have I visited a brothel. Not even in the fifty years of celibacy that followed the vanishment of my beloved Evangeline (well, fifty years of near celibacy, interrupted by a shameful dalliance with one of Frances's school chums in 1968 – but let's not go into that). Brothels are raging hotbeds of venereal disease, infested with lice and strains of gonorrhoea that can eat through the toughest prophylactic. (I remember how the Worcestershire First Battalion Regiment scratched constantly at the crabs residing in their pubes.) Though I was unfamiliar with the Frangipani Club and other iniquitous haunts, I was no stranger to the carnal delights of the female flesh. Marion Forte-Cannon would testify to that (once she had ceased, as she had melodramatically declared, the loathing of *every fibre* of my being). As would the many girls who shimmied up the drainpipe to my room in university halls.

'My dear Lieutenant,' I said, 'I believe you're confusing what it is to be a virgin with what it is to be a gentleman. Never in a million years would I go to the Frangipani Club, for I am the latter, I'll have you know.'

Charles guffawed and Spencer was silent, nostrils flaring as if from some detonation of rage in the nasal cavities.

'You saying I ain't a gentleman?' he said with a sneer.

How downright stupid that he, who'd just five minutes ago been describing the introduction of ping-pong balls to the delicate regions of a hooker called Heavenly Lotus, was protesting his exclusion from the rank of gentleman.

'I said no such thing,' I replied. 'I merely said that—'

''Cos you ain't no better than me, you public-school tosser. You can look down yer nose at the Frangipani

Club, but you ain't gonna find no posh ladies and croquet tournaments out here . . .'

'Now, steady on, old chap!' chortled Charles. 'No one is saying you are anything less than a gentleman. The very thought!'

The humidity merged with the lieutenant's drunken wrath, creating the atmosphere of a pressure cooker. I was convinced he was going to wallop me. I'd never been in a drunken brawl before (except the time I restrained a wild Max Montgomery from attacking Freddy St Clair at the Fencing Society ball) and had no desire to make up for this lack of experience. I was about to announce that I was off to bed, when there was a knocking at the door. The knocks came in staccato bursts, spaced at intervals.

'Ah ha! I know who that is!' cried Charles. 'Yes, yes, you may enter!'

The door opened and a young Chinese man slipped in like a quick-moving shadow. He wore the latex-splattered uniform of a rubber tapper.

'Detective Pang, welcome!' cried Charles.

''Evening, Detective,' said Spencer, hostility cast aside as he greeted the newcomer.

The man came and sat at the table.

'My loving Bolshevik salutes to you, Lieutenant Spencer, Resettlement Officer Dulwich.'

The man's locution was indistinguishable from that of an Englishman. To hear such refinement from a Chinese squatter was as strange as being spoken to by a cat.

'Ha, ha, ha, I'll give you a Bolshevik salute, yer cheeky sod,' said Spencer, laughing.

'Assistant Resettlement Officer Milnar, how do you do? I'm Detective Pang.'

The detective and I shook hands.

'How do you do?' I said. 'Crikey. You look nothing like a detective.'

'Detective Pang is the head of a thirty-strong network of undercover spies in the village,' said Charles.

'Thirty-strong!' I echoed.

'Whisky, Detective?'

'Oh, yes. Splendid.'

Detective Pang was as nondescript as the hundreds of other tappers in the village, and I'd no memory of having seen him before. With the bullish Spencer and the barrel-chested Charles either side of him, the detective seemed fragile and bird-boned, as if an enthusiastic bear hug would crush him. His cheekbones were high and feline and the low droopy folds of his eyelids made him seem half asleep (the opposite of vigilant; possibly integral to his success as a secret agent). As Charles ransacked the drinks cabinet for more booze, Detective Pang took a bag of sunflower seeds out of his trouser pocket. He nibbled the seeds as he sipped his nightcap, splitting them open with his teeth and discarding the striped husks on the table.

'How's the old intelligence gathering going?' asked Charles. 'What have the Min Yuen been up to lately? Spill the beans!'

'Up to their usual tricks, I'm afraid. We've had a

successful week, though, and have passed on the names of several Min Yuen suspects to Sergeant Abdullah.'

'Terrific result. Well done!'

'Ah, we have my wife to thank. The sewing circle she has joined has proved to be a goldmine of enemy information. The wives of the Min Yuen have lips as loose as their morals and are forever bragging of their husbands' criminal activities.'

The Chinese detective was so well-spoken and refined, I asked him if it was difficult to assume the identity of a common squatter.

'No, it's very easy,' he replied. 'I chew the betel nut and keep a hog and four geese. I talk with my mouth full and beat my wife. I have built my hovel from the same scavenged rubbish as the other squatters and have cut down on washing. No one here knows us from before, but they assume we're just random unfortunates caught up in the government resettlement scheme. I only visit the police hut and Resettlement Officer Dulwich in the dead of night. I am rude to the village police, and Sergeant Abdullah has had his men pretend to arrest me on two occasions to place me above suspicion. When you see me in the village, you must never approach me or talk to me, even though you are known for your friendliness, Mr Milnar. If anyone discovers that my wife and I are spies, the Communists will murder us.'

'What sacrifices you have made in order to pass yourself off as an ignorant squatter!' marvelled Charles. 'Sacrifices of the spirit, as well as in living standards. I propose a toast. To Detective Pang and his efforts in the war against Communism!'

'Hear, hear!' I cheered.

We lifted our glasses up to the burning kerosene lamp, and the whisky shone copper and gold. We clinked glasses and a tide of nausea rose within me.

'Thank you,' said Detective Pang. 'I am proud to be a Running Dog of Imperialism.' We all guffawed at this. 'Seriously,' the detective went on, 'I cannot bear to see Malaya – my Malaya – being torn apart by this foolish Communist agenda. It was bad enough when the Japanese were here.'

'I know how you feel, old chap.' Charles sighed. 'I was born here too. When I think of the golden, carefree days before the war I could weep . . .'

The detective was silent. He had nothing to say about the golden, carefree days before the war. Perhaps he was too young to remember. Spencer was slumped in his chair, eyelids flaccid and shreds of tobacco stuck to his chin. It was gone midnight and the suffocating heat was finally borne away by breezes, perspiration cooling against our skin. The booze had taken its toll on me as well as the lieutenant. Nausea came on like seasickness, and in a fanciful mood I imagined that the officers' hut was a ship tossed about on a stormy sea (the nautical illusion wasn't hard to establish, as the walls swayed and waves crashed in my ears). I imagined that Charles was the ship's captain, and Detective Pang his first mate.

'The trouble with Malaya,' said Captain Dulwich, 'is

that she has no Nehru or Gandhi to guide her to Independence. The Malays are lazy. Their patriotism is disorganized and they're not united enough against us. They're content to be cogs in our system. If the British leave they will flail and founder and the Communists will rush to the fore – just like when the Japs left. The British have no choice but to stay, or else the Communists will have you singing "Raise The Red Flag".'

The detective bit into a sunflower seed. He removed the husk from his mouth and let it fall among the other carcasses on the table.

'To defeat the Communists,' he said, 'we must turn around the minds of the immigrant Chinese so they are no longer loyal to Red China. Citizenship is the key. Otherwise they are against us. Their collective silence protects the enemy. How else can eight thousand bandits hold the country to ransom? This war will not be won by bullets and bombs, but by the conversion of hearts and minds.'

'Bollocks to the Communists,' jeered Spencer, snapping awake. 'Wait until Operation Starvation kicks in and the Reds come crawling out of the jungle for some grub. Me and my men are going to the Batu Caves next week. We've got the map coordinates for a bandit camp there. See if I don't bring back another sack of heads!'

'Not to belittle your efforts, Spencer old boy,' said Charles, 'but even if you wiped out every last Communist, Malaya is doomed. The British are leaving and she doesn't stand a chance without us. There's no hope of us staying either, for the Empire is rotting, and the rot is incurable and has spread to the bone.'

Independence, Empire, Communists, Emergency. The words shuffled meaninglessly in my head. I was too drunk to venture any opinions (though I wondered what became of this famous British loyalty when the Japs invaded – we certainly scarpered quickly enough then). Charles was born in British Malaya, and died in British Malaya, five years before Merdeka, with the conviction in his heart that the country was damned without Englishmen. Sometimes, when Charles's spirit comes to pester me, I try to correct this misconception.

'Your predictions about the departure of the British were wrong,' I tell him. 'Malaya gained her independence in 'fifty-seven and she's been managing jolly well ever since. You wouldn't recognize Kuala Lumpur today, Charles. It's a world-class metropolis with skyscrapers and stunning modern architecture. There are shopping malls and McDonald's and tube trains and six-lane motorways . . . The Chinese aren't Communists any more, Charles, they're entrepreneurs! You really ought to go and have a look. I think you'll be impressed.'

But Charles is mysteriously deaf to my accolades. Frustrated, I once pinched a travel agent's brochure and flipped it open under his nose.

'See, this is Merdeka Square, and this fireworks display is for the annual Independence celebrations . . .'

Charles yawned, patting his open mouth. 'Oh, put

your story-book away, Christopher. I'm too old for fairy-tales!'

It's as if the history of the world ceased for Charles when he passed away in 1953. Maybe all ghosts are impervious to events occurring after their death, their mental ectoplasm is resistant to current affairs. Nearly every day Charles promenades into my kitchen, announcing news fifty years out of date.

'I say! Did you hear they've killed the Bearded Terror of Kajang? They've strapped his corpse to the bonnet of a lorry and are driving him around the village to show the Min Yuen. Oh, how the mighty idol has fallen . . .'

'Do you fancy some monkey stew? That imbecile Spencer just shot it on a jungle mission. It was standing on its hind legs and he mistook it for a bandit. Ha, ha, ha!'

Sometimes I suspect Charles fakes his ignorance of Malaysia's progress. After all, he can see Adam and Julia (whom he refers to as 'the spawn of Beelzebub') and my ageing body (which he calls 'your withered bag of bones'). Perhaps he pretends not to see the photographs of modern-day Kuala Lumpur because they contradict the gloom-mongering predictions he made five decades ago. The more I think about it, the more likely this seems. Charles does so hate to be in the wrong.

On the evening of our drinking party Charles ranted on and on. Too drunk to listen, I was oddly transfixed by his nose, which had turned a startling shade of vermilion. Lieutenant Spencer was stuporous in his chair and, though he'd had quite enough, some self-destructive reflex kept him lifting glass to mouth. When he spoke it was in a patois of cockney and pidgin Malay, intelligible only to Charles.

'Mwargh bandits, me and my men'll sort 'em, makan haji eff off.'

'Ha, ha, ha, quite right, Spencer,' agreed Charles.

Only Detective Pang, compulsive nibbler of sunflower seeds, had his wits about him. I glanced at the overflowing ashtray on the table, queasy in the knowledge that many of the nicotine-stained filters were mine. My stomach lurched and I realized I had to leave before I vomited or lost consciousness or worse.

'Goodnight!' I said, my chair toppling over as I stood up.

Charles and the detective wished me goodnight back, and Lieutenant Spencer roared at me: *Bugger off!*

On the veranda I gulped the fresh night air like water in a land of drought. Bugs chirruped and a nightjar sang, the melody advancing through the treetops in an echolalia of birdsong. A two-man silhouette went by the perimeter fence, carrying rifles. As I stood there my view of the village tilted one way, then the other. I gripped the railing and wondered how the devil I was going to get back to my hut with all the blasted tilting. Woozy-headed, I started down the veranda steps. The next thing I knew I was sitting at the bottom, dazed and discombobulated, my buttocks throbbing as if they'd just had a good old paddle-whacking from the Latin master. I had fallen and my bum had bounced off every step (rendering it swollen and purplish for a week). *Whoopsadaisy!* I cried. Then I crawled a few yards over the trampled earth and was violently sick.

I didn't notice the figure on the veranda until after I'd vomited out the alcohol sloshing about in my stomach. The wooden boards creaked and I looked up, strands of hell-broth hanging from my mouth to the puddle I'd made on the ground. I recognized the height and girth of Charles and the firefly glimmer of his cigar.

'Are you all right down there, Christopher?'

'Right as rain, thanks.'

'I heard you fall down the steps.'

'Nothing sobers you up like a good fall.'

A loud burp came out of my mouth, catching me unawares. I wiped the stomach bile oozing down my chin on to the back of my hand.

'Well, I'd best be off to bed, then,' I said. 'I have check-point duty tomorrow.'

'Yes, and the Red Cross nurses are coming. You'll be assisting them and Evangeline Lim, won't you?' He pronounced the syllables of her name in a slow, knowing manner. 'Evangeline Lim,' he repeated. 'She has quite a history, that one. Detective Pang has been telling us . . .'

I did not like to hear him talking of her. I did not like it one bit. Another burp came out of my mouth.

'I'd like to take this opportunity to say that it is wonderful to have you here, Christopher,' he said. 'I can't think of anyone better suited to life in The Village of Everlasting Peace.'

I thanked him and wished him goodnight. Then I crawled all the way back to my hut on my hands and knees, without once looking round to see if the Resettlement Officer was still there.

5

Julia gallivants on the estate after dark and there is nothing I can do to stop her. Threaten her freedom and she bucks like a colt, unaware of the injury she could do to an old man like me. When I was Julia's age I romped on pastures of green. I climbed the highest trees, fished for pike in lakes, and competed in the Middleton Junior School conker tournament. When the rain chased me indoors I assembled model aeroplanes and thousand-piece jigsaw puzzles. These innocent pastimes are unfashionable nowadays. On the Mountbatten estate, glue-sniffing appears to be de rigueur.

What my hoyden of a granddaughter gets up to night after night I have no idea, but she returns home with the fading aura of an adventuress. Perhaps, through her twelve-year-old eyes, the Mountbatten towers are as magnificent as Babel, and the menagerie of council tenants, with their rainbow-hued tattooed skin and junk-food-fed obesity, as thrilling as the mythical beasts of the *Odyssey*. Perhaps she believes the glittering fragments of windscreen in the car park are diamonds, and the wacky-baccy smoke drifting from the heavy-lidded West Indians, zephyrs of holy incense. I worry about my granddaughter as she roams the concrete badlands of the Mountbatten estate. I tell her to stay indoors, but off she goes, every night, leaving her orthodontist appointment reminder cards on the mantelpiece to gather dust.

Waiting for Julia to come home tonight, I watched the street-lamp-lit estate from the living-room window. Fourteen storeys below, people were hunched against the cold, pushing illegitimate sprogs in prams or eating from bags of battered cod and chips. The late-autumn chill seeped through the windowpane and I was glad to be indoors, with every bar glowing on the gas fire, and *The Archers* on Radio Four.

'Well,' I said, letting the curtain drop back in place, 'I don't know about you, but I'm starving. I vote we start without her.'

Adam shrugged. An apathetic roll of the shoulders is the most the boy can manage these days. I fetched our supper from the kitchen and we dined in our armchairs, with our plates on our laps. I'd cooked gammon steak, tinned peas and carrots, and served it up with slices of buttered bread. Nutritious, well-balanced meals are important for growing children. When I lived alone I never ate such substantial fare.

As we dug in, the radio drama our substitute for

mealtime conversation, the front door banged. Then the bedroom door went as Julia ducked inside without so much as a *Sorry-I'm-late*. I set aside my plate and went to give the saucy madam a talking-to. Julia was sitting on her bed in her school blazer, her eyes mean and glittery with cheap make-up, her high ponytail stiff with mousse. She reeked of cigarettes, and her school blouse was missing a button or two, the heart-shaped pendant of her nine-carat Argos necklace visible against her breastbone.

'Julia,' I said, 'you were supposed to be home an hour ago. Your supper is ready.'

'I don't want any,' she replied.

'Whether you want any or not is beside the point. I go to a lot of trouble to make supper for you and Adam. And why is your shirt torn? They cost eight pounds each, those shirts. Where are the buttons?'

'Dunno,' she said.

The teenage ghost of Frances Milnar rolled her eyes.

'From now on you are to come straight home from school. Do you hear me? No more dilly-dallying on the estate.'

I made up a plate for Julia and put it on the sideboard, but she ignored my calls and stayed in her room. If the girl is this disobedient at twelve, I shudder to think what she'll be like at sixteen. Marjorie the case-worker says I must persevere, that the most important thing is for a family to stay together. But I am no good with children. It was the same story with her mother.

By the time I got back to my dinner Adam had nearly

74

finished, and was mopping up the leftover gravy on his plate with his bread. The boy was not alone, for mad Grace, sister of my beloved Evangeline, was dancing in front of the fireplace. Grace was dressed up in her finest cheongsam, the ribbon in her hair like a roosting butterfly with scarlet wings. I sighed. After my tiff with Julia, a visit from the village idiot was the last thing I needed. A daft smile on her pretty moon-shaped face, Grace reached down and lifted the hem of her cheongsam. Back in The Village of Everlasting Peace Grace took up her skirt for any man – Muslim, Buddhist, Christian or Sikh. Evangeline couldn't leave her sister alone for one minute, as Grace hopped into the jungle scrub with any fella who winked or whistled. Lecherous baying followed her wherever she went. The village children pelted Grace with stones, and women spat at her for encouraging their husbands to philander. Only the God-botherers Blanche Mallard and Marina Tolbin could find it in their hearts to be nice to her, babysitting Grace while Evangeline helped out in the medical hut, grooming her hair with the nit-comb and reciting prayers. Whether Grace's harlotry was playful innocence or sex-crazed lunacy, I couldn't tell. But my living room is not a go-go dancing club, and such lewd exhibitionism isn't allowed. As her skirt went higher I was irritated to see Grace had neglected to wear knickers.

'Stop that, Grace!' I scolded. 'For heaven's sake, behave yourself! Put your skirt back down.'

The silly goose ignored me, dancing to the jaunty

dum-de-dum-de-dum-de-dah of *The Archers'* theme tune, lifting her skirt and wiggling her bottom, as if to warm it by the fire. Adam stood up.

'Do you know what Julia gets up to after school?' I asked him. 'Do you know who her friends are? I'm going to telephone their parents and find out what's going on.'

Blank-faced, Adam clattered up his empty plate and cutlery. The boy does a good impersonation of a deaf mute when it suits him.

I wanted to shake him, but instead I lowered my fork and said: 'It won't do for you to be this way, Adam. I won't be here for ever, and you must look after your little sister when I'm gone. You must look after her and love her. If you do one thing in your life, Adam, you must love someone. Love is the only thing that matters.'

No sooner had I said the words than I was ashamed. They must have seemed insincere to a boy to whom I so seldom spoke. I think my candour was inspired by mad Grace, flaunting the sacred flower of her femininity by the fireplace. She reminded me of Evangeline and her daily battle to keep her younger sister out of the scrub. The strength of her devotion.

Adam looked me in the eye and spoke for the first time in weeks, the donkey bray of adolescence catching me unawares. 'Like you loved my mum?'

Then he left, and I heard the lock slide across the bathroom door. Tears of injustice stung my eyes. I took up my knife and fork and sawed at my stone-cold gammon steak.

'What does the boy know? The boy knows nothing! He wasn't even born when Frances ran away!'

No one heard me, of course. No one except mad Grace, who cackled and shimmied, lifting her skirt for everyone to see.

I met mad Grace and the God-botherers Blanche Mallard and Marina Tolbin in the autumn of 1951. I first saw the mission hut as I led a wheelbarrow procession of fence-mending equipment across the village. I knew at once that the hut was no squatter residence, for it had whitewashed walls and a trellis of Honolulu creepers around the door. A picket fence bordered the garden where a Saint Bernard panted in the shade of the papaya tree. An infant chorus of 'London Bridge Is Falling Down' drifted through the wire-mesh windows, bolstered by the operatic, bellow-lunged quavers and trills of what I imagined to be a Viking-hatted Valkyrie. I stopped in my tracks, then yelped as the wheelbarrow behind me ploughed into the back of my legs.

'Whose hut is that?' I asked the Tamil at the helm of the incendiary wheelbarrow.

The Tamil squinted over at the whitewashed idyll and said: 'Ah, that hut belongs to the Jesus People, come to turn the Chinese against the Lord Buddha. Two English ladies. They came last week. They are determined to convert everything that moves. Not even the chickens are safe.'

'Really,' I grumbled. 'Charles never keeps me up to speed on anything these days.'

How had the Jesus People managed to pass through the check-point, build their mission headquarters and begin indoctrination of the villagers without my noticing? I expect I'd been too busy to notice. Two weeks before, fifty army trucks containing two hundred evacuated squatters had rumbled into The Village of Everlasting Peace, and the ensuing chaos robbed me of the opportunity to think of anything else. What a nightmare. The government had sprung them on us with only a few days' warning. They had to live in tents as bulldozers and gangs of men with parang knives cleared the jungle so there was land on which to build huts.

The newcomers were very unhappy. Silence and hostility greeted my attempts to befriend them. And the few that did open up to me asked me to perform illegal feats.

'Master, please let my family go back. We've never helped the People Inside!' begged one old lady. 'You're a good man. You know we don't deserve to be here . . .'

I recited word for word, in Cantonese translation, from *The Handbook to the Briggs Plan*. I sang the praises of resettlement and sanitation, education and medical care; protection from Communist harassment and future prospects for grandchildren. But there was little in the inchoate mess surrounding us to inspire faith in such promises.

The old lady scowled. 'It will take more than your filthy lies to make me appreciate this dung heap of a concentration camp,' she said. 'Heaven has eyes, you know! And in heaven you will be punished, you wicked man!'

Every evening after supper I tumbled on to my camp-bed and slept like the dead. Charles stayed up till all hours, continuing to flambé his belly with brandy, alone but for the orchestral works of dead composers (Lieutenant Spencer was away on a mission to the Batu Caves). Once, passing the officers' bungalow on a mid-night visit to the latrine, I saw Charles whirl by the window in a solitary trance of ballroom dancing, arms encircling an imaginary partner. The next morning he was as sick and grumpy as ever. *What's so funny?* he snapped as I smiled at the memory of his drunken waltzing. Not that my teetotalism served me any better. My alarm clock woke me long before I'd slept off my exhaustion (how that tyrannical keeper of time clamoured for defenestration!) and my muscles ached twice as much as the day before.

Anyway, let's return to the Jesus People and their hut. Lowering my wheelbarrow, I instructed my team to make a start on the fence-mending without me (they veered over to the shade of the tulang trees for a siesta), then went to call on the missionaries. Nearing the cottage, I was cheered to see pots of scarlet hibiscus in the garden and the flower beds damp with the promise of further tropical bloom (a refreshing change from the yards of weeds and chicken shit). The Saint Bernard panted and thudded its tail, and one of the missionaries, Blanche Mallard, came out to greet me.

Blanche was tall and sturdy and the bun on her head was like a grey ball of yarn.

'Christopher Milnar, I presume,' she said, and we laughed and shook hands. After introducing herself and Humphrey the Saint Bernard to me, she invited me into the front room of the hut, where a dozen village children sat around a low table, colouring in pictures of biblical scenes and drinking orange squash. Religious tapestries hung on the walls and geckos darted to and fro, forked tongues flickering at spiders and flies. Chalking a prayer on to the blackboard was the second missionary, Marina Tolbin, a woman so ugly and hirsute I felt physically ill. Even now I remember her in chilling flashbacks of protruding teeth, furry moustache and moles like netherworldly creatures on her chin. It didn't take a qualified doctor to see that Marina had some hormonal imbalance or thyroid disorder. I squeaked 'Hello' and Marina stared wordlessly back. *Miss Tolbin is mute, the poor dear*, said Blanche, and I admit to a guilty relief that I was spared the ordeal of conversing with her.

Marina regained the ability to speak when she died. After a lifelong vow of silence it seems she has a lot to get off her chest. Her ghost pops up on the lavatory when I am in the bath and jabbers non-stop. Blanche is her favourite topic of complaint.

'Blanche always has the final say-so,' she says, 'and I have no say-so at all. She always takes charge of the exorcisms, even though I've frightened away hordes of demons in my time.'

I do wish she'd respect my privacy. I feel quite self-conscious performing my mandatory soap-and-loofah routine with Marina nattering on the lavatory. When Marina Tolbin was alive I thought her silence was of the utmost spiritual kind: a sacrifice of words so she could commune more devoutly with the Lord. But now Marina speaks aloud her cogitations, I know they scarcely deviate from the fatuous.

As the village urchins coloured-in scenes from the *Life of Christ*, Blanche praised their work in fluent Cantonese (*Very good, Ling Li, aren't you a clever girl!*) and gently discouraged acts of sacrilege (*Oh, no! The face of Jesus Christ is never blue . . . Blue is better for the sky . . .*). Marina Tolbin refilled glasses with orange cordial, as if afraid the little guests would run away if they were for a moment empty. The children were well behaved, except for one pipsqueak of a boy whose hand was down his trousers groping his juvenile tackle. Blanche scolded the boy. He was *not* to touch himself there! *Never, ever!* The boy removed his hand and Blanche nodded, satisfied, then told me that she and Marina were having trouble with a villager.

'Miss Tolbin and I experienced many trials during our long years as missionaries in Hong Kong,' she said, 'but never one such as this.'

Blanche led me through a click-clacking beaded curtain into the kitchen, where a Chinese woman sat at the table, the shrivelled newborn in her arms suckling at a bottle of milk. Like most women in our village, she was downtrodden and dirty, attending to her chores with a throng of little 'uns under her feet. The woman made a furious row when she saw me. She leapt up, spitting and cursing my ancestors. The baby squalled, shaken in her arms. Milk squirted from the teat of the feeding bottle and on to my cheek.

'Traitor!' she shrieked at Blanche.

'But he is not a policeman,' said Blanche.

'I know who he is!' the woman shouted. 'Even worse than a policeman. You've betrayed me! Jesus whore!'

I promised the woman that her troubles wouldn't go any further than the mission kitchen, and eventually she was calm enough to sit and jig her whimpering baby (though it was clear from the murder in her eyes that if she hadn't had a whimpering baby to jig she'd have done some serious violence to Blanche).

'This is Mrs Ho,' Blanche whispered. 'Her husband is an opium-eater and she is afraid he will gamble the baby away to fund his addiction. She wants the mission to adopt the child, to save him from a life of serfdom. But this is impossible! Miss Tolbin and I are too busy to bring up a child.'

'Opium is a police matter,' I said, *sotto voce*, 'and gambling is illegal in this village . . .'

'Stop whispering in your Foreign Devil tongue!' interrupted Mrs Ho.

'Mrs Ho,' I said, 'do you really want to give your baby away?'

'Better to give my baby to a good home than have him gambled into a bad one.'

'But surely it is better to keep your baby? Surely it is better to cure your husband's addiction?'

'One word to my husband and I will kill myself,' Mrs Ho said calmly. 'Then you'll have six children to find homes for.'

'Suicide is sin, Mrs Ho,' said Blanche, equally matter-of-fact.

'I promise to become a Christian and worship your Jesus God if you adopt my baby.'

'Mrs Ho, God does not bargain,' Blanche replied firmly. 'Faith is unconditional. When you are a Christian you will learn this. If you say your prayers every day, then the Holy Spirit will move within you. He will lend you the strength to overcome your problems.'

Mrs Ho was dissatisfied with this. There wasn't the time to wait for the Holy Spirit to move within her. The Jesus People had to take her baby *now*! She threatened to take her life once again and my patience snapped.

'Here's the solution,' I said: 'we arrest this husband of yours for the opium-eating and send him to prison. Then you and your children are safe. And we'll give you food rations to compensate for the shortfall in income, so you won't go hungry. Now, isn't that better than suicide?'

Mrs Ho's chair flew backwards as she stood up. She screamed, hexing my manhood with infertility (a hex that failed – my manhood is obviously a potent force to be reckoned with) and howling that if anything happened to her husband she'd set fire to the Jesus

Whores' hut and poison their dog. I feared for her crying baby as she thrashed in her selfish commotion. I promised not to say a word to the police and pleaded with her to hold the baby properly. But Mrs Ho wouldn't listen. Her tantrum chased me back through the strands of beaded curtain.

The classroom was silent but for the scratching of pencils. The circle of little 'uns looked up at me, eyes blazing with curiosity. I hoped that none of Mrs Ho's children had overheard the horrific threats their mother had made.

'It's no good. The kitchen is amok with demons!' said Blanche, as she walked me to the door. 'Such a furore! I only hope we can baptize Mrs Ho before it is too late!'

Blanche then invited me to join her congregation on the coming sabbath, but as I'd not been on speaking terms with God since the war I had politely to decline.

After saying goodbye to Blanche, I crouched in the garden to pet Humphrey the Saint Bernard, who thumped his tail, his pink tongue hanging out of his mouth. The poor old chap was dying in the heat. Why had no one thought of shearing his shag-pile fur? As I made plans to get hold of some clippers I heard a baby-voiced whispering. I turned to find myself eye-level with two urchins, peering at me through the fence pickets like midget jailbirds.

'If we go into that hut will the Jesus People give us orange drinks?' one of them asked.

'Yes . . . but I advise against it,' I said.

'Why?'

'I can't tell you.'

'Oh, tell us, tell us!' they cried.

I stole a cautionary glance back at the mission door.

'The orange drink is a witch's brew,' I said, 'a magic potion that will make you go to them every single day and listen to Jesus stories. It is too late for the children in there now. But you two must run and save yourselves . . .'

I thoroughly enjoyed my macabre joke, but had forgotten how susceptible the Chinese are to supernatural tales. The children listened wide-eyed, then one of them pointed over my shoulder and they both squealed. Their fear was strangely contagious and I hesitated to look round. Under the pink blooms of the Honolulu creeper trellis stood Marina Tolbin, holding a tray of orange squash. The urchins fled, leaving me to stand and shake my head and tut: 'Really, these children ought to learn some manners.'

The servant boy was on the bungalow veranda, sitting on a rattan chair and swinging his foot (the big toe of which was tethered to the ceiling-fan contraption) in a monstrous fit of the sulks. Around the side of the bungalow scuttled a headless chicken, fountains of blood spurting from its severed neck as chef Winston Lau chased it with a cleaver. The servant was so consumed by sulking he barely looked up.

In the office, Charles was wafted by the scalloped fan as he typed up the weekly village report. The story of Mrs Ho outraged him.

'We must call her bluff,' he said. 'We cannot let a squatter woman hold her life over us as a threat. Nor can we let opium-eating go on in this village.'

Charles assured me that Mrs Ho wouldn't find out her confidence had been violated. He would see to it that Mr Ho and the other drug fiends were caught in flagrante delicto. As I left, Charles dialled a number on the telephone and barked, *Get me Sergeant Abdullah!* And I returned to my volunteer team, trusting the situation was in good hands.

But there were no arrests. Not the next week, nor the week after that. When I asked Charles why the police were so slow, he spoke of an undercover operation to track down the opium ringleaders. *They're after the big boys*, he said, with a knowing wink.

Sometimes, when Charles comes haunting, I remind him of his whopping great lies. And he laughs and laughs, holding on to his massive jiggling belly as if it might explode. Charles often sets up his opium-smoking paraphernalia on my sideboard. He is especially fond of an Aladdin's lamp with a hollow rope attachment, devoting hours to sucking on the brass mouthpiece. Occasionally he uses more sinister tools of the trade – needles and syringes, weighing scales, morphia grains and vials of distilled water. He borrows my necktie to make a tourniquet around the venom depository of his arm. I close my eyes as he injects – I've always had a phobia of needles. I plug my fingers in my ears too, for I've come to loathe that sigh of intoxication. I have no desire to eavesdrop on his orgasm.

'This,' he says, eyes rolling back, 'is the most powerful weapon in the war against Communism. Not the hundreds of thousands of dollars of government propaganda and all that nonsense about hearts and minds. So long as the Reds want to outlaw this bourgeois indulgence, they'll never be loved by the Chinese.'

'Better a Communist than a dope fiend,' I muttered.

'Tee hee hee, tee hee hee,' giggled Charles, shutting his eyes and slumping into the arms of his toxic paramour.

The jungle settlement from which the two hundred newcomers had come was the last remaining source of food for the local Communists. Annoyed about their last supporters being corralled behind barbed wire, the 10th Independent Regiment of the Malayan Races Liberation Army upped their campaign of violence against The Village of Everlasting Peace. Grenades flew here, there and everywhere, blowing up the south watchtower and a few of our men besides. Dr Fothergill became adept at tweezering bullets out of our home guard, getting his patients shipshape so they were back on duty within a week. Conscious of the slit-throat fate of my predecessor, I kept to my hut after nightfall. I was lonely, I suppose, but I much preferred loneliness to boozing till all hours with Charles Dulwich and Lieutenant Spencer, back early from his failed mission to the Batu Caves, and in a filthy rotten mood after one of his squadron had blundered into trip-wire and got his legs blasted off.

One night I was woken by fists hammering my door. *Mistah Christopher! Mistah Christopher!* I fought my way out from under the mosquito nets and groped for the door bolt. There stood Special Constable Tahir, a young Malay of about seventeen, come to tell me I was wanted at the police hut.

'What for?' I asked.

Tahir told me they'd arrested a woman and she'd begged for me to be sent for. A week had passed since my visit to the mission and with a shudder I thought of the evil Mrs Ho. I asked Tahir if he knew who the woman was, and he smiled and shook his head.

'Hurry!' he said. 'But first, trousers!' alerting me to the fact I was stark bollock naked.

Special Constable Tahir and I jogged through the village, chasing the bobbing light of his torch over a steeplechase of ditches and fences. In the police hut, seated at the table, were Sergeant Abdullah, a pretty Chinese girl and the last person I'd expected to see in such circumstances – my medical-hut adversary, Evangeline Lim. Sergeant Abdullah, a night owl who often worked the graveyard shift, was chatting good-naturedly to the girls as we arrived. There was a large mahogany Go board on the table, its jade markers in complicated positions of attack and counter-attack. Sergeant Abdullah was sliding the jade markers about, describing the pros and cons of various moves to his silent guests.

'Ah! Number Two Man!' he cheered when he saw me. 'Come! Sit! Have a cup of tea.'

I sat down, panting slightly after my run. The pretty Chinese girl smiled as if to welcome me, but Evangeline stared into her lap, refusing to lift her eyes to meet my enquiring gaze.

'What's going on here?' I asked as Sergeant Abdullah poured me a cup of lemon-scented tea.

'We caught these nincompoops sneaking about by the fence *lah*. We searched them, but they had no food. They must have thrown whatever they were carrying over to the bandits. They can't speak English or Malay. The crazy sister cannot speak at all.'

'Sisters?' I said.

'She,' Sergeant Abdullah nodded at Evangeline, 'asked for you. And I thought, well, Number Two Man wakes up so early every morning, he won't mind coming here to translate!'

I glanced at the clock. It was quarter past two. The crazy sister (who I would later know as 'mad Grace') was in her late teens – decades younger than Evangeline, and more like a daughter than a sibling. Grace was as pretty and cherubic as Evangeline was haggard and unlovely. The only likeness between the two was their mysterious smoke-grey eyes. Grace's smile was that of a simpleton who thought it was perfectly fine to be arrested and brought to the police hut at quarter past two in the morning, as if the sergeant were hosting a tea party in their honour. Evangeline was as tense as her sister was carefree, lifting her chin as if all the dignity she had left was preserved in its tilt. *The nerve of that woman*, I thought, *dragging me out of bed just to stick her nose in the air.*

'Evangeline, why are you pretending you can't speak English or Malay?' I asked sternly in Cantonese. 'You are fluent in both.'

Blushing, she met my gaze. 'I need your help,' she said. 'You have to stop them from sending us to detention camp.'

Her voice shook with humiliation. It cost her greatly to ask for my help, and I admit to a devilish glee. (All those afternoons she'd arrogantly ticked me off in front of the Red Cross nurses! Oh, sweet revenge!) Sergeant Abdullah passed me their identity cards.

'Evangeline and Grace,' he said. 'Family name, Lim. Tahir says the younger one is a slut. Has trouble keeping her legs shut *lah* . . . Look at their Foreign-Devil eyes. I bet their mother had some leg-shutting trouble around the Holy Joes.'

There was a plate of biscuits on the table. The sergeant offered the plate to Grace.

'Here you go, chocolate biscuit. See if you have enough teeth in that nincompoop head of yours.'

Grace took a biscuit and grinned. The teeth studding her gums were small as milk teeth, growth stunted to reflect her mental age. Sergeant Abdullah offered the plate to Evangeline, who shook her head.

'What on earth were you doing out after curfew?' I asked.

'My sister ran away,' said Evangeline. 'She runs away all the time. I usually tie our wrists together with string

90

before we go to bed, so I wake up if she tries to escape. But tonight she cut herself free.' Evangeline lifted her wrist to show me the loop of string. She then lifted Grace's wrist, adorned with a similar bracelet of twine. 'When I discovered she was missing I went to look for her. I had to, Christopher, or else she'd have gone into other people's huts and got herself into trouble. I found her by the fence. Then the police caught us.'

'I see,' I said. The thought of Evangeline tying herself to her mentally handicapped sister every night depressed me. 'Don't worry. I'll explain to Sergeant Abdullah exactly what happened. You won't be sent to a detention camp.'

Evangeline's eyes flashed angrily. 'He won't believe me,' she hissed. 'My sister and I are guilty to him. Every squatter is guilty to him. He has no respect for us. See how he ridicules my sister. To send us away to detention camp means nothing to him.'

'Number Two Man, what is she saying? *Caw, caw, caw* – just like a crow.'

Sergeant Abdullah sipped some lemon tea, dunking his moustache in the cup. I glanced at Special Constable Tahir. Could he understand Cantonese? Apparently not. He stood by the door, eyes glazed, lost in cloud-cuckoo-land.

'One moment,' I said to the sergeant. Then to Evangeline: 'What do you want from me?'

'Tell the sergeant that you met me before in the medical hut. Say that I was desperate for sleeping tablets to drug my sister with. That even when I bind her to me with rope she manages to free herself and run away. It's true, Christopher – I've asked for sleeping pills, but they never have any. Sergeant Abdullah doesn't know that I speak English or help the Red Cross.'

'You want me to lie?'

'Look at her,' Evangeline said, gesturing to Grace. 'She knows nothing about the Emergency or Communists or the curfew, no matter how many times I tell her. We don't deserve to be punished.'

So I told Sergeant Abdullah what Evangeline had told me. Of her tying her wrist to her sister's every night, and of Grace escaping. Then I lied and told him that Evangeline had come to the medical hut several times begging for sleeping tablets to cure Grace's night wanderlust, and that we had none to give her. Sergeant Abdullah twiddled the corners of his moustache as he listened, and Grace babbled in her own private onomatopoeic language.

'Grace marches to the beat of her own drum,' I concluded, 'and, alas, it is the drumbeat of dementia.'

'Tell her,' the sergeant jabbed a finger at Evangeline, 'happen one time, OK. Happen again, and there will be trouble! Tahir, wake up! Take the time-wasters back to their hut.'

The relief in Evangeline's face was as fleeting as a subliminal frame in a film. But I saw it. For appearances' sake I uttered a few words of Chinese and she nodded. Tahir opened the door and the Lim sisters went quickly after him, without a word of thanks or saying goodbye.

The police-hut clock showed half past two. My mind was wide awake and I knew there was no hope of my getting back to sleep. I sighed, stood up and said goodnight to Sergeant Abdullah.

'Good of you to come, Number Two,' he replied. 'I will tell Number One what a good man you are. If it wasn't for those silly donkeys you'd be having your beauty sleep and I'd be beating Detective Pang at Go.'

In my heart there was a many-feathered explosion. *Detective Pang*? The door to the back room opened and the Chinese detective emerged from hiding. The detective gave me a polite nod and sat in the chair Evangeline had just vacated. I knew he'd heard it all. The walls were as thin as cardboard and no obstruction to even the lowest-decibel murmuring.

'Pang is excellent at Go,' said Sergeant Abdullah, 'but too bad for Pang he is not as excellent as I am!'

Elbows on the table, Detective Pang stared at the arrangement of jade counters on the board.

'Bold words for a man in such a fix, don't you think, Christopher?' he said.

'I don't know,' I replied. 'I don't know the rules.'

'Rules are important,' said the detective. 'If you knew the rules, then you'd appreciate the dilemma I am in.'

I don't recall what I said to that; I remember only the sensation of draining blood. I mumbled goodbye and stumbled outside, leaving them to their game and Detective Pang to the disclosure of my lie.

*   *   *

Sometimes, when I am ironing the bed sheets, or jotting the weekly shopping list on the back of a torn cornflakes box, I hear the crack, crack, crack of sunflower seeds. I look up and see the husks fall out of midair, as if from the beak of an invisible parrot, and scatter on the floor. This is the sly method in which Detective Pang makes his presence known. I am not happy about the mess he makes. The seed husks are very difficult to remove, resisting the rotating bristles of my carpet-sweeper, no matter how briskly I trundle it back and forth. Sometimes Pang appears as a detective, eschewing his tapper uniform for a slick brown suit and leather shoes. The detective sits in my armchair, one leg crossed over the other. Cool and debonair.

'That night was the beginning of the end,' he says.

'I know.'

'You may as well have lit a match and sent the whole village up in flames.'

'Now, look here,' I say. 'How was I to know? It's irrational to blame everything on me. You had the opportunity to tell Sergeant Abdullah the truth too. But you didn't.'

Detective Pang does not persist in his allegations, but his silence goads me into a fine old rant. I often get so worked-up that Adam gathers up his books and retreats to the bathroom (to read huddled under a heap of towels in the tub). Detective Pang regards me with mild curiosity as I bluster on in self-defence. The one-sided slanging match frustrates and wears me out – more so than if I were quarrelling with that slippery talk-aholic

Charles Dulwich. There is power in silence, and yet I cannot shut up. Even when the Chinese detective's contribution is so negligible I may as well be quarrelling with myself.

6

Every morning I cook porridge for Julia. And every morning my granddaughter pads to the kitchen, sleepy and sloe-eyed, in school uniform and stockinged feet, to watch the bubbling alchemy of oats and milk on the stove. The child is good as gold before she leaves for school, as if her rebellious alter ego has a lie-in while the rest of her washes, dresses and gears up for the day. No matter how bothersome my spectral guests the night before, I never fail to rise for porridge duty at quarter past seven. The wholesome nourishment of oats and a few morning pleasantries: this is my contribution to Julia's upbringing before she dashes out of the door.

As Julia spooned up her piping hot breakfast this morning, I wondered what she'd thought of Malaysia. Had she felt any connection to the land of durians and rafflesia and Chinese ancestors? Were there any genealogical stirrings, echoes of recollection in the portion of her DNA returned to its country of origin? Nervous of triggering painful memories, I'd avoided speaking of Malaysia before. But as several months had passed, and the worst of the grieving was over, I tentatively asked my granddaughter if she'd liked it over there. To my relief there were no tears or distress.

Julia licked her spoon and said: 'Malaysia was very hot. I had jet lag and couldn't sleep for weeks. Madame Tay took me to do outdoor t'ai chi in the park to make me sleepy. In the park there was this pond with hundred-year-old turtles in it. I was stroking one of the turtles and it bit my finger off.' Julia showed me the forefinger of her left hand, severed above the top-most joint. Really. Hundred-year-old carnivorous turtles. What a lively imagination she has! Adam says the finger was slammed in a door.

'Did your brother like it there?'

'Dunno. Adam had diarrhoea and prickly heat. He had jet lag too, but he didn't want to do t'ai chi. Said it was girly.'

'Did you get on with Ayah?'

'She was scary! She nagged Mum like she was a child.'

'Oh yes, she's an old battleaxe, isn't she?'

Madame Tay was my daughter's ayah for sixteen years – an ill-chosen surrogate mother who taught Frances to be scornful of her English father. I'd have sacked the conniving witch, if Frances hadn't loved her so.

'Mum reckoned she's going to die soon anyway.'

'Julia. You mustn't talk like that!'

Heaven forbid! The thought of Madame Tay levitating about my council flat gives me the screaming habdabs. Let us pray that her potions of belladonna and bat's gonads help her outlive me by years.

After scraping her bowl clean Julia went to the bathroom to brush her teeth and metal brace, a task she performs with such vigour the bristles of her toothbrush are splayed flat within a couple of weeks. After she'd rinsed, gargled and spat, Julia grabbed her satchel, shouted, ''Bye, Granddad,' and tore out of the door. I watched from the kitchen window as she crossed the estate, tall and raw-boned, with a gangling, clumsy stride (she must have inherited that gaucheness from her father; Frances was very graceful at that age). I watched my granddaughter lope away, knowing she will return to me tonight a different girl. Resentful and sullen. A stranger. Outside my flat Julia belongs to the estate. To the smashed-up telephone boxes and stolen cars. Until she straggles home again my granddaughter belongs to whatever claims her. And I fear there are many things eager to claim the likes of a twelve-year-old girl.

At least I don't have to worry about Adam running wild. Though that's not to say the boy's not a worry. It's not normal for a fifteen-year-old boy never to speak, not have any friends and rarely go outdoors. Yesterday, returning from his weekly trip to the library, Adam came home reeling under the weight of an 18-inch black-and-white TV. I'd never owned a television before and wasn't sure if I wanted the so-called 'opium of the masses' in my living room. But keen for Adam to have a hobby other than reading I said, *You can put that on the sideboard.* Adam had cleaned out his post-office savings to make the junk-shop purchase, and at first I feared he'd been fleeced. He sculpted an aerial out of a wire coat hanger, then spent half an hour twisting it about until there was a picture decent enough to watch. The first programme we saw was a quiz show (which, owing to the on-screen blizzard, seemed to have been filmed on location in Siberia). I enjoyed the quiz very much, and when Charles Dulwich came strutting along, scandalized by our new acquisition (*I say! What the devil's that? Where've you hidden the projector . . . ?*), I was so engaged in the number puzzles and the witticisms of the host, I ignored the peeved Resettlement Officer until he went away.

When our nicotine-stained angel came home she gave a whoop of delight and sat down on the sofa in her puffa jacket. I'd cooked sausages and mash for dinner, and we ate with our plates on our laps, spell-bound by the snowy landscape of the TV screen. In the flickering monochrome light I could see the fluctuating emotions on my grandchildren's faces: Julia giggling at every comic moment, widening her eyes at the slightest bit of dramatic suspense; Adam blushing, eyes down-cast during romantic clinches, smiling darkly at tragic happenings. For three hours we sat in the living room, suffused in the glow of cathode rays. And despite my initial reservations, I am quite looking forward to the same again tonight. How nice it was to have the three of us spending time together, like a family.

After I'd lied to Sergeant Abdullah to protect the Lim sisters, I was certain that Detective Pang had reported me. I steeled myself for the tap on the shoulder, the summons to the police hut. But none came. Why was my day of reckoning not forthcoming? Had Detective Pang decided my storytelling was for a good cause? The best way to eliminate my suspense was to ask the man himself.

As Detective Pang had warned me not to approach him in public, there were few opportunities to talk to him. But about a week after our encounter in the police hut I saw him alone, dragging a billy goat by the horn along a deserted trail. The goat was stamping its hooves and kicking up a spindrift of dust, and the detective was hitting the struggling creature with a bamboo carpet-beater. The goat dropped to his knees and Pang's thrashings became so vicious I thought the bamboo carpet-beater would snap. Why was the detective putting so much effort into the cruel perform-ance when there were no witnesses to his imitation of a villager? I took a deep breath to shout his name, but the cry froze in my throat as a man wielding a broom ran over to him. I recognized the man, for Ah Yeop was a known Communist sympathizer (and latterly one of my spectral interlopers, forever bragging about the three sons he sacrificed to the Malayan Races Liberation Army and their collected acts of terrorism). When I saw

Ah Yeop I knew my chance to find out why Detective Pang hadn't reported me had passed. I watched instead as the Min Yuen member and undercover spy beat the goat unconscious, then hauled the creature away by its hind legs.

On rainy days the villagers couldn't go rubber tapping. They could do little more than shake their fists at the disobliging sky and curse the day's lost wages. It was on such a day of rain and idleness that I filched a heavy padlock and took it over to Evangeline's hut, dashing through the drowned village in thonged slippers, through crashing sheets of rain. The torrential rampage made a mud slide of the path, and more than once I slipped and soiled my trousers. My umbrella sprang a leak, and by the time I reached Evangeline's hut I was woefully drenched.

I peered through the wire netting of the window to make sure I had the correct hut. Grace was sitting on an upturned beer crate and sucking her thumb, and Evangeline's head was bowed as she worked at a Singer sewing machine, inching a length of fabric under the quick-stabbing needle, her foot tapping the pedal as the bobbin of thread spun round. Evangeline made her living as a seamstress, going from door to door collecting clothes for mending and taking orders for made-to-measure garments. But clothes were not a priority for the impoverished villagers and Evangeline had a hard time making ends meet. When Grace saw me she took her thumb out of her mouth and cooed.

Evangeline glanced up from her sewing, surprised, then self-conscious. When she opened the door her face was lined with irritation. I shut my broken umbrella and regretted not asking permission to visit. The rain pelting the zinc roof was loud enough to wake the dead, and we shouted to communicate.

'Hello.'

'Hello.'

'What are you doing here?' she asked in English.

'I've brought a padlock for your door, to stop your sister from escaping again. I've brought tools too, and I can fix the brackets if you like.'

I lifted the sturdy padlock from my bag and held it up. Evangeline swung the door wider and I stepped inside, shivering and dripping on the beaten-earth floor.

'I'll get you a towel,' said Evangeline.

The sisters lived in the most ascetic of huts. Bamboo-mat bedding and wooden crates were the only furniture, and the sewing machine dominated the room. As Evangeline rummaged about in a tea chest at the back of the hut, I said hello to Grace, who smiled and slurped on her thumb. Evangeline dug out a threadbare towel from the tea chest. She beckoned me closer and, instead of passing me the towel, flung it over my head and vigorously tousled my hair. I was embarrassed at first, my head fiercely rumpled by Evangeline's strong and competent hands. And no sooner had I begun to enjoy the warm, domineering rub-down than Evangeline whipped the towel away and declared me dry.

Kneeling by the door in mud-spattered trousers, I disembowelled my tool bag and selected a nail from the old tobacco tin. Striking the first hammer blow, I realized that the wood was very brittle and weak, and Grace could easily prise out the nails if she wanted (though I doubted she'd think of it). When the first bracket was secured, I took a little breather and asked Evangeline, who was standing, arms folded, a pace or two behind me, if she missed being a high-school teacher.

'Yes,' she said, 'but I have to look after Grace now, so I cannot go back to Kajang and teach English.'

'What a pity,' I said. 'Who looked after Grace before?'

'Our parents, but they are dead now.'

'I'm so sorry.'

At a loss for what else to say I resumed the lock fitting. When I finished I showed Evangeline how to work the padlock and gave her two copies of the key. Evangeline thanked me and offered me a cup of water, which she poured from the lukewarm kettle. We stood awkwardly together as I took a copper-tasting sip. The austerity of the hut was troubling. There was no shrine or joss-sticks or knick-knacks to make the place look like home.

'Do you like to read, Evangeline?' I asked.

'Yes.'

'Resettlement Officer Dulwich has a terrific library in his bungalow. Austen, Conrad, Dickens . . . I can lay my hands on anything you want.'

'No, thank you,' said Evangeline. 'I don't want to read any of those books.'

Those books . . . Her tone of voice was as if I'd suggested pornography. Babbling softly, Grace crawled off her beer crate and on to the bamboo matting. She yawned, revealing the stumpy teeth in her gums, and tilted her head to gaze ponderously at her sister and me.

'How old is Grace?' I asked.

'Twenty-three.'

'What's wrong with her? If you don't mind my asking . . .'

'She drowned when she was a child. She died, then came back to life, but came back brain-damaged.'

'You must have your work cut out caring for her. She seems to demand your constant attention . . .'

Evangeline sighed and rubbed a dog-eared corner of her eye. 'Sometimes she's demanding, sometimes peaceful like this,' she said. 'She was worse when she was younger.'

We were quiet for a moment. The percussion of rain on the zinc roof made it seem as though we were inside a kettledrum. Grace continued to gaze at us as she lay on the bamboo matting. She bent her legs, the pale scar on her knee like a little caterpillar wriggling to her shin. By then I'd heard of Grace's infamous promiscuity, but there was nothing 'come-hither' about her lack of modesty. She moved unconsciously, her limbs seeking a more comfortable arrangement in the sticky heat. I never understood how men could take advantage of her the way they did. Though she encouraged her defilement, Grace had the mind of a child. And there is something very wrong with the conquest of an infant.

'Does anyone ever help you with Grace?'

'The Jesus People take her when I help the Red Cross.'

'Are you and Grace Christians?'

'No.'

'But you have Christian names.'

'Yes.'

'Do you have Chinese names too?'

'No.'

'That's unusual.'

'Yes.'

I lifted the cup to my lips and found it dry. Everything about Evangeline, from her reticence to her barricaded arms, made me feel unwelcome. It occurred to me that she hadn't even bothered to thank me for the night I'd rushed to the police hut to help her. The rain had slowed to a feeble pit-a-pat-pat and children ran out of a neighbouring hut, screaming after the morning cooped up indoors. I told Evangeline that I had to leave for tiffin. I told her that I was too busy to help in the medical hut that week, and would she pass on my regards to the Aussie nurses? Evangeline nodded, relieved, and I gathered up my tools and left.

As the sun made its debut in the sky I was glad to be outside, away from strange Evangeline and the smoke-hued fascination of her eyes. I splashed in puddles and hoped that Winston Lau wasn't dishing up fish-head curry for tiffin again.

* * *

Due to the coercive nature of the Briggs Plan, the Chinese community were very hostile to it. The belief that New Villages existed under police dictatorship was widespread, as was the misconception that the Chinese community were being persecuted by the British, as they had been persecuted by the Japanese during the Occupation. Such attitudes were unhelpful in the war against Communism.

The government wanted the Chinese to play a more active role in their liberation. They wanted to show that the so-called dictatorship of the proletariat, as advocated by the Reds, was nothing more than the dictatorship of the Malayan Communist Party central committee. The government wanted to give the Chinese what the Communists were out to deny them: democracy.

Resettlement Officer Dulwich and I received a government directive stating that, as part of a pilot scheme to give the ex-squatters the power to manage their own affairs, The Village of Everlasting Peace was to elect a village council. The trouble was that, with the exception of the few ex-urban Chinese (such as my beloved Evangeline), most of the squatters had lived their whole lives in jungle settlements and were un-educated and ignorant of such political ideals. Therefore, before the village elections could be held, the Chinese had to be taught about democracy, so the need for a village council would be fully appreciated. With this objective in mind, thousands of dollars were spent on a brief documentary explaining the democratic process, which was to be shown in tandem with the Hollywood film *Tarzan* – the glamorous bait with which we were to draw a large audience to our village meeting.

On the day the documentary was to be shown, an Indian projectionist drove his van of equipment up to the officers' bungalow. The projectionist, whose name was Vorpal, had been hired by the government to tour the New Villages of Selangor with a Cantonese-dubbed version of *Tarzan*. Charles invited him to join us on the veranda for a *stengah* or two.

Vorpal sipped his lemonade and joked about the behaviour of the elders in The Village of Eternal Prosperity, which he'd visited the night before. When a celluloid tiger had sauntered across the screen, some of the elders had wailed and run away, afraid the tiger would leap into the audience. We had a good laugh at this and I asked Vorpal if the village meeting had been a success. The projectionist shrugged and said he didn't know. He couldn't understand Cantonese and politics bored him. For a man at the forefront of such a pioneering democratic scheme Vorpal was very apathetic. It was a pity the 10th Independent Regiment of the Malayan Communist Party didn't take his apathy into account when they ambushed his van outside Kajang three weeks later and slit his throat. Vorpal's corpse was bound in ribbons of celluloid and dumped at the gates of the resettlement camp where a film screening was scheduled for that evening.

By late afternoon preparations were under way in the village square. A crowd of spectators gathered as we hoisted up the cinema screen (the majestic sail of our maiden democratic voyage!) and Vorpal set up his projector. A police truck drove around the village, loud-hailing a reminder to everyone of the lifting of the curfew and the evening's cinematic extravaganza. Tilly lamps were hung like fiery fruit from the tulang trees bordering the square, and as the event was a prime target for Communist saboteurs the home guard patrolled in force, rifles strapped on and eyes peeled for any monkey business.

At six o'clock the invasion of the square began; first a hesitant trickle, then a human landslide, villagers spilling in as folk-ballads of the motherland plink-plonked from the cinema speakers. Children ran pell-mell, bouncing yo-yos, hitting the shins of antagonists with sticks, and *ai-oooh*-ing, awed by the vast screen. The elderly shuffled in on the arms of kindly neighbours, and mothers distributed blankets, woven mats, paper fans and other comforts of home. Friends and neighbours hailed each other (*Hey! Third cousin, come and sit by me!*) and I greeted the rowdy masses, smiling and crying *Hello!*, delighted to see the villagers brought together by something other than misfortune and unanimous loathing of the British administration.

In the mass of bobbing heads and wagging tongues I spotted Evangeline and mad Grace. Grace was in a very animated state, eyes darting everywhere as she stood up to chase after whatever sparked her interest. Evangeline had her sister's wrist in a tight grip and every few seconds yanked the wayward Grace back down in an unhappy tug-of-war that lasted all night. Near the front of the square the missionary Marina Tolbin stood in the midst of a sea of urchins, whose hands were thrust out like beggars'. The idolatry of Marina Tolbin confused me, until I saw she had a bag of sweets and was scattering the confectionery like birdseed. The little ones (and a few bigger ones bereft of dignity) dropped to their knees and scrabbled after the lemon fizzes and bonbons. It was such a lamentable show of greed that Marina put the bag away. The children who hadn't managed to procure sweets for themselves pawed at the hem of her skirt and mewled like kittens. This must have caused Marina some distress, but she sat in the deckchair next to Blanche and pretended not to hear.

When the square was full, Resettlement Officer Dulwich stood upon a beer-crate podium and read a speech to the crowd. The assembled villagers resembled a monster of a thousand heads, and a very ill-mannered monster at that, paying scant attention to Charles and the awkward stream of Cantonese issuing from his loudhailer. Even after the film started the audience refused to settle, chattering and commenting on everything that appeared on the screen. I stalked up and down, flashing my torch and *shush*-ing trouble spots like a militant usher.

The film was a jolly caper in which Tarzan the beefcake and Jane the buxom belle fought war-mongering

African tribes with the assistance of a troupe of well-trained chimpanzees. It was nothing like the Edgar Rice Burrows novels of my boyhood and failed to hold my interest for long. Voyeur of the shadows, I watched the villagers instead, the rows of Asiatic faces illuminated by the moving Technicolor images as the projector reels spun round. When the vine-swinging Tarzan crashed into a tree the thousand-headed monster laughed as one. When a tiger pounced across the screen the thousand-headed monster let out a gasp. The shadows of moths frolicking in the projector light interfered with the picture and Vorpal squirted them with repellent spray, so they flew off with poison-laden wings. And the moths weren't the only pests, for the children discovered the joy of shadow puppetry. First there came a single rabbit, wagging its long ears and hopping up and down to everyone's giggling amusement. Then a whole Noah's Ark of shadowy animals. For every shadow puppet a dozen torch beams swooped upon the audience, for the home guard were enjoying the Cantonese-dubbed film as much as everyone else. They dealt with the matter severely, seizing the culprits by the ear and slinging them under the tulang trees.

After Tarzan had conquered the African tribe and brought the film to its exciting climax, Charles requested that everyone remain sitting. The thousand-headed monster groaned. It was half past eight – bedtime for most, and bladders needed emptying. In this climate of discontent the documentary flickered into being. Whether it was any good or not, I don't know. I was busy rereading my speech and jittering with nerves. I'd read the speech in English translation to Charles that afternoon, pacing back and forth in the sauna heat of the bungalow as he sat flaccid in his wicker chair. Charles shut his eyes as I read aloud, and when I paused between sentences my gaze would stray to the open lower buttons of his shirt and the pale blancmange of his paunch.

'Forgive me, old chap,' he said with a yawn, when I'd asked for his verdict, 'it's too damn sticky to applaud.'

Encouraged thus, I climbed upon the wooden crate podium at the end of the documentary. *Hey, there's that big-nosed devil Christopher*, villagers called. *Hey, Christopher! Can we go home now? We've got to go to work in the morning*. The night was humid as ever and the underarms of my shirt patched with damp. The projector lamp illuminated the screen still and my pupils flinched in the glare, the audience diminishing to an impenetrable mass of darkness and eyes. In the expectant hush, my speech began. I described the importance of the village council, and the process by which it was to be established. I declared it a momentous day for The Village of Everlasting Peace.

'We need twelve nominations,' I said. 'Those who wish to nominate, please raise your hands. When we have twelve candidates you may go home.'

I hadn't used a loudhailer (believing such contraptions to distance the speaker from the audience) and with an aching throat I shaded my eyes and squinted into the darkness for a hand held aloft. The shadow-masked masses also peered to see who'd defy the People Inside and support the hare-brained Foreign Devil scheme. One brave and solitary hand went up as a villager called Timmy Lo made a self-nomination. I knew Timmy Lo well, for he was a good man – a stalwart digger of ditches and builder of huts, pulling the weight of two and a half men. Timmy and I were good chums and it always cheered me to see his affable, round-as-a-cantaloupe face. As Special Constable Tahir jotted down Timmy's name there was a hissing in the audience, like air let stealthily out of a tyre, but to my relief no more objection after that.

But I'd underestimated the ominous threat of that hiss. Timmy Lo was not the scree preceding the avalanche of nominations. He was the one and only candidate of the night. For another twenty minutes I paced before the villagers, calling for nominees and arguing the hypothetical good of democracy. And with the tick-tock of every minute my humiliation deepened. I felt as though I were pleading with a lover who wanted nothing more to do with me, a lover whom I repulsed (oh, bitter taste of things to come!). The villagers became bolder in their mutterings and curses. They may have been in the square against their will, but they still had the freedom to move their tongues.

'Who is this impostor?' a woman cried. 'Where is Mr Christopher, our friend?'

'Hah! That'll teach you to befriend an Imperialist whore!' heckled an unseen man.

'My boy will piddle his pants in a minute!' another voice piped up.

Cheeks aflame, I searched the crowd for a lifted hand, desperate as a sailor lost at sea scanning the horizon for land. Who were my allies? Not the yawning home guard. Not Vorpal the projectionist, impatient to pack up his equipment and leave. Not Resettlement Officer Dulwich, flipping open his silver pocket watch to inspect the time. I knew why the villagers were scared. I could smell the rotting stench of the invisible bandits crouched in the crowd. I could see the red stars of their invisible berets as they pressed invisible blades to throats. Through their spidery network of minions and spies the Communists were omnipresent; the Min Yuen, the diseased heads of the thousand-headed monster, malignant and inseparable. The villagers were terrified, and though I understood why, I wanted to hurl my wooden crate podium at them in frustration.

'You will all remain here until we have twelve nominations!' I shouted. *'Twelve!* Not one less! No one is allowed to leave, not even to go to the toilet! Even if we have to sit here all night and all day tomorrow. This brave man here is your example!' I pointed at a cringing Timmy Lo. 'You must unite and stand up for yourselves against the Communists . . . !'

When the ghost of Charles is in a malicious mood (is there any other kind?) he teases me about the failed village meeting, and my lapse into dictatorship.

'What an appalling little tyrant you were!' he says, laughing, from the upholstered throne of my armchair. 'What a snotty-nosed little tantrum! What illogic possessed you? One cannot discipline a bank of butterflies by swinging a sledgehammer at it! And in the name of democracy no less! Ha, ha, ha! Democracy! As if the Chinese give a monkey's about democracy. All the Chinese want is to be jolly well left alone.'

His lazy-mindedness really gets my goat. How dare Charles dismiss a whole race of people? Once again, I make futile appeals to historical evidence to cure him of his prejudices.

'Only a year or two after you died every New Village in Malaysia had a successful, democratically elected council. Including The Village of Everlasting Peace. The Chinese want political representation as much as anyone else. So much so they campaigned for it on the streets of Kuala Lumpur in the sixties . . .'

And does Resettlement Officer Dulwich listen? Of course not. He smiles patronizingly as I speak, then continues to dishonour my motives for haranguing the villagers.

'Oh, it was unbearable to watch you!' declared Charles, with a glee implying the opposite. 'How dark the recesses of your Nietzschean soul! Tell me, Christopher, was it really your passion for democracy that made you so tyrannical? Was it really the best interests of the villagers you had at heart? Or were you just determined that everyone yield to your megalomaniac will?'

'Oh, do be quiet, Charles. I wasn't nearly that bad!'

'Well, we all know what happened next . . .'

After I'd lost my temper and swung my sledgehammer (the herd of butterflies seething but uninjured), a hand came to rest on my shoulder.

'C'mon, old chap,' said Charles, 'this is never going to work.'

He was right. One only had to listen to the wails of dismay. I stepped aside as Charles announced in broken Cantonese that the villagers were free to go. The exodus was indignant. Gathering limp and drowsy children, the villagers left in a plague of fury, with much rancorous spitting, ten times quicker than they had arrived. I felt the departure of the angry hordes so keenly it was as though they were trampling me under-foot. Cheered by the sudden reversal in popularity, Charles waved the masses off. He came up to me and imparted some kind words. I did not hear them. I stared, crestfallen, as Timmy Lo petitioned Special Constable Tahir to remove his name as a nominee. In less than ten minutes the village square was empty, but for some peanut shells and a small forgotten child, bawling for its mother.

The siren for the late curfew was howling when I arrived back at my hut. I sank to my knees in the darkness, burying my head in my hands and making other pathetic gestures in the pantomime of despair. I was very angry. Angry at the Communists, angry at the villagers, and most of all at myself. The chorus of night creatures caw-cawed and tu-whit-tu-whooed in ridicule as I stripped off and lay on my camp-bed. And though I expected the evening's miserable outcome to fuel hours of insomnia, I fell swiftly into oblivion minutes after shutting my eyes.

Hours later I was woken by a banging on my door. *Evangeline* – the four syllables rang out in my mind, preceding any other thought or awareness of time and place. The banging had a knock-on effect in my heart, which gave a succession of shuddery thuds as I tumbled out of bed and groped for my trousers, eyes casting about in the pitch-darkness of my hut. *Who's there?* I called. I threw the door open on its creaking hinges and saw a girl – not Evangeline – with a shawl over her head, kneeling in the moonlight a few yards from my hut. The shawled girl was sobbing, and when the swinging door banged against the hut wall she glanced up, her face wrenched with grief and sodden with tears. Her eyes were red weeping lesions and her mouth a sobbing wound. In her lap was a bundle of rags.

'Who are you?' I demanded. 'What do you want?'

The young woman didn't answer, only wept more furiously. It must have been three in the morning and I was more irritated than concerned. I had no telephone and would have to escort the blubbery wreck down to the police hut. I went and crouched by her, touching her shoulder, hoping to reassure her and encourage her to speak.

'Why did you knock on my door?' I asked. 'What are you doing here?'

Her tears were silvery in the moonlight, slithers of glittering brine. Snivelling, fingers trembling as if frost-bitten, she fumbled open the cloth bundle in her lap. My head eclipsed the moonlight as I leant to get a better look, squinting to separate what she'd unwrapped from the shadows. What I saw was oddly familiar: thin and pale – like the chopped bones Winston Lau set aside to boil for porridge broth. The acid taste of nausea flooded my mouth as I made sense of what lay in the rags. I swallowed hard.

'Whose fingers are they?' I asked.

The slender digits were amputated before the knuckles, pale and blanched, the cloth maroon with blood.

The woman said, 'My husband's.'

One of the fingers rolled away from kith and kin, out of her lap and on to the ground. I did not pick it up. The woman wept with hysterical abandon, and I realized that I did not have to ask who her husband was.

7

Adam takes the bus to see her in the afternoon. Her phone is cut off, so he never knows if she'll be in. If no one answers the door he waits in the stairway outside her flat until it gets dark.

He knows the way from the gates of the Mountbatten estate with his eyes shut; every block of flats and concrete paving slab, the route mapped in his head. In a few weeks, though, most of the estate will be gone. The council have admitted defeat, admitted that the maze of social planning has failed, gone amok, and are moving in with bulldozers and wrecking balls and a blueprint for regeneration. As he walks to his sister's, Adam gazes up at the tower blocks earmarked for demolition. He stares at the block where he lived for two years with his grandfather, behind a triple-bolted door on the fourteenth floor. He remembers the baby squall, the racket of other low-income lives vibrating through the walls.

Julia knows they are knocking down the estate. The council sent her a letter. She ripped it open and read it, slowly, through pinned pupils. Then she went to the window and opened the curtains for the first time that week, blinking at the landscape of stone. As a teenager she mucked about in the stairways of every high-rise, smoking fags, vandalizing the lifts with felt-tipped pens, daring her friends to bang on letterboxes and run away. The tower she lived in dominates the estate like a concrete tumour. She stared at the charred, burnt-out flat on the twelfth floor, the England flags hanging proudly from window ledges, and the lines of tattered baby clothes. She closed the curtains, murmuring that it was about fucking time. Then she lay on the sofa, on her side in her dressing gown, crossing her arms over her breastbone as if to pull an invisible blanket around her. She sank into the cushions, into the amniotic fluids; seven stone of skin and bones and a map of scarred, misshapen veins. She's an empty husk of a girl; her body chambers of air, the bowels and stomach barren for days. An abandoned chrysalis, butterfly flown. Adam dreams of carrying her out of there – a recurring fantasy of his – to take her into the car park, into the back of a waiting car. He wants to drive her away from London, lock her in a room somewhere and watch over her as she burns and sweats. He dreams of her rapid recovery, the last beads of poison evaporating from her brow. He imagines her compliant, grateful, determined to help herself – smiling weakly as he brings orange juice to her bedside. Adam thinks it through and it seems so easy. But when he sees her it's the hardest thing in the world. The council aren't touching Julia's block – it's one of the few that they aren't bringing down. Adam was gutted when he heard.

He stares up at the perpetually drawn curtains on the third floor. He stands there, hands burrowed in his pockets, as swings steered by children flinging their heels fly back and forth across the way. On the balcony passageway outside Julia's flat a boy crouched in a shopping trolley is launched at the far wall by his friend. The impact of steel against bricks, the juvenile scream and jarring of bones makes Adam wince, but he says nothing as the dazed and injured boy climbs out and his laughing friend climbs in.

Adam knocks on Julia's door. She answers in a bulky knitted cardigan and jeans. He shifts awkwardly on her doorstep. Every time he sees Julia he thinks she's grown paler and lost more weight, that her eyes have sunk deeper in her head. In the first instant of reunion Adam sees what others see: the genderless anorexic, the leper queen; the shrink-wrapped skull daubed from a palette of ochre and grey. Then the image is gone and he sees her as Julia again.

'Happy birthday,' he says.

'I thought it was tomorrow.'

'No, today.'

Julia's pale eyes flicker towards the carrier bag that Adam has brought.

'Come in.'

The flat is smoky and smells to Adam of homeless-ness, though Julia and Rob have lived here for three years. While Julia is in the kitchen, boiling a saucepan of water for tea, Adam opens the curtains, shadows rising up from the carpet like a flock of birds. The carpet, with a pall of fag ends and ash, is studded with glittering ring pulls, and the stains are like dark continents on a map of a foreign planet. On the window ledge, next to an old shoelace tourniquet, a clock ticks loudly, the second hand quivering, power-less to advance. Adam shuts the curtains again, preferring things in the poverty of light.

Julia returns and presents Adam with a chipped mug of tea. They sit opposite each other on the two sagging sofas.

'Twenty-fucking-two,' she says, sighing.

'That's not old.'

'Oh, c'mon, I can hear the shovel hitting the soil.'

Sometimes when Adam visits she is agitated, smoking irritably, listening out for a knock on the door. She'll snap at Adam, spittle flecking her lips as she blames him in some illogical way for her gnawing dis-comfort. But on her birthday Julia is in a good mood – stoned and calm. Her eyes are tiny pricks of dark in a sea of pale blue; opiates binding to neurotransmitters, corrupting the biochemistry of her blood. Adam has done his research and knows pretty much everything there is to know about her drug of choice – except, of course, how it feels. He wishes her happy birthday and passes her the carrier bag.

'Oh, Adam, you shouldn't have!'

Polythene rustles as she peers inside. There are sterile packets of 0.4mm needles, syringes, disinfecting swabs, cotton wool, a bottle of bleach. Julia pulls out the miniature birthday cake in its box; shop-bought confectionery, thick with sugary icing. She reads aloud the piped message.

'Many Happy Returns, Julia.'

She rips open the envelope of the birthday card with hopeful eyes. There's nothing in the card but what Adam has written and, briefly pissed-off, her face hardens. Then she smiles and dutifully stands the card on the arm of the sofa.

'Thank you,' she says. 'That's really lovely of you.'

She leans over and kisses Adam, her dry lips chafing his cheek as he breathes in mildew and scalp. He thinks of the weeping blister at the edge of her mouth with a guilty shiver of repulsion. Julia sinks back on the sofa, dragging fingers through her limp hair, ploughing furrows of grease.

'Did Rob get you anything nice?' Adam asks.

'Dunno. He went out this morning. Hasn't come back yet.'

'How's your week been?'

'Oh . . . OK . . .' answers Julia vaguely, her horizon of time narrowed to the hours it takes to score and relieve the pangs of addiction. 'How's things with you?' she asks.

'OK. Same as usual, I s'pose . . .'

Adam sips his tea and tastes the sourness of the milk.

So long as Julia makes the effort to brew cups of tea for him, all is not lost. He watches the bony spider of her hand chase an itch from throat to collar-bone, the bone-white ridge of her knuckles. Julia is ageless and never the same. Sometimes she's an emaciated child, vulnerable and frail, her thin wrist threatening to snap from the weight of a cigarette. Other times she's decades older, calculating and mean, looking to cheat you if given half the chance. Today she drifts in between, not quite the hostile stranger, but not quite his sister either.

'Have they cleared out Granddad's old block yet?'

'Yeah. There's no one left now 'cept for squatters.'

The spider scuttles under the cardigan sleeve and scratches, nails harvesting dead skin. Adam takes the black-and-white photograph he has brought out of his jacket pocket and passes it to her.

'What's this?' she asks.

Adam doesn't say anything. Julia lifts the photo closer to her face, squints and frowns. Though the picture is turned away from him Adam sees the two smiling schoolgirls made from monochrome patterns of darkness and light. One of the girls grips the handlebars of a bike, her hair dark and feathery, and her freckles paintbrush-splattered flecks. The girl squints, at odds with the glaring sun, and Adam knows that she is his mother at sixteen; nine years younger than he is now, six years younger than Julia. The second girl – an English girl – smiles timidly at the camera lens. The English girl is large, unwieldy, taller by a foot. Her curly blonde hair springs about her head like a clown's wig, every follicle a slave to humidity. Both girls wear a school uniform of a white blouse and a grey pleated skirt. The photograph came with a letter two days ago through the post, and Adam has looked at it a thousand times since. Sunlight from the last century leaps from the faces of the teenage girls. The light glitters from the silver bell of the bicycle, flows through the aperture and into the dark chamber of the camera. Adam thinks of that moment of shutter-click; the moment his mother and her wallflower friend were immortalized in black and white.

'That's Mum, isn't it?' says Julia.

'Yeah. It was taken in 1969, in Kuala Lumpur.'

'Where d'you get this?'

'The other girl in the photo sent it to me. Says she's an old schoolfriend of Mum's. She wrote me a letter, says she wants to meet up.'

'What for?'

'I don't know.'

'How'd she get your address?'

'I don't know . . . Phone book?'

Julia passes the photograph back to Adam. She takes a cigarette out of the packet on the table and places it between her scuffed lips. She sparks a flame on the disposable lighter, then slouches back on the sofa. The sleeve of her cardigan slides up and Adam sees a rash like a thousand tiny razor nicks on her forearm.

'What's her name?'

'Sally Hargreaves.'

'I don't like it,' Julia says. 'Mum said she hated that

school. She said she never had any friends there – that all the other girls were snobs and bitches. It's weird. This Sally person must be after something.'

'I don't have anything to give her.'

'Then why's she bothering you? She might be mental.'

'Since when d'you have anything against mental people? What about your mates? The one who barks at the skirting board and shoots up in his jugular?'

'Adrian's Rob's mate, not mine, and what's he got to do with anything? I'd leave this woman well alone if I were you.'

'But she was a friend of Mum's . . .'

'So she says. She might be lying. There's no way of knowing if she's telling the truth or not.'

Her objections stop there. Her eyelids falter and her head droops so Adam can see the scraggly parting in her thin blonde hair. He is used to Julia nodding off mid-sentence, words floating away. It used to annoy him. He used to prod her, nag her awake (*I've come all the way here to see you . . .*). But he realizes now she has little control over the ebb and flow of consciousness. He's learnt not to take it personally.

He stands up, removes the cigarette smouldering between her fingers and stubs it out on a plate of toast crusts on the floor. He takes the photograph, puts it back in his pocket, whispers 'Happy birthday' and leaves.

8

When Sally's father asked her to accompany him to
Kuala Lumpur, she had wanted to say no. She was a
timid girl. She'd left boarding school after a bout of
glandular fever at the age of eleven, and had been
home-tutored ever since. Sally had no friends her own
age. She hid in her bedroom night after night, listening
to classical music and reading *Jane Eyre*. The furthest
she'd ever travelled before was Marseilles, and she'd no
idea where Kuala Lumpur was (though if she'd had to
hazard a guess she'd have said India). Had a fortune
teller predicted that Sally would live and die in
Cricklewood without ever travelling elsewhere, she
wouldn't have minded. What Sally did mind, however,
was being separated from her father. Sally's mother
had died when Sally was a baby and it had always
been just the two of them. A year was a long time
and she'd miss her father very much. The only way to

avoid the sorrow, she reasoned, was to go with him.

In January 1969 the Hargreaves moved into a spacious, two-storey house on a street of expensive, gated residences in Petaling Jaya, Kuala Lumpur. The house had marble floors, air-conditioning and, in the front yard, Trixie and Tinkerbell, a pair of Dobermann guard dogs Mr Hargreaves installed that Sally was so frightened of she lobbed food at them whenever she left the house – pork dumplings, cold cuts of ham, bunches of green bananas – anything to distract the Hounds of Hell as she ran to the gate.

Like most expat households the Hargreaves had a live-in maid, a Malay girl of Sally's age called Safiah. Safiah had a pretty, cherubic face and a thick mane of black hair and Sally knew little about her other than that she was very hard-working – forever sweeping, or standing on tiptoe on the banister to dust away cobwebs, or scouring the bathroom floor. Safiah was very cheerful and smiley, and with hopes of friendship Sally borrowed a Malay–English dictionary from her father and approached the servant girl as she knelt in the yard, scrubbing laundry in the wash tub. Standing awkwardly by the washing line, Sally attempted to talk to Safiah, riffling the dictionary pages as she foraged for words. Safiah was confused at first, then she erupted into giggles. She giggled and giggled and Sally was so mad she nearly threw the dictionary at her idiotic giggling head.

Mr Hargreaves also hired a cook, a Chinese woman called Yok Ling. Yok Ling was a much sought-after chef, recommended to Mr Hargreaves by an acquaintance at the Royal Selangor Club, and one of the conditions of her working for the Hargreaves was that they allow her to spirit-proof the house first, shifting tables, chairs and the china cabinet in accordance with the principles of feng shui. Yok Ling's English was excellent, though her tactlessness often made Sally wish she was as mute as Safiah (*Oooh! You are a fat one* lah! Yok Ling cried when introduced to the boss's daughter: *I am going to have to cook extra for you!*)

Mr Hargreaves was at work until after midnight most nights, and Sally spent her first week in Kuala Lumpur alone. Most days she slept until noon and spent her afternoons sprawled on her bed reading Georgette Heyer novels. Yok Ling rang a bell at mealtimes and Safiah would bring Sally's food to the dining-room table, before squatting in the doorway to watch her eat (as though it were feeding time at the zoo). Sally whiled away the evenings lying in a cool bath, listening to Cantonese pop-songs on the radio. She wept into her pillow before she went to sleep. She desperately wanted to tell her father that she had changed her mind. But it was too late.

Mr Hargreaves hired a chauffeur to ferry Sally to and from school every day and though the twenty-minute journey to the prestigious Amethyst International School for Girls was her first trip into central Kuala Lumpur Sally was too nervous to look at the early-morning streets. She sat rigidly on the leather-upholstered back seat, her new blouse tucked into the waistband of her new pleated skirt, an empty satchel on her lap and a fearful rhythm in her heart. When the car passed the gates of the Amethyst school, Sally's first sighting of the colonial-era mansion of wood and woven bamboo did nothing to calm her nerves. With the car parked a little farther down the street, Sally turned to look out of the rear window and watched the girls flitting through the gates; tall girls, short girls; one girl pedalling a bicycle, another speedily hopping on crutches; girls monogamously arm-in-arm. There were girls in every stage of adolescence, from skinny prepubescence to the fullest bloom of womanhood; every shade of hair, from palest blonde to Arabian black. The pupils of the Amethyst school seemed frighteningly 'other' to Sally – as though they belonged to some secret sect of girlhood. In the flagstone yard a gang of older girls shared a surreptitious cigarette, shooting casual looks of disdain at the younger non-smoking pupils. Girls gossiped around the earthenware pots of flowers, or queued to jump a long skipping rope, chanting rhymes Sally had never heard before. The driver, who'd been silent throughout the journey, eyed his passenger in the rear-view mirror; *Missi, we already here* lah*! You better hurry or you'll be late.* Sally pulled the handle and inched open the door. But overcome by an irrational fear of the distance to the kerb, she slammed it shut again and squeaked to the driver, *One moment, please!*

Eventually, after the bell had rung and the yard was empty, Sally left the car and scuttled into the school building. The secretary led her to the fifth-form class-room, where the form tutor, Miss Ng, brought Sally to stand next to her on the teaching platform. The class of sixteen-year-old girls hushed their chatter about the Christmas holidays and stared at the larger than average newcomer, who stared back at them, fighting the powerful urge to throw up. How slim and pretty they were. How well-groomed and fresh-looking, as though lightly misted with dewdrops. Sally blazed with self-consciousness, her classmates' inquisitive eyes like ants crawling over her skin. Whatever must they think of her? Of her weight? Of her wild tumbleweed hair (unsmoothed by the nightly applications of olive oil, singed from the unsuccessful attempt to iron it flat that morning)? Miss Ng asked Sally to introduce herself and, blushing, Sally whispered her name. *What did she say?* a voice called from the back row. Miss Ng repeated what Sally had said and sent her to an empty desk.

The majority of Sally's classmates were British or Australian, with a few mixed-race girls of dual national-ity thrown in. To Sally's horror the classes were very lively. She sat meekly at her desk as the lessons moved swiftly along, praying she would not be called upon to speak.

The bell rang for lunch at half past twelve. There were seven tables in the dining hall, one for each class, and lunch was a refined affair with silver cutlery, napkins on laps and tea served from teapots. Miss Ng presided over the fifth-form table, and three lunch monitors served the rest of the class vegetable consommé, asparagus, new potatoes and slices of chicken, and then little bowls of vanilla ice for dessert. A wild anxious fluttering in her belly prevented Sally from eating a single bite, and as her classmates chattered she stared at her plate, feeling as though she could no more join in than converse in Tagalog. Fortunately, after the soup course, the girl sitting next to Sally came to the rescue. *Do you like Cliff Richard?* the girl whispered (as if whispering the codeword for a secret underground organization). *Yes, I do*, Sally lied. The girl flashed a broad metallic grin and said her name was Melissa. After lunch Melissa took Sally to the library, where she showed off her Cliff Richard scrap-book; the pages were crammed with magazine clippings, song lyrics and fan-club letters. As Melissa reverentially turned the pages, preaching the gospel of Cliff, Sally stared at the snaking metal wires harnessing Melissa's teeth – the work of a mad visionary of an orthodontist. Melissa was a crashing bore and listening to her was torturous, but in the terrifying wilderness of teenage girls she was a friendly face, and Sally was grateful.

Later that day, after her chauffeur had dropped her home, Sally stood in the yard, her mind galloping. Why had her father chosen such a posh school? The lessons were too difficult and her classmates too pretty and accomplished. Back in Cricklewood, where she'd been home-tutored surrounded by the potted palms of the conservatory, Sally had been the star pupil. But at Amethyst she was the class dunce, the lumbering class elephant. Sally dumped her satchel (bulging with text-books and assignments she didn't understand) on the ground, and there and then decided not to go back. She'd look in the *Encyclopaedia of Tropical Maladies* and fake the symptoms of some illness until her father got her a private tutor. Inner peace somewhat restored, Sally tiptoed past the Dobermanns, snoozing in the afternoon sun, to rinse her hands under the standpipe. As water splashed over her sticky fingers and into the drain, Sally heard a *clank, clank, clank* at the gate. Trixie and Tinkerbell heard it too, and leapt up, barking, heavy metal chains dragging across the yard as they ran over to the small Chinese girl rattling a stick back and forth across the railings. The girl smiled at the snarling dogs and rattled her stick faster. She wore the same blouse and grey pleated skirt as Sally, and Sally guessed she was a student in one of the years below. Laughing, the girl tossed the stick high over the gate into the Hargreaves' yard. Trixie and Tinkerbell lunged after the stick, tails wagging.

'Hello,' said the girl. 'You're the new girl. I saw you in my class.'

Though the girl looked pure Chinese, her English accent was perfect. Sally had no memory of having seen her at school that day.

'How d'you get here?' Sally asked.

'Flew,' came her breezy reply.

Sally asked her if she lived near by, and with an unsubtle shiver of distaste the girl said, God, no; she lived above a shop in Chinatown, and had just come to

Petaling Jaya to visit her mad aunt. She pointed at the Christian hospice at the end of the street.

'She lives over there,' she said, 'in that loony bin. When I was a baby she covered herself in petrol and set herself alight. They chucked a bucket of water over her to put the fire out and she had a heart attack. She's OK now, though she's paralysed down one side and disgustingly scarred.'

Sally didn't know what to make of this information. She wiped her damp hands on her skirt and went nervously up to the gate. She asked the girl her name.

'Frances Milnar,' she said, slipping her small hand through the railings. '*Enchantée*.'

Sally asked Frances if she'd like to join her for afternoon tea, and Frances laughed, showing off her tiny vampirish teeth. For a moment Sally thought she was laughing at her offer, but then Frances announced she was starving, adding in a mock sophisticated drawl that tea would be *absolutely divine*. Sally unlatched the gate and let her in. Frances was tomboyish and scrappy-looking; five-foot nothing and flat-chested as a ten-year-old. She had short hair that she tucked behind her ears, small almond eyes, and freckles on her snub nose like the speckling on a bird's egg. Frances skipped over to Trixie and Tinkerbell, and the chained beasts reared up to paw Frances' school uniform and lick her giggling face. Sally was horrified. Her friend of less than five minutes was about to be mauled to death by her own dogs! But they merely sniffed her and smothered her with loving, slobbery licks.

The ceiling-fan blades gently chopped the air of the dining room. Sally lifted the wicker cage on the table to uncover the jug of lemonade and the plate of red-bean pastries.

'Wow!' said Frances. 'Are all these cakes for you?'

'They're for my father too,' Sally replied, defensively.

There was only one glass, so Sally called for Safiah, who padded to the doorway, barefoot and giggling. Sally pointed at Frances and mimed drinking out of a glass.

'That's Safiah,' Sally said, as the servant disappeared into the kitchen. 'She never speaks.'

When Safiah returned, Frances spoke to her in Malay, and Sally, listening as the servant girl strung together sentences of three words or more, was peeved that she hadn't made a similar effort for her on the afternoon of the Malay–English dictionary.

'What did she say?' Sally asked, as Safiah crouched by the door jamb.

'She says she is very happy here. She likes working for you and Mr Hargreaves very much.'

As they drank their lemonade and chatted, Frances laughed to hear that Sally had quit boarding for good at the age of eleven. Though Frances had spent her childhood in Kuala Lumpur, when she was ten her expat father (*He's English, but I don't look half-caste, do I?*) sent her abroad to be educated in Hampshire. Frances did not adapt well to boarding school life. She returned to Malaysia for the Christmas holidays and when the holidays were over refused to go back.

'I climbed up on to the roof of my house, and stayed up there for two weeks. I threw stones at anyone who tried to climb up after me. My father thought I was on hunger strike, but my ayah secretly brought me a plate of noodles twice a day. In the end my father promised not to send me back to boarding school in England and I climbed down.'

'How did you go to the lavatory?' asked an incredulous Sally.

'I had a chamber-pot. Madame Tay emptied it for me. Or I'd chuck it out in the street.'

Sally gazed admiringly at Frances, who held her cake in both hands and nibbled it like a monkey, her eyes glittering with disobedience and adventures to be had. Frances asked Sally where her mother was. With downcast eyes and a sorrowful tone of voice cultivated over many years of practice, Sally told Frances that her mother was dead. Agnes Hargreaves had died in childbirth, and Sally had never known her. Telling people about her dead mother used to be Sally's guilty pleasure. *Poor motherless Sally Hargreaves* – it was almost a mark of distinction. Accustomed to the awkwardness and pity of others, Sally was sorely disappointed by Frances' reaction.

'Mine too!' she cried triumphantly. 'I could tell, you know,' Frances added, 'that you had no mother.'

This irritated Sally. She demanded to know how.

'Oh, I always can.'

Then, very abruptly, Frances scraped back her chair and said that she had to go and visit her mad aunt, because the nuns wouldn't let her in after six.

Sally walked her to the front gate.

'Do come for tea, next time you visit your mad aunt,' she said.

Frances shrugged and said: 'I only see her once a month. That's about as much as I can stand.'

She gave a little wave as she slipped out of the gate and Sally was crestfallen. But no sooner had Frances started off down the road than she turned round again and, skipping backwards a few steps, shouted: 'Why don't you come with me to Chinatown tomorrow? It's a lot more fun than around here.'

Sally nodded and Frances smiled, dimpling her cheeks, her little vampire teeth on display.

'See you in school!' she cried.

And Frances ran off to the hospice, leaving Sally to latch the front gate, her fingers trembling with joy.

9

'Adam . . . Jules ain't here.'

Rob surfaced in the doorway, squinting as if the daylight corroded his retinas. The chain was broken and the door opened narrowly, Rob's plimsoll and bony shoulder wedged behind it – a feeble precaution against forced entry. When he saw it was Adam he eased up, lifted his hand and scratched his red-rimmed nose, the sleeve of his baggy jumper swamping his thin arm.

'Where's she gone?'

'Shops.'

'Shops?' Adam echoed.

'Yeah.'

The tarry edges of Rob's teeth showed themselves, his tongue slothful in his mouth. He'd answered the door because he'd expected someone else and he wanted Adam gone as quickly as possible.

'When will she be back?'

'Hard to say. This evening?'

Rob's squint eased up and Adam could see the pale blue of his irises, his pupils microdots of dark. Rob is a decade older than Julia and over the years has come to look more like her brother than Adam ever will. They have the same eyes, the irises haloes of splintered ice, the same dirty blond hair in lank ponytails; the same rotting teeth and matching his 'n' hers trackmarks. They've succumbed to the same degree of weight loss, a similar bone structure emerging underneath; identical bumps of skull and hollows beneath the temples, as though they were a twin birth, delivered by forceps squeezed too tight. No matter how alike they look, though, they will never be equals. Rob scores for Julia, fixes for her, looks after her. His fists have pummelled her stopped heart back from the brink of death (after delivering the shot that nearly killed her). Adam hates him. He hates the obnoxious swagger of him. He hates that his sister is so dependent on this weasel of a man.

'D'you mind if I wait inside?'

The words almost stuck in Adam's throat. He wanted to barge past Rob and find his sister. But things aren't so easy. Rob only has to click his fingers and Julia would agree never to see Adam again.

'Would if I could but I've got some mates round. Sorry, Adam.'

Adam heard the low thudding music and murmur of voices coming from the living room. He'd seen these get-togethers before, where everyone's slumped about like they've got muscular dystrophy, staring at their shoelaces for hours on end. He knew then that Julia was in there, and had to remind himself that she was not some victim. For all he knew she'd remembered he was coming and asked Rob to send him away.

'Tell her I came, then.'

'Will do. I'll get her to give you a call.'

No such thing had happened in the last three years, but Adam nodded and Rob lifted his hand in a swift, mocking salute, before letting the door slam shut.

After leaving Julia's, Adam went over to the Mountbatten high-rise, the keys to his grandfather's old flat jangling in his jacket pocket. The rehousing of the tenants was nearly over and outside the tower block a large council sign gave notification of demolition on 28 January. The main entrance was locked, and Adam strolled backwards, craning his neck to take in the twenty-eight floors.

He did a tour of the ground floor, peering in the windows, hands cupped around his eyes. Stripped of furniture, most rooms were stark as prison cells, though a few of the walls had been transformed into graffiti canvases; egos unleashed from spray-cans in a chaos of tags. Some of the graffiti was very impressive – works of imagination and skill – and Adam wondered why the artists had gone to so much effort, knowing that in eight weeks the tower would be rubble and dust.

Adam pushed open a window with a broken lock, climbed up and jumped down on the other side. He went up the fourteen flights of echoing stairs and down the corridor to the flat where he'd lived with Julia and his grandfather. He twisted the key in the lock and went inside for the first time in eight years.

Everything was the same and not the same. The left-behind furniture was the same, the upholstery in the same dilapidated condition as when they'd lived there, but the rooms were smaller, as if the ceiling had descended and the walls inched stealthily inwards. Adam wandered from room to room, memories of living there stirred up by the cracks in the bathroom tiles and the rings of limescale in the kitchen sink. The room where he and Julia had once slept, side by side on the narrow beds, smelt of unwashed bodies, and in the bathroom stale piss choked the throat of the toilet. Adam stood in the kitchen, remembering the silent leakages of gas from the faulty cooker, and the charred patch on the ceiling where the flames in his grandfather's frying pan once leapt five feet high. The silence of the fourteenth floor suffocated Adam, and he heaved the force of his hearing into it, ear-drums taut, listening for footsteps, or voices, or the distant slam of a door. But there was nothing, not even the wind.

In the living room Adam lowered himself into the armchair where he once sat for seven- or eight-hour stretches, every day for two years. His elbows jabbed the armrests and his head settled in the hollow in the floral upholstery (a perfect fit – as if the chair had been waiting eight years for the prodigal grandson's return). Spurred by the physical déjà vu, Adam tried to re-enter the mind of that sullen fifteen-, sixteen-, seventeen-year-old boy. He no longer understood what motivated his exile, what day-to-day endurance such loneliness demanded. The other armchair used to be his grandfather's. Adam remembered the never-ending melodrama of the old man's imagination; the invisible cast of thousands, persecuting him for hours on end. Years after his death Adam still wakes in the night to the old man's bewildered croak. When this happens his stomach bottoms out, and for a moment he believes he's trapped in the council flat again, as his grandfather paces, shouting at nobody in the room next door. Adam is frustrated at his younger self. He and Julia didn't have to live like that. But he hadn't known any better. He'd been too afraid (and, Adam suspects, not quite right in the head himself).

But there were lulls to the madness, tranquil inter-ludes during which Adam's grandfather was genuinely likeable. Sitting opposite Adam, his cardigan buttoned up over his shirt, slippered feet shuffling closer to the gas fire, Christopher Milnar would remark: *Look at you reading those books! You'll be as clever as old Socrates before long* . . . But his grandfather never pressured him to go to school, just as Adam never pressured his grand-father to see a doctor about his illness. The two hermits just left each other to get on with it. Occasionally Christopher would talk about Frances. How she broke his heart when she ran away and how he hired a private detective to track her down. When he discovered, a decade later, that Frances was in London, he moved to

England to be near her and his baby grandson. Christopher wrote letters seeking reconciliation and sent her cheques for hundreds of pounds on birthdays and Christmases. Frances returned the letters to sender via the Royal Mail and refused to let her father see his grandchildren. Adam's grandfather kept up his letter-writing campaign for fourteen long years – until Frances' death in 1995. *That stubborn child never did tell me what I'd done wrong,* he grumbled to Adam, *but I wouldn't let her forget me – not so long as I had money to spare for postage . . .*

Adam knows how stubborn his mother could be. More than ten years have passed since they walked out on Jack Broughton. He doesn't remember the date exactly, but knows it was springtime, after the clocks had gone forward. Frances broke the news to them one tea-time, when he and Julia were sitting on the sofa, eating from plates of spaghetti on toast on the low coffee table. Julia was engrossed in whatever was on the telly, and spaghetti hoops slid off her fork prongs, staining her school blouse with splotches of tomato sauce. Frances was perched on the arm of the sofa, not eating, not watching TV. She was wearing her nurse's pinafore, which was unusual, as Frances always changed as soon as she got in from work (before she opened the bills or put the kettle on – as if she couldn't stand the lingering odour of hospital and sickness). Adam noticed that Frances still had on her stark white uniform, with the clip-on watch hanging upside-down from her pocket, but said nothing. He was unhappy at school and said less and less back then.

The front door slammed and Jack passed by the window, a bounce in his stride as he set off for the pub. His hands were shoved deep in his pockets and the wind lifted his sandy hair from his receding hairline. Adam glanced up as Jack went by, then returned his attention to the telly, unaware that he'd just seen his stepfather for the very last time.

Frances lifted the remote control and clicked off the TV. The children's heads snapped irritably towards their mother.

'Oi!' said Julia. 'I was watching that.'

'Listen,' said Frances. 'We're getting out of here. We're going to Malaysia. I've packed our suitcases. We're going tonight.'

'What?'

Adam shook off his television stupor.

'Are you serious?'

Of course she wasn't. Adam knew that people didn't just walk out of everyday life like that. Especially not their mother.

'Yes,' said Frances.

'Are we going tonight? By aeroplane?' Julia squealed.

'Yes.'

'For how long?'

'I don't know.'

'Just for a holiday?'

'I don't know.'

'More than a fortnight?'

'I haven't decided yet.'

For the first time in months Adam looked carefully at his mother. At the sprinkling of grey in her hair, and her eyes dark and haggard with sleeplessness. But he knew better than to be deceived by her shattered appearance. Frances was ready for the children's protests. She was ready to put up a fight.

'Are you having a mental breakdown?' he asked.

'No.'

'Then why are we running off to Malaysia?'

'I am sick of things the way they are. It's time for a change.'

'Bit of a drastic change, though, isn't it, taking us to Malaysia?'

'It's what I want to do.'

'Aren't you forgetting that we have school?'

'If you're so worried about school, Adam, you can stay here with Jack.'

Adam shut up. He wasn't *that* worried about school.

The mention of Jack set Julia off. 'Is Dad not coming?'

'No, he's not.'

'But then he'll be here by himself. He'll be lonely without us!'

'Have you told him?' Adam asked.

'No.'

Julia stood up, knocking the edge of her plate so her half-eaten spaghetti on toast overturned on to the carpet. She opened her mouth, as if to object, then closed it. She sat down again. Frances didn't shout at

Julia for upsetting the plate. She told them both to go upstairs to clean their teeth while she did the washing-up.

They went up the stairs in silence. Adam was not especially bothered that they were leaving Jack behind. Adam had lived with Jack Broughton since he was two. There was no malice in the man, but no affection either. Jack was selfish like a child and indifferent to father-hood, even when it came to his own daughter. Adam and Julia brushed their teeth over the bathroom basin. As Julia zigzagged the toothbrush about in her foamy mouth, she kept catching her brother's eye in the mirror, her gaze exploding with excitement and incredulity. Adam ignored her, but when Julia, a vigorous tooth-brusher, accidentally prodded him with her elbow, Adam cheerfully elbowed her back. Going to Malaysia meant not going to school and Adam suddenly felt freer than he had in months.

After rinsing and spitting they went downstairs, where two leather suitcases sat in the hall. Frances had her summer jacket on and a dash of lipstick on her lips, and was ordering a minicab on the phone. Adam spotted the damp patch on the beige carpet, from where she'd sponged up the mess of Julia's dinner. He unzipped his rucksack and dumped out his school books. The empty rucksack was abnormally light on his shoulders, so he picked up a travel scrabble set and one of Jack's paperbacks – *Chariots of the Gods* by Erich von Däniken – to restore it to its usual weight. Julia had fetched her peach drawstring make-up bag from the bedroom. She was strictly forbidden from wearing make-up until she was fourteen, but that didn't stop her from spending her pocket money on cosmetics. Bursting with blusher, glitter sticks and compacts of iridescent beads of powder, the little make-up bag heaved. Julia's ambition was to be a make-up artist, and most evenings she practised applying false lashes and lipstick, until she resembled a juvenile drag queen.

'Why're you taking that crap? You're not allowed to wear it and you don't even know how to put it on properly.'

Julia narrowed her eyes at Adam. 'Shut up, Adam. You're just jealous because you're gay and want to wear make-up too.'

'Julia, for goodness' sake,' said Frances, sighing, 'come here and let me try to get the knots out of your hair. Why don't you brush it once in a while, eh?'

Julia went obediently to her mother, who rummaged in her handbag for a thin plastic comb. Though Julia was barely eleven she was already inches taller than Frances, who reached up and tugged the comb through her scowling daughter's hair with fast, efficient strokes. Many times Frances had threatened to take a pair of scissors to Julia's messy hair, but the thought of the tantrum this would provoke exhausted her.

'Did you tell our schools we're going on holiday?' asked Adam.

'No,' said Frances.

Julia's head jerked back as the comb sank its teeth into a knotty snarl. 'Owww!'

'For goodness' sake, Julia, hold still!'

'What about the hospital? Do they know you're leaving?'

'No.'

'Won't you lose your job for that?'

Her lips a thin line of determination, Frances wrenched the plastic comb down the length of her daughter's hair. Julia's chin wobbled and her eyes watered. A champion cry-baby, she could weep for hours non-stop, screwing her face up with aggression, howling as salty bombs detonated in her tear ducts.

'I want to say goodbye to Dad!' she sobbed. 'It's wrong not to tell him. It's out of order. He'll be lonely on his own.'

Outside, a cabby honked his taxi horn, engine idling.

Sternly, not a trace of sympathy in her face, Frances disentangled the comb from Julia's hair and turned Julia to face her. She seized her daughter by the arms, as if to convey her firmness of mind through the grip.

'Listen,' she said, 'your father won't be lonely. He's got his mates down the Brewery Tap. And I put a six-pack of beer in the fridge. That'll keep him busy. Come on now, Julia. Don't be sad. Don't you want to come on holiday? I'm going to take you where it's lovely and sunny. You can send your dad a postcard when we get there. And it won't be for ever.'

Julia sniffled back her tears.

'Now put your coat on and go outside. The taxi is waiting.'

Julia went to the door, the drawstring bag of

glittering trophies she was too young to wear dangling at her side. She took her coat down from the hook.

'You too, Adam,' Frances said. 'Coat. Door. Go on!'

Adam went to the hallway, but as he took his coat he glanced back at Frances. He saw her pick up her hand-bag and breathe a sigh of relief. He saw her take off her wedding ring and put it on the table.

Frances Broughton, née Milnar, was forty-three years old when she left Jack Broughton. It was a decision she arrived at quietly, with no breakdown, no hysterical weeping or prescription of pills. Up until the day they left for Malaysia, Frances had been regular as clock-work; up at six every morning, bran flakes eaten and children's packed lunches made by half past. She'd tidied up whatever mess Jack had left when he got in the night before (be it empty beer cans or the remnants of a take-away kebab) and was off to work by seven, for eight hours of whatever nurses are underpaid to do. The house was always clean, the clutter picked off the floors, and school shirts ironed and bed-sheets washed. She gave Adam his monthly haircut, took him to the doctor when he was sick, and wrote countless notes excusing him from PE. Every night she battled against Julia's phobia of soap and water, coercing her into the bathtub (then shouting a checklist of what she mustn't forget to wash through the bathroom door). She nagged her children half to death and, though she wasn't affectionate, they sensed they were loved, in a matter-of-fact, unsentimental way. Only Jack she left alone. She never forced Jack to have a bath (though he needed one more than Julia) or made him doctor's appointments (though he woke every morning to murderous coughing fits, catarrh rattling like a caged beast in his chest). Frances left the dirt to accumulate behind his ears. She left him to pass out unconscious on the sofa. She cooked dinner for him, and if he ate it he ate it, and if he didn't she threw it away. Jack was like some bothersome lodger; a feckless, layabout eldest son. Adam never credited him with the ability to break her heart.

10

Though Frances Milnar had attended the Amethyst International School for Girls since she was twelve, Sally was her first friend there. Sally was amazed that the other girls didn't adore Frances as much as she did, but as she witnessed more of her behaviour she began to understand why. First and foremost a child of Kuala Lumpur, Frances was impatient with the Western affectations of her peers. She thought her schoolmates girly and pathetic; scorned the way they swooned over pop stars and fussed over their appearance. Frances was arrogant. She said exactly what she thought, even if it was staggeringly rude. Before Sally arrived, Frances had spent four years wandering the corridors of Amethyst alone; hanging out on the school roof after lunch and sailing paper aeroplanes over her enemies in the yard. Sally couldn't believe that Frances hadn't gone to pieces from loneliness – that she hadn't capitulated to peer pressure and smoothed the conceited edges of her personality to make a friend or two. But Frances gave no outward signs of suffering and made no effort to make herself the least bit likeable. *We don't have time for that*, she snapped at Melissa, who'd brought in a Cliff Richard LP to lend Sally. *Go away!*

Frances's lack of success at Amethyst was academic as well as social, and she was bottom of the class for several years (a position she was ousted from by the arrival of Sally, who bumped her up the rankings to twenty-third place). During lessons Frances wriggled at her desk, yawning and jiggling her foot. She'd spend an entire period diligently unpicking her skirt hem with her compass or gnawing her fingernails to the quick. Frances's inability to concentrate irritated most teachers (*Miss Milnar, would you share with the rest of the class exactly what you find so fascinating out of the window*). Perhaps Frances's fidgety attention deficit was due to some learning difficulty (dyslexia, to judge by her spelling). But in 1969 her condition went undiagnosed, as the teachers assumed stupidity and Frances spent her school-days bored.

Frances lived with her English father (a businessman whose business she was unsure of) and her ayah, Madame Tay, above the Good Fortune Fabric Emporium on the outskirts of Chinatown. To get upstairs Sally and Frances had to pass through the fabric store, much to the annoyance of the young manageress (who, after a ten-year-long feud with Madame Tay, made a sniffy show of ignoring Frances).

The manageress sat on a stool by the cash register, her shapely legs peeping through the slit in her cheongsam as she perused fashion magazines and misted her immaculate beehive with hairspray. The aisles of the Good Fortune Fabric Emporium were lined floor to ceiling with bolts of silk, and the temptation to trail her fingertips along the shimmering rolls was often too much for Sally. *Don't touch!* the young manageress would shriek, and Sally would whisk her fingers away, as if from hot coals.

The Milnar apartment was a refuge from sunlight, every room a chamber of shadow, redolent of sandalwood and tiger balm. Sally never once saw the window shutters open; it was as if the furniture would disintegrate if touched by light. In contrast to the shady apartment the kitchen, a lean-to of corrugated iron sheltering the sink and stove from the elements, was up on a sunny roof terrace, which overlooked the alleys behind Sultan Road: the slatted metal fire escapes bolted to the backs of shop houses, the dirt-streaked walls, and lines of laundry stiffened to parchment by the sun.

When Sally first met Frances's ayah she was tending to a pot simmering on the stove and ignoring the flea-bitten stray cats slinking along the balustrade, mewling at the top of their lungs. The kitchen was hot and bright, with bundles of pak choi wrapped in newspaper and a bucket of shellfish on the large wooden table. Madame Tay was in her fifties, and the same height as Frances (though a great deal stouter), with a fiercely permed crop of black curls. When she saw the girls she threw down her ladle and spoke to Frances in an abrasive flame-tongued Cantonese, as if severely ticking her off, though she lovingly stroked and petted her teenage charge, eyes shining as she smoothed a flyaway tress. Over her months of visits to Sultan Road Sally discovered the ayah's affection for Frances was inexhaustible. Madame Tay gave the impression of living for the young girl alone, and Sally came to understand how Frances had acquired her cast-iron self-esteem – her ayah's constant deluge of love assuring her of her status as a divinity. Frances, the bored, limp recipient of Madame Tay's fussing, introduced her to Sally and at once the smiling woman pinched Sally's chubby arm and poked the tubby roll above her waistband. Sally, indignant, widened her eyes at Frances, and Madame Tay accompanied her transgressions with a spitfire of words.

Sally asked what she was saying, and Frances translated.

'She says that she pities you for befriending a devil like me.'

Most days after school Sally and Frances went to Chinatown, where they weaved in and out of the market stalls of Petaling Street, dodging rickshaws and motor scooters and vegetable carts towed by hunched old men. The market traders hawked their wares at Sally, thrusting at her bamboo-leaf parcels of sticky rice, too-small wooden sandals and, once, an entire roast duck, swinging upside-down by its charred feet. *Hello*,

Hello, English missi! What you wan' drink, eat? Rambutan for you? or they'd shout, *Scarf! Scarf! Scarf!* waving the cheap fabric in her face. In the marketplace, where she was known to everyone as the 'half-and-half girl', Frances was in her element, skipping from stall to stall and bantering away (*Hello, Ah Wang! How're you keeping? Sold many melons today?*) and laughing as she translated for Sally what they'd said (*Ah Wang says you're very big and I've got to watch you don't gobble me up!*). The market was always crowded with haggling customers and traders. Even the beggars of Chinatown had an admirable work ethic, chanting and playing the harmonica, the one-legged man dancing his hopping dance and rattling his bowl of coins in the afternoon heat.

One afternoon Frances took Sally to Slaughter Row, the nickname Chinatown locals had given the arcade of butcher stalls behind Petaling Street. Sally halted at the entrance to the arcade, staring at the rows of butchers industriously hacking away, their knives raised in carnivorous mastery of the lower-animal kingdom. *Go on!* Frances urged her. *You won't see much from here!* Sally stumbled forward, past the metal coops stuffed with scores of live chickens. The arcade was adrift with feathers – as though in the aftermath of a violent pillow fight – quills sticking to the butchers' aprons and Frances's dark hair. The girls stood watching as every few minutes a butcher yanked a squawking chicken out of a coop, deftly chopped off its head, then dunked the carrion in boiling water and stripped off the feathers at lightning speed. The stench of carnage was everywhere and by the late afternoon enough poultry had been killed to fill whole sacks with bloody combs and feet. Oh, those poor massacred chickens! There and then Sally vowed to become a vegetarian – a resolution that lasted three days – and swore never to eat fish again either, as there were fish stalls in the arcade, with swordfish and cuttlefish piled up in the stinking heat, gills fluttering in slow suffocation. Slippery fish oil anointed the cobblestones and Sally was splattered with carp juice as a fishmonger shook his wet hands. Ugh! But it was the cow's head that finally sent her fleeing for the exit. The head sat on a table at the far end of the arcade, flayed of its skin so the pulpy flesh was exposed. The cow's bloodshot eyes glared accusingly at her, as though she'd been the one who'd murdered it and cut off its head. Hand clamped over her mouth, Sally lurched away. Giggling, Frances skipped after her into the scorching street.

'Look at you, Sal! You're green! Where did you think roast chickens came from? Did you think they fell out of the sky in a baking tray with roast potatoes?'

Frances then stuck out her hands, waggling the scabby chicken feet she'd stolen. She poked the claws at Sally's throat and cackled at her screams.

On Friday nights Sally stayed over at Frances's. They'd spend the evening sitting on the bedroom window-ledge, drinking from a hip flask of whisky and pretending to smoke cigars stolen from her father's study (Mr Milnar was away on a month-long business trip to Brunei and Sally had yet to meet him). They wore tatty Panama hats as they dangled their legs over the street below, and Sally's first acquaintance with Frances's mysterious father was the scent of his sweat and aftershave in the hat band. As they spied on the night-time to-ings and fro-ings of Sultan Road, Frances told macabre tales about the people coming out of the Petaling Street market.

'See that girl there? She's got webbed fingers and a stumpy tail 'cos of inbreeding. Her half-sister is also her mother and her grandfather also her father. Ayah says the family are possessed by demons and I'm not to buy anything from their bakery . . . And that man there, the one with the limp, he's the chef of this swanky restaurant. He buys orphaned babies from Thailand and cooks them for gangsters who believe eating babies makes you live longer. D'you know eating nothing but babies can make you immortal?'

'What a disgusting pack of lies!' Sally laughed. 'You ought to be ashamed!'

Widening her eyes, Frances breathed, 'But it's true!' and continued to spin her urban myths, gaily depicting her neighbours as cannibals, freaks and vampires.

They silenced the radio after midnight, clicked out the light and stumbled through clouds of cigar smoke to bed, where they'd lie together under the canopy of mosquito nets, the room swaying in their drunkenness. As Sally's eyes adjusted to the dark, she was able to distinguish the shape of her friend: the hillocks of her knees; the ridge of collar-bone and the rise and fall of her chest under her camisole. The girls always lay awake until they'd sobered up. They wouldn't let each other sleep – one murmuring as the other began to drowse, nudging her bedmate back to consciousness.

Sally remembers little of those nocturnal conversations and the dreamy silences in between. But she recalls the darkness was permissive of anything, tolerant of any aberrant words or thoughts that popped into their heads.

'When's your dad coming back from Brunei?' Sally once asked, after weeks of Mr Milnar's absence.

'Tuesday,' said Frances. 'But I wish he would stay there for ever.'

Sally lay on her side, elbow on the mattress, head in her hand. Frances stared at the ceiling. It wasn't the first time she'd expressed sentiments like this about Mr Milnar. Sally couldn't imagine wishing her father exiled to another country. What a sad thing to wish for.

'Why do you hate him so much?'

'Because.'

'Because what?'

'Because he's a murderer.'

'Oh?' Sally said casually, expecting this was another one of Frances's absurd tales. 'Who did he murder?'

'My mother. When I was a baby.'

Sally narrowed her eyes. 'Y'know . . . it's not funny to joke about stuff like that. My father would be really hurt if he overheard me saying that about him. And it's disrespectful to make things up about the dead. Especially your mother.'

'I'm not making it up.'

'Right. And I suppose he killed her to sell her kidneys on the black market.'

'If you don't believe me, fair enough. But if it wasn't for him she'd still be alive today.'

'If your father's a murderer, then why isn't he in prison?' Sally asked.

'Because he didn't do it in cold blood – he's not a murderer in the eyes of the law.'

'C'mon, Frances,' Sally said impatiently, 'you can't have it both ways. Either he killed her or he didn't. How did she die?'

There was a long silence, then Frances said: 'I don't want to talk about it. Please don't mention it again.'

This was fine with Sally, who thought Frances's storytelling had crossed the line from funny to disturbing. The lie was ludicrous, yet at the same time part of Sally believed her – felt a thrill of fear to be in the home of a murderer. The room was quiet and tense with mutual irritation. When Frances spoke again, her words chimed in the dark.

'Promise you won't tell anyone at school.'

'Don't worry,' Sally replied, 'I won't.'

They were outside a herbalist when their careers as petty criminals began. Piled up along the shop front were sacks of dried sundries – beans and lotus root and woven baskets of candied mango and papaya. As they lingered, dithering over whether or not to go in, Frances whispered: 'I dare you to steal some sweets.'

Sally glanced at her, wondering if she'd misheard. She had coins in her purse and had no desire to steal anything. She glanced in the shop. The assistant was busy at the counter with his pestle and mortar, and no one else was paying them any attention. Not wanting to pass up an opportunity to impress Frances, Sally dipped her fingers into the basket of dried fruit and scooped up a fistful before moving into the street. She broke into a trot, pandemonium in her heart, convinced she'd hear the shout of *Stop, thief!* at any moment. They turned into an alleyway and Sally's knees shook with relief when she realized they hadn't been followed. She unfurled her fist to show Frances the sweets she'd stolen, which glistened like sugared jewels in her palm. And, grinning her baby vampire's grin, Frances unclenched her own fist, to show off her copy-cat theft.

They stole more and more recklessly; light-fingered thrill-seekers, filching and pilfering wherever they went. They flitted past diners in the hawker centres and pinched chopsticks from plates (while the diner had turned his back to greet a friend or to check his lottery ticket against the winning numbers on TV). They thieved from the fruit carts, stuffing pineapples into their satchels, cheering 'Happy National Pineapple Day!' as they handed them out to passers-by in the street. They became the opposite of pickpockets, smuggling stolen lollipops and paper fans into handbags, giggling to imagine the victim's surprise when they reached for their wallet, only to find a bright yellow starfruit, or some lychees nestling like eggs against the pocket lining. Once Sally was caught in the over-ambitious act of sneaking up behind an old lady to balance a mango on her sun bonnet. The mango wobbled on the bonnet for a second, before toppling forwards into the basket of the woman's push-bike. Baffled, she picked up the reddish-yellow fruit and held it up towards the Foreign Devil culprit, who was now legging it from the scene of the crime.

One day after school they made the pilgrimage to the Guandi temple, the shrine of Kuan Ti, the Taoist god of war. At the temple gates a group of beggars sat, bony arms outstretched, rattling tins for alms. Frances glided through the gates as if she had neither seen nor heard them, but Sally hesitated, her eyes meeting those of an ageless man in rags, with matted hair and a misshapen proboscis for a nose. The man shouted at Sally in Malay and grabbed the hem of her skirt. Sally couldn't have panicked more if her skirt had caught fire. She tore the hem free and ran into the temple, shuddering in disgust.

Sally had always found Chinese temples ostentatious and the Guandi temple was no exception. Banners of red and gold were draped everywhere, and dragons perched on the jade-tiled roof, tails coiled round the temple pillars. Joss-sticks burned in great brass urns and spirals of incense gently snowed ash from the ceiling. A furnace incinerated origami cars as offerings for the afterlife, and vases and golden statues dazzled the eye. It was as if the Chinese feared the slightest hint of austerity would offend the gods. On a marble bench at the side of the temple, Sally and Frances sat and watched as the caretaker swept ash from the tiled floor and a row of men bowed their tonsured heads and waggled incense sticks at the altar.

'It's mostly businessmen that come here,' Frances said. 'They're praying for money and success in the business world.'

'I thought this temple was for the god of war,' said Sally.

'It is. The businessmen think they're warriors.' Frances snorted her contempt, then gave Sally a sly, sidelong smile. Sally knew what was coming.

'I dare you to nick one of the cakes from the altar.'

Sally glanced at the offerings of fruit and little pink cakes. She'd no steadfast opinions on God and the status of His existence, but thought it wise to avoid sacrilegious behaviour until she was firmly committed to atheism. Frances clucked a few times and fanned her elbows in a disheartening chicken imitation.

'Scared old Kuan Ti will come after you with his sword?' she scoffed. 'Since when were you Buddhist?'

Sally *was* scared – even though in the hierarchy of religions she thought Buddhism inferior to Christianity or Islam. If they had to steal from a Buddhist god, why not the goddess of mercy? Surely she would be a far safer bet.

'I think it's lame to steal from temples,' Sally said.

'OK,' Frances said. 'If you won't do it, I will. I'll take a cake and give it to the beggars outside. Watch!'

Frances strode to the altar. She stood for a moment, head lowered before the golden statue of the god of war as though in silent prayer. Then, hands flying out, Frances swiped a couple of cakes and whirled round so fast her grey pleated skirt flared behind her. Stolen offerings in her hands, Frances hurried to the temple gates, the cocksure confidence that had taken her to the altar no longer in evidence. She'd almost succeeded in her getaway, but, reaching the threshold of the shrine, she rushed smack bang into a tall, blond man in a linen suit. The man caught Frances by the shoulders and steadied her, before both parties stepped back from the collision.

'Frances,' he said, 'what do you have there in your hands? What are you playing at?' The man towered over her.

Frances flushed and said nothing.

'Frances, answer me this minute. Did you take those from the altar?'

'They're for the beggars,' said Frances stubbornly.

'You've more than enough pocket money if you want to buy cakes for the beggars. There's absolutely no need to go about stealing. This has to stop, Frances. I've only been back five minutes and already I've had nothing but complaints about you. Now, put those back where you found them.'

That must be Mr Milnar! thought Sally, *Frances's father!* The Aryan-looking man was completely unlike how she'd imagined Frances's father to be. Mr Milnar was very handsome; firm-jawed like the heroes on the covers of her Harlequin romances, he had a distinguished hump-back nose and elegantly receding fair hair. Though he was forty-ish, he had the clean-cut air of a public-school boy about him. He looked nothing like the murderer Frances claimed he was. Mr Milnar watched sternly as his sulky daughter replaced the cakes on the altar. And as he nodded to himself, satisfied the crime was undone, Sally felt herself fall slightly in love with him.

Mr Milnar frowned as Sally approached him and she guessed her feelings weren't reciprocated.

'Who are you?' he said.

'Sally Hargreaves, sir. I'm in the same class as Frances at school. We're friends.'

'Ah yes, I've heard about you. You and Frances are fast acquiring reputations as trouble-makers here in Chinatown. You're nowhere near as discreet as you think you are!' He looked Sally up and down. 'And it's not as if you're inconspicuous, is it?'

Sally hung her head, blushing red as a brick.

'No, sir.'

'A fine friend you are, encouraging Frances to steal!'

They left the temple in disgrace. Mr Milnar flung some coins to the beggars, then ordered the girls into the back seat of a stuffy overheated Morris Minor parked outside, ignoring Sally's protests that she could make her own way home.

They drove to Petaling Jaya in silence, the scorching leather upholstery searing the back of Sally's legs. She was deeply ashamed, but beside her Frances fumed as if she'd suffered a great injustice. Frances didn't speak for the entire journey – not even to say goodbye when Sally was dropped off at her home. And Sally realized it was the maddest that she'd seen her.

11

Over the years the biochemistry labs have become Adam's second home. He belongs there, like the odour of halogens, the hum of the fume cupboards, and the iodine splashes on the benches. Every morning before the first session of practicals, he wheels a trolley around his appointed lab, pausing at intervals to set out volumetric flasks, pipettes, stoppered bottles of 0.1 molar sodium hydroxide. Adam is efficient and methodical, completing his tasks like an automaton, thoughts free to roam elsewhere.

When the biology undergraduates straggle in, tugging white lab coats on and whinging about deadlines and hangovers, Adam withdraws into the clutter of the preparation room, to the perpetual de-ionizing trickle of the distiller. Throughout the morning gum-snapping students in oversized safety glasses knock on Adam's door; *Where are the 50ml cylinders? Where are the latex gloves?* More often than not Adam will stop whatever he's doing and direct them back to the cupboard under their bench.

Most of the other laboratory technicians are women, a decade or two older than Adam. At break time he joins the circle of comfy chairs in the tea-room and listens to the chatter about families and last night's TV while steam from the electric kettle fogs the windowpane. Adam likes his colleagues, though he can't endure their mundane chit-chat for longer than it takes to gulp down a mug of coffee. The other technicians like Adam too. They like the youth he takes for granted, and are intrigued by the diffident way he carries himself – like an outsider, a mysterious refugee. They like his shyness – the way he blushes and stutters and gets the syllables of words back to front. They think it's endearing that Adam is often stage-struck mid-sentence or mid-word, as if he lacks the confidence to finish his lines. The women technicians mollycoddle Adam, flirt with him, relishing his obvious discomfort. Every one of them projects upon Adam a romantic back story of their own invention, to explain his notorious timidity. Three of Adam's colleagues regularly fantasize about seducing him; of bursting into the stock-room where he eats his lunch and knocking him off his stool; of popping open their lab-coat stub buttons and peeling off knickers and support tights to let him fuck them – gleefully betraying their husbands to shatter the boy's celibacy (or virginity, as some imagine).

What would Adam think if he knew about these

daydreams? If he knew what these middle-aged women wanted to do to him, as he sits among the shelves of hazardous chemicals and stacks of scientific catalogues, eating the bread and cheese he brought for his lunch? Adam would probably be a little embarrassed, a little scornful, though amused enough to smile. But he wouldn't dwell on it for long as his habitual obsessions return to haunt him: his ex-boyfriend Mischa and his sister and Rob. If one of his colleagues *were* to take the initiative and barge in, grabbing him by the lapels, Adam would be annoyed. He likes to be left alone at lunchtime to brood. If it were a girl who exiled herself in this way the other technicians would be offended. They'd wage a whispering campaign until the offender meekly returned to the tea-room. But Adam is forgiven his solitariness because he is a man, and his co-workers have long taken it for granted that men are different.

Some nights he leaves his flat and walks. He'll walk into the city, cold draughts of air ventilating his lungs, the austere slap of the pavement against the soles of his shoes, the stone vaulted architecture belonging to him alone. Or he'll walk to a street of restaurants, slowing to stare at the candlelit diners – the woman in the silk scarf, lifting a forkful of linguine, throwing her head back to laugh at her male companion. Sometimes Adam goes further east, over the flyover to Stratford, past the mosques and churches, night sky impaled by steeples, to the dingy bedsit land of Romford Road (where he lived after his grandfather died and swore he'd never go back to, though he often does). On these city rambles Adam loses track of time, ceases seeing, only maintaining the level of perception necessary to avoid colliding with lamp-posts, drunks stumbling out of pubs. Only after he has retraced his steps back to Mile End, to flop exhausted into bed in the early hours, do the muscles in his legs begin to ache. When Adam walks, introspection staves off fatigue, distracts him from other night prowlers and the possibility of violence. To walk is to remember, and possessed by memories of Mischa Adam has traversed every inch of London. He has meandered along the banks of the Thames to Hammersmith, mind cast back to the nights of lying awake beside him as he slept, his heart speeding in fear of being discovered as a fraud, inept at intimacy. Ill-equipped for something as simple as happiness. Adam has lost his way in the suburbs of Essex, taking wrong turning after wrong turning, remembering Mischa's coarse tongue tracing the outline of his spine, fingers blossoming into touch. Mischa's childhood memories are lodged in Adam's mind. Mischa the clown, the class chatterbox, exiled to the hall by his teacher, only to get another bollocking minutes later for joking with passers-by. The pale scar above his left eyebrow, from the time he flew over the handlebars of his bike, in a street in Cambridge when he was eleven years old.

The memory of infatuation is as bittersweet as yesterday. The shadows under his eyes, his stomach turning over, words freighted by fear. Mischa came and went like a firework, a chrysanthemum of light, before vanishing from Adam's life. Resign yourself to it, Adam thinks. Get over it. Walk it off. Like a drunk walking off inebriation in the cold.

12

The Broughton family, minus Jack, left Heathrow airport early one morning in April 1995 on a flight to Kuala Lumpur. For thirteen hours they flew against the spin of the earth, the aeroplane scudding through darkness and oceans of cloud, before soaring into the sunrise of the East. Frances had swallowed a sleeping pill in the departure lounge and lost consciousness before the plane left the runway (seat-belt clipped on, chair aligned for take-off), but Adam and Julia didn't sleep a wink the entire journey. The furthest they'd been before the midnight flit was Southend-on-Sea and the long-haul flight was an adventure.

A taxi drove them from the airport to the shop house on Sultan Road where Madame Tay had lived alone for twenty-five years. She was waiting outside when the taxi arrived, sheltering from the sun under a lacy parasol. When Frances saw her old ayah she gave a cry and flung open the passenger door. She fell out, scraping her hands and knees, staggering up the roadside gutter on to the kerb. From the back seat Adam and Julia watched as their mother doubled over in her nurse's pinafore, hands pressed to her mouth, shaking as though hysterical with laughter. Madame Tay's parasol fell and rolled in an arc as she shuffled over to comfort the prodigal daughter. Frances collapsed into the frail old woman's arms, sobbing in broken Cantonese.

As he and Julia climbed out of the cab, Adam dug his fingernails in his palms and swallowed hard. They'd never seen Frances cry before. She clung to Madame Tay as if she were the last person on Earth, the tightness of her grip bruising her arms (though no pain registered on the ayah's face). Frances and Madame Tay embraced, blind to all onlookers: the stunned children, curious shoppers, the taxi driver impatient for his fare, and the Good Fortune Fabric Emporium manageress, patting her bouffant grey hairdo and smirking at the messy scene.

Adam and Julia lugged the suitcases up the stairs and Madame Tay put Frances to bed (their own mum – forty-three years old and put to bed like a child!) before turning her attention to the children, unconditional love beaming from the wrinkly depths of her face. Madame Tay had twenty-five years of bottled-up affection to squander, and the object of her doting was Julia (Adam privileged with the privacy and dignity afforded to teenage boys). The old ayah launched herself at Julia, who climbed on top of wardrobes and dived under beds to escape her insatiable liver-spotted arms. As Madame Tay kissed and cuddled her and massaged stinky tiger balm into her mosquito bites – which swelled all over Julia like mumps – Adam got the impression she wanted to eat her alive.

Madame Tay couldn't speak English and communicated with them by shouting very slowly in Cantonese, as though they were retarded Chinese children. They picked up some of the language this way and were soon able to recognize the words for dinner time, bedtime, bath time, and wake your mother (or *Mei Mei ah!* as Madame Tay called her). When Madame Tay wasn't chasing Julia she was cooking up on the roof-terrace kitchen, or cleaning the apartment, or watching Hong Kong soap operas with bizarre plot lines. Adam was ambivalent towards her. Sometimes she seemed little more than an innocuous old lady with ill-fitting dentures and a diaphanous cloud of hair. Other times Madame Tay seemed sinister and he was paranoid she had mind-reading powers and could tell when he'd been bad-mouthing his mother or wanking in the bathroom. Adam and Julia's caginess around Madame Tay wasn't helped by the sleep deprivation of the first week. Both cursed by over-sensitivity to disrupted circadian rhythms, they were badly jet lagged, tossing and turning night after night, eyes burning holes in the dark. Tired and apathetic, they rarely ventured out, and the apartment became like some shadowy nether realm between waking and sleep as they wandered listlessly, napping in unsatisfying fits and starts. Every night at eleven o'clock they went to the bedroom they shared (an arrangement they were far too old for, though neither objected when Madame Tay showed them to the room) and lay on beds veiled by mosquito net mantillas. The darkness gave free rein to the unquiet of wakefulness; the mangling of sheets and frustrated sighs; the hourly flush of the toilet after restless bladders had leaked a thimble of urine; shallow breaths never plunging beneath the surface of consciousness. A few times the sleep-starved Julia cried. She'd sit up and sob, calling out to Adam, *I hate it here! I want my dad!* and Adam would go to her, sweeping aside the netting to sit beside her. He'd give her shoulder a squeeze and reassure her he couldn't sleep either. One night, when Julia wept, Adam hugged her – something he hadn't done for years. She was slippery with sweat, her skin searing as though her homesickness was burning her up inside. In his arms Julia was all gangling bones, her shoulder-blades jutting sharply through her thin vest. Her sobs subsided as he soothed her. She shifted closer to him, touched her face to his, her tears wetting his cheek. She hooked her arm round Adam's neck, and slackened, so her weight would pull them both down on the mattress. Adam teetered for a moment, unsure of whether to let himself fall. He thought of how nice it would be to lie with her, for their bodies to press together. But then, sickening, and with a strange ache of heart, Adam unhooked his sister's arm from his neck and lay her down alone. He turned his back on her and lifted the mosquito nets to get back to his own bed. *Go to sleep*, he said, as if that wasn't the problem, and Julia began to snivel again. Adam lay awake listening for a while, guilty and irritated, but less than an hour later the insomnia broke and they both slept until noon the next day.

During the time her children were wretched with insomnia Frances slept like the dead. She slept around the clock, literally dragging herself out of bed to eat the meals Madame Tay had cooked and stumbling back there as soon as she'd laid her chopsticks down. At first Adam and Julia were jealous of their mother: all she had to do was lay her head on the pillow and that was that – out like a light! But as the sleeping continued, the envy became anxiety. No matter how long Frances spent in bed, sprawled like a lazy starfish, or a swastika of arms and legs, her appetite for sleep was never sated. When Frances spoke she sounded drunk, slurred with fatigue, tongue drained of strength. She'd never been that way back in London. Back home she was always vacuuming, nagging, the knife a blur as she chopped vegetables. She'd eaten her breakfast on her feet, pacing the linoleum as she spooned up her bran cereal. But in Malaysia, helping Madame Tay with the chores, faded headscarf tied over her greying hair, Frances tired in minutes, abandoning feather duster and broom to go for 'a lie down'. The children harassed her during her brief hiatuses from sleep – *You've slept the whole week! Are you ill? Drink some coffee!* – and Madame Tay quietly took over the duties of motherhood, making Adam and Julia eat their vegetables, sending them to

177

bed at eleven and wagging her finger when they fought.

The sleeping bothered Julia the most. She invented excuses to go and wake her. *Mummmy . . .* she'd whine in a babyish voice, tugging Frances until she lifted her head from the pillow and squinted as if trying to recognize the lanky girl with the skinny blonde plaits. Julia usually asked Frances for permission to go across the street and buy ice cream. And Frances would mumble her consent, waving towards the handbag on the dresser. *Take what you want,* she'd say, eyelids fluttering shut. This liberal attitude to ice cream frustrated Julia. Ice cream wasn't allowed. Not every day. And definitely not an hour before dinner. And on the rare occasions it was allowed, Frances counted out the money, warning the recipient to return with change.

'She wasn't even sleeping. Just lying there with her eyes open,' Julia told Adam as she licked her flavourless cone. 'I saw.'

Though Chinatown was on their doorstep Adam and Julia spent most days lazing indoors, cross-eyed with boredom. Stuck with each other, they played hours of blackjack and poker, until Adam shuffled decks in his dreams. When they were sick of cards they persuaded Madame Tay to unlock their grandfather's study (the grandfather they'd been told was dead, but was actually alive and living two miles from their home in east London). The study was a museum of Mr Milnar's scholarly past, the shelves stacked with reference books, geographical surveys and travel memoirs; the filing cabinets stuffed with sheafs of foolscap covered in Chinese calligraphy, some characters practised hundreds of times per leaf, as though Mr Milnar had been in a hypnotic trance. On the desk was an Olivetti typewriter with a desiccated ink ribbon, a yellowing wad of manuscript paper (the palimpsest of a letter composed in Mandarin on the topmost layer) and a globe that squeaked when spun on its axis. Adam and Julia spent hours rifling through the old man's stuff, pulling out drawers and reading his private correspondence (*Look at this!* they'd cry, waving a photograph of their grandfather in a loincloth and Iban warrior headdress, posing before a jungle backdrop). Imaginations whetted by the roomful of artefacts, Adam and Julia regressed to the role-playing games of their childhood. They adopted secret code-names and pretended to be the CIA, shooting each other in the hallway with their grandfather's fountain pens. They found a magnifying glass in the bureau drawer and, dressed in his moth-eaten suits and panama hats – Julia with a brown felt-tip moustache on her upper lip – made believe they were detectives. It was the most fun Adam had had in ages, but he was deeply embarrassed to be playing with his little sister at the age of fourteen, and whenever the burden of shame became too much he gave her a Chinese burn.

One afternoon, returning from a trip to the ice-cream vendor, they befriended Malay twin sisters, whose father owned the furniture shop down the road. Adam has forgotten their names, but remembers they were twelve and a half and spoke fluent English in playful lilting tones. Though non-identical, the twins had the same squishy noses (that looked as though they'd been launched by catapult and landed *splat!* in the middle of their faces) and identical scars on their upper lips left by corrective cleft-palate surgery. Behind their backs Adam called them 'the Harelip Twins', and though they were quite ugly he liked to tease them and pull on the thick ropes of plaits dangling down their backs. The twins left for school every morning at seven thirty and were home again at one fifteen, when their father put them to work polishing furniture in his shop. Adam and Julia would call for them after two, and with a nod from their father the twins would join them in the street. Adam and Julia tried to initiate the Harelip Twins into their secret world of gangsters and policemen, but the twins preferred gentler, unimaginative pastimes such as hopscotch and hand-clapping games that Adam hated (though he always mooched around, partly because he had nothing better to do and partly to bask in what he imagined to be the Harelip Twins' love rivalry for him). The twins had had a strict religious upbringing and displayed an innocence that shocked Adam and Julia (who'd chant *fuck* thirty times in a row just to frighten them). Adam and Julia taught them about London, bragging of gangland shootings, teen pregnancies and kids stabbing one another up at school. The twins, who'd also been spoon-fed fear from an early age, responded with the cautionary tales of

Kuala Lumpur, warning Adam and Julia about the kid-nappers lurking around every corner, ready to bundle people into sacks, to be butchered in the kitchens of Chinese restaurants.

After three weeks of bed rest Frances was still exhausted, surfacing for meals puffy and pillow-creased, her hair mussed up as she stared at the children in mild detachment. Her lethargy rubbed off on Adam, who began to devote hours to lying on his bed.

'C'mon, get up!' Julia shouted. 'How can you just lie there? You're becoming like Mum!'

'Get lost, Jules. Go and play with the Harelip Twins.'

'I will! It's much better without you there being sarcastic anyway!'

His sister gone, Adam stagnated, not even moving to scratch an itch. He stared at the dust glittering in the blades of light coming in through chinks in the window shutters, every minute suffused by the scent of furniture polish and the ticking of the clock. The city became a fog of sound: of horns beeping, the *put, put, put* of motorscooters, and foreign shouts. Sometimes, out of nowhere, panic would charge up in his chest. How long were things going to be this way? For the next month? The one after that? Frances's nurse uniform, washed and ironed by Madame Tay, was hanging in her cupboard. Adam had a strong feeling she was never going to wear it again; that she'd found her true vocation vegetating on the bed. It was all wrong. It was wrong that they'd taken off without telling Jack. It was wrong that he and Julia had missed weeks of school. It was wrong that their mother had become a selfish invalid. Adam blamed Malaysia. Once they were back in England, Frances would be back to her old self.

During the fourth week of the holiday Julia's battle against Frances kicked off. She waited until lunchtime, when Frances had left the safety of her bedroom and had no choice but to listen.

'Muuum . . .'

Frances ignored her, slurped a noodle between her lips.

'Muuum . . . Muuum . . .'

'What?'

'When are we going home?'

'I don't know.'

'Can we go back next week?'

'No.'

'The week after that?'

'I don't know.'

'Why not? Why can't we go back?'

'Julia, shut up.'

'But what about school? Me and Adam have to go to school. It's against the law if we don't go.'

'She's right,' Adam chipped in. 'It's illegal.'

'It won't kill you,' said Frances, 'to miss a few weeks.'

'Are you going to divorce Dad?' Julia asked.

'No.'

''Cos I don't mind if you are. I don't mind seeing him only at the weekends. But you should go back to England and tell him.'

Noodles dangled down Frances's chin. She slurped them up and chewed.

'It's so unfair . . .' Julia whined. 'I miss Dad. You're just keeping us here because *you* want to be here, though me and Adam have fuck all to do! It's bang out of order!'

'Julia, shut up. I have a headache.'

'You always have a headache. Are you sick or something?'

'Yes. I'm sick.'

'Well, you'd better go to the doctor and sort it out, then!'

As Julia argued with Frances, Madame Tay sneaked stir-fried green beans into Julia's rice bowl. She'd got in three chopstick loads before Julia noticed. She glowered at Madame Tay.

'I don't want any!' she hissed, shoving the bowl away.

'For Christ's sake, Julia! Don't speak to Ayah like that.'

'I don't care. She pisses me off,' said Julia. 'She's an evil cow. And so are you for making us stay here. I want to go home!'

Tear ducts detonated and Julia thumped the table and shrieked: *You've kidnapped us! I miss my dad!* She stormed up to the roof-terrace kitchen, slamming every door and banging up the stairs as loudly as someone three times her size. Then she stomped back down again, not wanting her fury to go unheard. By then Frances was locked away in her bedroom and, angered by her hasty retreat, Julia hurled her weight at the door, screaming that Frances was a kidnapper and child abuser and a shit mother. Julia attacked the door for half an hour, blonde hair flying as she punched and kicked, throwing her body about as if she didn't care what bones she broke as she haemorrhaged fury. Back in London Frances wouldn't have put up with five minutes of Julia's tantrum. She'd have smacked her and sent her packing. But things were different in Malaysia. *What are you looking at? Piss off!* Julia shrieked at Adam, before she crashed, weeping, on her hands and knees. Adam was impressed. He'd never seen such a savage tantrum before. He never knew she could be so psychotic. But after a while Julia's howling got on his nerves and he went to call for the Harelip Twins. When he returned, several hours later, Julia was still crouched outside their mother's room, but pathetic as a kitten, quivering with the residual spasms of sobs. When Madame Tay clashed saucepan lids to announce supper, the bedroom door opened and Frances barely glanced at her daughter as she stepped around her into the hall.

Julia kept it up for the next two days, harassing Frances at lunch, before flying into a self-destructive rage and spending the afternoon screaming and battering the bedroom door. On the third day Julia changed tack, and after lunch chased Frances into the bedroom before the door could be locked. Adam heard them fighting in there, the mattress springs creaking as Julia bounced on the bed, Frances shouting at her to get down. Adam heard Julia scream and went to the hall. Frances was pushing Julia out of the door, a firm but weary expression on her face, and Julia lashed out at her mother, gouging her cheek. With a cry of pain Frances shoved Julia, forcefully, so she fell on her bum and banged her head against the hallway wall. Though the violence frightened him, Julia's look of shock was so comical that Adam laughed. Concerned she'd seriously hurt her daughter, Frances stepped forward to get a better look, and Julia sprang up and charged at her. Frances quickly recoiled, slamming the bedroom door shut just as Julia grabbed hold of the door jamb. There was a moment of silent shock, before Julia screamed; not her usual exhibitionist, temper-tantrum scream, but the genuine bewildered scream of a child in pain. Frances opened the door and Julia crumpled into a ball of pain, gripping her mangled fingers as she rolled on the floor. There was blood dripping everywhere, and Frances knelt down, all over Julia, her eyes wide and frantic, the most awake Adam had seen her in weeks. *Julia, Julia, Julia*, she begged, *show me your fingers* . . .

They took Julia to the hospital in a taxi, a towel sopping up the blood from her injury, and when they brought her back late that evening half the index finger of her left hand was gone and the rest were splinted and bandaged up, so her hand was like a swollen paw.

Frances bought Julia ice cream. She told Julia she was very sorry about her finger. And Julia, being Julia, forgave her. But when she asked when they were going back to England, Frances still had no reply.

13

It was 20 February 1969, the date of Frances's seventeenth birthday. They'd skipped afternoon lessons that day (after forging notes claiming a dentist appointment and the death of a great aunt) and gone to the Lake Gardens' butterfly sanctuary, returning to Frances's at six o'clock, grubby and grass-stained, damp blouses hanging over skirt waistbands. Mr Milnar was home early from the office, and the parlour floorboards creaked as he seesawed in the rocking chair. He stood up as the girls entered, folding a newspaper dense with Chinese hieroglyphics. The sight of Mr Milnar alarmed Sally, who feared their truancy had been rumbled. *We must destroy the evidence!* she thought, glancing at Frances's jar of butterflies (a glass mortuary of winged corpses picked off the sanctuary floor because they were too pretty to go to waste). Mr Milnar, however, did not seem cross.

'Happy birthday, Frances,' he said.

Sally was confused. Frances hadn't mentioned it was her birthday.

'We're going to have dinner at the club tonight to celebrate.'

'Oh, why?' scowled Frances.

'Because it's your birthday and this is what we do every year, that's why,' said Mr Milnar. 'And it's too late to do otherwise now, because Madame Tay has gone to see her friends and hasn't cooked us any dinner. The table is booked for seven. You've ten minutes to go and scrub up. And your, er . . . friend too.'

Mr Milnar sat in the rocking chair and shook open his Chinese newspaper to signal the end of discussion.

As the girls went to the bathroom to wash, Sally whispered: 'You never told me it was your birthday! Why didn't you say so?'

'Don't worry about it,' Frances said. 'It's probably not even my birthday today. My father picked this date because my mother wasn't sure when I was born. My birthday could've been last Tuesday, for all I know.'

Not knowing your own birthday? Sally had never heard of such a thing.

'How can your mother not know when you were born? She was there, wasn't she?'

'She was living in the jungle and lost track of the days.'

'What was she doing in the jungle?'

Frances shrugged. 'Yuck, the club . . .' she said. 'I hate that phoney place.'

The girls splashed tap water on sunburnt faces and combed their messy hair. Frances refused to change out of her sweat-rag of a blouse, declaring that her father could like it or lump it (he did neither – he didn't notice), and when they were ready Mr Milnar called a taxi, which let them off outside the Moorish domes of the Malaysian Supreme Court. The sun was setting as they crossed Merdeka Square, the sky blushing crimson behind the Royal Selangor Club's mock Tudor façade. Sally hadn't been to the club before, but its reputation had led her to imagine the ladies and gentlemen of the Kuala Lumpur élite swanking around, chomping cigars and drinking out of champagne flutes. She was rather disappointed by the balding expats playing bridge in the lounge. The restaurant, a sea of white tables laid with silver cutlery and damask napkins fanned in accordion pleats, was empty but for a woman drinking alone at the bar, her elegant back to the rest of the room. The head waiter, a Malay with Brylcreemed hair, hopped about like a rabbit trussed up in a waistcoat and bow-tie, taking Mr Milnar's jacket and pulling out chairs for the girls.

'*Tuan* Milnar, always a pleasure,' he cried. 'Who are these charming young ladies you have here tonight?'

'My daughter Frances and her friend. It's my daughter's birthday.'

The head waiter flashed Sally an obsequious smile. 'Happy birthday, Miss Milnar. How old are you today?'

'No,' Mr Milnar corrected impatiently, 'the other one.'

'Oh! I do beg your pardon! Happy birthday!'

Frances gave the waiter a shadow of a polite smile, then opened the menu. Sally watched the birthday girl's eyes flickering across the list of appetizers, the crooked parting in her hair shining in the light of the chandelier. Mr Milnar was reading the menu too, and Sally took the opportunity to admire his pale Scandinavian eye-lashes and his splendid hump-backed nose. How strange and nerve-racking it was to be sitting mere inches from the object of her feverish daydreams (since the day she'd met Mr Milnar in the Kuan Ti temple, Sally's imagination had churned out every possible romantic scenario leading up to Mr Milnar's eventual marriage proposal, gallantly bent down on one knee in the Lake Gardens' Pavilion). The only family likeness Sally could see, as her gaze shifted from father to daughter, was the shared look of arrogance. Frances smouldered at the menu, as if selecting a dish from the high-priced array was a torment. She dug her elbows into the tablecloth like a bad-tempered child, and Sally felt a twinge of annoyance. *Sit up properly!* she wanted to say; *Wipe that pout off your face!* The years of expensive school fees Mr Milnar had paid in the hopes of moulding an agreeable young lady out of Frances had evidently gone to waste.

The drinks arrived and glasses clinked in a birthday toast. Cherry cola bubbles fizzed up Sally's nose. She'd never heard the Milnars have a conversation before and was curious to know what they'd talk about. But before either had the chance to say anything a woman called huskily: 'Hello, Frances! Fancy seeing you here! Christopher! How are you?'

They looked up and saw a girl in a black crochet shift dress. The woman drinking the cocktail at the bar hadn't been a woman after all, but seventeen-year-old classmate and foreign diplomat's daughter Delilah Jones.

The fifth form was dominated by a clique of five girls and the clique in turn dominated by the invincible Delilah Jones. She was the first girl that Sally had noticed at Amethyst – even though Sally's desk was three rows behind her and she could only see the back of her head. Sally's eyes were drawn to her chestnut hair, glossy and thick and somehow outshining the hair of her classmates. And then there was her voice: sonorous, husky and achingly mature. A voice that stood up to Mrs Pritchett's academic shrill as they debated the imagery in *Paradise Lost*. A voice that was destined for the élite of society. All morning Sally longed to see the face that yielded such a voice and was not disappointed when Delilah glanced round. Though not quite beautiful, Delilah was striking, with dark intelligent eyes and obscenely full lips, and while her masculine eyebrows and crooked nose would have ruined the looks of a lesser girl, Delilah made these imperfections work.

Standing, smiling, before the birthday party, Delilah flicked her chestnut hair. At five foot ten Delilah was the same height as Sally, but unlike Sally she held her back poker straight, as if every inch was deserved. The hair flicking was a habit of hers at school, though she was never prone to twirling strands around her fingertips and wistfully gazing into the distance. Delilah Jones was not a dreamer. She was quick and smart as the crack of a whip. She'd gained an A level in Latin at fifteen and in the fifth form was studying for A levels in French and German. She was applying to study PPE at Oxford, and once she was in would bring the institution to its knees. No one doubted it.

Delilah was no bluestocking, though. She had a deathly glamour about her, and having lived in New York, Hong Kong and Paris made no secret of the fact she thought Kuala Lumpur a primitive city and a frightful bore. The other girls in her élite group of friends were Francesca, the child of an Anglophile Cambridge-educated sultan; Lillian and Meredith, Eurasian twin daughters of a Perak palm-oil plantation owner; and an English rose called Rebecca. Sally was enchanted by them all, but none of them was as legendary as Delilah, the nonchalant eye of a hurricane of rumour and myth. She was deflowered at thirteen, it was said, by a diplomat friend of her father's in New York. She had had an affair with a married man, whispered another source, but changed her mind about eloping after he'd confessed to his wife. The more outrageous the rumours the more believable they were: Delilah had invited two builders into her home and paid them fifty dollars to sodomize her; had bullied Catriona Peterson in the lower sixth until she drank a bottle of nail-polish remover and had to leave school without A levels; she howled when the moon was full; had a set of retractable glow-in-the-dark claws . . . Sally was hooked on the scandal and terrible beauty of Delilah, and Frances was the only girl she knew who didn't share this fascination. Sally had been full of questions about their illustrious classmate. Did she have a boyfriend? Where did she live? Frances neither knew nor cared. Sally had never seen them so much as pass the time of day before, and was surprised to hear Delilah greet Frances so warmly, as though they were great friends. Delilah shone her smile at Frances, and Frances nodded grimacingly back, before shooting Sally an indiscreet, meaningful look, as if to say: *See! This is why I don't like to come to this phoney club!* Delilah elected to ignore Frances's rudeness and spoke instead to Mr Milnar.

'Christopher, did you receive an invitation to Daddy's party next week?'

Christopher? How could she speak to a man twenty-five years her senior as though they were equals?

Mr Milnar cleared his throat. 'Invitation?'

Delilah put her hand on her slim hip, smiled a 'don't play innocent with me' kind of smile.

'I made certain a copy was sent to you. Wrote it out myself.'

'Ah, yes, I do recall . . .'

'Good! So you'll come, then?'

'Forgive me, but I think I have a prior engagement. Please pass on my apologies to your father and tell him I will ring him in the week.'

'But you don't have to come at seven on the dot,'

Delilah cajoled, the knowing smile never leaving her lips. 'You can come at whatever time you like. You know how our parties are, things are liveliest after midnight . . .'

Oh, leave him alone, Sally thought. *He doesn't want to come to your stupid party!* But despite her irritation, she couldn't help admiring Delilah's bravado as she chattered on. There was no self-doubt or nervous tremor in her voice. And how lovely she was in her crochet shift dress, as though she'd just stepped out of a *Vogue* fashion spread. Sally wondered if Frances shared her outrage. Frances was stabbing the ice cubes in her cherry cola with her straw, as though she were trying to drown them.

'. . . so you have no excuse!'

'Thank you, Delilah. As I said, I shall see on the evening.'

'Well, we'd be delighted if you came. It's always a pleasure to have you as our guest.'

Delilah beamed at Mr Milnar, and Mr Milnar smiled back in obvious discomfort. Delilah fluttered her fingers in a coquettish wave and turned to go. Mr Milnar looked relieved by her departure, but shaken and pale. Hunched over her glass Frances slurped noisily through her straw. Sally could hardly believe she was seventeen (or thereabouts). She was so immature. But then, they were all children compared with Ms Jones.

Sally had never dined with Mr Milnar before and when the food arrived she sat very stiffly, chopsticks trembling with performance anxiety. Mr Milnar tucked a napkin into his shirt collar and with a murmured *bon appétit* began selecting titbits from each dish. Conversation was negligible, with Frances speaking only to Sally in pig Latin. Mr Milnar took no notice of his daughter's rudeness as he ate, nor of her tense, chubby friend, who was so intent on making a good impression that she took only dainty bird-like mouthfuls from her plate. Sally's attempts to be ladylike backfired, however, when a fish bone got caught in her throat and, too self-conscious to cough, she tried to dislodge the bone by swallowing. She keeled over, a choking shade of violet, and Frances leapt up excitedly to perform the Heimlich manoeuvre. And all Sally could think as Frances walloped her trachea free of the bone was how silly Mr Milnar must think her.

Once the plates had been cleared away, the waiters wheeled out a cake fizzing with sparklers, and sang 'Happy Birthday' to a bashful Frances, who puffed out the candles to a smattering of applause. As the smoke wafted from the candle wicks Mr Milnar stood up and announced he had to go and speak to an acquaintance at the bar.

When he'd gone, Sally said to Frances: 'Delilah Jones was coming on a bit strong, wasn't she? She was like a bloody steamroller. And I can't believe she was calling your dad "Christopher"!'

'That's his name.'

'I know, but isn't it a bit rude of her?'

'I don't know. They know each other from parties, I suppose.'

'He doesn't seem to be much of a partygoer, though, your father. He didn't seem at all keen on going to Delilah's shindig – not that that stopped her from going on at him!'

'She doesn't care. She's relentless. She's spoony over him.'

'She fancies him?'

'She used to phone our house all the time. Sometimes she'd ask to speak to him. Sometimes she'd just listen to his voice, then hang up. Once, before Christmas, she came over. I was in bed, but I heard Ayah let her in. She went to Father's study. I could hear her shouting in there.'

'Really? What was she shouting?'

'I couldn't hear properly. Mad, hysterical stuff. She was only in there for ten minutes, and when I heard him helping her back down the stairs I went and crouched by the banister for a look. Delilah was drunk and crying and falling over with her miniskirt up to here.' Frances drew her hand level with her chest. 'My father had his arm around her to keep her upright, and she kissed him. Suctioned her mouth to his like a sink plunger.'

'Did he kiss her back?'

'No, he pulled away. He told her off. Practically carried her outside and put her in a taxi. She was bawling.'

Sally needed a moment to absorb this information.

The Great Delilah Jones, drunk and disorderly and acting like an idiot.

'I can't believe she just came over here and invited him to her party like none of that had happened.'

'I know. She has no shame. And talk about bad taste in men!'

Sally feigned a nod of agreement. 'You can't stand her, can you?'

'Not one bit. And I can't stand *him* either. They deserve each other.'

'Finished eating now, girls?'

They glanced up. Mr Milnar was back from the bar. It was impossible to tell how long he'd been standing there and how much he'd overheard.

'Yes,' said Frances, pushing aside her slice of birthday cake, flattened to marzipan and icing sugar putty with her fork prongs. 'Can we please go home now?'

A week after Frances's seventeenth birthday the fifth form sat their mock O levels. It was an excellent year for Amethyst, with most pupils getting straight As and a few luminaries, such as Delilah Jones, passing mock A levels too. There were only two failures in the class. Though they'd heard rumours of the approaching exams, Sally and Frances hadn't bothered to revise. After reading the results posted on the class notice-board they sneaked off to the toilets and in the privacy of a cubicle split their sides laughing, communicating between splutters of mirth: '*What d'you get for maths?*' '*F . . . How about you?*' '*I got an E.*' '*An E! What a clever clogs!*'

'You're both pathetic!' sneered a girl in the next cubicle but one, and Sally howled. For the rest of the day a flicker of eye contact was enough to set them both off again. Even after final bell, when the fifth-form failures were summoned to the headmistress's office, they *still* could not control themselves.

'This will not do,' said Mrs Pritchett, headmistress of the Amethyst International School for Girls since 1951. 'I have discussed your grades with your subject tutors and have organized a timetable of after-school classes that you will attend for the next ten weeks until exams. You will both put your heads down and study. No pupil graduates from Amethyst without pass grades! Do you understand?'

Not even the formality of the office and the formi-able Mrs Pritchett could cure the girls of the giggles. Sally hung her head to hide her smirk, but the presence of her partner-in-crime was irresistible as nitrous oxide. A wayward snort of laughter escaped her nose, and she clamped her hand over the offending orifice, quaking with laughter. *Out!* ordered a disgusted Mrs Pritchett, frowning as the girls hiccuped past her to shriek in the corridor.

The last laugh, however, was reserved for Mrs Pritchett. She watched from her office window as Sally and Frances raced out into the sunny courtyard and tore open the letters addressed to their fathers. Their jaws dropped in outrage and disbelief.

'Maths classes! Twice a week after school,' Frances gasped. 'Science classes twice a week. *And* we have to report to the library every lunchtime. I can't believe this! That bitch Pritchett! She may as well handcuff us to our desks!'

When both patriarchs had read the letters – Mr Milnar having received the torn fragments of his copy from the Good Fortune Fabric Emporium manageress, who saw Frances scatter them in the street – they had a brief telephone symposium and agreed to ground their daughters until the O levels were over in June. Sally and Frances were spitting with rage. Oh, the injustice of it! Why couldn't everyone just leave them to fail their exams in peace? Frances took the curfew harder than Sally (who'd spent most of her adolescence shut up in her bedroom anyway). To Frances, school was a prison she agreed to be incarcerated in between the hours of 8.30 and 3.30, so long as she could do as she pleased afterwards. Now the only incentive to get through the day was gone Frances sank into a depression. Too old for rooftop hunger strikes, she stomped about the apartment, glaring at her father whenever he was in eye-shot. She threatened to quit school altogether; to leave home and get a job. But far from ready to be an emancipated adult, Frances confided to Sally that the sweetest revenge would be to sit the stupid exams and fail the whole bloody lot.

The first after-school revision lesson was maths with Mr Leung. Frances and Sally sat in the stuffy classroom, muffling yawns as Mr Leung chalked tetrahedrons and polygons on the blackboard, hands flying about as he lectured on axis of symmetry with mind-boggling enthusiasm. Up from the yard below came the sound of the netball club: the stampede of plimsolls as they ran laps to the pips of Miss Van der Cruisen's whistle. For the first time in her life Sally wished she was running laps too. Anything to get out of extra maths. Frances carved up her desk top with her compass, staring mutely at Mr Leung and his avid spectacle-magnified gaze. Mr Leung was in his late twenties and a funny-looking man; though acne-studded and bum-fluffed like a teenage boy, he had hair that receded far back on his crown, like a cockatoo's crest. He was a good teacher and though most girls made fun of him and his pimples they were often swept up by his passion for the cosine rule and universal significance of pi. But not Frances. *Frances, what is the difference between a rhombus and a trapezoid? How would one go about finding out what this exterior angle is?* To every question Frances shrugged and Mr Leung had to turn to Sally for the answer (which she guiltily supplied, colluding with the enemy). Because of Frances's abstention, the lesson dragged, and they were all thankful when the hour was up. Though she'd been difficult and rude, Mr Leung spoke kindly to Frances as she scraped back her chair.

'Apply yourself a little, Frances, and you'll find maths a lot more interesting. We are all sacrificing time to help you because we think you are achieving less than you are capable of. The exams may seem pointless to you now, but the qualifications will help you once you have left school.'

Frances flung her books in her satchel and stormed out of the class.

'Thank you very much for the lesson, Mr Leung,' said Sally, hurrying after her friend. 'See you Wednesday . . . 'Bye!'

'Are you all right?' she asked as she caught Frances up in the hall.

'Who asked Mr Leung to sacrifice any time for us?' she fumed. 'Not me! He can keep his precious time. I hate the way he pretends to be so calm and reasonable. He's a sadist. He gets a kick out of boring us to death with equilateral triangles.'

Some of the netball club ran up the veranda steps and turned a few illicit cartwheels. In the courtyard a girl in a wing defence bib held open a sack which her team-mates lobbed orange balls into.

'He's only doing his job, Frances,' said Sally.

'I'd rather he didn't.'

'Well, it's only ten weeks,' said Sally. 'That's no time at all really, is it? You mustn't over-react. If you weren't so stubborn things would be easier.'

Frances said nothing in self-defence. She jerked her chin towards the car parked outside the school gates.

'Look,' she said. 'There's your driver. He's probably been waiting ages. You'd better go.'

The timetable of after-school classes had Frances and Sally studying maths on Monday and Wednesday, science with Mrs McPhee on Tuesday and Thursday, and English literature with the Evil Pritchett on Friday.

They also had to report to Mrs Iqbal the librarian every lunchtime, who was to supervise their prep. As the weeks of tuition progressed, a change came over Sally. She began to make sense of the periodic table; the difference between a volt and an ampere; a metaphor and a simile. She began to do some work, handing in the bare minimum at first, then tackling her assignments with genuine pleasure. The only drawback to this awakened love of learning was the stress of keeping it secret from Frances, who was determined to drag her heels. Frances turned up fifteen minutes late for every lesson, with lame excuses about stopped watches and jammed locker doors; she handed in her homework on torn jotter pages, illegible with ink smears and rubbings-out. She dropped an essay on *The Taming of the Shrew* on the classroom floor and watched with satisfaction as the pages were trampled by the procession of girls on their way to morning assembly. No amount of nagging would make Frances mend her sloppy ways. They could boss her about until they were blue in the face. Frances was adamant she wasn't going to learn a thing.

Towards the end of March, Sally went down with stomach flu. The nausea came on during a history lesson, when her forehead became speckled with mysteriously cool beads of sweat. The room swayed as she lifted her hand to ask permission to be excused, and Miss Ng's voice was dim as an underwater echo. Sally crashed to her knees in the toilet cubicle, hugging the porcelain bowl as stomach contractions purged the enemy within. For a good forty-five minutes she knelt there, head thrust well into the toilet bowl, a lion-tamer tickling the tonsils of the beast. During the break a second-year pupil heard her puking and called the school nurse. Sally was sent home, where she spent the next seven days in the dark seclusion of her room, at the mercy of gastric flu.

Her stomach roiled like an angry sea, rejecting Yok Ling's chicken broth with tidal waves of nausea. She was so weak and jelly-limbed that Safiah, the giggling servant girl, had to help her to the bathroom. Every evening Mr Hargreaves popped his head round the door – *How's my petal? Feeling better today? Don't worry, I won't come in when you're so fragile* – then quickly retreated from his delirious daughter and her vomit-stained nightie. Frances telephoned twice, but Sally was too wiped out to take the calls. Sally's immune system bid farewell to the last of the flu germs on Sunday night and on Monday she was well enough to return to school. Frances dashed up to her in class and seized her shoulders as if to check her friend was real.

'Oh, I'm so glad you're better. I've missed you!'

'I've missed you too,' said Sally.

'You've lost weight!'

'No! Really?'

'Oh, yeah, loads!'

Sally decided the week of lying in bed feeling rancid as sour milk was worth the affection on her return. For the rest of the day she and Frances were thick as misfit thieves. There was a change in Frances. She'd let her defences down, stopped acting as if everyone was out to get her. Her aura was no longer spiky and negatively charged. When Sally asked what she'd missed in science, Frances got out her biology notes. The pages were dated and ordered, and the usual spidery madness of her handwriting was tamed, so as not to inflict a headache on the reader. Frances had even drawn diagrams of plants in cross-section, and coloured and labelled the reproductive parts.

'Are these yours?' Sally asked her.

'Yes.'

'But you've done all the questions . . . And got some of the answers right.'

'Hard not to when everyone's breathing down my neck.'

The last lesson was games and Frances and Sally were in the changing room as the bell went. Already showered and dressed, Frances combed her damp hair and Sally sat on the bench, shrouded in a towel, having successfully passed Miss Van der Cruisen's post-shower inspection. While Delilah Jones and her clique paraded about the changing room in fragrant clouds of talcum powder, naked and shameless as Lady Godiva, Sally, who found showering after games an ordeal, had devised a showering routine around exposing the least amount of flesh to the least number of people. As Frances crouched to buckle her shoes, Sally sighed at her underwear hanging on the peg and the thought of wriggling into it under her towel.

'Can you tell Mr Leung I'll be late for maths?' she said. 'I've still got to get dressed.'

'There's no maths today. Mr Leung's not here,' said Frances.

'But I saw him this morning coming out of the first form.'

'Mrs Pritchett said to say it's cancelled. We can go home early.'

'Oh, OK.'

'I'll see you tomorrow. I've got to go and help Madame Tay with the chores.'

Since when has Madame Tay made Frances do chores? wondered Sally.

'OK, see you tomorrow, then.'

Alone among the rows of empty pegs and benches and the odd forgotten sock, Sally finished dressing as Miss Van der Cruisen locked up (*Last again, Hargreaves!*). The bus stop opposite the school had no shelter and as Sally waited there the sun blazed through the cotton of her blouse and seared her scalp with a maddening itch. The other girls at the bus stop were playing leap-frog or spinning in dizzying circles, and Sally watched the mad dance of shadows as she faced the other way. *Hurry up, bus,* thought Sally, flinching as the girls shrieked like prehistoric birds of prey. As she licked a moustache of perspiration from her upper lip she noticed a thin dark shadow appear alongside her own, appearing so stealthily it seemed to seep up through the ground. The owner of the shadow spoke.

'Hallo, Sal. How's tricks?'

Though they sat desks apart in class, it was the first time Delilah Jones had ever spoken to her. Overcome by shyness, her tongue faltered.

'Um, OK.'

'Bloody hot, isn't it?' said Delilah.

'Yeah, it's horrible.'

'The bus is bound to be hotter, though. It's always like an oven in there.'

Delilah smiled a jaded smile. Her hair was swept back in a ponytail, and Sally thought there was something of a beautiful hawk about Delilah, with her steeply arched eyebrows and beakish nose.

'Off home, are you?' Delilah asked.

'Um, yeah. I'm knackered.'

'Me too. I've got a ton of prep to do for maths tomorrow, though. It's going to take me ages.'

Sally's wonky smile of sympathy went unseen as one of the girls mucking about behind them banged into Delilah, who stumbled off the kerb into the road. When the girl saw who she'd knocked off balance she gushed apologies, bowing and scraping as she dusted off Delilah's fallen satchel. The girl's friends watched in uneasy silence.

'Be careful,' said Delilah, straightening up and taking back her bag. 'You could have pushed me into the path of a car.'

Delilah turned to Sally with a wry smile.

'Don't you usually have a maths class after school on a Wednesday?' she asked.

Sally nodded, surprised that Delilah knew of the affairs of a nonentity like herself.

'Yes, but it's cancelled. Mr Leung's not here today.'

'But I saw him and Frances go into the classroom about fifteen minutes ago,' said Delilah. 'You'd better hurry. You don't want to miss your lesson.'

Sally could see no point in going to a class that had started fifteen minutes ago, but somehow felt as though Delilah had issued her with a command. She thanked her and went back through the gates.

Sally saw them first through the glass partition in the classroom door. Frances was sitting in her chair, and instead of pacing about on the teaching platform, frantically scribbling sums on the board as though he'd half an hour to save the world with algebraic formulae, Mr Leung was perched on the edge of the desk next to her. Twenty minutes of the allotted lesson time had passed, but Frances had none of her books out. Mr Leung was talking animatedly, and Frances was very still, as though hypnotized by the wild choreography of his hands. Mr Leung's voice sounded different, and as Sally pushed open the door she realized he was speaking Cantonese. Mr Leung quickly stood up. He raked his fingers through his sparse crest of hair, his spectacle lenses magnifying his surprise.

'Sally,' he said, 'I thought you'd gone home. Is your stomach ache better now?'

Sally looked from Frances to Mr Leung, from Mr Leung to Frances. *Now I understand*, she thought bitterly. Frances's gaze said many things at once – *What are you doing here? Go away! I'm sorry* – but above all it pleaded complicity. Frances looked sheepish. Frances *never* looked sheepish – not even after her father had caught her stealing from the Kuan Ti shrine. *It doesn't suit her*, Sally thought.

'Come and take a seat,' said Mr Leung. 'We got so side-tracked by our discussion that we haven't even started yet . . .'

'Actually,' Sally said, 'I'm feeling sick again. I think I shall go before I throw up.'

The hallway was blurred with anger as she marched away from the classroom. Out on the veranda she paused, waiting for the patter of footsteps as Frances chased after her to offer an apology, an explanation. But none came.

14

At ten past eight on Monday evening I left my flat and, chaperoned by stale smoke and the fumes of the unwashed, descended fourteen storeys in the lift. The ground-floor exit doors were smashed, shattered glass cobwebs clinging to the security mesh, and as I pushed through the doors into the night the wind rushed smack-bang against me. I clinched my belt tighter as that frigid mistress slid her icy fingers beneath my coat and chilled my ankles and slippered feet (where a pair of socks wouldn't have gone amiss). I'd much rather have been indoors with a mug of Ovaltine, toasting my toes by the gas fire. But enough was enough and I had to tell her so.

The estate was dreary, the tower blocks sequestered by gloom. A gang of Afro-Caribbean lads were gathered under a street lamp, nodding to a couple of boys migrating towards them with larger-than-life limps (what a strange trend it is, this hobbling gait, as if pretending damage from childhood polio). I hurried on, slipper-slapping the paving slabs as I stared into the faces of passers-by, regretting my lifetime's carrot abstinence as I squinted to see if they were Julia.

On past the Mountbatten tower, ear lobes bitten by cold. On past the Linton low-rises and the estate mural, a twenty-foot menagerie of many-coloured faces – cocoa brown, lemon yellow and candyfloss pink – smiling widely in multiracial harmony and community *esprit de corps* (a mural that may as well have been of unicorns and fairies for all the truth it contained). As I took a short cut through the car park of Dr Chopra's surgery the hairs on the back of my neck stiffened with a prickling discharge of ions. They seemed to stiffen apropos of nothing, but a backward glance confirmed my follicles justified in their behaviour. A man was crouched in the surgery garden, incompetently hiding behind a dead shrub. My heart went shuddery with the memory of my last mugging (on my seventieth birthday, it was, the perpetrators schoolboys, beginner thugs, as eager to get the rite of passage over with as virgins in a whorehouse). Jittery with remembered pain, I quickened my step, but after a second glance at my stalker fear gave way to irritation. Teenage thugs would have been preferable.

'I can see you,' I muttered in Cantonese. 'You're fooling no one behind those bushes. Go away. I don't have time to talk to you. I am looking for my granddaughter.'

'Ha! So now you know how it feels to have loved

ones cruelly snatched from you by Imperialist Oppressors,' said Comrade Kok Sang of the Malayan Races Liberation Army. Kitted out in red-star beret and olive-green uniform, he leapt from the shadows and sped a few paces closer to me. Heaven knows why he bothered hiding. Perhaps after so many years of sneaking about in guerrilla warfare, stealthiness is second nature. He had a home-made rifle strapped on and the pouches of his terrorist belt were stuffed with ammunition. The poor chap was lousy with jungle sores, but, apart from the weeping lesions, Comrade Kok Sang was in pretty good shape for a bandit. As the cold wind blustered, he shimmered with the heat of equatorial climes.

'There are no Imperialist Oppressors on the Mountbatten estate,' I said. 'Nor are there any left in Malaysia.'

'What do you call yourself, then?' Kok Sang shouted. 'The people's friend? Timmy Lo was your friend, wasn't he? And look what happened to him!'

I stopped by the estate playground, a demolition site any responsible parent would forbid their child from entering. The swings were broken, chains wound round the frame so the seats were out of reach, and the slide was mangled as if by the jaws of a metal-crushing machine. On the Mountbatten estate the lure of destruction is strong and nothing stays unmolested for long. I circled the knee-high wall, scurrilous with graffiti, and Comrade Kok Sang cleared it in one guerrilla-style leap to land abreast of me.

'You think you are our friend because you speak our

language?' he yelled. 'That you are one of us because you fornicate with our women? Ha! You speak Chinese like an idiot gargling mud. And our women joke about your clumsy Running Dog technique and laugh at your inferior penis. You will never be anything other than our enemy . . .'

I ignored the rest of what he said, not wanting to lend my ears to such nonsense. On the playground roundabout a group of teenagers slouched. As the carousel of thugs revolved I counted six of them, all shaven-headed, their faces so darkly smudged with shadow I couldn't tell their ethnicity. One of the boys had his arm around a pale wisp of girl huddled against his jacket. Surely not Julia? Faint-heartedness hindered closer investigation.

I listened carefully to the teenagers' banter. What aggressive voices they had, snarling at one another as though in a vicious quarrel. They spoke in a hybrid of London slang and West Indian patois I couldn't make head or tail of. The girl said nothing.

Tentatively, I called: 'Julia . . . is that you?'

The boys on the roundabout looked over at me. Laughter ensued. *Julia . . .* they croaked, *Julia . . . is that you?* I wasn't surprised. It's the sort of thing one expects from the guttersnipe mouths of Mountbatten. The girl snuggled deeper into her boyfriend's jacket and said nothing to confirm or deny whether she was Julia. I refused to let the gang intimidate me.

'If you see Julia Broughton,' I said, 'tell her her grandfather is looking for her.'

'Yeah, we know dat bitch Jules, we'll tell her . . .' a boy lisped back.

I left the park. To my irritation Comrade Kok Sang hadn't gone away. He'd been listening to my exchange with the teenagers with keen interest.

'See! See!' he cried. 'The people won't listen to you! Why should they? Through violence and oppression you stole our land. We are fighting to return Malaya to the people.'

'Malaya was returned to the people a long time ago.' I sighed.

Why was I squandering my breath arguing with him? Like all those who died during the Emergency, Comrade Kok Sang is stubbornly resistant to any posthumous historical event. As far as he is concerned Independence never happened. As far as he is concerned the only hope for Malaya is the ascendance of Communism.

As I continued to search for Julia he bombarded me with insults – *Foreign Devil* this and *Imperialist Oppressor* that – taunting me all the way back to my flat. And I knew then that Comrade Kok Sang wouldn't be gone until his accusations had worn me out, spinning dark Saturnian rings round my eyes, as I suffered late into the night.

After the kidnapping of Timmy Lo, his wife Mabel sank into a deeply catatonic state, broken by outbursts of wild gibberish about locusts and the moon. Mrs Lo's mental deterioration came as a blow to the police, for

Mabel had witnessed the bandits in the act of mutilating her husband, and somewhere in her fractured mind was the key to their identity. Mrs Lo was taken to convalesce at the Jalang town hospice, tended to by Spanish nuns in the hope that she would recover her senses. In the meantime the police began an investigation, interviewing villagers who lived near to the unfortunate Timmy Lo.

As the abduction was a consequence of the bravery Timmy had shown at the village meeting, sick with the guilt of partial responsibility I attended every interview. Inspector Lam of the Special Branch came from Jalang town to head the investigation. The inspector, a Chinese urbanite and middle-aged bachelor, was less than congenial as he went from hut to hut, puckering his nose at the boiled-cabbage smells and the squelch of animal muck underfoot, and frowning at the gurgling toddlers as though they were germ-ridden vermin. Not that Inspector Lam's disgust made any difference to the villagers' attitude to the authorities. Even if he'd handed out lollipops and let the snotty-nosed little 'uns clamber up into his lap, the villagers would have remained steadfast in their refusal to talk. They played dumb with a vengeance. The inspector may have worn silver cuff-links and slicked his hair with Yardley lavender oil, but it wasn't enough to earn the villagers' co-operation. Inspector Lam went into the interrogations hard and fast, but came out limp and frustrated.

'Did you hear anything the other night?' he asked Ah Fang, neighbour of the abducted Timmy Lo.

'What night?'

'The night Timmy Lo went missing.'

'Who?'

'Timmy Lo. The man who lived in the hut next door to you for the last nine months.'

'I don't know him.'

'You thick-as-pig-shit imbecile! Everyone knows he was your best friend. Tell me what you heard! Did you hear any bandits sneaking into the village?'

'What village?'

'This village! This village! The Village of Everlasting Peace!'

The peasants yielded not one speck of useful information, goading Inspector Lam into a beetroot fury and bringing out his violent streak (though my stern throat-clearings made him limit his abuse to one strike per interviewee).

At the end of the day the inspector declared: 'Never have I met such simpletons. I'd rather ram a goat-pen stake through my head than return to this resettlement camp again.' And hailed a trishaw back to Jalang town.

The following day a government courier cycled over to The Village of Everlasting Peace with a parcel of mimeographed questionnaires – one for every household. The questionnaires asked two questions:

Do you know who kidnapped Timmy Lo?

Do you know who is helping the Communists in the village?

I helped with the distribution, reading out the questions to the illiterate villagers, and the next day the sheets were collected in a secret post-box so as to safeguard anonymity. Resettlement Officer Dulwich and I upturned the metal box and sifted through the mound of white paper that fell on to the floor of the officers' bungalow. Three quarters of the questionnaires were blank. A few villagers had taken the trouble to write messages in English – *Death to Imperialists! Die! Die! Bloody bastard liars!* – with liberal dosings of the f-word. More specific allegations were made in Chinese – for example (translated): *The person helping the Communists in The Village of Everlasting Peace is that big-nosed devil Christopher, and what's more he is having homosexual relations with Prison Officer Dulwich*. Many used the paper to showcase their artistic talents, with drawings of elephants, the honourable Chairman Mao and a monkey on a unicycle. The most cooperative reply was written in tidy cursive and said, *We are very sorry but we do not know who kidnapped Timmy Lo or who is helping the Communists in The Village of Everlasting Peace, from Miss Mallard and Miss Tolbin* – which was no help to us at all.

The failure of the questionnaires was the final straw for the District War Executive Committee. *The collective silence of The Village of Everlasting Peace calls for a collective punishment,* they said. *The hours of curfew will be brought forward from seven o'clock in the evening to two o'clock in the afternoon. The period of extended curfew is to last for a week.* And guess which unlucky bugger was appointed harbinger of the bad news . . .

I stood in the back of a pick-up truck as it bumped

over the rutted, debris-strewn trail and around the village. I read out the government directive in Cantonese and Hokkein translation through a loud-speaker, until I was reciting it verbatim. As the afternoon sun flayed my shoulders and my voice boomed, villagers surfaced in doorways to howl in out-rage (*Two o'clock! Two o'clock! Curse that Timmy Lo for making all this trouble for the village!*) and children threw stones at my back. The buxom Aussie nurses Madeleine and Josie, both of whom are deaf to Cantonese, came out of the medical hut and waved as if to a passing dignitary. In the shadows behind them stood my beloved Evangeline, her arms crossed and lip pensively bitten. The First Battalion Worcestershire Regiment were in the village to work on the school hall, which was progressing at a rate of one plank per week. They hooted and wolf-whistled when they saw me, one soldier yanking down his khaki pants and mooning me from the rooftop. The truck bounced through the check-point and out to the market gardens, the thank-less task of spreading bad tidings not yet done.

Round and round the village we went, and I repeated the news of the punishment curfew until my throat was parched and my tonsils ached. Confusing the messenger with the origins of the punishment, villagers clobbered me with the evil eye, and by the time the truck stopped outside the police station and the tail gate was let down for me I was giddy with heatstroke and in very low spirits after my hour as the object of communal hatred and blame.

The day after news of the disciplinary curfew had been loudspeakered about the village, the siren blared at quarter to two. Sergeant Abdullah and I inspected identity cards at the check-point as the rubber tappers and hoe-carrying market gardeners trooped back into the resettlement camp for fifteen hours of stagnating under hut arrest, the children unable to play Bandits versus Colonialists (or the ever-popular Tarzan versus the African Devils), the mothers and fathers unable to play mah-jong with the neighbours or go for a twilight constitutional. Eyes narrowed to slits as identity cards were handed to me for inspection. Gobbets of betel-nut juice were spat on the ground by my feet.

Irritated, I turned to the moustache-twiddling sergeant and said: 'Why are they angry at me and not the men who kidnapped Timmy Lo? Don't they care that a man's life is at stake? Over one thousand people in this village and not one of them has had the guts or integrity to come forward with information. Timmy Lo was one of the people. Yet none of them cares whether he lives or dies.'

'Timmy is already dead *lah*,' Sergeant Abdullah said. 'Why keep him alive? What good to the Communists is a man without fingers? Just another mouth to feed.' He clapped my shoulder in friendly condolence. 'Ah well, Timmy is in the arms of his Lord Buddha now.'

The kidnapping of Timmy Lo wasn't the only affair to bludgeon village morale, as during the week of curfew Detective Pang and his network of undercover spies made an unsettling discovery. Let me first of all say that in 1952 terrorist attacks on resettlement camps reached a crescendo as the Malayan Races Liberation Army reacted furiously to the segregation of the squatter community. The Village of Everlasting Peace, however, had a relatively easy time of it, with only the odd sporadic grenade exploding over the perimeter fence, and not one throat-slitting since that of my predecessor, the late Ah Wing.

One evening Kip Phillips, manager of the sandbag-fortified, trip-wire-booby-trapped Bishop's Head plantation, drove his armoured truck over for a round of gin slings with Charles and me. As the gramophone needle lifted from the last strains of 'Clair de lune' and the mechanical whirring of insects reclaimed the night, Kip Phillips patted his bullet-proof vest – a frequent unconscious habit of his – and said: 'Quiet, this village. Almost too quiet, if you know what I mean . . .'

Kip Phillips was correct in his suspicions. Detective Pang's investigation into the charmed, incident-free nights of the home guard was already under way. And what he discovered had us reeling in shock.

Twenty of our home guard had made a non-aggression pact with the regional regiment of the Malayan Races Liberation Army – a complicit agreement that bandits be let in and out of the village, and the home guard in exchange be spared gunfire and all the other little skirmishes that make night patrol so perilous. Every night for months the Reds had had free rein of The Village of Everlasting Peace, consorting with the

Min Yuen, stealing and extorting, and having sex-famished reunions with lovers and wives.

A list of names was compiled and the treacherous guards arrested. As the accused were handcuffed and marched out of the village some frothed at the mouth, swearing innocence in the name of Allah. Others went willingly, smiling as if to say, *Ah well, the game's up* ... The strong-arm of government censorship prevented the debacle of the corrupt guards from reaching the national news. But nothing could stop the news of the bloody cull from reaching the ears of the villagers. Many cackled in glee. *Good for nothing mata-mata! Betraying their country because they're too lazy to fight!* I felt terrible for those villagers who'd wanted protection from the Communists and had been badly let down.

Shortly after the mass sackings Charles and I were dining on the veranda, serenaded by a vinyl airing of Mendelssohn's 'A Midsummer Night's Dream', when Sergeant Abdullah came to see us. He sat with us and accepted a dish of beef stroganoff (a much sought-after and celebrated tinned import) with a *Thank you, Number One Man*. The sergeant ate as if racing against the clock, finishing before Charles and me, then lifting the plate to lick the mushroomy sour-cream sauce. He hiccuped and wiped his moustache with a napkin.

'We are twenty men less now because of those chicken-shit bastards,' he complained. 'Last night my men were doing eighteen-hour shifts. They are falling asleep standing up. I have to run and poke them and

222

shout *Wakey, wakey!* The village is very weak now. If the Communists wanted to attack they could cause a lot of damage . . .' He paused and smiled at me. 'Number Two Man,' he said, 'what do you say to helping us with night patrol? You can go up into the watchtower for a week or two until we recruit more guards. No more check-point duty in the morning and night duty until one or two o'clock instead. What do you think?'

I thought it a silly plan. The Crown Agency for Colonies had employed me for my knowledge of Cantonese; to improve relations between the Foreign Devils and the Chinese. To be exiled in the watch tower would be a waste. Why couldn't they recruit some boy from a nearby kampong to go up in the watch tower?

'But I am needed at the check-point,' I said. 'There are fewer guards now and none can speak Chinese. It's taking longer and longer to search the tappers every morning. They are getting to the plantation later and later and losing wages.'

'Never mind about the tappers,' said Sergeant Abdullah. 'They are never happy. Always complain, complain, complain – give me a bloody headache! After what happened it is hard to know who to trust any more. And Pang doesn't know one hundred per cent if all the traitors have been caught . . . But we know we can trust *you*, Number Two Man. From the watch tower you can keep an eye on everything that goes on.'

Charles, forelock draped across his sweaty brow, was slumped in his chair, as if flattened by his enormous belly.

'I think it's a marvellous idea. A few late nights will do Christopher good,' he said, as though I were a child. 'It's disturbing, the moronic hour he rises every day.'

Sergeant Abdullah nodded, in agreement with anything that would get me up in the watchtower.

I sighed. 'How long do you need me for?'

After the sergeant went, I lingered on the veranda, but the pleasure of my last sips of beer and Johann Sebastian Bach was impaired by Charles's saturnine remarks. Dark septic-feathered ravens wheeled overhead as Charles indulged his usual bleakness.

'They disgust you, don't they?' he said. 'The deceitful guards.'

'Yes, of course,' I said. 'Don't they disgust you?'

'No. Every one of us is weak and capable of betrayal. To be disgusted by the guards is to be disgusted by one's inner self. Nothing sickens us more than what we fear within.'

'You shouldn't tar everyone with the same brush as those lily-livered guards,' I said. 'I for one certainly won't be negotiating with any bandits.'

'How defensive you are, Christopher' – Charles was smug, as if I'd played into his hands – 'and how self-assured. Integrity is far easier in theory than in practice, you know.'

I lifted my bottle, draining the last of the yeasty foam. Charles had put me in the mood for the solitude of my hut. As I lowered the empty bottle I saw Police Lieutenant Spencer charging towards us, his pugnacious eyes screwed tight as monkeys' arseholes, and swarthy sweat patches under his arms. The policeman clomped up the veranda steps, shooting Charles a hurt, cuckolded look. He smacked a mosquito imbibing the blood of his neck, and flared his nostrils in my general direction.

'Gin sling, Percival?' Charles called cheerily, though his face fell as Spencer stormed the bungalow as if to deal with a hostage-taking situation.

'Oh, do be careful!' he cried. 'My beautiful record!'

There came a hideous warping as the gramophone needle gouged across the vinyl incarnation of Bach's Suite No. 3 in D Major. Then a satisfied silence. Charles whimpered, and Spencer thudded back on to the veranda, jaw grinding, fists clenching and unclenching at his sides, his skin pale and incandescent as candle wax. Spencer was a man tormented by the twin demons of jealousy and opium withdrawal – though I'd no idea of this at the time. Ignorant of his romance with Charles, I hadn't an inkling that I was a cattle prod to the green-eyed monster living inside him. I thought he had a bee in his bonnet about the classical music.

'Oh, do sit down, Percy!' Charles said. 'What the devil are you so uptight about? Christopher was just leaving.'

This was true: it had been my intention to leave. But it was bloody rude and presumptuous of Charles to voice it for me. I got up and said that Charles was quite right, and with much harrumphing Spencer sat in my chair and began rolling a fag. And off I went, not sorry to leave their company.

The ghost of Charles has since apologized for his bad manners. Of course, Charles's motives were ulterior to the making of amends; the apology not an anti-histamine to his bee-stung conscience (Charles's conscience is alabaster, devoid of nerve endings), but a knife, prising the lid from a can of worms. He was sitting at the kitchen table at the time, my layabout grandson snoring in the next room. Charles had a napkin tucked in his collar, and was smiling as Winston Lau, the poker-faced chef, stooped over him, ladling rice porridge into his bowl.

'Gosh, I am sorry for hurting your feelings that night. You went off in such an awful huff!'

'No, I didn't. I couldn't have cared less.'

'Oh, Christopher, there's no need to pretend you weren't upset. I assure you, it was nothing personal. It's just that three's a crowd. Especially when the third wheel is a boring puritan. Old Percival may have been the son of a Stepney chimney-sweep, but at least he knew how to have a good time. We got ourselves gloriously drunk, inhaled blue clouds of heaven into our lungs, and fucked and fucked and fucked until we were sick! While you were hunched at your desk, dipping pen nib in ink pot to transcribe your beloved dictionary, Spencer, the naughty snake-charmer, had his underwear round his ankles, ramming his seven inches into my hole. Oh, we were awash with semen and opiates – delirious with pleasure. Ever felt a man's balls jiggling against your buttocks? Had your shit compacted by a good hard cock shunting against your entrails . . . ?'

'Certainly not,' I said. 'If you had such a wonderful time together, why don't you go and find Spencer now?'

I sincerely hoped Charles would be hit by a pang of nostalgia for those orgiastic days of yore, and bugger off in search of the lieutenant. No such luck. Charles groped his belly, his pupils vanishing as the whites of his eyes rolled round.

'Argghh . . . they got me . . . the ruddy Reds got me in the guts . . .'

The accent was more Antipodean than cockney, but Charles chuckled at his poor mimicry. He sipped a spoonful of rice gruel.

'Hmmm . . . Winston! This porridge is sublime! You have really surpassed yourself. This is simply to die for!'

Charles's brow furrowed as his teeth crunched. He plucked a chicken's foot from his mouth. Winston's ghost stood beside his sycophant of a master, reptilian and beady-eyed, cold-blooded as a snake.

'Have I ever mentioned, Christopher, that our friend Winston here was a Communist? Oh, yes! Comrade Winston here was an important member of the village Min Yuen. But we didn't let politics get in the way of our friendship, did we, Winston? Our friendship transcended petty politics. Comrade Winston here knows of the horrors I endured when the Japs had me imprisoned in Changi. Comrade Winston has seen me in my darkest hour. When I first arrived in The Village of Everlasting Peace days went by when I could do nothing but lie on my bed and dream of liberating thick spurts of blood from my wrists . . . Oh, come now,

Christopher, don't pull that ghastly face! Don't tell me you've never had a touch of the doldrums before. Never ogled the knife drawer with the urge to slash your wrists to ribbons. Anyway, as I teetered at the edge of the abyss, Winston, bless him, made me a gift of some hashish. Deliciously potent stuff that made me dream the sweetest of dreams when smoked before beddy-byes. After that Winston brought me opium and a bamboo pipe to smoke it from; then a beginner's dose of morphia, which he taught me to inject into my veins. Thanks to Winston I've sampled many delights in generous abundance. *Do you remember what a chaste dabbler I was to begin with, Winston?* Good old Winston, that sly fox, he upped the dosages . . .'

'Winston Lau turned you into a drug addict!'

The silent angel of death hovered at Charles's shoulder. Was that a faint smirk I saw on his lips? Surely not. Winston has too much self-control to smirk.

'I can't believe you're so naive. Winston took advantage of you. He was the opposite of a friend. And besides, Charles, you committed suicide in the end. The drugs solved none of your problems.'

'Oh, shush now!' Charles flapped his hand dismissively. 'There's no need to be so damning. It was a mutually advantageous relationship and the opium served us both well. Communists are against such decadence as a rule, but Winston saw how my depravity could be used against me. As I soared with angels each night, Winston ransacked the office to update the Min Yuen on our administrative plans. A herd of rhinos could've stampeded through the bungalow and I'd have been none the wiser. But let's not focus on the negative. Winston was a marvellous friend to me and I am grateful. And let us not forget his excellent culinary skills. The fiery curries of cunning! The dumplings of duplicity! Winston Lau was a loyal servant to the end, and never failed to replenish my veins. Not for decades have I endured the agony of sobriety . . .'

'The agony of sobriety! You weren't the only one the Japs had in the bag, you know. That's no excuse for the wacky baccy and whatnot. You ought to have been stronger and got by without the drugs. You knew what Winston was up to. You were practically his accomplice. You were just as spineless and irresponsible as the sacked guards. You undermined every effort in the War against Communism. You . . . you . . .'

Charles grinned like a cheeky schoolboy. 'Oh, Goldilocks . . .' he sighed, 'you're so sexy when you get worked up.'

A quarter to midnight and my granddaughter not yet home. I keep vigil, an abandoned bride with a cheap veil of net curtain over her head, the windowpane a sheet of ice. As I gaze outwards, the dark appears to be in descent, like volcanic ash, mantling the estate below. I indulge a favourite pastime as I wait: rehearsing a telephone call to social services, to be made at a later, as of yet undecided, date. *Julia is becoming worse and worse . . . Twelve years old and already a tearaway . . . I am too old to cope . . . I want her off my hands.*

Imagination is the Devil. Fifty times an hour I hear the rattle of the front door, my granddaughter's shoes on the mat. The devious shadows beyond the domes of street light metamorphose, assume the form of a twelve-year-old girl, before dissolving into shadow again. Before common sense has a chance to object, I unlatch the window, fling it far and wide, and throw my pyjamaed chest over the sill. The wind buffets the lacy curtains behind me, and I grip the ledge, arms rigid, knuckles white. Electrocuted bride.

'Julia Broughton!' I holler. *'Come home!'*

My plea sweeps over the quietude of the night, soars across the landscape of tower blocks.

Beside me Comrade Kok Sang is laughing. 'Hah!' he cries. 'Your daughter has learnt of what a fiend you are. She is ashamed of her imperialist father. She has run away to join the fight to overcome the poverty of the masses. She is gone for ever and you have only yourself to blame!'

'Granddaughter, not daughter,' I correct. 'My daughter is dead.'

The factory-made curtains flutter, billowing out like a majestic cape. The freezing cold sends a shudder through me, a peristalsis through my core. Comrade Kok Sang laughs a staccato *ha! ha! ha! ha!* comic-book-villain laugh, and I remember a humid night in the watch tower, not four nights after I'd begun night patrol. My rifle was aimed out of the watch tower at a bandit, a mere pygmy of a lad, wriggling under the perimeter fence. The bandit held a bundle of feathers, a dead chicken gripped by its wrung neck. The poultry rustler was in trouble, his shirt hooked on a barb of wire. As he struggled to free himself, the bloody-plumaged bird flapped about, brought back to life by its murderer's panic. The boy was an easy target, a sitting duck, so foolishly close to the watch tower he needed "*is 'ed seeing to*' (as Lieutenant Spencer would say). And yet the carbine shook in my hands, the trigger slippery with the sweat of indecision. *Shoot him*, I commanded myself, *shoot his foot. One must shoot any bandit on sight.*

'Why didn't you shoot him?' asked an incredulous Special Constable Ahmed when he came to relieve me from night duty.

'Why the devil didn't you shoot him?' yawned a hungover Charles at breakfast.

'Why didn't you shoot him?' scolded Sergeant Abdullah in the afternoon.

'Why didn't I shoot him?' I lament as the clock strikes midnight, fifty years too late.

In the night sky above the Mountbatten estate hovers Comrade Kok Sang, a bright and ghostly constellation, eyes shining like celestial birthday candles.

'Why didn't you shoot me?' He laughs. 'Why didn't you . . . ?'

15

'See how he shakes with demons. They do not grant him a moment's peace,' whispered Marina Tolbin, the hawk-visaged missionary.

'The heathen embraces them,' observed Blanche, best friend of Marina and arch rival in the battle of the sanctimonious. 'He is a willing host. We have no choice but to perform the rites.'

'But he does not want the demons expelled. He has grown fond of them and will resist.'

'True. But we must do our duty. He killed our Humphrey, and next time he might kill a village child.'

Gimlet-eyed and pendulous of jowls, the witches' coven of two watched me from the living-room door-way. Two battleships in flowery frocks, Blanche's steel-grey bun imperious on her head, and Marina gorgonesque as ever, her mere propinquity to a mirror enough to crack it.

I was hunched on the edge of my fold-out bed, shivering like an alcoholic in the latter stages of cold turkey. My dentures chattered like a wind-up toy and my hands were suspended midair, as if by invisible strings, twitched by a wicked puppeteer. They are occurring more and more frequently, these shaking fits. I ought to arrange a check-up, but I've never cared much for doctors (especially that condescending pill-pusher Dr Chopra). I wanted to tell the missionaries that I hadn't murdered Humphrey, but I knew my voice would not be steady enough. As I shook, the Sisters Grimm continued to whisper and err, misinterpreting my affliction as Unholy Tenure. And then, as suddenly as it had begun, the shaking stopped.

'Whatever gave you the idea that I killed Humphrey? I can't even stomach rare steak, let alone decapitate a dog. I dare say the culprit was a bandit, or a Buddhist, fed up with all your baptisms. Or maybe the gambling, opium-eating husband of Mrs Ho . . .'

The missionaries took no notice of these sensible suggestions. They were convinced it was me and that was that.

'Ooh, to hear him speak! He is the mouthpiece of Satan!'

'Beelzebub, master of demons commands his tongue! Let us be upon him.'

They left the doorway, proceeding towards me, the sacrificial victim, defenceless in my flannel pyjamas.

'The Lord Jesus rebuke you, the Lord rebuke you. In

the name of Jesus of Nazareth, rise up and walk!' cried Blanche.

Though I'd intended to ignore the silly exorcism, the strangest thing happened. The words of the scripture literally stung my skin, as though I were being rubbed in nettles. I confess I 'freaked out' (as Julia would say). Snarling, I lashed out at the missionaries, swinging my arms as if fending off a swarm of killer bees.

'Bugger off, you vile witches!' I screamed. 'You evil crones! Out of my flat! Who said you could come here?'

Marina plucked a vial of holy water out of thin air. She sprinkled a few drops on my forehead, where it hissed and sizzled like hydrochloric acid.

Blanche Mallard, holding the Bible out before her like a shield, intoned: 'The Lord rebuke thee! O demons, be gone from this man for we go by the commands of God.'

I howled profanities and gouged my cheeks in despair. What had come over me? Perhaps there was a demon or two knocking about inside me after all.

'O heathen, be strong in the name of the Lord and the power of His might,' she droned on.

I threw a blanket over my head and hid in the scratchy-wool darkness. The God-botherers broke into a chant, and I writhed under my bedspread, fingers plugged in ears, until I could take it no more.

Determined to scare the missionaries off for good, I threw off my blanket with an almighty roar. A volcano-like venting of fury. And it worked. When I looked around me the exorcists were gone and Adam was hovering by the sideboard. As usual the boy was an anaemic, acne-pustuled fright to behold. But aesthetic cruelty of adolescence aside, there was something different about him. It took me a moment to work out what it was. Adam was afraid.

'Oh, I do apologize, Adam. Honestly, these fits will be the death of me. But as you can see I am quite all right now.'

I stood up in demonstration of my mental and physical well-being, sinews of shame quivering in my legs. The teenager retreated from the living room with cautious backward steps, wary that the beast in flannel pyjamas might pounce upon his vulnerable back.

The bedroom door slammed and I hung my head. And pleased by the deteriorating relations between my grandson and me, my demons gurgled contentedly within.

The watch tower was in the south of The Village of Everlasting Peace, a garret held aloft by rickety twenty-foot-high stilts, yards from the border fence. The tower was roofed by a thatch of palm leaves and widely fenestrated on every side. A ladder, many of its rungs loose or gone astray, reached up to a trapdoor in its floor. The garret, though comprised mostly of windows, was dark and stiflingly hot. The whiff of urine made me think of an aerial latrine.

The afternoon before my first shift Special Constable Ahmed gave me a guided tour. Ahmed and I were the same age, but he was already husband to three wives and father to eight children (a feat sanctioned by the polygamous laws of Islam). Though these complex domestic circumstances seemed demanding of a beyond-his-years wisdom and maturity, Special Constable Ahmed was exceptionally juvenile, laughing and farting loudly as he climbed the watch-tower ladder a few rungs ahead of me. Up in the garret I commented on the odour of urine. Ahmed jabbed a finger at a jar in the corner, containing a liquid the colour of bouillon stock.

'Special Constable Ibrahim's wee-wee,' he said. 'He thought it was wrong to wee out of the window. You can throw it away if you want. He's gone now. He won't mind.'

'How could Ibrahim think it wrong to urinate out of the window, but OK to let bandits into the village?' I mused. 'Where's the moral consistency in that?'

Ahmed shrugged. He pointed to various objects in the room.

'That is the bell you ring if you see a bandit,' he said. 'There are the binoculars . . . torch . . . prayer mat . . .'

My attention strayed to the magnificent view. From our lofty perch the rubbish pyres, stagnant ditches and sullen humanity shrank to insignifance, and the Midas touch of sun on the quarter mile of corrugated-iron rooftops transformed our shantyland into a city of silver. For the first time ever, I thought The Village of Everlasting Peace was beautiful. The opposite view was of the rainforest, stretching for miles and miles, lush and green and many fathoms deep. The canopy was thickset and fertile, giving the impression it would spring like moss as I strolled over it, among the frolicking birds of paradise, to the other side of the hills. I leant over the splintered, rough-hewn ledge and breathed a deep breath, inhaling nature at her most exhibitionistic, almost tasting the sap of the hundred thousand trees. In the vastness of the jungle one sensed the presence of the Creator (a feeling this infidel of an Englishman associates more closely with the animist beliefs of the indigenous people than with some bearded chap in the sky). Seeing my reverence, Special Constable Ahmed came and stood by me, sweeping an outspread hand along the scenery, as if conducting an orchestra in slow motion. His fingertips brushed the horizon, where the emerald green of the rainforest met the sky.

'Bandit country,' he said. 'The jungle, not the people, is the Communists' number one comrade. If there was no jungle to hide the Communists there would be no Emergency. When you see a bandit crawling out of the jungle, you must shoot him . . .' Special Constable Ahmed shaped his hand into an imaginary gun and fired it at a skin-and-ribcage dog sniffing at the fence. '*Bang, bang, bang!* You see? And if you see any villagers out after curfew, you must shoot them too . . .' The Special Constable spun 180 degrees to the village and fired the gun at some chin-wagging old women who were queuing at the standpipe, oblivious of the imaginary bullets speeding towards them. '*Bang, bang, bang!* You see? Easy. You'll like it up here. It's nice and quiet. The best place in the village.'

'If this is the "best place in the village", then how come all the guards have refused to come up here?' I asked.

'Refused?'

'Sergeant Abdullah came to me as a last resort, didn't he? No one else wants to work here at night. Why?'

Ahmed laughed, nuggets of gold glittering in his back teeth. 'The other guards are scared. The *hantu* – ghosts – come out of the jungle and visit this watchtower.'

It was then my turn to laugh. 'Ah ha, I see. Has anyone actually seen these ghosts?'

'I have. Ibrahim has. Many people have.'

'What do they look like?'

'The same as us, only dead.'

'How very scary! So how come *you* can stand to be up here and not the other guards? You must be made of pretty stern stuff.'

Ahmed nodded. 'The *hantu* come to me and I tell them: "You are scary, but not as scary as my wives when they need money to go to market!"'

'And what do you suggest that I say when the *hantu* come to me?'

Special Constable Ahmed stared at the jungle, considering what would be appropriate for me to say when encountering the spirit world. 'They won't come to you,' he decided. 'You are an Englishman. They leave foreigners alone.'

At twilight I climbed the scantily runged ladder to commence my shift in the watchtower. I took up with me a flask of tea and a tiffin-carrier of ham and Dijon mustard sandwiches prepared by Winston Lau (the opium-mongering chef had given a rare gem of a smile as he handed me the tiffin-carrier, tickled by the thought of desecrating the Muslim-frequented watchtower with sacrilegious meat). Before I could settle in to my new quarters, though, I had to get rid of Special Constable Ibrahim's piss-pot, which sloshing jar I carried down the ladder with much disgust. After a good hand-scrub with carbolic soap at the standpipe, I returned to the garret.

I'd expected the vigilant demands of lookout duty to keep me occupied, but the novelty of scanning the jungle scrublands with my binoculars quickly wore off. An hour into my shift I was so bored I wished for the jungle ghosts to change their opinion of Englishmen and come and keep me company (never has the adage *Be careful what you wish for* rung so true!). The night became treacly black and I lit some citronella incense, though the malaria-tainted drinkers of blood and kamikaze moths were undeterred. The night patrol trooped by and I hailed them from my lookout, hoping to engage them in some boredom-alleviating banter. But the exhaustion of an eighteen-hour shift had fleeced them of good humour, and only one or two of them gave me an apathetic wave. Before midnight I got caught short and discovered the illicit pleasure of pissing far and wide out of the window. How satisfying to fire a golden cannonade into the night and hear it patter on the ground twenty feet below! But other than the thrill of spending a penny (and I sweat so much in the heat I rarely had the chance to), night-watchman's duty had few perks and I was driven near insane with nothing to do. When Special Constable Ahmed came at two o'clock from his bar-tending job at the Jalang Club, I damn near hugged him I was so relieved.

The following night I stocked the watchtower with ammunition for the war against tedium: playing cards, a solitaire board and a bag of marbles, Proust's *A la recherche du temps perdu*, a Chinese dictionary, a sheaf of paper, a calligraphy brush and a pot of ink. Thus occupied, I found the clock hands shook off their lassitude and resumed a normal pace. However, on my fourth night up in the watchtower I was so immersed in my calligraphy I almost missed Comrade Terrorist Kok Sang of the 10th Independent Regiment wriggling under the fence with a garrotted chicken in his thieving clutches (of course, Comrade Kok Sang was just an anonymous bandit to me then, having only introduced himself posthumously). By the time I'd swapped my calligraphy brush for a rifle and dithered long and hard about whether to shoot, he had leapt into the leafy armour of the jungle. I hadn't even rung the bell.

I left the watchtower at two a.m., the night hyper-active with cries and croaks and the high-frequency vibrations of the natural world, my embarrassing gaffe at the forefront of my mind. The lights of the officers' bungalow were blazing and a faint ivory tinkle could be heard – Charles and Lieutenant Spencer still up and no doubt tight as bastards. I identified the piano music as Liszt's Ballad, a favourite of mine, and halted in the moonlight, the melody stirring my senses into an agreeable melancholia. The last time I'd heard the nocturne I'd been sitting on the veranda steps at dusk, striking matches, one after the other, and watching them blacken and shrivel in the heat of a bright orange flame. I was suffering from a bout of homesickness, or, rather, the sickness of unbelonging – of living in the village drowning in bad blood. The music suited my mood. My private thoughts were interrupted, however, by Charles's heavy tread on the wooden boards behind me. Charles can sniff out sadness like a bloodhound a fox.

'Music such as this provides sanctuary for the soul,' he murmured, 'provides companionship in sorrow and dignifies self-pity. It burns with indignation on behalf of the listener and all the petty injustices he has endured . . .'

Oh, the black raven doth soar! In a few words Charles had stripped the music of its transcendence and made me feel rather foolish to boot. I saw the lights of the bungalow go out and I wondered if Spencer was under the Resettlement Officer Dulwich's joyless tutelage, adopting the manifesto of sadness as his own.

Guided by torchlight I trudged on, crossing a footbridge on the brink of collapse, and passing a large pyramid of sawn-off lead pipes left behind by the Public Works Department, toads ribbiting in the pipe-tunnel mouths. Passing the officers' bathing hut, I heard a noise. A snuffling, scuffling noise, as if someone was dragging a corpse around while breathing heavily through a gas mask. Then there came a thwack and an enormous splash as the water barrel overturned. As the hour was too late for bathing, my mind immediately turned to bandits. I'd once transcribed an MCP advisory pamphlet on personal hygiene, with passages on the importance of regular washing, shaving and teeth-cleaning for Communist morale. Perhaps guerrillas were raiding the bathing hut for toothpaste, razors and soap. The noise was rather loud and indiscreet for thieves, though, and I considered it might be some jungle animal – perhaps a trapped porcupine, thrashing about in frustration. Nervous of encountering a bandit's flashing blade or the sharp quills of a rampaging porcupine, I went round the back of the bathing hut and banged on the wall.

'Who's there?' I shouted. 'I have my gun.'

In truth all I had was my tiffin-carrier containing some sandwich crusts and was regretting my intervention, when the door of the hut banged open with such force that the walls shook. I peeked around the side of the hut and caught sight of a man streaking behind a row of nearby shacks. A curfew violator, I supposed. I proceeded cautiously round to the front, to see what damage had been done, flashing my torch around the crime scene until it came to rest upon a bare-legged girl in a dress, crouched behind the toppled-over water barrel like a child playing hide-and-seek. Though the girl must have sensed the torch beam, she kept her face hidden in her hands, as if she believed that banishing the world from her sight would, in turn, banish her from the sight of the world. In any case, there was no need for me to see her face. I knew who she was.

'Grace,' I said. 'What are you doing here?'

Grace spoke no language but baby-talk, and wasn't going to start babbling on my account. Hearing her name, however, she realized the invisibility ruse had failed and removed her hands from her beaming face. There was a purplish bruise on her cheek, and her lips were bloody and swollen, as if split by the toothy kiss of an over-amorous Romeo. She stood up, blinking a little in the torch glare, but smiling, happy as a clam. Her dress was wet and torn and clung to her thighs, but her cherubic face bore no trace of guilt or knowledge of wrongdoing. Smiling at me, she put her hand between her legs and rubbed herself, the glint of sexual delinquency in her eyes. Irritated, disgusted and slightly aroused, I grabbed her arm and hauled her roughly outside.

'What happened to you, Grace? Who did this to you? Have you no pride?'

Grace's eyes clouded over, her face as pale and empty as the moon. I bristled at the inconvenience of having to escort her back to her hut. It never occurred to me that Grace might have been the victim of a sexual assault, or in need of medical attention. Attitudes to such things were different then. I doubt the police would've shown much sympathy anyway. Grace didn't

243

seem the least bit traumatized and was known for her promiscuity. Manacling her elbow, I steered Grace in the direction of her home – a good ten minutes' walk away.

As I tugged her along Grace stumbled with none of the virtue implied by her name. We hadn't got very far when a figure came hurtling out of the darkness. My Evangeline, cloaked in moonshadow. Barefoot, frantic and wild-eyed in my torchlight. She panted, shuddering hard, but she didn't pause to recover her breath. She flew at us, swinging her arm and striking Grace's cheek with the whipcrack force of her open palm. Grace bucked like a horse startled by lightning, wrenching her elbow from my grip. She turned to flee but Evangeline lunged, grabbed a fistful of her dress and fell on her, pushing her younger sister to the ground. Evangeline pummelled Grace with bare-knuckle punches, the poor simple girl wailing and fending off the blows with flailing arms. Evangeline was a blur of violence, a creature of eight arms, her face hideous with rage. I was afraid she'd lost her mind. I girdled Evangeline from behind, pinning down her arms and hauling her off her sister. Unfortunately for Grace, Evangeline clutched a handful of her hair, dragging Grace along with us through the dirt. When I finally freed Grace's tresses from Evangeline's fist, the kicking, screaming momentum of aggression shifted on to me. She thrashed like a hell-cat in my arms, kicking my shins with her bare heels.

'For heaven's sake!' I gasped as she battered my sternum with her elbow. 'The guards will hear and you'll be sent to a detention camp.'

Evangeline stiffened at the mention of detention camp. Wary of a resurgence of violence, I kept hold of her, clamping her arms in my backwards embrace. The tenseness of her body dissolved into shaking, her breath coming in sharp sobs. The worst of the hysteria over, I twisted Evangeline to face me.

'See those huts over there?' I nodded to the hunched, misshapen row of shacks a stone's throw away. 'Everyone who lives in those huts is now awake. The commotion you made woke them.'

The thin wail of an infant drifted through the dark. The windows were dark gaping mouths and the sensation of being watched was overwhelming, as if every pair of eyes delivered a tiny electric shock. Grace huddled in the earth, whimpering and rocking back and forth on her heels. Her knees were grazed and dirt-encrusted, her face a bloody swollen pumpkin. She cowered from her sister, touching the raw and tender spot on her scalp from which her hair had been torn. Evangeline trembled, not far off whimpering herself.

'I am sick of this!' she said. 'I am sick of looking after her. I forget to lock the door just once . . .'

I concede I had seen none sicker than Evangeline. Resentment poisoned her blood, and the violence had purged her of not one drop.

'Well, what good will come of beating your sister to a pulp?' I hissed. 'For goodness' sake pull yourself together. Now is not the time. Look!'

Scything along the darkness of the trail were three circles of torchlight, swaying in the distance like luminous spectres. Fortunately, Evangeline's break-down was not so severe that she didn't grasp the urgency of our situation. *Over there*, she said, pointing towards a ditch. Together we shoved and bundled the cowering Grace towards the chest-high trench. Evangeline and I lowered ourselves in and Grace fell in after us with a splash. The errant sisters and I crouched ankle-deep in the filthy water, the surface a flotilla of mosquito larvae, effluent scum and other vile flotsam. The stench made me gag, and I held my nose so the odour was less pervasive. Grace grizzled softly and Evangeline silenced her, clamping a hand over her mouth and muttering fiercely in her ear.

The guards had seen us jump down into the ditch. I knew it in my bones. My eardrums were taut with listening for footsteps, waiting for the swoop of torch beams upon us as we squatted like dirty animals in our hiding place. Paranoia taunted me with illusory sounds: whispers of *Mistah Ingerris* and the tittering of guards sneaking up to the ditch. However, when the night patrol did eventually pass us by (much louder than the phantom footsteps of my imagination) the tenterhooks withdrew from my heart. They were a pro-cession of men dead on their feet; somnambulists, their numb muteness only broken by the odd wheeze, a tarry cough. When they were far enough away I climbed out of the cesspit, shoes squelching, the foul wetness cling-ing to my trouser turn-ups. I then lent a hand to Evangeline and Grace and helped them out too.

I saw the Lim sisters back to their hut in a furious

silence. How had they managed to embroil me in such a shambolic episode? I didn't utter a word to Evangeline, whom I blamed entirely for everything, and Evangeline knew better than to speak to me. The mooncalf Grace smiled as she followed us, the throb of bruises all she retained of the night's misadventures. I said a few terse words in parting at their door – *Make sure this never happens again* – before turning my back. It was remarkably cold of me, but I wanted my displeasure to be known and was determined to wash my hands of the pair thereafter.

That night I slept fitfully, in a turmoil of dreams. I dreamt the guards of The Village of Everlasting Peace filed into my hut, a dozen or so men, with gouged hollows where their eyes ought to have been. They gathered around my camp-bed, where I lay terror-drenched and paralysed, their empty sockets glaring at me.

I dreamt I was up in the watchtower and a gigantic moth flew in; a lepidopterous beast with the wing-span of a serpent eagle. The moth flew in wild circles, then crashed into the kerosene lamp so it smashed to the floor and set it on fire. The moth dive-bombed me and I remember the shiny armour of its thorax and the blue iridescent beads of its eyes, bulging large as apples. I drove it off with a calligraphy scroll, beating at its wings so the scales disintegrated into mottled-grey powder, which, falling, invigorated the kerosene flames like some flammable dust.

I dreamt I lay in the darkness, breathing in the hot viscous air, when a whorish naked Grace lifted my mosquito net and climbed on to my mattress. Grace straddled me, sheathing me, sliding her tight slippery warmth up and down on my Judas erection. I lay back in horror and arousal as Grace writhed, moaning in the throes of lust. She molested me with damp stumpy hands, groping my chest and leaning close so I could smell the sour-milk smell of her succulent flesh. She bit my cheek, pressed her parted lips to mine and probed me with her muscular tongue. I could not fight her off. Invisible forces pinned me down as Grace the succubus, the harlot-rapist, leant back, moaned and fondled her small breasts, clenching and quickening her rhythm, manipulating me towards an orgasm filled with incestuous sickness.

I dreamt that a stranger came and slid a sheaf of papers under my door.

I woke to a hot bright morning. Flies attracted by the lingering stench of ditch buzzed merrily about my feet. A trip to the bathing hut was in order. As I yawned and stretched and collected my towel I saw, with a strange sense of déjà vu, an envelope bearing my name on the floor. I dropped my towel and pounced upon the letter. And it wasn't until I was tearing open the seal that I realized how many questions I had and how badly I wanted answers.

16

Charles Dulwich appeared by the fireplace in his seer-sucker suit, Little Lord Fauntleroy curls poking out like the springs of a disembowelled clock, a dangerously smug smile on his face.

'Guess who I've just seen!'

The gas fire was off to save money and I sat in the armchair under a pile of blankets, my breath a pale cirrus mist. Charles, the lucky bugger, was immune to the bitter chill. Whereas I'd lost sensation in my toes, Charles was sweating like a pig on a spit. He plucked a hanky from his pocket and delicately patted his fore-head. A drop slid down the slope of his nose to the tip, where it hung with a menacing quiver before plummeting to the carpet.

'Aren't you going to guess?' he asked.

I had better things to do than play Charles's silly guessing game. For the past five minutes I'd been trying to drink my toddy of hot milk and whisky. My hand trembled as I gripped the mug, the amplitude of shaking increasing the higher the mug was lifted, until boiled milk slopped over the rim and scalded my knuckles. At this point the mission had to be abandoned and the mug lowered to the safety of the trestle table.

'Spoilsport,' Charles accused.

The children were asleep in the bedroom and I was loath to wake them by quarrelling with Charles. Julia has been so naughty of late that every night she sleeps peacefully under my roof is a blessing.

'I haven't the foggiest. Who d'you see?'

'Guess. It won't be any fun if I just tell you!'

I was dubious that there was any fun in it for me at all, but I said: 'Police Lieutenant Percival Spencer.'

'Ha, ha! Old Periwinkle! I haven't seen the Boy Wonder and his amazing flying intestines for half an eternity.'

'He was here looking for you the other day . . .'

'Have another guess!'

'Oh, I don't know, Charles . . .'

'Go on!'

'Kip Phillips from the Bishop's Head plantation . . .'

'Ha, ha! Wrrrong! Guess again.'

'Give me a hint. Was he Chinese, an Englishman or Malay?'

'The person, who is of the non-male gender, is of Chinese blood.'

My heart gave a nasty lurch. 'Evangeline?'

A vampire feeding on the anxiety of others, Charles smiled, then sank his fangs in deeper. 'Haha, *you wish*! I haven't seen that knackered old donkey and her mad trollop of a sister since heaven knows when.'

'I'd appreciate it if you would kindly refrain from speaking of her like that.'

'Oh, c'mon, Christopher, she was hardly a paragon of feminine virtue. You *do* know about the slutty Lim sisters and the Japanese, don't you?'

Blankets tumbled to the floor and my dressing gown came agape as I stood up and pointed to the door.

'Shut up! Get out!'

Charles was not remotely cowed. 'Calm down or you'll wake the snivelling brats next door,' he said. 'Seeing as you're so hopeless at guessing, I will describe her. She is as tall as your armpit and seventeen years of age. She has raven silk hair and almond-shaped eyes; hazel and gold-flecked in sunshine, deepest brown in the shade. Tawny-limbed and no breasts to speak of. Her school uniform a grey pleated skirt and cap-sleeved blouse . . . Have you guessed who she is yet? Here's another clue: she was smoking one of your cigars. Yes! The disobedient child was blowing smoke rings out of her bedroom window and across Sultan Road for everyone to see. Really, Christopher. Just because she was born out of wedlock doesn't mean you ought not to teach her some manners.'

I was winded, my solar plexus punched by an invisible fist. Weak-kneed, I sank down on to the armchair again.

'Frances.'

'Yes. Well done. Got there eventually.'

'But how did you recognize her? You've never seen Frances before. You died when she was a baby. Your lives scarcely overlapped.'

I often forget that common-sense logic is irrelevant in the topsy-turvy realm of the dead.

'Of course I recognized her,' Charles said impatiently. 'She has her mother's scheming slitty eyes.'

'What did she say?'

'I spoke to her first. I said: "Your father won't approve of you smoking, young lady."'

'And she said?'

'She was foul-spoken as a drunken sailor on shore leave. She told me to fuck off and mind my own business, because her father was *dead*!'

'No,' I protested limply.

'Yes!' Charles was saucer-eyed in faux-astonishment. 'Seventeen years old and swearing like a trooper! What kind of school have you sent her to, Christopher? A finishing school for scrubbers and fishwives? You should demand your fees refunded. I said to her: "You cheeky cow! Your father is not dead, but living a life of impoverished misery on a council estate in east London with your bastard son and feral slut daughter . . ." "He's not my father!" quoth she, a patricidal rage in her eyes. "He is a liar, a murderer and a Foreign Devil!" Then she stubbed her cigar out on the wall and left the room.'

Oh, those terrible teens! Frances was a delightful child, who liked nothing better than to sit on Daddy's lap and listen to Orang Asli folk tales, but as soon as she hit puberty she became a stranger. I remember the brooding silences that stretched for weeks on end, her secret world of Chinese whispers with Madame Tay. Her cold shoulder, her eyes a perpetual roll of contempt. Sometimes I'd forget, reach out and pat her head as our paths crossed in the hall. Only to be reminded of the status quo by a shudder of repulsion that tore my heart in two. My child rejected me and my pitiful stabs at affection. Avoiding her lessened the pain, so I kept to my study. I kept myself aloof.

'My dear fellow,' said Charles, 'whatever did you do to make your daughter hate you so?'

And leaving that knife twist of a question lingering in the air, Resettlement Officer Dulwich vanished from the fireplace in a clichéd puff of smoke.

Believe me, I'd like nothing more than to reverse the chronology of blunders. But time moves stubbornly forwards, distancing me from my crimes, yet bringing them closer, to greater prominence in my mind. My darling Frances. If only I could atone for what I have done. But you never gave me the chance.

I stowed the letter in my trouser pocket, reading it in spare moments throughout the day, sneaking it out like an alcoholic with a secret hip flask. I pored over the letter while supervising a bare-chested volunteer team, machetes hacking at undergrowth that had sprung up overnight (as if the Communists had scattered magic beans by the fence). I shuffled the pages in the bungalow while Charles had his afternoon siesta, snoring like a wildebeest in his rattan chair. By dusk the letter was worn from handling – from my habit of furrowing the pages between finger and thumb, so they puckered with crow's feet and furled at the edges (and now, after many decades, the document is soft as suede, the ink faded, and each page in quarters, detached along the folds).

That evening the letter accompanied me to the watch tower – garret of light adrift in the sea of night – to be read in the paraffin-lamp haze, my shirt clinging like damp papier mâché to my back. Over the years I have memorized every sentence, and do not have to retrieve the letter from its shoebox in the hallway cupboard to see the script that blossomed from the fountain pen. Every word echoes in the authorial voice, sombre with the dark annals of history. The years have not lessened its impact.

Christopher,

My sincere condolences over the failure of the village meeting. I want you to know the meeting was destined to fail. Earlier that day bandits waylaid the tappers at the Bishop's Head plantation as they carried their pails of latex to be weighed at noon. The People Inside ushered them to a clearing and warned them of the consequences should anyone cooperate with the plans for the village council, slit- ting the throat of a dog in demonstration of what they would do. Why Timmy Lo did not heed these warnings I do not know. But he is now dead.

*I write to you, Christopher, because it is barely six
o'clock in the morning and already rumours of you and the
Lim sisters are flying about the village. I write to you
because I do not want to involve the police in this matter.
Before I discuss last night's imprudent actions, however, I
want to address a conversation I overheard between you
and Evangeline Lim in the police hut, on the night of
12 September. No doubt you are aware that I overheard
you both. Perhaps you are wondering why I did not report
you . . .*

Detective Pang made me feel like an ant scurrying about beneath a magnifying glass. When one considers this goose-pimply sensation of being under surveillance, what happened next that night seems downright absurd. However, the birth of love is often coupled with the demise of reason. And as I hover in the shadows, watching over my younger self, I can pinpoint the very beginning of the demise. It began with the creak of wood.

The creak came from a ladder rung. The noise startled, but did not alarm me, as no bandit would be stupid enough to climb up to the watch tower, and I assumed it was a guard or policeman too lazy to announce himself. I peered through the open trapdoor at the shadowy figure ascending in the darkness. 'Who is it?' I called. 'It's me,' came the reply, and I remember how my heart sank and lifted at the same time.

Evangeline surfaced, levering her body through the trapdoor on arms so thin I feared they'd snap. She clambered on her knees, then to her feet. She gazed at me, self-consciously running her fingers through her cropped hair. I thought of my resolution to have nothing more to do with her. I thought of the letter and how incessantly she'd been on my mind since I'd read it. I knew then I had no hope of keeping my resolution, less than eighteen hours old. Evangeline was fated to enter my life, with or without my consent.

'What the hell are you doing here?' I asked. 'Why not just turn yourself in to the village police and be done with it! And where is Grace? Run away again, I suppose.'

'Grace is with the Jesus People tonight,' said Evangeline.

Evangeline's trespassing into the watch tower evoked the memory of a long-forgotten childhood sweetheart, the stubborn, freckled and marmalade-pigtailed Myfannwy Price, who braved verbal abuse and the pelting of apple cores to climb up to my tree-house and declare her true love. The past was recurring, though in its repetition my heroine was decades older and dressed not in knee-high socks and gingham party frock, but a worn cotton smock ready for recycling as dishcloths. My eight-and-a-half-year-old Princess of Pembroke-shire had come back to me as an eccentric Queen of the Orient, the freckled beauty of yore reincarnated with craggy eyes and a thin and down-turned mouth. The paraffin lamp cast my beloved in an unflattering light, darkening the mauvish bruises under her eyes, deepening the time-furrowed wrinkles. But if I could go back I would change none of it. I would have Evangeline before me again in all her haggard glory. I would not have it any other way.

'Look, I don't want to lose my job over this,' I said. 'Go back to your hut or I'll call the guards.'

Evangeline was deaf to my empty threat. 'Did the way I beat my sister last night disgust you? Did it sicken you?'

'I was unimpressed, to say the least. And I'm even less impressed by your compromising me – for the third time no less! – by violating Emergency regulations to sneak up here.'

'I went to the Jesus People today and told them that I cannot cope with Grace any more. I told them of the bad feelings I have towards her. They said they would take her for the night, to give me time alone to read the Bible and find God. The Jesus People say that once I have found Him I will learn to love my duty to Grace. But I have been reading and reading, Christopher . . .' she laughed bitterly, 'and He is nowhere to be found.'

'Well, you certainly won't find Him up in this watch-tower,' I said. 'Though, I dare say, if you continue to sneak about the village after curfew, the guards will pump you full of lead and then you'll make his acquaintance in Kingdom Come.'

Evangeline was unflinching at the prospect of being gunned down by the Security Forces. Her forehead shimmered in the heat and her eyes blazed like some-one in the grip of an *idée fixe*.

'They tell me God will cure me of my resentment,' she said, 'but it is getting worse and worse. I have to do everything for Grace. Every day I wash and dress and feed her. I cannot leave her unattended for a second, or she will wander into people's homes and make a mess and steal their food. I have constantly to keep her away from the men who think her body is the property of the masses. Grace will always be a child. She will never grow up and live apart from me. I told the Jesus People that sometimes when I hear her breathing next to me in the night I wish for it to stop. I think how easy it would be to put a pillow over her head. They told me God will save me, God will give me strength, but . . .'

I bit my tongue. Evangeline was on the verge of tears and experience had taught me a few sympathetic words would be enough to trigger the deluge. Call me cold-hearted, but if there's one thing I can't abide it's a weeping woman. From age eleven onwards I've had the good sense to recoil from this childish medium of self-expression. Yet all the women I've known turn on the sprinklers with shameless abandon – well into old age! After all Evangeline had survived during the war, I was shocked that the mundane burden of caring for her sister threatened to bring her down. The Village of Everlasting Peace was overrun with downtrodden humanity and the Lim sisters were no worse off than anyone else.

'I appreciate it must be hard taking care of your sister,' I said, 'but you really have to pull yourself together, Evangeline. Everyone in this village has a tough life of it. There are women with a tribe of little 'uns to look after and no husband to help them because he's buggered off into the jungle to join the People Inside.'

I'd hoped to lessen Evangeline's self-pity by reminding her of the hardships of others. But this only stoked the embers of her rage.

'What do you know, Christopher? What do you know of our lives! I have seen how tough *your* life is, you and your fat alcoholic friend gorging yourselves on roast duck and listening to music on your veranda . . .'

Her arrogance was breathtaking. Who was she to accuse me of leading a life of privilege? Evangeline had violated several Emergency regulations to come and harangue me in the watch tower and yet had the audacity to behave as though she were in the right.

'Do you honestly think I am living it up here in this village? I work damn hard – for sixteen hours a day or more, mucking in wherever I can. I even live in a wooden hut just like the rest of you.'

'But you are not like the rest of us. You can walk in and out of the gates when you want. Go wherever you want at any time of day or night. You are so proud of yourself! You think yourself so moral and worthy to be here, to be friendly to the natives, but you are just a tourist.'

'Really? A tourist? And what kind of holiday destination is The Village of Everlasting Peace? Do you honestly think I have come here for pleasure? To see the sights?' I was spitting with rage, a baptism of salivary flecks. 'What do you want me to do? Relinquish my British citizenship and become a bloody rubber tapper?'

'I want you to make me feel alive again.'

I stifled a nervous laugh, the statement of desire immediately changing the atmosphere from one of conflict to aching uncertainty. Evangeline's gaze was riveted to mine, her pupils engorged by the stimuli of darkness, challenging me to look away. I felt as gawky as a schoolboy to whom women are a species apart. Self-conscious of everything, from the epiglottal slam as I swallowed, to my bony, oversized wrists dangling at my sides. My breathing was laboured, the thudding valves of my heart loud as galloping hoofs. The chasm between two statues standing apart to the intimacy that Evangeline had insinuated seemed too wide, too perilous, to leap. Though Evangeline had spoken her desire, her body language was that of a fortress dense with invisible thorns. Where was the permissive pout? The seductive quirk of the eyebrow and the coquetry that made the transition to romance a thing of ease?

I had begun to wonder if I had misinterpreted her meaning, when, in a fever of doubt, Evangeline said: 'What is wrong? Am I too old?'

'No, no,' I said, shaking my head.

I closed the distance between us in a stride. Too shy to look Evangeline in the eyes I reached for her hand. I lifted it, cradling it in both of mine. I caressed her palm with my thumb, tracing the fate, life and heart lines, stroking her fingers, each crease of joint, up to the seamstress calluses that sat roughly on her fingertips. I bowed my head, pressed my lips to her palm. Then

I kissed her mouth and I still remember the softness of her lips, and my relief that we had begun.

Like you, Christopher, I am aware that the police are often too quick to send villagers to detention camps without sufficient evidence, and I wanted to investigate the background of Evangeline Lim before deciding whether to report the incident. The findings of the investigation are as follows:

The Lim sisters are orphans. During the Occupation their parents were murdered by the Japanese – their throats slit because of rumours that their father, a furniture-shop owner, belonged to a secret society that raised funds for the Malayan People's Anti-Japanese Army. There is no record of Mr Lim having been a member of any secret society and it is likely the rumours were fabricated by the Kempeitai informers, for reasons unknown.

After the murder of their parents both sisters were forced to work in a comfort house for Japanese soldiers. They were enslaved there for a year or more, but a few months before the end of the war they managed to escape. They fled from Kajang to the jungle, to the Chinese squatter camp of Jing Jang, to live with their maternal grandmother, Old Mother Wu.

When the Japanese surrendered, the Malayan People's Anti-Japanese Army surged out of the jungle to claim responsibility for the liberation of Malaya. Determined to seize power in the aftermath of the Occupation, the MPAJA went to most small towns and kampongs, where they were greeted by the Chinese with enthusiasm and

admiration for enduring the rigours of jungle life and
resisting the Japanese. They tore down Japanese flags and
replaced them with Communist Party hammer-and-sickle
banners. They rounded up villagers of all ethnicities for
public meetings and long self-aggrandizing speeches about
how they had driven out the Japanese. The dominant
theme of the MPAJA meetings was revenge upon those who
collaborated with the Japanese, and until the return of the
British there was no higher authority to stop them. During
a period now known as the Fifteen Days of Terror the
MPAJA held numerous 'People's Trials'. Those found guilty
were killed – mutilated and butchered before the mob.
Many went into hiding.

When the MPAJA arrived at Jing Jang, Evangeline was
heavily pregnant and the squatter settlement was rife with
rumours that the father of the child was a Japanese
general, whose mistress Evangeline had been. Of course,
the unborn baby was undoubtedly of Japanese origin, but
the bastard child of a hundred soldiers of rank and file,
and certainly not the product of a consensual affair.
Unfortunately the Malayan People's Anti-Japanese Army
did not take the oppression of the brothel worker into
account when they rounded up the Japanese 'collaborators'
of Jing Jang . . .

Fragments of the letter echoed in my head as I kissed
Evangeline. I embraced her beneath the watchful gaze
of dead Japanese soldiers. I held her in spite of them.

I remember the electric hum of beating wings and
the trickle of sweat like a blade of grass tickling the

nape of my neck. I remember the taste of metallic salts and the shy probing of tongues. I brushed my lips along Evangeline's cheekbone, kissed the tiny thread of blue that pulsated in her temple. My hands roamed the surface of her, exploring her contours in blind cartography. Oh, she was no voluptuous beauty, my Evangeline, the loose cotton of her dress sheathing a figure that was pitifully lean. I moved my hands from her jutting hips to the knife-handles of her ribs, acquainting myself with every underfed angle. Evangeline's hands hung limply at her sides, taking none of the liberties with my body that I took with hers. When she met my gaze she was solemn, as if she took the business of seduction very seriously indeed. This unnerved me, and in a clumsy banging of foreheads I moved in to kiss her again.

We went from standing to lying down, from clothed to unclothed. I remember the grey squalor of her bra, covering breasts that were barely there, its sad dinginess as I removed it. Her torso was dissected by silvery lines, shimmering in memory of child-bearing; the striations fine as snail trails, as though an army of molluscs had slithered over her in the night. As I knelt above her, Evangeline kissed my throat, sliding her emollient hands over my chest, the sparse hairs and desire-inflamed patch of skin beneath my collar-bone. Not even then, as my breathing quickened, did the dead soldiers leave us in peace. I laid a path of kisses over her flank of stomach, her hardening nipples, and my tenderness was overshadowed by anger. How many

263

hundreds of Japanese had Evangeline lain beneath? How many had unclothed her as I had? Raped and defiled her? Ghosts. They were now ghosts. Surrendered corpses heaped on funeral pyres, dumped in mass graves, left to rot in deepest jungle. But I could see the invisible crescents of bite marks, whorls of savage fingerprints, the weals where they'd prised her open. I wanted to be gentle, the antithesis of everything she had endured, but my hands were everywhere, clutching her hair, her breasts, pushing her thighs apart. Evangeline flinched and I asked if I was hurting her. She did not speak, but fumbled at the buckle at my waist.

. . . and put them on trial. They were paraded about before the settlement, their alleged crimes shouted out. The residents of Jing Jang were appointed jury, and the verdict determined by the baying of the mob. Punishment was exacted on the spot and the methods of execution were numerous. Suspected Japanese informers were tied to trees and had their eyes gouged out in front of screaming wives. Guts were spilt with the jab and twist of a bayonet, and those who were persecuted by the Japanese during the Occupation were encouraged to mutilate the corpses. Many had suffered at the hands of the Japanese and the corpses were unrecognizable by the time they had finished.

In the midst of these bloody reprisals the pregnant Evangeline had her wrists and ankles tied together and was hung over a bamboo pole. The MPAJA guerrillas carried her about the settlement as huntsmen carry wild boar out of the jungle, and her crimes were shouted out as she hung and wept, her bound wrists and ankles bearing the weight of her pregnant body. Though the judgement of the mob was harsh the intervention of her grandmother prevented her murder. After Evangeline had suffered an hour or so of humiliation, and had been dropped several times, she was cut free of her bindings. She went into labour soon after, and gave birth to a stillborn baby boy. The squatters of Jing Jang all agreed that the MJAPA had done Evangeline a service by ridding her body of evil.

The return of the British ended the Fifteen Days of Terror and normal life was resumed. In spite of all she had suffered Evangeline did not leave for Kajang or to start a new life elsewhere, but stayed with her sister and grandmother. Over the years her hard work and resilience has earnt her a quiet respect but even after resettlement Evangeline remains stigmatized and an outsider.

After the night of 12 September we kept the Lim sisters under surveillance and they have no affiliations with the Communists. They are left alone by villagers and bandits alike. When the British returned, Old Mother Wu swore that she would avenge the men who had tortured her granddaughter. Her neighbours laughed at the notion of this old lady exacting revenge on the Communist guerrillas, but were silenced when, days later, Evangeline's torturers' remains were found in Jing Jang. Shortly before she died, Old Mother Wu made another oath, to protect her grand-daughters from beyond the grave. That superstition holds such sway over ruthless bandits is hard to believe, but one must remember that superstition is a powerful force among the Chinese.

I am not going to report last night's incident, but I write in warning to you. I urge you to keep away from the Lim sisters. I am not superstitious, but they reek of bad luck . . .

The *reek of bad luck*. I breathed it in as Evangeline lay beneath me on the rough and splintery floor. I breathed in our ill fate and the condemnation of the stars, infused with the scent of jasmine at her neck. I would die to conjure it up again, that intoxication of the senses. Had I known how short-lived our carnality was to be, how long-enduring the lovelessness to come, I would have savoured every last molecule of her, grown inebriated on her sweet brine. My memory of that night occurs in staccato bursts of heat and eruptions of flesh. The damp hollow at the base of her throat, the shadows cast by her tilted chin. Her teeth glistening, tarnished and chipped. Perspiration stung my eyes and cast her in a diaphanous haze. Though she moved with me, arched her back and dug her callused fingertips in my shoulders, she made no sound other than her breathing. Perhaps I was inattentive. I could not silence my thoughts. The corpses crowded into the watch tower and jeered as my beloved and I writhed together on the floor.

A spike of poison rushed through my veins and I cried out, clasping Evangeline's shoulders in a throb of rage. I was sweat-drenched, light-headed, as if the watch tower had moved to a mountain top, a thinner altitude.

The corpses were gone, though I knew I had not subdued them for long. Blinking, eyes smarting, I gazed upon Evangeline as she lay, mute and trembling, on the rough and splintery floor.

17

I woke in my armchair to a miscellany of aches and pains, my bladder a swollen water balloon on the verge of bursting. The lamp was on and though the mantelpiece clock was tick-tocking loudly, the hands were spinning fast as helicopter blades, and the hour a mystery. I got up out of the chair, stiff neck and aching back reproaching me for not setting up the fold-out bed, and hobbled to the bathroom in my pyjamas (muttering *Come alive, damn you!* to my cramped foot). I was desperate for a wee, so you can imagine my annoyance when I clicked on the bathroom light and saw Lieutenant Spencer hogging the lavatory, his shorts bunched up around his hairy ankles. The creepy-crawlies of the Malayan jungle had invaded the bathroom too, the floor a wriggling blanket of centipedes, millipedes and flightless cicada. The lieutenant was pallid and shaking. He was hunched like a philosopher deep in thought, forearms resting on his thighs.

'Marvellous,' I said. 'Have they been serving that dodgy curry at the officers' mess again? Or have you been over-indulging your vices with Charles? I need to wee. How long are you going to be exactly?'

The lieutenant's backside retorted with a splutter, then an explosion. The pneumatic splatter went on for ages, as if he were purging himself of his entire intestinal tract. Poor quivering Spencer slumped against the cistern. A silent moan escaped his lips. I pitied the poor blighter. You'd think the afterlife would spare the deceased such vulgar earthly sufferings. But as far as I can tell, the indignities of life recur with gleeful vehemence. As usual, the lieutenant had that whopping great hole where his guts ought to have been. How strange that a man so thoroughly eviscerated should suffer from a gastrointestinal complaint. But the spirit world is rife with such illogic.

'Are you all right there, Lieutenant?' I asked, superfluously.

'No, I ain't,' said Spencer. 'I've got the cholera. Charles has it an' all.'

Spencer was as wilted as a dying lily, pores weeping tears of perspiration. *What now?* I wondered. Thanks to my conscientious hand-washing regime and cast-iron immune system I never caught the cholera. But having assisted the Red Cross when the epidemic hit The Village of Everlasting Peace, I knew the standard treatment: antibiotics; rehydration salts diluted in a cup of boiled water. But I had none of these in my bathroom cabinet, and even if I had, Spencer was a ghost and I doubted he would be able to ingest any of it.

'Chin up, old chap,' I said. 'You'll live. At least you did at the time. You recovered very quickly, if memory serves correctly. You have bowels of steel.'

'Oh, fuck off, Goldilocks,' groaned Spencer.

He hunched over his thighs again, shaking like a space shuttle preparing for take-off. By now the pressure of my bladder was unbearable and warning sirens resounded in my head. How on earth was I going to get Spencer off the porcelain shrine when he was convinced he was dying of cholera and determined not to budge? Ordinarily I'd accept this hierarchy of need without demur, but Spencer was already dead, whereas I was alive and needed to pee *in extremis*. That decided me. A millipede crunched under my slipper as I stepped towards him.

'Um, Spencer, would you mind scooting off the lavatory for a moment or two? My bladder has been misbehaving of late, and I'm afraid there might be an accident if I don't empty the damn thing . . '

From the lieutenant's nether regions came the flatus eruption of indifference. I'd half a mind to go over there and relieve myself on top of him! (After all, whatever non-corporeal substance the lieutenant was made of would be no obstruction to the tinkling of my watering spout.) But I couldn't bring myself to do it. Even after the savagery I'd encountered in the Malayan jungle, I was an incurable gentleman. I would not, could not, piss on old Percival when he had Asiatic cholera. I reluctantly sized up the washbasin before making one last appeal.

'C'mon, Spencer old boy, it won't take a minute. Then the lavatory's all yours for the rest of the night.'

It appeared this was one last appeal too far. The policeman's head reared up, pale and serpent-like, his eyes red-rimmed and Satanic.

'Look 'ere, you posh tosspot. If it weren't for me, tigers would 'ave eaten you and orang-utans would 'ave 'ad your eyes out. So bugger off and let a dying man 'ave a shit in peace!'

Sighing, I pulled the light cord, leaving in the dark the man who'd saved my life and the wriggling wall-to-wall infestation of myriapods and annelids. My foot tingling with pins and needles, I tottered back to the living room and set up the cumbersome fold-out bed. I lay down and pulled the blankets up to my chest, determined to ignore the angst of my bladder. But I nodded off to dreams cataclysmic with tidal waves and biblical floods, and in the morning woke to cold damp sheets, my need to urinate taken care of itself.

Falling in love changed the relationship of my senses to the world. Love abstracted me from the here and now – the there and then. I'd eat a three-course meal without tasting a single bite, type out a letter to the District War Committee, as dictated by Charles, and not register a word of what was said. I became accident prone, bashing my shins and promenading into doors, mottling my skin with navy bruises; stars and tweety-birds circled my concussed bonce. Eros heightened my compassion for others, made my heart an organ of unspeakable tenderness, my ribcage useless armour. I saw beauty in the hoary faces of old women, and the destiny of children, busy gambling with bottle tops, to grow up and fall in love and beget children who'd do the same. I sympathized with my enemies and every glower that came my way. Love makes humanitarians of us all. And it also makes us smug fools. And there were none more smug and foolish than I.

After our first night together Evangeline confessed to the missionaries a deepening spiritual crisis and a need of further solitude to study the Bible and seek the Lord. This proved irresistible to Blanche and Marina, and they agreed to babysit Grace every third or fourth night. In exchange for the babysitting, Evangeline offered her services as laundress and charwoman, helping with chores and joining them for daily prayers. The spiritual crisis was fictitious, of course, and spending so much time at the mission was purgatory for my beloved. Long reconciled to a Godless universe, on her nights of freedom Evangeline would climb up to the watch tower and sin herself into damnation with me.

Our secret romance was a gender reversal of the Rapunzel fairy-tale as I waited anxiously in the watch tower for Evangeline. When she was late I was filled with dread. The crack of gunshots, like firecrackers during Chinese New Year, catapulted me to the window, my heart imploding as I scanned the darkness with my binoculars. When Evangeline came through the trapdoor unscathed, I would smother her with kisses, denying her even a moment to catch her breath.

In the heyday of our love Evangeline came to see me half a dozen times. Half a dozen two-hour visits. Twelve hours. A pathetically brief length of time to have spent with the love of my life. And yet the thousands of hours I've devoted to recollecting these visits have made Evangeline an omnipresence in my mind. Every moment is enshrined in memory. Conversations, word for word. Her nakedness as she shed her dress. The knuckles of spine as she curved away from me, the childlike way she hugged her knees to her scrawny chest. The creases in the laughing corners of her eyes. The petals of flesh, moist ridges sheathing my fingers as they delved inside her. The shadow of a fallen eyelash on her cheek, the instant before I brushed it away.

I made a soft nest of blankets on the splintery floor. I brought her tins of peaches in syrup, Turkish Delight and Cadbury's chocolate. I loved watching her eat, licking icing sugar from her fingers and sprinkling morsels for the ants. I made sure our rendezvous were light-hearted. I never asked her about her life before The Village of Everlasting Peace, and never mentioned Detective Pang's letter. I wanted us to be happy together, to create a refuge from the past. Instead I shared my daydreams of our future in London.

'We can go sightseeing in an open-top double-decker

bus. We can go to Trafalgar Square and Piccadilly Circus and the Houses of Parliament. You'll have to wrap up warm, mind, because it is bitterly cold in the wintertime and you won't be used to it. It snows as well. You've never seen snow, have you? We can make a snowman and go tobogganing on Hampstead Heath. I think I'll become a teacher and lecture in Mandarin at UCL. Or an author. I'll publish my memoirs of Malaya and the Emergency and we'll be filthy rich off the royalties.'

'What will I do?'

'Anything you like. You could teach Chinese or Malay. Or you could be a lady of leisure and do nothing all day long but soak in the bathtub and stuff yourself with rum truffles. I will love you just the same.'

'What about Grace?'

'We'll hire someone to look after Grace full-time. I will buy a large house so there's plenty of room. The houses in London are very grand. The shacks in this village are about the size of their back-garden sheds.'

Evangeline squeezed me in anticipation. 'I can't wait to go. I can't wait to leave this country behind.'

'My contract is up in six months. Then we'll elope and scandalize everyone! Knock 'em all for six!'

I joked about us growing arthritic and snowy-haired together, and teased Evangeline, my senior by thirteen years, with predictions of my one day ferrying her about in a wheelchair. It was not out of shame that we kept our relationship a secret. To make it public would have made life harder for both of us. Though she never spoke of it Evangeline was still considered an ex-mistress of the Japanese and to be romantically linked to an Englishman would stigmatize her further (she even forbade me from visiting her hut, lest her neighbours see). And as for me, well, I was happy to do without Charles's ribald jokes.

My love for Evangeline was so consuming that it was appallingly late in the day before I noticed the ascendance of the *vibrio cholerae* in The Village of Everlasting Peace. Such an epidemic had been inevitable of course. The village was a cesspit, the filth of human habitation rising week after week. The drainage system was in the same unfinished condition as the day I arrived (despite our telephone calls to the Public Works Department). Over the months my judgement had lapsed and I'd come to regard this public health risk as acceptable, when it was anything but. There was a Buddhist funeral for a dead child, smoke billowing from the bonfire of her clothes. The queues at the village checkpoint diminished as those who fell ill stayed home. No sooner were the sacked guards replaced than there was another shortfall due to sickness. Though I'd been scheduled to leave the watch tower that week, Sergeant Abdullah insisted he couldn't let me go.

The day the epidemic broke I had breakfast alone on the veranda. *That lazybones Charles!* I thought. But I didn't go and wake him. It made a nice change to eat my scrambled eggs and ketchup without Charles wincing across the table at me as if I were somehow responsible for his fiercely pounding skull. I hummed along to an old Glenn Miller ballad on the radio as our treacherous cook appeared with a fresh pot of Earl Grey.

'Winston,' I said, 'where is Mr Dulwich this morning? Is he still in bed?'

'Eh?' The secret agent of the insurgency lifted his eyebrows, under orders to feign stupidity at all times.

'*Tuan* Dulwich,' I said. 'Where is he?'

Winston nodded to Charles's bedroom window and clattered up the plates.

In the office the remnants of an orgy cluttered the table; bottles drained of alcoholic contents, booze-soaked cigarette papers and various items of dope-smoking paraphernalia (which I naively mistook for sophisticated tobacco pipes). Though the quantity of empty bottles would seem excessive to a social tippler, for a piss-artist of Charles's calibre it was all in a night's wassailing. Charles was never too hungover to make an appearance at breakfast. Even when he was sulphur yellow and unable to lift his aching head. *Has the old devil finally drunk himself to death?* I mused. I knocked on his bedroom door. *Charles? Charles?* There was no reply, so I tentatively pushed open the door and went inside.

The fumes hit me first. What an eye-watering stink! The odour of mucking-out time at the stables. The room was dark and Charles and Lieutenant Spencer lay inches apart on the bed, breathing open-mouthed in the swampy heat. They wore identical string vests and a cotton sheet was draped over their legs; hobbity feet poked out at the bottom, hairs sprouting from the horny toes. Though it was dim, I could see both men were cast in a pallor far removed from the usual whisky burn of their cheeks. Beside the bed stood a metal bucket, from which the death stench emanated.

'Charles . . . Charles, are you all right?'

Charles slept on, eerily peaceful. Spencer whimpered, like a dog having a bad dream.

'Charles!'

I tugged his swollen big toe (the ingrown toenail was in urgent need of chiropody).

Charles sighed and, without bothering to open his eyes, said crossly: 'Christopher! Will you stop ringing that blasted bell! Can't you see I'm not well?'

Lieutenant Spencer woke at the sound of his master's voice. He glared at me out of the angry cracks of his eyes.

'That Goldilocks . . . ? Gerrout! This room's private!'

Both men lapsed back into a stupor. Tiny droplets beaded their pallor and they were both fever-bright, as if the cholera bacterium produced an evil luminosity, shining within. Now I come to think of it, the swiftness with which Charles and Spencer succumbed to the Asiatic cholera is rather suspect (especially considering Charles's strict abstinence from fresh fruit, liquids less than 7 per cent alcohol and any physical contact with the villagers whatsoever). Now Winston Lau's true identity is known, I am certain of foul play.

I dialled the Jalang town surgery on the office

telephone and requested Dr Fothergill. I said it was a matter of urgency. The receptionist informed me that the doctor had already packed his medical case and left for the village. She told me that the Red Cross were also to be expected before noon.

Operation Cholera under way, a flock of pretty young Red Cross nurses came in clean white pinafores, Red Cross hats pinned atop their neatly coiffed hair. My Antipodean lovelies Madeleine and Josie came too, but I was assigned to do the rounds with two English novices, Enid and Perdita, the former a staid brunette, and the latter a runaway debutante who'd come to Malaya intent on scandalizing her well-to-do family (though her torrid, scatological new occupation had so far scandalized only herself). There was no infirmary in the village and no beds left at the Jalang town hospital, so the sick were quarantined in their huts. Roughly one in three households were affected, the invalids to be found lying listless on bamboo mats. Though from my limited knowledge of pathogens I knew that cholera was a water-borne disease, at times I was convinced I could detect the illness, as if the sick breathed out a miasma of bacteria, which gathered in oppressive clouds and wafted from hut to hut.

Our Foreign Devil medical team had a mixed reception as we toured the village. Some households welcomed us with offers of rice and freshly brewed tea. Others were suspicious we were government spies. In every hut the nurses would solemnly recite the five commandments for the treatment and containment of the cholera, which I translated into Cantonese with an equal degree of solemnity: *Boil water before drinking. Keep the sick indoors. Administer antibiotic pills and rehydration salts to the sick. Do not throw the waste of the sick in the village drains or latrines. Wash hands after touching the sick or the waste of the sick.*

I was impressed by the Chinese peasants' stoic attitude towards the illness. Mothers cared calmly for their poorly children (with none of the melodrama and gin-quaffing despair characteristic of the Milnar family matriarch), and invalids stayed in their sickbeds with forbearance and a minimum of fuss. The immigrant Chinese are a hardy and resilient breed. After leaving the shores of China to seek their fortune in Malaya, they'd survived exploitation by the white colonialists, persecution by the Japanese, the bloody reprisals of the MPAJA, and then internment in resettlement camps by the British. The cholera was just another hardship in the long line of hardships that comprised their collective history. The village was not without its martyrs and exhibitionists, though: those who howled for the mercy of the Lord Buddha and squatted to void their bowels, indifferent to the appalled audience. Poor Enid and Perdita had a rude awakening to the grotesqueries of human suffering, as the sick haemorrhaged waste from every orifice. But the two beginner nurses became tougher and more efficient by the hour, and by the end of the epidemic were as shock-proof and professional as veterans.

Dr Fothergill was called to attend to the moribund. The doctor always arrived out of breath and ruddy-cheeked, equipped with his medical case and dressed in pinstriped trousers and waistcoat over his shirt (a bold fashion statement in the tropics). Without a sideways glance, he would march to the back of the hut and press his stethoscope to the patient's weakly beating heart. The doctor would listen intently for thirty seconds, then, adjusting his toupee (which seemed to make his scalp intolerably itchy in the heat), he'd announce his findings: *Christopher, tell the mother her child will improve in a day or two . . . Nurse, soak a flannel in water and place it in this man's mouth . . . chop chop!* And on one unhappy occasion, flipping open his silver pocket watch to check the time: *I pronounce this man dead at three twenty-three.* Hundreds of villagers were taken ill, but only a few died. Though every death is a tragedy, considering how quickly the disease engulfed the village, I think we got off lightly.

Of everyone in The Village of Everlasting Peace, the missionaries seemed to have the most rewarding time of it during the cholera epidemic. They cancelled their Bible lessons, put on their best flowery dresses and floppy sun bonnets and went canvassing for the Christian faith among the sick. (*In their darkest hour people need the Lord!* said Blanche.) They went door to door like travelling salesmen, presenting themselves with compassionate smiles and offers of prayer. The Christians were delighted to see them, of course, but the non-Christian households turned them away.

Refusing to accept defeat, the missionaries returned to homes that had rejected them with a basket of fruit scones (that Marina had baked at great expense, with ingredients purchased from the Kuala Lumpur Cold Storage). The heathen villagers were curious about the scones and Blanche and Marina were able to bribe their way past many Buddhist altars. Once they'd gained entry Marina would kneel before the defenceless sick, holding open a biblical picture book and turning the pages as Blanche narrated tales of Jesus in Cantonese. The pair could go on for an hour or more, and if the invalids became delirious Blanche would round up an urchin choir to stand outside and sing rousing hymns. The children had memorized the hymns syllable by syllable, and as they sang the lyrics lapsed into Chinese tones – a strange new language, beautiful to my ears (but probably ill appreciated by those doubled over with stomach cramps).

On the fourth morning of the epidemic the anti-Christians took their revenge. I was drinking a cup of tea on the veranda when I saw the sight that haunts me to this day. The morning sky was grey and rain was pattering softly. On the jungly hills shreds of mist floated motionless, wisps of cloud snagged upon the tallest treetops. It was a lovely tranquil scene, not even spoilt by Charles, snoring like a tone-deaf trombonist in his bed. I was using these stolen moments to think of Evangeline, when I saw an apparition on the muddy village trail: a lady in white, baptized by raindrops, her dress billowing behind her as she ran, her arms lifting an unidentifiable object above her head. As the lady streaked by the bungalow I saw it was a very distressed Marina Tolbin. I stood and called to her. *Miss Tolbin! Miss Tolbin!* The missionary didn't hear me. Had she gone mad? Where was she running to, pell-mell in her nightdress? What was the dark substance dripping down her arms? What was she holding above her head like some sacrificial offering for the pagan gods? As she veered off the trail I realized that it was the severed head of Humphrey the Saint Bernard.

Fearing Marina had lost her mind, I rushed to the Jesus cottage. Blanche was kneeling in the garden, where Humphrey's headless cadaver lay in a pool of blood.

'I forgive them for what they have done,' she said, sad but resolute. 'I forgive them and love them even as they cast stones at us. I will continue to do my duty and save their damned souls from the conflagration of Hell.'

Poor old Humphrey. Never again would he lie, panting, in the shade of the papaya tree or . . . Come to think of it, that was the only thing I ever saw old Humphrey do. I helped Blanche indoors and brewed her a pot of tea. Then I went to notify the police. An hour later Marina returned with Humphrey's head. The missionaries weren't so sentimental that they wanted to give Humphrey a Christian burial. When some villagers knocked at the door and timidly asked permission to cook Humphrey's remains (offering to bring portions of the cooked meat for the bereaved), they let them (though they declined to partake in the feast). After

Humphrey's corpse was carted away in a wheelbarrow, Blanche and Marina shut themselves away for the rest of the day, the evangelical zeal knocked out of them.

The demise of Humphrey disturbed me. How awful to think the perpetrators were still at large in the village. Assisting the Red Cross on their rounds, however, I was cheered to see, recovered and pottering about, villagers who had been feverish and shaking days before. Even Charles was well enough to resume his rattan throne and boss the sarong-wearing servant boy, who pouted as he served his master glasses of medicinal gin.

That evening I paced the watch tower restlessly, as if allergic to keeping still. I'd seen Evangeline in the back of the Red Cross van that afternoon as Nurse Perdita and I were taking an inventory of stock. The runaway debutante was counting vials in the medical refrigerator when Evangeline climbed into the van to fetch some antibiotics for the Aussie nurses. As Evangeline took a bottle of pills, she whispered in Cantonese that the missionaries had agreed to take Grace for the night. Then she was gone, out into the midday sunshine. Removing her head from the refrigerator, Perdita remarked that I was looking frightfully pleased with myself. Then she smiled and batted her lashes (for the ex-society girl had her singleton eye on me). I couldn't wait for the evening. After days of touring the stifling huts and breathing sickness into my lungs, I was drained, conscious of my own mortality. What could be more rejuvenating than to take my beloved into my arms and breathe the fragrance of her skin? To lose myself in her embrace and dissolve the boundaries between us. As I paced the watch tower, impatient for her, I saw a movement from the corner of my eye. I lifted the binoculars and focused the lenses on the boundary fence. A bandit was crawling into the village. *What fool does he take me for?* I wondered. (Of course, Comrade Kok Sang of the 10th Independent Regiment was right to take me for a fool; my mind had hardly been on the job.) The man was struggling, his jacket snagged on the barbed wire. I snatched the rifle and calmly aimed it at the bandit's foot. Though I'd had some shooting practice with the home guard, I'd little confidence in my marksmanship. I'd expected to miss. I'd expected merely to make a loud bang and frighten him away. So I was surprised to squeeze the trigger and, along with the gunpowder blast, hear a human cry of pain. The muscles of my face hardened as I lowered the gun. *So that's what it feels like to shoot a person*, I thought. I did not feel guilty or upset. Only the desire to shoot again. The injured bandit was now crawling backwards, out of the village. I couldn't see where the bullet had gone in. I rang the alarm bell to alert the guards and aimed my rifle again. Loud footfalls came hurrying up the rungs of the ladder. Evangeline threw open the trap-door in a breathless panic.

'Don't!' she cried.

'It's all right,' I said, 'I've caught a bandit.'

Evangeline wrested the gun from me and rushed to the window. An empty jacket hung from the fence like a drab abandoned chrysalis. The bandit was nowhere to be seen. A commotion of voices could be heard, coming from somewhere near by. The guards were shouting in Malay.

'Oh God,' I said to Evangeline, 'we've got to get you home. This place will be crawling with guards in a minute.'

Evangeline was unconcerned by the guards. She turned to me, eyes blazing.

'What have you done?' she screamed. 'What have you done?'

18

Adam and Julia lost interest in the Friday-night film and drowsed on the sofa, Julia worn out from a hard day's truanting and Adam from compulsive page-turning and bibliophile flights of the mind. Julia hugged a cushion, legs curled under, bottom resting on her heels. Adam dozed with his head thrown back, throat exposed, as if bared to a knife. There was an enchanted quality to their slumber, as if they'd taken a bite of the same poison apple, or the sandman had sprinkled them with magic dust.

The wind gusted by the fourteenth floor, swift as a greyhound racing round a track. The TV signals blustered away, the picture a cryptic fuzz, every other word a mystifying buzz. My grandchildren had been watching a Hollywood action movie starring some indestructible hero with an East European accent. A hail of bullets perforated the static, whizzing and pinging and defying the laws of physics. Special effect. Explosion. Special effect. Explosion, explosion, explosion. None of the pyrotechnics disguised that the film was a very dreary affair.

I shuffled over to the TV and clicked off the volume. Then I sat and watched the children as they slept. Adam has the beginnings of a moustache, faint as caterpillar fur on his upper lip. I'd teach him how to shave, but it's optimistic to expect a boy who's worn the same holey jumper for six weeks running to pick up a razor. *Adam, you tramp! You stink!* complains Julia. *Have a bath!* Advice she ought to follow herself. The odours of the estate cling to my granddaughter. Fags, epoxy resin and fish-and-chip wrappers. Both children are a source of olfactory offence. They make my flat smell like a homeless shelter.

A helicopter plummeted from the sky, propellers thrashing wildly as it spiralled across the TV screen. A stuntman dived from the hatch, machine guns blazing in freefall. The rip-roaring action sequence shuddered on the fluorescent screen, the living room strobe-lit, the aerial a lightning rod in an electrical storm. And as I watched the film, with no idea who were the goodies or who were the baddies, my estranged daughter appeared.

Nothing could have prepared me for it. My heart arrested for a count of three, and my breath stalled in my throat.

'Frances,' I wheezed.

'Father,' she said coolly.

She wore her school uniform, her skin pearly and phosphorescent, as if she too were a discharge of speeding cathode rays. Strands of her dark pageboy hair hung in her eyes and the smattering of freckles on her nose. How old was she? Thirteen? Fourteen? The same age as her acne-blighted agoraphobic son? I knew from the supercilious look on her face that the Cold War had begun. The years she was a distant stranger under my roof.

Frances interfered with the TV signals, the picture deteriorating into a meteor shower on the moon. Twenty-five years had gone by since I'd last seen her. She was a beautiful child. A sanctimonious child, disdainful of the compromises I'd made to give her a comfortable childhood. Able to live by her convictions because her sheltered life threw up no challenges to them. She turned to watch the sleeping siblings and I saw the profile of her snub nose.

'My children do not look well.'

I was startled to hear her call Adam and Julia her children. How could this virgin child claim that those two strapping adolescents were the product of her taut, never-lived-in womb? Adam and Julia were her siblings, her classmates, her peers. Never her children. My daughter fixed me with her critical gaze, and I knew no punches were to be pulled.

'You have not been feeding them,' she accused.

How outrageous! Child or not, one could not deny her maternal ferocity.

'Of course I feed them. What do you take me for?

Julia always has her porridge in the morning, and I cook them both supper in the evening. I try my best, but it is difficult to raise children at my age. Adam won't go to school and Julia comes home when she pleases. Believe me, I'd put them over my knee and give them a good spanking if I could . . . But my arthritis is bad this winter and my wrist seizes up.'

Adam stirred. He opened his eyes and looked at me. I half-expected him to see his mother and make some loud exclamation of surprise. But he didn't. This must have made our quarrel appear somewhat one-sided.

'Look what you've done! You woke my son,' said Frances. 'Why does he look so pale and sickly? Why are his eyes so haunted and bruised?'

Her hands were on her hips; on her face, a look of anger. For a child of four foot ten and a hundred and one pounds she was very intimidating. Not even the demure lace frills of her ankle socks diminished the effects of her sabre-rattling.

'Adam refuses to go outdoors,' I said. 'He has decided to renounce the world and live an ascetic life of the mind. I have reported him to social services but they say there's nothing they can do.'

Now Julia woke, her eyes lazy and slitted like a cat in the sun. Brother and sister slouched as they watched me, loose-limbed as two abandoned marionettes.

'You were a terrible father,' said Frances, 'and now you are a terrible grandfather.'

'Now, hold on a minute . . .'

'This flat disgusts me. There is damp everywhere and no food in the cupboards.'

'Frances . . .'

Her young eyes glittered with contempt. 'You took my mother away from me.'

'Frances,' I pleaded, 'you judge me too harshly. I had to make some very difficult choices. I agonized . . .'

'Why are you crying, you selfish man? Your tears won't bring my mother back.'

I lost my temper. There is only so much blame I am prepared to take. 'Get out, get out!' I shouted. 'You ignorant child. Go away!'

The look on her face was murderous, just like the time I told her she was grounded until the O levels were over.

'Go away? And leave my children in the care of a mad old man! You are unfit to serve as their guardian.'

'Mad, am I? Who is the pot to call the kettle black? If you're so concerned about the welfare of your children why did you kill yourself? That was jolly selfish of you, wasn't it? If they're miserable and motherless and stuck with me in this damp council flat, then it's your fault. They had nowhere else to go.'

I'd hoped to draw Frances's attention to her hypocrisy, but she wasn't listening. Her twelve-year-old daughter had risen from the sofa and had lifted a porcelain Buddha from the mantelpiece – one of my few souvenirs from Malaysia.

'Shut up!' she shrieked. And smashed the ornament against the gas fire.

Julia fled the crime scene, the holy Siddhārtha in smithereens. Adam winced from the safety of the sofa.

Frances shook her head, her mouth a thin disapproving line. 'Look what you've done,' she said.

And satisfied with the seeds of malice sown, my estranged daughter vanished, leaving me with Adam, who stared into the fuzzy vortex of the television screen as if therein lay the solution to our broken home.

'What have you done?' Evangeline screamed.

What had I done?

She grabbed the torch and jumped down the trapdoor. What had I done?

'Evangeline,' I said, 'wait!'

Her gaze was black as thunder, irritated and impatient.

'What's going on? Do you know that bandit?'

'Yes. I have to go after him and see if he is OK. He won't make it back to the camp with a bullet in his side. He will die.'

I stared at Evangeline, not caring a damn whether the bandit died. The only thing that mattered to me were the fractures that had appeared in the truth. She had tricked me into thinking she was someone she wasn't.

'You're a Communist.'

'No. You must trust me.'

'Bloody hell! How can I trust you? You have been coming here to distract me, haven't you? So guerrillas can sneak in and out of the village. You've been lying to me.'

The truth occurred to me as I spoke it. I was furious enough to hit her. I'd have given anything to have her come back to me, to hear her vehement denial and whispered love. But Evangeline's priorities lay elsewhere. She started down the ladder.

'Wait! The guards are by the fence. They will shoot you!'

There was a clatter as she slipped down a few rungs in her haste. A gang of guards stood where the bandit had been, rifles aimed at the scrubland, bickering like old women about whether to go and hunt for him. I bounded down the ladder after Evangeline, knowing that if they saw her alone they would shoot. When I reached the ground Evangeline was racing back into the village. I chased her along the main trail to a section of fence dangerously close to the police station. Evangeline was squeezing through a hole with the skill of a contortionist when I caught her up. I expected her to fly off again once she was on the other side, but she turned and lifted the chicken-wire mesh so I could follow. Then we ran together, across the no man's land and into the jungle.

Before that night my acquaintance with the jungle was limited to my Sunday hiking expeditions with Kip Phillips, the rubber-plantation manager. Kip was a splendid host to the rainforest, and we hiked deep in the jungle, where the canopy was so dense it was like rambling through a twilight realm. As he guided me through the labyrinth of leaves, Kip would show me a tiny exquisite flower hidden amid the mass of vegetation and teach me its Latin name, or he'd squat by a cluster of fungi and with a chuckle indicate a jungle tortoise's teeth marks in a mushroom. Kip was forever handing me strips of bark and sticky buds that gave off strange medicinal aromas when rubbed between my fingertips. He'd list the ailments they treated and describe the techniques of preparation. But mostly we hiked in silence, the forest floor breathing its muggy halitosis of rotting flora and fauna, clinging to Kip and me till we were damp-skinned as amphibians. Some of the trees were more than a century old, and as my gaze travelled up the colossal trunks I'd be dizzied and awed.

Though peaceful and companionable, our hikes were never completely free of anxiety. Wary of Communist ambushes, Kip insisted on rigging me out in one of his home-made bullet-proof vests and he was never without a rifle, which he aimed at the slightest trembling of foliage, finger hooking the trigger and a fierce look in his eyes. One afternoon a pygmy squirrel made the mistake of cavorting too noisily in some bushes. Before I'd even registered the disturbance, Kip had cocked his rifle and sent a bullet through its tiny rodent heart.

'Bloody Reds,' hissed Kip, quaking with fury and remorse. 'They've turned this jungle into a bloody war zone.'

The jungle at night was a different world: dark and subterranean, as if we'd descended into the bowels of the earth, the sweltering heat rising from rivers of molten lava. Evangeline ran ahead along the claustro-phobic trail, the stiff branches she charged through whipping my face and arms. Through the shrinking tunnel of leaves I stumbled after her and the flashlight, struggling to keep up. Parasitic vines slithered from the treetops, hairy tendrils flaying my shoulders and neck. Shallow roots and buttresses tripped my every other step.

'Evangeline!' I shouted. 'Slow down.'

Her torch hung by her side, illuminating the ground as she waited. From the waist up she was shrouded in darkness. As soon as I caught up she was off again.

'Evangeline, stop!' I panted. 'What the hell has been going on over the past few weeks? Why've you been coming to the watch tower? I want to know the truth.'

'We can talk later. We have to keep going. I have to make sure he made it back to the camp.'

'Camp? Evangeline! Are you taking me to a Communist camp? Are you out of your mind? I'll be killed!'

Evangeline stopped and turned. She squeezed my shoulder with her small callused hand.

'Please, Christopher,' she said. 'I will not let anything happen to you. I have to know how badly he is hurt. Come on . . .'

For another twenty minutes or so we continued to beat a path through the jungle. Darkness devoured the way we had come, the gallery of foliage shifting to conceal the trail. But even if it had been daylight I doubt I would have known the way back to civilization. The wild bandit chase disorientated me, as if I'd been blind-folded and spun around for a game of blind-man's buff. The maze of leaves narrowed, became more con-voluted, and eventually we came up against a wall of jungle so dense we could only progress an inch at a time, battling against the sharp-clawed undergrowth. The rot of organic matter intensified in the knot of jungle, as if it concealed some carnivorous rafflesia with bloody meat in its jaws. Smothered by leaves, the torch-light was no brighter than the belly of a firefly.

'Are we lost?' I asked Evangeline.

'No, keep going,' she said. 'It will open up again soon.'

She was right. After five more minutes of under-growth thick enough to asphyxiate a man, it came to an end. We tumbled into a clearing, hands and faces marked by stigmata from the foliage; the cuts of thorns and grass-blade nicks. For a while we could do little more than tremble and take insatiable breaths of air, gulping it down regardless of the poisonous stench.

A shimmer of moonlight came into the clearing. I looked up and saw an aperture in the rainforest roof, framed by a silhouette of leaves. As the pounding of my heart subsided, the high-decibel clamour of invisible insects teemed in my ears. There must have been a million of the critters, oscillating their creepy-crawly parts so the stridulations merged into that of one solitary beast. There came a blood-curdling monkey screech and the arboreal croak of tree frogs. When Evangeline skimmed the flashlight along the periphery of the clearing, spiders and scorpions scuttled back into hidy-holes to watch us out of crepuscular eyes. The torch beam darted nervously, as if Evangeline feared that if it were to settle for more than a second it would set the leaves ablaze.

'Looks like he isn't here,' I said.

'If he was badly injured he would have collapsed on the trail,' Evangeline conjectured. 'We have not seen him, so he must be OK.'

'We can go back, then.'

'No.'

'What?'

Evangeline turned her back on me. She flicked the torchlight on and off, reminding me of how the village police flashed their torches at a bush of scintillating fireflies, mimicking their mating call (they claimed this made the flies sexually frustrated).

'What's going on?'

Evangeline ignored me. I strode over to her and put my hands on her shoulders, confident my touch would snap her out of her strangeness.

'Don't touch me.' She pulled her shoulders free and moved away.

'Evangeline, what the hell is going on? You must tell me, this minute!'

The torch clicked off, plunging us into blackness. I saw the dark shape of her, pacing through the kettle-steamy heat, the shadows of the clearing parting for her, as if to avoid contamination. I reached out, raking the empty air, then grazing the thin cotton of her dress.

'I said, *don't touch me.*'

I lowered my hand. Cantonese? Why was she speaking in Cantonese? Our language was English. Moths stirred in the recesses of my stomach. Why was she acting like this?

'What's come over you? Why are you being so cruel?'

'Do you find me cruel?' Cantonese again. 'How come you feel the little cruelties so much more keenly, Christopher? What about the cruelties that you help inflict? What about imprisoning people in a concentration camp? Surely that is worse.'

I was furious. What had politics to do with us?

'This again! I thought we'd taken care of this! You know I am just doing my job.'

'And does doing your job mean you no longer have a mind of your own? If you had any conscience you would have left months ago. Instead you look about the village and pat yourself on the back for a job well done.'

'This is stupid, Evangeline. It's ridiculous to blame me. Everything – the Emergency, Resettlement, the New Villages – is beyond my control. I am not the British Administration. I am just one man. I am here to do what I can, day in, day out, to protect the villagers from the Communists and make life better for them.'

'Don't you ever question what you do, day in, day out? Villagers are dying because of how lousy the conditions are, because of what the British Administration has done. Because of what you – glorified prison warden – help to do.'

I took a deep frustrated breath. 'We are working hard to return Malaya to its people,' I said, 'to make her independent. This is the reason I came here. It's wrong to make a scapegoat of me.'

'If you don't see the harm of your actions, then you are blind.'

'Blind? Don't talk to me about blindness, Evangeline. The Communists have brought nothing but suffering and misery to the people. More so than the British.'

'I am not a Communist.'

'No,' I said, 'you are just the Communists' whore.'

This viciousness brought a stab of sweetness. We circled each other like warring tigers, our faces masks of darkness, from which the voices of strangers emerged.

Evangeline laughed. 'That's more like it, Christopher. Now you're being honest! Why are the men never whores? What name is there for a man who lies to a woman about taking her back to his country to get what he wants? Lies, lies, lies . . . You make me sick.'

'I never lied. I meant every word.'

'And I am not a whore.'

'Then, I don't understand. If you hate me so much, and think me a prison warden, then why did you come to the watchtower? For yourself? For the Communists? How do you know that bandit? Why are you talking in Chinese? For whose benefit? Is he near by?'

Silence.

'Come on, Evangeline. We are above this, you and I. Turn on the torch and let me see your face. I don't believe you hate me. I don't believe this is you.'

Silence.

'Do you love me?'

Silence.

'Come on, Evangeline . . . turn on the torch and let's go back.'

There was a faint breeze, the stirring of conscience. A sharp intake of breath, and like the shattering apart of glass the tension broke. Evangeline was crying. A victory that brought me no joy. She hid her face in her hands and shook. *Now we can go back*, I thought grimly, and moved to steady her in my embrace. But before I reached her there was crashing in the undergrowth. And before I could turn to see what was going on, one side of my body was overwhelmed by pain and I was screaming on the ground. Never in my life had I known such agony. The whole of my consciousness was subjugated to it, and I was only dimly aware of myself writhing and screaming, and of the boot viciously kicking my back. After a while the kicking went away and I lay in the clearing, stunned and breathing stunted breaths. I called for Evangeline, but she was gone. The moon had gone too and the clearing was so dark I couldn't tell whether my eyes were open or closed.

I lost consciousness and, when I came to, the clearing was suffused with the grey light of dawn. Pain shrieked below my ribs. I gritted my teeth and lifted my head a fraction of an inch, almost expecting to see a crimson mist above my torso; a fine nimbus of blood. My shirt was soaked red and cleaved to my skin, resisting slightly as I pulled it up. The wound was three or four inches long and scalpel-thin. What had been lacerated? Kidney? Liver? Spleen? There were some dark leaves stuck to the skin surrounding the wound . . . Oh, no, not leaves, but leeches! – pulsating as they drank from the gash. Nauseated, I tore the blood-glutted leeches off me, ripping them to bits where the suckers remained stubbornly welded to my flesh. I wiped the slime and leech-muck off my fingers and on to the soil. Then I lay very still, so as not to aggravate the pain. It was very cold and damp and I realized it was raining, the canopy drumming as raindrops slid from one leafy precipice to the next. Through the hole in the rainforest roof, drops like shards of glass fell and stung my eyes.

The pain came and went in powerful tides. When it was at its worst it induced in me a dazzling synaesthesia, a magnesium flare in my mind. And in the split second that white light drenched my consciousness came numbness and ephemeral reprieve. Then the pain would surge again from nothing, igniting nerve endings one by one.

As I lay there in the spitting rain, I fell prey to hallucinations. I imagined the nearby bushes were shaking as Evangeline and my assailant hid, gloating and spying on me. I heard their laughter in the percussion of the rain and glared at the offending bushes, jaw clenched in anger and humiliation. Minutes later I imagined that Evangeline crept into the clearing to kneel beside me. She took my hand and pressed it to her soft cheek, weeping for forgiveness. The

Communists had taken Grace hostage, she said, and had forced her to betray me. But now she was back and would never leave me again. She wept and covered my face with kisses moist with tears and begged and begged me to forgive her. And, weeping too, I forgave. I forgave and forgave and forgave until my heart bled with joy. Then my beloved was gone, and my joy turned to bitter disappointment because Charles Dulwich had replaced her, puffing on a cigar and lording it over the clearing in his rattan chair. Charles gave me a stern talking to. Serves you right for being such a dupe! What did you expect, taking up with a low-breed Communist bitch? Haven't you learnt by now that humans are born into this world to cheat and lie and damage one another? It was the first and last time in my life that Charles's pessimism has ever consoled me.

After an hour the rain stopped and sunshine sifted through the mosaic of branches and leaves. The miracle of the sun on my skin lent me the strength to prop myself up on my elbows – a manoeuvre that was agony, but rewarded me with the feeling that I was alive. Had the rain continued to batter me I'm sure I'd have lost my will to live and quickly died. I looked around the clearing, defeated. To claw my way out of that fortress of leaves, as I had clawed my way in, was impossible. I couldn't even stand. As the sun heated the jungle, steam rose from the soil and the rotting odour strengthened. Here and there the canopy dripped, and to my left a trickle of rainwater slid down a liana vine. Slowly, agonizingly, dying of thirst, I dragged my carcass towards the vine. But when I was halfway there the trickle dried up and I collapsed, flat on my back once more, exhausted by mere inches of progress.

The canopy twittered with birdsong and crashed as some tree-bound creature hurtled from bough to bough. How I envied the wildlife up there in the parapet of leaves. The canopy was the zenith of the rain-forest, a leafy amphitheatre of exotic feathers and finery. As I lay amid the millipedes and grubs I was keenly aware that I'd sunk to the very depths of the jungle hierarchy; the morass of decomposition, the strata of decay. When it comes to death, nature is ever fair and egalitarian, and if I were to die in that clearing, earthworms and saprophytic fungi would reduce me to the same nutrient-rich soil that every dead animal becomes. The only possible deviation to this fate would be if I were to be swallowed by a giant python. Then my masticated remains would reside briefly in its carnivorous intestines, before being shat out on to the forest floor.

My heart shrivelled up in hopelessness. I thought of the jungle-craft that Kip Phillips had taught me on our Sunday-afternoon hikes; how to make a rodent snare; how to build a fish trap out of twigs; how to identify edible fungi and so on. I remembered Kip telling me, as we huffed and puffed up a steep trail, that if one is lost in the rainforest the wisest thing to do is to bang a stick on a tree buttress, as a buttress can amplify a bang so it travels for a distance of three miles. Kip had demon-strated with his rambling stick, striking the buttress of an ancient tree as though it were a gong. The effect was loud as gun blasts.

'If you are lucky,' said Kip, 'a search party will take a compass bearing of the bang and come and rescue you. But be careful!' he warned, wagging his finger. 'Buttress-whacking is a means of communication for the Reds. You might accidentally bang out a secret Communist code!'

The most formidable buttress in the clearing lay just beyond a fly-buzzing thicket. The buttress was four feet in height; a sinuous wing of wood, strange and extra-terrestrial. I was weak and enervated and every movement brought great pain. But if anything could amplify a bang to within range of a search party, that buttress was it.

I dragged myself on my back, inch by painstaking inch, the angry mouth of my wound screaming in protest. As the heat of the day mounted, more and more flies came out of hiding to buzz under a nearby thicket. The thicket was en route to the buttress and, as I heaved myself along, a few flies drifted over to me, translucent wings whirring. I furiously batted them away, repulsed by the thought of them laying eggs on me and fly larvae burrowing into my wound. Halfway to the buttress, searing pain forced me to stop beside the fly-besieged shrubs. Gritting my teeth, I willed the pain to subside so I could move on. It was then that I noticed the leather flask, half buried in the mulch under the thicket. The Hallelujah refrain from Handel's *Messiah* chorusing from above, I grabbed the flask, unscrewed the lid and tipped the contents down my parched throat . . . only to splutter and cough and spit it all out again. Whisky! – as filthy and acrid as petrol. I tossed the flask aside and lay on my back again, head turned sideways to see what else was hiding under the thicket. And as I stared and stared through the branches and maelstrom of flies, the nest of shadow stirred and became a human face.

I turned away and gazed up into the lofty marquee of leaves. Then I turned back, to check what I'd seen was real and not a hallucination. The dead man was covered in flies. They crawled out of his parted lips and roamed the contours of his face and glassy eyes. The flies droned and droned, and I stared and stared, my breathing ragged. I felt the kiss of flies on my cheeks, but did not brush them away. The putrescence that had lurked in my nostrils since entering the clearing the night before suddenly had a new significance. I dry heaved, once, twice, but my empty stomach had nothing to offer the soil. The man had not been dead long – his skin undecayed, waxy and pale. The corpse was too thin to be Timmy Lo, and too recent a kill. The worms had made a banquet of Timmy weeks and weeks ago.

Then recognition came. Triggered by the sharpness of his cheekbones and vulpine tapering of his face. Slowly, the death mask began to correspond with my memory of the last time I'd seen the face alive. The corpse stared at me with dead eyes.

'Well, Detective,' I murmured, 'you were wrong about Evangeline not being a Communist. You were about as wrong as you can get. Why ever did you write that letter?'

Then it occurred to me Detective Pang hadn't been wrong. He hadn't written the letter. He wasn't the only person in The Village of Everlasting Peace literate in English. I knew of at least one other person – skilled enough to teach the language to high-school students, no less. The intention of the letter, according to its author, was to warn me away from Evangeline. Yet by convincing me of her non-involvement with the Communists and making me sympathetic to her plight, it had succeeded in doing the opposite. If the true aim of the letter had been to pave the way for love and deception, then it had accomplished this very well.

I ask Detective Pang about the letter when he comes to my flat. The detective pretends not to hear, preferring to scatter sunflower-seed husks over the carpet, or retune the dial of the kitchen radio to shrieking para-normal frequencies. I suspect he is embarrassed that Evangeline discovered, then assumed, his true identity. Poor old Detective Pang. So good at his job until they found him out. Did they march him into the jungle at gunpoint? Or was he lured to the imperialist slaying ground, as I had been, by some treacherous village floozy? Detective Pang is very reticent on the subject of his death, so I doubt I'll ever know.

After travelling with me from Kuala Lumpur to London in 1980, Evangeline's letter now lives in a shoe-box in my hallway cupboard. The document is an antique now; fallen to pieces, burnt by air to the colour of straw. Once upon a time reading the letter upset me and I'd lie awake for hours afterwards, full of scalding emotion and eruptions of bile. But not any more. Before I left The Village of Everlasting Peace in 1953, I investigated Evangeline's background, consulting official documents and villagers who had known her. The letter had given a factual account of the events of Evangeline's life during and shortly after the war. Her epistolary revelations were true, the only falsehood the *nom de plume*.

Clever Evangeline. Not a week goes by when I don't take that letter from the shoebox and turn the pieces over in my hands. By now I know the damn thing by heart. Every loop of handwriting and dot and dash of punctuation. Every lapse of grammar, misspelt word and inky smear. I know that letter better than the wrinkles of my own face. It's all I have left of her, you see.

I let the branches fall and obscure the detective once more. Then I continued dragging myself to the buttress – much to the chagrin of my boot-clobbered back and screaming wound. The throb in my side had a speeding tempo, a diabolical rhythm, and progress was slow. When I reached the buttress I collapsed against it, ear pressed to the wood, as if listening for a heartbeat. My poor broken body was spent and I hadn't even begun.

There was a heavy stick within reaching distance. I grasped it in both hands and beat the buttress with force. The thwack of it resounded through the jungle, and I was certain every creature within a quarter-mile radius had heard. Heartened, I beat out a slow arduous rhythm, with a long recuperative pause between each bang. I feared the hollow thuds would summon axe-wielding Communists to come and finish the job. But it was a risk I had to take. As the hours passed and the patterns of light shifted across the ground, strength faded in my arms and my palms were slippery with weeping blisters. But whenever I felt the urge to give up, I'd think of the corpse under the shrubs and hit the buttress with renewed vigour. So long as I had the stick in my hand and was able to bang it, I had a lottery ticket and a chance to live.

All of my human will was condensed into hitting the buttress. I thought no profound thoughts about the nature of life and death. Had no memories of England, or my childhood, or my dear old mother and sisters. I thought only of pain and endurance and Evangeline. The monotonous rhythm was hard to sustain and I was kept going by contradictory desires – the desire to see Evangeline and resume our love, and the desire to have revenge upon her. 'It's A Long Way To Tipperary' as sung by the First Battalion Worcestershire Regiment echoed in my head. Even after a fitful mid-afternoon doze, the song was there upon waking, like a headache that wouldn't go away.

The day passed in stark thirst and pain, and by dusk my arms were useless – any noise I made inaudible beyond the clearing. I lapsed back into delirium and

Detective Pang crawled out from under the shrubs to offer some words of encouragement. But it was no good. No one had come. The battle was lost. Darkness was returning me to the womb of the earth and I was certain that the violent fragrance of decay came as much from me as the murdered detective.

So I tossed the stick aside, the clearing as black as the bottom of a grave, each passing minute another spadeful of soil.

19

Tendrils of smoke unfurled in my nostrils and I sneezed awake. Cold grey dawn and excruciating pain. My body slumped against the buttress; bones aching, every cell of me panting with thirst. To have survived another day left me underwhelmed, to say the least.

My eyes were blurred as steamed-up glass, and I blinked and blinked, afraid the loss of sight was permanent. Slowly the fog lifted and I saw a man standing in the clearing. I squinted at his muddy boots and woollen socks. Camouflage uniform and bull-neck. Gold buzz-cut capped with an olive beret. Part Billy Bunter, part snarling pit-bull face. The man dragged on his cigarette, then blew the smoke up towards the hole in the canopy, as if puffing a signal for help. Lieutenant Spencer grinned like a pumpkin on Hallowe'en.

'Hello, Goldilocks.'

Size eleven boots rooted to the ground, the

lieutenant flickered like a candle flame in a draught. It occurred to me then, with sinking heart, that my deus ex machina was a hallucination. The stiff hinge of my jaw creaked to let out an enquiring croak. Spencer dragged on his roll-up and squinted at me, piggy-eyed, as his nostrils spurted smoke.

'Wotcha doing lying on the ground for?'

The bloodstain spread from sternum to groin, my clothes filthy and dark, I patted my wound and smiled with a touch of pride. Trying to focus on the lieutenant gave me a splitting headache. His face shifted as if viewed through a kaleidoscope; a slowly revolving Picasso of eyes and jug ears, stubbly chin and nose.

'That pansy little cut!' scorned the mouth on his forehead. 'The village ain't even a mile away. You could have hiked it. Took me twenty minutes to get here.'

The pain surged in offence. I gritted my teeth, my hand closing around the large stick I'd tossed near by.

Lieutenant waggled his roll-up at my clenched fist. 'Little drummer boy, are we now?'

The policeman laughed as I lay debilitated by my near-fatal stab wound. I've never understood the urge to mock a man when he is down. What a cheaply won sense of superiority. The tinnitus of flies gathered around the thicket. I pointed my stick and said the detective's name.

The lieutenant jerked an eyebrow. He crouched by the shrubs, lifting the branches to peer underneath. He stared for a good long while, then let out a low whistle.

'Dearie me,' he said, 'now that ain't a pretty sight.

Your old slyboots girlfriend do that to him, did she?'

He flicked his cigarette butt under the bushes. Was Evangeline back in the village? The question was a strangled whimper in my throat. The lieutenant came and squatted by me. He flipped open his knapsack and uncapped a water canister. He tilted the canister to my lips and I gulped and gulped, water streaming down my chin. Oh, it was glorious! Spencer laughed and I didn't care. I couldn't gulp it down fast enough. I could feel my stomach bloating and my cells hydrating one by one, intoxicated by the elixir of life.

'Well then,' said Spencer when the water was gone, 's'pose I ought to piggyback you home. But first things first . . .'

The lieutenant delved into the knapsack once more and removed a first-aid kit. He took out a small glass vial and a syringe. He tugged a hanky from his pocket – crumpled and filthy, as if used to polish his boots – and gave the needle tip a wipe.

'Now then, Christopher,' he grinned as the needle pierced the foil lid of the vial, 'have I got a treat in store for you!'

The voyage out of the jungle came to pass in a dreamy haze. The good lieutenant and I were weightless, borne along by a flock of angels and harpsichord music. The savage undergrowth parted like the Red Sea as the lieutenant cradled me in his arms. Why he grunted, cursed and wheezed as he did was a mystery to me.

The weeks of hospitalization were also hazy. Sterile

sheets replaced the decaying jungle soil and my blood-stained clothes were exchanged for a backless hospital gown. They pumped me with donated blood, and tubes drip-fed me and rinsed the septicaemia from my arteries and veins. For a while my kidney flailed and floundered, the medics uncertain whether it would heal and resume functioning.

Every night I woke in an orgy of screaming, clawing the bandages from my mid-section, convinced that maggots had infested my wound. I slapped the nurses who came to calm me and head-butted the night porter, disturbing the other patients on the ward. The hospital staff wanted to bind me to the bed like a mental patient, but Charles made a fuss and had them move me to a private room. During the day hallucinations and spells of madness enlivened my drug-fuddled state. I confused the nurses tending to me with Evangeline and, forgetting her betrayal, would pull them to me and kiss them full on the lips. I'd pinch their bums and slide my hand inside their brassières during my sponge baths (which, to my mortification, I mistook for caresses of a more intimate nature). Convinced one long-suffering female doctor was the love who'd forsaken me, I chucked my dinner tray at her, splattering her with peas and gravy, and shouting every disgusting insult that came to mind. Thank God those nurses had a sense of humour. When I recovered they'd tease me. They'd wink at me and say: 'No kiss for me today, Christopher?' And I would blush, grateful they'd seen the funny side.

When I was better the police came to interview me. I recounted every detail of my affair with Evangeline and the events of the night I was stabbed and abandoned in the jungle. I was not the first government official to have had a liaison with a resettlement camp internee and no disciplinary action was to be taken against me. It was put to me kindly, however, that if I wanted to return to old Blighty to put my ordeal behind me, that would be perfectly understandable. And what a temptation it was, the chance to flee the heat and mosquitoes and knife-wielding Communists. But I was determined to stick it out. *It's my duty to stay for the remaining months of my contract*, I said, without the faintest premonition that I was to stay in Malaya for another twenty-eight years.

And so I returned to the kingdom of ramshackle slums and backed-up drains. I'd been hospitalized for nearly two months, but not much had changed. I resumed my role as Assistant Resettlement Officer as if I'd never been gone.

Though my fugitive beloved was very much alive and on the run (with a $100,000 bounty on her head), I was haunted by her. I saw her everywhere. Queuing by the standpipe, sowing seeds in her market-garden plot, wandering through the village with a basket of clothes for mending. I was busy from dawn to dusk, but from time to time a strange paralysis would sweep over me and I'd be lost in the memory of her (brought to, God knows how many minutes later, by the repetition of my name and fingers clicking in my face). Evangeline was my waking thought and the last thing on my mind at night. It became a secret vice of mine to go up to the watchtower and stand in the emptiness, listening out for echoes of the past.

The missionaries unofficially adopted the wayward Grace and I went to see her at the Jesus cottage once a week. Blanche Mallard was rather cross about my complicity in Evangeline's fib about needing solitude for Bible studies and to seek the Lord. But she forgave me, relishing her subtle reminders that I'd been punished for my sins. Though the other sinner had fled, Blanche assured me of the even-handedness of divine retribution.

'The Lord has seen and He has judged! The jungle may shield her from the eyes of the government, but not from the eyes of our Heavenly Father!'

Grace replaced the late Humphrey in the missionaries' affections. They scrubbed her pink with carbolic soap and dressed her in Marina's prim cast-off blouses and ankle-length skirts. They often left Grace and me alone together in the Jesus cottage kitchen, behind the beaded curtain. Seated across the table, Grace would fidget and rock her chair on its hind legs. She'd rest the sole of her bare foot on the table edge, showing off the frilly bloomers they'd made her wear. Grace was blank as a Noh mask. But if I smiled she would mimic me, like a baby gurgling in a pram. As sermons, psalms and words of scripture droned in the classroom next door, I'd lean close to Grace and speak to her in

Cantonese. Where has she gone? Did she ever really love me? When will she come back? Grace would wince, twisting from the intensity of my gaze. Or she'd yawn hugely, baring her stumpy, gappy teeth. Sometimes Grace would cease fidgeting and trap me with an unflinching stare. And in that stare I'd be reunited with Evangeline. The gyre of smoke-grey irises so familiar to me, and something else – something living behind the eyes. I'd leave the Jesus cottage then. I'd resolve not to go back. But then another week would go by, and I inevitably would.

I returned to The Village of Everlasting Peace an object of communal ridicule: the Foreign Devil seduced and tricked by a woman of the Min Yuen; the hypocrite who broke the rules he enforced. But as days became weeks became months my determination not to quit my job earnt me a grudging respect. I was solemn, hard-working and logical in my approach to things. The romantic, happy-go-lucky Christopher Milnar who'd arrived at Kuala Lumpur airport was gone – died in that jungle clearing.

'I miss the old Christopher,' lamented Charles. 'You're such a misery guts these days.'

Charles was a fine one to talk, of course. In 1952 he was so heavy of heart, the organ dragged along the ground, aorta and ventricles clogged with dust. Charles had handed the reins over to his demons. The bad mood that plagued him in the mornings now lasted all day. No one liked him much any more, except

Lieutenant Spencer, who was loyal as a dog. But the former Raj orphan and Changi POW was unable to accept Spencer's love graciously. He was a condemned man and anyone who loved him was condemned too. Drunken abuse shattered the night as he turned on his dearest companion. Charles yelling, glasses smashing, chair legs splintering across Spencer's back. Spencer was the stronger of the two, but I very much doubt that Charles was the one stabbed with filthy syringes or shoved through the veranda railings and chased out the village gates by the speeding bullets of an antique handgun (a family heirloom, once belonging to Charles's grandfather, Thomas Dulwich Esquire). But again and again Spencer went back to the officers' bungalow, the battered housewife whose fidelity to the beast survived every brutal attack.

'You made each other so unhappy,' I said to Charles, as he swilled a glass of whisky in my armchair the other night. 'Why didn't you have the courage to break it off?'

'Unhappy!' scoffed Charles. 'Whatever are you talking about? *You* were the unhappy one, Christopher. We were having an absolute ball!'

I stayed in The Village of Everlasting Peace for another year. The insurgency raged. The burnt carcasses of ambushed trucks cluttered the roads, and tin mines and rubber estates were bombarded with grenades, shrapnel glittering in the morning sun. THIS RUNNING DOG LED BRITISH IMPERIALISTS TO ARREST OUR PEOPLE declared the sign hung from a villager strung from the perimeter fence.

My wound healed into scar tissue. I grew a moustache and people said it aged me. Sometimes I taught English to the children in the village school. Cat Dog Horse. A B C. One Two Three ... Sometimes, during checkpoint searches, I'd discover notes written in Communist code in a hollowed-out pineapple, tube of toothpaste, or bicycle pump. Sometimes Charles and I would eat our supper in silence, staring at the flamingo-pink ebbs of the sinking sun. And so the year went by.

One morning in January 1953 I went to breakfast to see Charles washed and shaven and in his chair. Charles was smiling, trouser braces hitched over his recently ironed shirt. I hadn't seen Charles smile since October 1952 and was right to be suspicious.

'Good morning, Christopher.'

'Good morning, Charles.'

'How are you today?'

'Same as usual.'

'Jolly good.'

Charles lifted his coffee cup and drank, eyes smiling at me over the rim (old red-eyed Devil, whisky spiders scuttling out every night to spin webs of blood). I buttered my roll and added a dab of jam. I shook open *The Straits Times* and began to read. But it was no good. Charles's smile was impossible to ignore.

'What's the matter, Charles?' I snapped. 'You look like the cat who's got the cream.'

'I have some news that might interest you.'

'Oh?'

'I received a telephone call from the Jalang town police station this morning. There was a raid on a bungalow in Batu Pahat last night. When the police burst in three men made a dash for it and were shot dead. The others were arrested. There were two women in the bungalow, one of whom, you'll be interested to hear, was Evangeline Lim, hiding in the back room with a baby. They arrested her.'

'Arrested?'

For 364 days Evangeline had been out of sight but omnipresent in my mind. I had obsessed and obsessed over her, until she was no longer a creature of flesh and blood, but a thing of myth. My monomania had made Evangeline a lesser god. How could she be captured? How could they handcuff a deity?

'Yes, arrested.' Charles's grin was bursting at the seams. 'The police are hardly going to slap her on the wrists and send her on her scheming whoring way, are they now? I say, Christopher, you've gone deathly pale! You don't still hold a candle to that murderous wench, do you?' Charles widened his eyes, though he knew perfectly well.

'Where is she?'

'They are holding her at Jalang town police station. She is under interrogation.'

Interrogation: a euphemism for cigarette burns and electric shocks; for suspects stripped naked and spat on and dunked in barrels of water. Strong men

318

and women had committed suicide in police custody.

'Jesus . . .'

'Why are you so concerned?' asked Charles. 'Need I remind you that this is the same woman who tricked you and left you for dead.'

Charles was amused. I hardened my face to lessen his satisfaction.

'What are the charges?'

'The charges are numerous,' said Charles. 'Membership of the Communist Party, running away from The Village of Everlasting Peace, the attempted manslaughter of Assistant Resettlement Officer Christopher Milnar . . .'

I nodded.

'The last charge carries the death penalty,' said Charles. 'If you testify against her, the woman is as good as dead.'

The trial of Evangeline Lim took place at the Selangor Magistrates Court on 18 February 1953. I arrived at nine o'clock and sat with the five other witnesses, all of whom were Surrendered Enemy Personnel. The court-room was large and panelled in dark wood. Though the ceiling whirred with fans, the room was oppressive and as hot as an oven; a taste for the guilty of the perdition to come. The missionaries and Grace were there, sitting in the public gallery. The missionaries wore white gloves and church-going hats, and waved cheerily when I glanced round. ('Look! There's Christopher,' Blanche said to Grace, as if they'd come to see me in a play.)

Also in the public gallery was a Chinese journalist in horn-rimmed spectacles, scribbling in his notebook, and some British men – detectives from the Special Branch, who'd gathered the intelligence leading to the raid on the bungalow in Batu Pahat.

There was no jury at Evangeline's trial. The local population, who were often anti-government and had Communist allegiances, were not considered trust-worthy enough for jury service, and Evangeline was to be tried by the old Assessor system. Mr Justice Morrison was to preside over the trial, and two assessors – one Malay, one Chinese (both English educated) – were seated either side of him. Evangeline was late. As the courtroom waited I twitched as if I'd drunk a gallon of coffee, my shoe tap-tap-tapping and a tic agitating in my temple. The other witnesses were relaxed, the trial a welcome day out of jail. They made good-natured complaints about the broken-down air conditioning and broiling heat, and made fun of Mr Justice Morrison's white curly wig. They gossiped about me in Hokkien: what's wrong with this Foreign Devil? He's making the whole bench shake. You'd think that he was the one on trial!

At nine thirty Evangeline Lim was escorted into the Selangor Magistrates courtroom by two female prison wardens. When I saw her my heart banged like a slammed door. I was on fire, my cheeks blazing, flames licking the ceiling. The courtroom murmured to itself. My beloved was barefoot and wearing a blouse and cotton slacks. She'd changed. Her greying hair was now chin-length, pinned back with tortoiseshell combs. And she looked older, her skin lined as if she'd aged a decade in a year. She wasn't nearly as pretty as I remembered. The opposite of pretty, in fact. But I ached for her nonetheless. Evangeline's eyes skimmed the benches before she took her seat. She must have seen me (the lone Caucasian, the man with the flambéd cheeks) but her face bore no trace of recognition. I wanted to rectify this, to shout and shout until she acknowledged me. And when a scream did pierce the ears of the courtroom, for one disorientating moment, I thought it was me. Grace was screaming at the top of her lungs in the public gallery, the missionaries flapping about, trying to silence her. Evangeline's was the only head in the courtroom not to be turned by the commotion. She stared into midair, her face a vault, from which not a mote of emotion escaped.

One by one the witnesses were called up to the stand. And one by one they identified Evangeline as the ranking party official Small Cloud and described the specifics of their acquaintance with her. The Communist Party defectors testified in a perfunctory manner, scarcely breaking into a sweat when cross-examined by the lawyer for the defence. I, on the other hand, sweated torrents, the ceiling fans mocking me with their redundant whirring as I fidgeted on the bench. Evangeline held her head high as the surrendered Communists gave evidence against her (only once narrowing her eyes when a witness claimed that she had supplied him with hand grenades). During the breaks in court the Surrendered Enemy Personnel were taken to a private room, where they smoked and drank chrysanthemum tea. Unable to eat or drink, I wandered the corridors of the courthouse until the trial started up again. When five o'clock came I realized that I would not be called to the stand that day. Court was adjourned at a quarter to six and I left the Selangor Magistrates Court exhausted, without a word to anyone.

I spent the night in a hotel in Kajang, the lamps blazing in my room as I lay awake until dawn.

I imagined Evangeline dying. Dangling from a noose of rope, stool kicked from under her feet. The brittle snap of her neck, truncated gasp from her strangled windpipe. The light-headedness as oxygen seeped from her brain. And then nothing, I presumed. A corpse hanging from the gallows. I could not comprehend it, the eternal snuffing out of life. For Evangeline, who had lived and breathed and cared for her sister and washed clothes in the village stream, to no longer exist. I would not testify. I would leave tomorrow. But I knew my loyalty was to an illusion; to a woman who had left me for dead.

I bathed at sunrise, ladling water over insensate flesh. Then I shaved away the night's shadows, the eyes staring out of the mirror smudged dark with sleeplessness. The razor scraping my stubble bit my cheek. Rinsing away the blood in the basin, I thought what sweet relief two quick slashes of the blade would bring.

* * *

Three hours later I was in the witness stand, an exhumed corpse of a man, describing my relationship with Evangeline from beginning to end, omitting nothing, except that I had loved her.

The lawyer for the defence said that my testimony was motivated by revenge for a love affair gone sour. Evangeline had not lured me into the jungle. Fuelled by one-man heroics, I had chased after the bandit alone. The consequences of my stupidity embarrassed me, so I blamed Miss Lim. I was confident the assessors would not believe him. His was the strategy of the desperate, of a side with nothing to lose. As her lawyer made these audacious claims Evangeline seemed dissociated from the proceedings, as if she wasn't listening. What a co-incidence, I said, for Miss Lim to vanish on the night of my attack. What a coincidence for me to have stumbled upon the corpse of Detective Pang on my own. The lawyer continued to accuse me, and though I didn't lie once, when I left the stand an hour later I was trembling with shame.

When Evangeline stood in the dock I was struck again by how old and plain she was; a woman not a single head would turn for in the street (except mine, of course: my head will never cease to turn for her). Though English was the language of the courts and it would have been in Evangeline's favour to speak it, she used an interpreter and testified in Cantonese – a decision that baffles me to this day. When the prosecution asked her to confirm or deny whether she was a Communist, Evangeline denied it. Though she had been forced to live among the Communists she'd never met the witnesses. She accused them of perjury; identifying her as Small Cloud to receive free pardons. They were out to save their own skins, she said, and not to be trusted. Evangeline's defence was a denial of everything. When the prosecution cross-examined her about the night I was stabbed I expected the lies to continue. But they didn't.

'Yes, I led Assistant Resettlement Officer Milnar into the jungle,' she said, 'but I had not meant him to be harmed. The bandit he shot was a boy I had grown up next door to in Kajang, and I chased after him to make sure he was OK. I brought Mr Milnar with me so he could help. The trail we followed is used by Communists, but it is also well known to local squatters. I did not know the boy was going to attack Mr Milnar. When Mr Milnar collapsed and the boy began kicking him, I tried to stop him, to pull him off, but then he turned on me. He put the knife to my throat and forced me to go back to the camp with him. I was afraid for Mr Milnar, but I was also frightened for my life and the life of my unborn child.'

Evangeline went on to say she had stayed, very reluctantly, at the Communist camp, because she knew she would be arrested if she returned to the village, and she did not want to give birth to her baby in a detention camp. She then went to live in Batu Pahat, to work as a housekeeper for a Communist official. Not because she was a Communist, she said, but because he provided a home for her and her child, and she was tired of living in the jungle. The lawyer for the defence was ashen. It was not the defence they'd agreed upon, the script they had rehearsed.

The next morning the two assessors delivered the guilty verdict and Mr Justice Morrison sentenced Evangeline to death by hanging. Evangeline staggered, then let out a scream. A scream that, *The Strait Times* reporter claimed, *conveyed her anguish to each and every one of us*. Evangeline keeled over and the prison wardens caught her arms to prevent her from sinking to the floor. As they frogmarched her to the door, Evangeline turned to the public gallery and called her sister's name. Grace shouted back at Evangeline, actual coherent words – *Wait for me! Wait for me!* – and lunged at the balcony rail, heedless of the twelve-foot drop. The missionaries grabbed her arms, so for a moment the sisters mirrored each other, straining against the human shackles that held them back. The prison wardens had little patience with this and dragged Evangeline to the door. They passed the bench where I was standing and Evangeline met my eyes for the first time in over a year. And in that instant I knew she hated me and would hate me to the grave.

I agreed to take the child out of guilt. Saving the daughter from the orphanage to make some reparation for the nails hammered in her mother's coffin. Charles laughed his head off when he heard. I was a dunce, a dolt, a dunderhead. The baby was no more mine than

Chairman Mao's. Not that I let his opinion bother me. By then I'd already written my letter of resignation.

The baby was being looked after by an Anglo-Indian woman, the wife of a Scottish policeman who lived on the outskirts of Jalang. The woman, whose name was Betty, wore a sari as bright as a parakeet and had a smudge of red on her forehead. She fetched my daughter as I waited in the parlour of her house.

The baby knocked the breath out of me. Betty gently lowered the carrycot to the floor, and the little girl, naked save for a cotton nappy, waggled her feet and threw some punches in the humid air. The baby smiled – not at me, but at the world at large, reaching out her arms, impossibly tiny fingers clutching and pulling at the invisible threads tangible only to the recently born. I smiled awkwardly at my daughter. She made me nervous. She was so fragile. I was bound to snap those little finger joints as carelessly as I'd snapped my reading glasses the week before. (*Look, perhaps I ought to come back for her in a couple of years, when she is a bit bigger*, I wanted to say.) Betty beamed encouragingly. The baby had a button nose and brown eyes lidded with Evangeline's epicanthic folds. Her skin was pink-toned like mine, but what settled for me any doubts about paternity were the blonde tufts on her crown (tufts that would darken to black before her second birthday). I peered closer, breathing the milky talcum-powder fragrance of her skin. The sight of my hulking great face must have been disagreeable to my daughter. She whimpered, causing me to fear that she'd sensed my inadequacy as a father. Betty lifted her out of the cot, gold bangles jingling and jangling as she jiggled the baby and cooed.

'Oh, you poor silly thing!' sang Betty, 'You poor silly thing! Do you want to say hello to your handsome father?'

Smiling, Betty held the child towards me. My hands flew up as if to fend off a blow.

'Not right now, thank you. I shall, uh . . . hold her later . . .'

Later, much later, alone together in a Kuala Lumpur hotel room, I would cradle my daughter in my arms for the first time. And my daughter would howl like a human air-raid siren. Later she would vomit out her formula milk and I would bathe her in the sink, hand supporting her weightless skull, terrified of drowning her. Later I would spend a good quarter of an hour grappling with a safety pin, trying to put her in a nappy. Later, in the bleary-eyed hour before dawn, I would stare at her demoniac screaming mouth in awe. Surely this wasn't normal infant behaviour. What had I done to make the child hate me so? But that was later.

'You do know how to care for a baby, don't you?' asked Betty. 'How often to feed it, how to change a nappy . . . ?'

'I expect I shall muddle through.'

I realized I did not know her name. I asked Betty what she was called.

'Heavenly Orchid.'

I sighed. I'd thought Evangeline had more sense than that.

'It's quite popular for Chinese girls,' Betty assured me.

'But it's hardly suitable for a doctor or a lawyer now, is it? We must think of a proper name for her. What names do you like?'

'When it comes to English names I have always liked Frances,' said Betty. 'I knew a woman in Penang called Frances who died of typhoid during the war . . .'

'Frances . . .' I said. 'Yes, I like it very much. I think that is what I shall call her. Thank you.'

Betty was reluctant to let me go, delaying my departure with advice on feeding times, milk temperature and bum rash. She gave me a knapsack stuffed with nappies and lotions which I strapped on my back. I lifted the cot and Frances waved her arms and legs. As I gave Betty a firm farewell handshake in the yard, two macaques climbed down from the mango trees and stood a short distance behind her.

'Good luck.' Betty smiled. 'Good luck.'

I set off down the hot and dusty road, my daughter, my acquaintance of twenty minutes, swinging in her carrycot by my side. Before the bend in the road I glanced back and Betty was still there in her bright coloured sari, the macaques standing behind her with their tails pointing stiffly in the air. She smiled and waved, and with my free hand I saluted her, before we turned and left for good.

I peel a carrot with the paring knife, spilling shavings on the chopping board as I dig in the blade. Boiled cabbage, carrots and fried liver is our supper tonight – a supper Julia may or may not come home to eat. Dusk is gathering beyond the window, a landscape of grey. Adam sleeps in the bedroom, has been hibernating under the duvet for thirty days now. They are getting worse and worse, those children. Disintegrating in their separate ways, though I suspect the origins of decay are the same.

There is a shiver of antagonism in the kitchen, an atmospheric pins and needles. Who has come now? I turn and see and the clocks of Mountbatten strike hard upon my Judas heart. My beloved stands by the table, her frock too thin for the December chill, her furious beauty unmarred by a scowl. The paring knife is frozen in my hand, a carrot shaving caught in the blade. Evangeline stares, her eyes unblinking. And my cheeks flush and my heart flutters as if I have been caught stealing or telling a lie.

She absentmindedly thumbs the corner of a French textbook, the pages sticky with Ribena spilt by her homework-loathing granddaughter. *Who are you?* I ask my elusive love. I thought I knew her once, when we met high above the sleeping village, lakes of shadow merging on the rough-hewn walls. But now I don't know. The silence teems with decades of uncertainty.

Evangeline's chest heaves as if she has run a great distance. On the day she died, I wheeled Frances in her pram to the Lake Gardens' butterfly sanctuary. Frances giggled when the butterflies landed on her, delicate wings opening and shutting, feelers twitching, probioscises dipping the nectar of her infant skin. I kept the truth from her for years and years.

Does Evangeline blame me for what happened to Frances too? So long as I am entombed in flesh I'll never know. Evangeline flees interrogation, vanishes in the blink of an eye. Only once my heart has ticked to the end of its allocated ticks will I be able to fly off in pursuit of her.

When that day comes I'll resist the urge for quarrel and recrimination. Who betrayed whom, and who left whom to die. None of that matters any more. We'll exist again in our moments of happiness, perfect as snowflakes before they melt.

The front door slams and Evangeline's eyes soften in the fading December light. And as the tiles swell beneath us, I savour our precarious truce. It is the closest thing to reconciliation we will have for a long time.

IV

20

Adam was in the kitchen when the door buzzer went. A pan of spaghetti was boiling on the hob, and the tumble-drier rumbled with gentle thunder, tossing sheets. The radio was tuned into a long-wave French station, the panel debate accompanied by a snake-hiss of static, a high-pitched whine. Adam doesn't know French. The foreign syllables moved up and down the scale like musical notes; masculine basso, feminine chimes, cymbal clashes of conflict soothed by the mellifluous host. On the way to the intercom he clicked off the radio, silencing his eloquent Gallic guests.

'Hello?'

'Adam, it's me, Jules. Can I come in?'

Adam hadn't heard his sister's voice through the intercom before. Disorientated, he said, 'Jules. You all right?'

'Yeah, fine.'

'Come up.'

Adam buzzed her in. How did she know his address? Adam had scribbled it down for her soon after his tenancy began, but that had been years ago. He was surprised she'd hung on to it so long, that it hadn't been lost in the tides of junk that besieged her flat. Why had she come? Money, of course. Irritated, he steeled himself. But when he opened the door, he was so happy to see her his vigilance disappeared. Julia gave him a lopsided smile and walked into his arms. Released from the hug, she conscientiously stamped her shoes on the doormat, peering over Adam's shoulder and into his flat. The flat was practically a studio, separated from the tiny bathroom and kitchen by folding accordion doors. Everything was clean and functional; the stripped wood floor recently mopped, cushions plumped, and the sofa throw smoothed of wrinkles. The computer desk and bookshelves were dusted, CDs stored in a rack. The dark windows were opaque with condensation coalescing into drips that glided to the sill.

'You like it nice and warm, don't you?' Julia said.

'It's the tumble-drier,' said Adam, 'and I'm cooking pasta.'

Julia sat on the sofa. The naked 100-watt ceiling bulb exposed what the decaying shadows of her flat had concealed: the yellow sclera of her eyes and the bloody-edged scabs that scavenging fingers never let alone to heal. Too much scalp showed in the parting of her hair and as she tucked some limp strands behind her ear Adam saw the cigarette burns bejewelling her knuckles.

She was so thin she was painful to look at. A skimpy vest was all she had on under her denim jacket, her skin tinged blue like skimmed milk, ice crystals thawing in the blood.

Adam offered her a cup of tea, a bowl of pasta (a memory flashed of his sister crying and bolognese smeared, smacked by Frances for playing with her food). But Julia, her appetite blunted for years, wanted only water. Adam went to the kitchen and turned off the gas ring under the boiling pan. He held a glass under the shrieking tap.

'Where d'you sleep?' Julia called.

'That sofa folds out into a bed . . .'

'Comfy?'

'It's all right.'

'You live alone?'

'Yeah.'

'No one special in your life, then?'

'No.'

'Thanks . . .'

Julia took the water, throat undulating as she gulped it down. Adam wheeled the swivel chair out from under the computer desk and sat opposite. Julia was on her best behaviour; back straight and gaze clear and direct, as if Adam were interviewing her for a job. It was false and out of character and Adam preferred the stoned, apathetic mood of her flat. The rims of her sticky-out ears were wind-chapped and raw (ears that, as a paranoid teenager, she'd taped back every night for a year). She hadn't had a fix in a while – she had that lustre about her. The tiny jerks and tics of a speeding metabolism, aching to be suppressed.

'How d'you know where I live, Julia?'

'You wrote it down for me. Remember?'

Julia passed him an old bus ticket and Adam recognized his scrawl on the back. She reached sideways across the sofa to place her empty glass on the bookcase. There were two framed photographs on the shelf: one of Julia, aged eight, astride a BMX, a pink-gummed gap in her grin where her eye-teeth had been; and the other of Frances, smiling as she cradled baby Adam, arms bare in her summer dress, dimple-cheeked and youthful under her thick bouncy fringe. Adam had found the photos in one of their grandfather's shoeboxes after he'd died, but only put them out the week before. Julia glanced at the pictures briefly, disinterested, as if they were of strangers, someone else's family.

'Mind if I smoke?'

Adam shook his head and passed her an ashtray. Ancient shreds of tissue, dilapidated as cobwebs, spilt from Julia's pocket as she fumbled for her Benson and Hedges. The match flared and the cigarette trembled as she sucked in the flame. Amputated forefinger clamped the filter to middle finger, and Adam stared at the smooth regenerated skin, the severed tip having been reduced to heat and bone-ash in a hospital incinerator over a decade ago. Julia tugged the stream of tar and phenols into her lungs, satiating one of her lesser, legal desires. Adam dislikes the claustrophobia of cigarette smoke and never smokes indoors himself.

'Why've you come, Julia?'

'I wanted to see you.'

A lie. Julia would never travel across the city, hopping on and off buses and navigating unknown streets, for the sake of seeing him alone. He got the feeling that Rob was pacing three floors below, muttering and sneering at Adam's neighbours as they scurried past him with carrier bags of Marks & Spencer's ready meals.

'I wanted to talk to you.'

'Is Rob with you?'

Julia looked offended. 'Rob doesn't know I've come here,' she said. 'I wouldn't ever let him know where you live. Anyway, I've left him. That's why I'm here.'

'Left him?' echoed Adam.

Adam sensed her agitation, sparks flying from nerve endings, flaying her under the skin. She cared about her next fix, not breaking up with Rob. She was too dependent on Rob, and he on her. They were Siamese twins; respiring through the same pair of lungs, the same heart pumping blood around the same diseased body. But even if it were a lie, he couldn't let her down. Julia had never expressed sentiments about changing her life before. He had to encourage it.

'You can stay here,' he said. 'I'll take some time off work and help you come off. I'll take care of you.'

'That's not what I want, Adam.'

'But where else can you go?'

'There's this crisis centre. They put you on a two-week detox programme, but they don't have a bed free for another four nights. I'm going to stay in a hostel until then.'

'But why not stay here? It's safe and clean here. In a hostel you'll have to sleep in a room with a load of strangers. They let anyone in.'

'I have to do this my own way.'

Adam was silent, thinking of how to persuade her.

'The hostel is fourteen pounds a night.'

'You can stay here for free.'

'I'll be using, Adam. I'll be using till the programme starts.'

'It doesn't matter.'

'Yes, it does.'

Julia coughed into her fist, chest revving like a car that won't start. She stubbed her cigarette out in the ashtray.

'Why now?' Adam asked. 'Why are you leaving him now?'

'He wants me to go on the game.'

She wielded the fact bluntly, with no emotion in her voice. Adam had tortured himself with the thought hundreds of times before, but was shocked to hear it said out loud. He realized that, as much as he had hated him, he'd trusted that Rob had some minimal decency. Trusted that he'd never bully Julia into selling herself to anyone who could scrape together a few quid. But it had happened. Julia had left him. But Adam still felt sick.

'Julia,' he said, 'stay here. I don't mind you using.'

'I can't. I don't want to mess things up for you.'

'Look at this place. There's nothing in my life to mess up. Nothing that matters more than you.'

'I can't.'

'Stay for just one night.'

'I have to do this on my own.'

'Promise me you won't go back to Rob.'

'I won't, I promise. I don't want to go near him.'

It was her earnestness that made Adam doubt her. As a teenager Julia had lied every time she drew breath, without any tell-tale flickers of guilt. He knew that sincere, wide-eyed, clear-as-water gaze. He had two options. Refuse to give her money and risk not seeing her again; or give her money and have her come back. Adam went to the jacket hanging on the back of the front door and rummaged in the pocket. (*She hasn't left Rob – she made it up because she knows you hate him, and now she wants her cash reward.*) He opened his wallet. There was roughly thirty quid in there. (*She's already on the game – has been for years. You're pretending not to know because you can't stomach the truth.*) He scooped out the notes and coins and gave her the lot. (*Rob is waiting outside for her. Go to the window. Look . . .*)

Julia thrust the money into her pocket, afraid the sight of her counting it would tempt her brother to ask for it back.

'I'll pay you back soon as I can.'

'Don't worry about it,' he said. 'If you come back tomorrow, I'll give you some more. I get in from work about six. What's the address of the hostel you're staying at?'

She told him and Adam jotted it down. 'You'll go straight there, won't you? And if it's shit you can come back here. It doesn't matter how late it is. Please don't go back to Rob, whatever you do.'

'I won't.'

Julia stood up, eye on the door, impatient to leave. She buttoned her jacket, the denim dirty and thin.

'Do you want to borrow a jumper? It's freezing out there.'

She let him give her a jumper, which she draped over her arm. She said goodbye and went. Adam listened to her footsteps receding down the hall.

Alone in his flat, empty wallet hanging open in his hand, Adam was motionless. The city devours people, secretes them in its darkest crevices, thousands missing every year. There was much worse out there than Rob.

21

Frances's lie about the cancelled maths lesson confused Sally. Frances hated maths. She hated Mr Leung too. So why leave Sally out, like a child too selfish to share her toys? The next morning the girls had swimming first lesson, for which Sally had forged a note from Mr Hargreaves saying that she had her period (in reality the thought of her father knowing her menstrual cycle was too horrific to contemplate). As Miss Van der Cruisen scanned the note with a snort of disbelief (*Your third period this month, Hargreaves! What fertile ovaries you have!*), Frances scuffled up alongside her with a similar forgery to submit for ridicule.

The fraudsters sat on the shady poolside bench as their classmates, anonymous in goggles and slick red caps, swam warm-up lengths, limbs churning up the water like a spate of shark attacks. The poolside air drizzled humidity, settling on their skin like silt. 'Bless

341

you,' said Frances, when the chlorine fumes tickled Sally's sinuses into a sneeze. Frances gnawed her fingernails. Sally opened her biology textbook and pretended to read.

'Are you really on the rag?' asked Frances.

'No,' replied Sally, without looking up from the frog's digestive system on page 92.

'Me neither. I just wasn't in the mood for swimming today.'

'Hmmm.'

For a good ten minutes neither girl said a word. The fifth form queued to practise diving, one by one climbing the ladder, the board arching as they strode to the end and, in a flash of thighs and ballerina toes, plunged head first into the pool. They struggled to the surface, doggy-paddled to the side and heaved themselves out; then, waddling and plucking the clinging fabric of their navy one-pieces from their buttocks, they joined the queue again.

The silent treatment worked. Frances blurted that she was sorry. She knew it was wrong of her to have lied about the lesson being cancelled, but it was very important that she was alone with Mr Leung. She and Mr Leung had become friends while Sally had been ill with stomach flu. Mr Leung was teaching her about politics. Frances had become *very passionate* about politics, and if Sally had been there she'd have had to forfeit her ad hoc politics lesson for a normal algebra lesson instead.

Sally was dubious. 'Do you fancy Mr Leung?' she asked.

Frances didn't flare defensively as she'd expected, but remained calm. 'You don't understand,' she said. 'In the last few days Henry has taught me so much! I feel as though a switch has been flipped in my brain and I finally see things the way they are. The situation in this country is awful. Really awful.'

'Henry?' Sally gawped. 'Mr Leung lets you call him Henry?'

'I told you. Henry and I are friends now. He has been educating me. He has helped me to realize how tough things are for the Chinese; how we are denied jobs, access to higher education and land, and treated as second-class citizens . . .'

'You're not a second-class citizen, though,' said Sally. 'Your father is very rich and a member of the Royal Selangor Club.'

'Just because we are better off than most doesn't mean I'm not aware of the suffering of the Chinese community. Henry has helped me to realize lots of things about my own life too. Like how my father wants to turn me against my Chinese heritage by sending me to an English school.'

'But you live in Chinatown,' said Sally, 'and you live with Madame Tay. She teaches you about Chinese heritage, doesn't she?'

'My father wants me to be English. He wants me to graduate from an English university and marry an Englishman, like all these girls here.'

'And what's wrong with your father wanting the best for you?'

Frances sighed. A spray of chlorinated water splashed up from a nearby swimmer, douching their shins.

'But it's not what *I* want. I want to stay here, in Malaysia. But this country has to change. We need a proper democracy. The Alliance have dominated since Independence and right now Malaysia is run by the Malays, for the Malays.'

'You've got Chinese in government,' interrupted Sally. 'I've seen them on TV.'

'The Alliance is a party of privilege and the Chinese politicians in it know nothing about the everyday working-class Chinese. They represent the rich middle classes, who accept the Malays' constitutional special status to keep the peace. Meanwhile the poor suffer, are denied jobs, land, education ... That's why the Democratic Action Party is so important. They represent Chinese from every walk of life. They stand for a Malaysian Malaysia. They are campaigning for the eradication of exploitation of man by man, class by class, race by race.'

Exploitation? Eradication? Constitutional special status? Sally was speechless, mystified by rhetoric. Frances, meanwhile, was radiant, exhilarated by her recent discovery that she belonged to an oppressed minority. Her eyes shone black as liquorice. Sally had never seen her so thrilled.

'But won't the Chinese being in charge, and thinking the Chinese are better, be just as bad as the Malays being in charge and thinking they are better?' asked Sally.

'You haven't been listening! We don't think we're better. We only want equal rights and an end to discrimination. The DAP is not anti-Malay. They are campaigning to end rural Malay poverty too – an end to poverty for everyone!'

'Like the Communists?'

'Henry says it's Humanism, not Communism.'

'Mr Leung's in the DAP?'

'Henry's very committed. Now that the elections are only a few weeks away he is at the campaign office seven nights a week. He says that I can go down there and help.'

'But you can't, Frances. You're grounded until the O levels are over.'

'I don't care. This is more important. We've to stop the persecution of the Chinese.'

'Persecution?'

'Henry says the Chinese are the Jews of Asia.'

Sally let out a loud gasp. She generally slept during history lessons, but she knew sacrilege when she heard it.

'You can't say that! Millions of Jews were killed in the Holocaust.'

'And millions of Chinese were killed during the war too. Henry says—'

'*Henry says, Henry says* . . . Don't you think for yourself any more?'

'I was wrong to think you'd understand.'

Frances shook her head in sadness and frustration, and Sally bit her lip so hard she tasted blood. She understood all right! Mr Leung had brainwashed Frances! Frances had never cared about any of this stuff before, but now she was carrying on like the DAP's number-one activist. The fifth form were treading water in the deep end, pink scrubbed faces lifted to receive Miss Van der Cruisen's wisdom on backstroke technique. Laughter tinkled as Miss Van der Cruisen mimicked the clumsy stroke of a weaker student.

'I have never fitted in at this school,' Frances murmured, as if her new political awakening had shed light on the reason why.

'Well, that's 'cos you never talk to anyone,' said Sally, 'and you're very rude. It's not because you're Chinese. Cynthia Wong in the third year has loads of friends.'

'I never wanted to come to this school. My father made me come here.'

'Well, I doubt that any of us *wanted* to come here . . .'

'He's disgusting. He knows the situation in this country is unfair, but thinks the Malays should keep their special privileges. He says *all hell will break loose* if the other races have equal rights. It's cowardly to know things are wrong, but to be afraid to change them.'

And on Frances went, ranting about the unfair quotas for government jobs and university places, the National Language Act of 1967 and land reservations for Malays. Sally knew she was perfect for a trial run of Frances's new political opinions, none the wiser if she fluffed her lines or got her facts wrong. The bell chimed for the end of the lesson and the swimmers hoisted their pale gleaming bodies up on to the poolside tiles, biceps and triceps flexed against the gravity of the water. Red plastic caps were snapped off heads, and wet ropes of hair wrung out. And as Frances lectured her ignorant friend, for the first time in her games-skiving career Sally wished she'd endured the humiliation of a swimming costume and spent the hour in the pool.

During her months in Kuala Lumpur, Sally had turned a blind eye to newspaper headlines and slogan graffiti on walls; turned a deaf ear to political rallies and electioneering; turned off the TV at the spectacle of debating politicians. Though Chinatown was Sally's after-school haunt, she didn't prefer the Chinese to the Malays, or the Malays to the Chinese. Both races were equally 'other' to her, thought of in terms of stereo-types: the Malays cheerful, indolent and work-shy; the Chinese industrious, money-grubbing and sly. Though Sally knew of the separateness of the communities, any interracial tension had escaped her notice. She asked her father's opinion (Mr Hargreaves was a champion of equal rights after all, employing both Chinese and Malay servants and paying them equal wages). Mr Hargreaves frowned, scratching his bald pate as if to facilitate thought.

'Well, dear, the Malays are very much the dominant race, aren't they? And they're not very fair to the Chinese and the Sikhs, are they? But we mustn't poke our noses in. We left Malaysia to manage her own affairs in 1957 and they've been getting on quite nicely without us. We must let these people sort it out among themselves. And as for Frances, we all go through funny phases. Believe it or not I was a Trotskyite at Oxford, barking on about Communism every chance I got! Don't worry, silly old Frances will come round. In the meantime, it's tremendous fun to be young and fired up . . .'

Frances begged Sally to be her alibi when she volunteered at the Democratic Action Party campaign office (since her grades had improved Mr Milnar allowed Frances to have dinner at Sally's once a week), and Sally agreed – a decision she sorely regretted when Mr Milnar called the Hargreaves' residence, putting her through the heart-clenching ordeal of imitating her friend on the telephone. The DAP voluntary work indoctrinated Frances in the opposition party ethos until she could rattle off the election manifesto verbatim (detonating in Sally a thousand and one yawns). Nonetheless, not wanting to be left out of things, Sally asked if she could volunteer at the DAP campaign office too.

'You can't,' Frances said.

'Why not?' asked Sally.

'Because you're English.'

'So are you! You're dual nationality! Besides, I thought the DAP weren't a racist party.'

'They're not. But it's inappropriate for an English person to volunteer. The message of the DAP is freedom and equality, and Malaysia has been freed from the shackles of colonialism for years now.'

During maths lessons Sally fumed at Henry Leung. She hated him so much she had to break her hatred of the maths teacher down, loathing one segment at a time: the mad professor's crest of hair; the yucky pimples on his chin; the buniony wrists and trouser turn-ups flapping above his weakling ankles. Twice Mr Leung was so flustered by the glaring student in the third row, second desk from the left, he had to stop teaching mid-sentence. Chalk hovering over quadratic equation, he asked Sally if anything was troubling her. Sally narrowed her eyes, letting the evil Svengali know she saw through his nerdy maths teacher disguise. Slowly, she shook her head. And Mr Leung nervously resumed teaching, though the girl's stare was enough to turn a man to stone.

One Saturday in April Frances telephoned Sally and invited her to sleep over.

'My father is away,' she said. 'Come over and we can drink whisky and mess about like old times.'

Flattered, Sally wheedled permission from her father. But once in Frances's bedroom she wished Mr Hargreaves had been stricter. Sally had been tricked into attending a DAP rally where the sole speaker was Frances Milnar (in her new activist's get-up of vest, dungarees and militant red bandanna). Sally swigged from a hip flask stolen from Mr Milnar's study and sulked.

'The Chinese have been abused by every ruling power in Malaysia. Exploited by the British. Tortured by the

Japanese. Accused of Communism and locked up in detention camps by the British again. And now trampled on by the Malays. Henry says we are just beginning to fight back. To realize that suffering is not the fate of the Chinese. To take power into our own hands and create a new multiracial nation.'

A flame of whisky shot down Sally's throat and the warmth of the stolen liquor spread across her chest. *Absinthe makes the heart grow fonder – C. Dulwich, 1948.* Sally traced the etching in the flask's silver with her fingertip, wondering who C. Dulwich was and what 'absinthe' meant. As she sprawled on the bed, Frances paced like a caged animal, from wardrobe to door, door to wardrobe, ranting, frustrated by the rules that governed her seventeen-year-old life, preventing her from giving one hundred per cent of her heart, body and soul to the campaign.

Sally was sleepy and bored. Though the ceiling fan spun like mad, rattling and threatening to tear loose from its bracket, the breeze was negligible and she felt as if a great dog were panting its muggy breath over her. Sally threw back her head and yodelled a massive yawn. When she finished her yawn she was amazed to see Frances still pacing and talking to herself, oblivious to her boredom. *Enough!* thought Sally.

'You're in love with Mr Leung, aren't you?' she said.

Frances blushed. For the first time in days the wind dropped from behind her sails. There were no lines in the DAP election manifesto to counter such an allegation.

'I don't know,' she admitted.

'What about him? Is he in love with you?'

'I think he likes me, yes.'

Frances smiled self-consciously at her toes. Sally smiled too, hoping the non-participation of her eyes wasn't too obvious.

'Wow,' she said, trying to inject her flat tone with enthusiasm. 'Has he said anything to you? Kissed you or anything?'

'No,' said Frances, shaking her head a touch too ruefully for Sally's liking, 'He would never . . . not yet anyway. Not while I'm still his student. But he says he's leaving Amethyst at the end of term. And so am I. He wants to be a candidate for the DAP and I'm going to help him . . . I . . . I don't know how I know he likes me. I just do. You know when you just know?'

Sally nodded, though she had no idea.

'Anyway,' Frances blinked the sun spots of adoration from her eyes, 'the elections come first. We must focus on making Malaysia an equal society for all. And once that has been accomplished, we'll see what happens.'

'But . . .' Sally flailed for grounds to object to the romance, 'isn't he really old?'

'He's not that old! He's only twenty-nine. That's only twelve years older than I am. My mother was thirteen years older than my father.'

'Yes, and look at what a success they made of that.'

Frances flinched at this wasp-sting of sarcasm. 'That's not funny,' she said.

But she forgave Sally in a heartbeat, inoculated

against snideness by the chemicals of infatuation. Frances bounced on the bed, hugging her knees to her chest, untying and retying her red bandanna as she analysed every possible sign of the maths teacher's attraction to her. Every look, gesture and word. Sally's jealousy was an acid haze, sharpening with every breath. Why did she feel so jilted?

The adult Sally Hargreaves understands the mechanics of jealousy better than her teenage self. She can now put up her hand and own up to her only-child selfishness, the deleterious effects of an adolescence spent in the wilderness of solitude. Sally was an emotional infant, not happy that Frances was happy, only seething at the loss of her friend. Her confidante's hostility didn't escape Frances's notice and before long the mutual resentment was stifling, each girl withdrawing into her own silence.

They stood back to back as they changed for bed, as if preparing for a midnight duel. The darkness of the bedroom was usually a whispering darkness, tactile with messages traced on each other's backs. But after the light blinked out nothing more was said. They lay apart on the mattress, bodies suffocated by heavy, slow-moving tides of heat. Sally listened to Frances's shallow wide-awake breathing. She didn't blame her for not wanting to talk.

Much later they were woken by the clattering of stones, a fistful of gravel pitched up against the fortress of sleep. The mattress springs creaked as Frances sat up.

'What was that?'

'What was what?' mumbled Sally.

The slats of the window shutters rattled again, as if the sky were raining scree.

'That – there!'

Sally yawned, groggy and incurious. Let whoever was throwing stones throw stones. They'd get bored eventually and go away. Frances had a more confrontational attitude. She leapt energetically out of bed and sprang across the room. She threw open the shutters, as if to catch the person unawares.

'You!' Frances cried. 'What do you want!'

The stone-thrower hollered something back. Sally couldn't make out the words, but the voice was unmistakable: that majestic drawl, the husky edges as ragged as torn silk. Only one person she knew owned such a voice. Frances turned excitedly from the window, her cotton camisole shimmering like satin in the glow of the street lamp.

'It's Delilah! And she's drunk!'

Needing no further encouragement, Sally padded to the window. Two storeys below, Delilah stared up from the empty street, her mahogany hair cascading in soft waves over her shoulders and the straps of her black evening dress. Though her face was porcelain and composed, her posture betrayed her drunkenness. She staggered and swayed, heels clipping the pavement, a lone drunken tap-dancer under the street-light dome.

'Gosh! She's sozzled!'

Sally could hardly believe her eyes. The Queen of Amethyst, who glided to her every destination like some heavenly creature, lurching about, three sheets to the wind!

'What do you want?' called Frances.

'I've come to see Christopher,' Delilah said, cut glass and authoritative, the disciplined muscle of her tongue sober and precise.

'He's not here,' Frances said.

'Then I shall come inside and wait for him.'

'He's on a business trip to Hong Kong and won't be back till Tuesday.'

'Then I shall wait until Tuesday!'

'Don't be stupid. I think you should go home.'

'Let me in or you'll regret it!'

'Ooooh!'

Frances laughed, and Sally felt a hot bolt of shame, as if she were Delilah's surrogate conscience.

'Maybe we should call her a taxi,' Sally whispered. 'Or let her come inside and have some coffee to sober up,'

'No way,' Frances hissed. 'Look at the state of her!'

'Exactly. Look at the state of her. We can't just leave her in the street.'

'Yes, we can. She found her own way here, and she can find her own way home. *Go away, Delilah! My father's in Hong Kong! Go home!*'

Frances reached over the ledge to pull the shutters to and Delilah crouched down. For one shocked moment Sally thought Delilah had squatted to urinate. But the Amethyst Queen quickly stood up again and swung her arm in a great arc, opening her fist at the highest point, so stones and gutter dirt flew up to the open window.

The girls shrieked, lifting hands to gravel-stung cheeks as the grit pit-pattered across the bedroom floor. Sally's eyes watered, flickering with bits of sand. She tasted dirt in her mouth.

'She's gone mad!' said Frances. 'Who does she think she is?'

Another volley came in through the window and scattered, pinging over the floor. Sally stood to one side and Frances dived into the bathroom, from which came the sound of gushing water.

'Oh my God!' said Sally. 'You aren't . . .'

Water slopped over the rim of the bucket as Frances re-entered the bedroom and marched to the window, stony-faced with intent. She heaved the bucket up to the ledge and flung out the contents with all the strength in her arms. An amorphous wave leapt through the air, momentarily liberated from gravity, before crashing down in the street.

Delilah screamed as though impaled by a bucket of knives. Everything clung to her: hair plastered to her scalp; black velvet dress sopping wet against the willowy length of her. She had the slippery look of a new-born calf, soaked in the amniotic fluids. Her collar-bones stuck out like angry blades, her ribs prominent as her chest heaved in fury. She seethed up at them, spitting with her eyes. Sally guessed that the water had sobered her up. Faces appeared in the upstairs window of the gambling house across the street. Delilah plucked at her evening dress, sodden against her thighs, as if she couldn't believe her humiliation was real. In one ruthlessly efficient act

Frances had reduced Delilah to a B-movie swamp creature. It couldn't be done. Yet it had been.

'If you dare come here again, I'll chuck another bucket over you!' threatened Frances.

She slammed the shutters, what became of Delilah on the street no longer her concern. Light from the bathroom slanted across the bedroom floor. The girls stared at each other, stunned by what had just happened. Then they dissolved into giggles, tension dissipating.

'Did you see her face?'

'She looked like she was going to explode!'

'Like a human volcano . . .'

'Has she gone? Quick, check!'

'She's gone!'

'She must hate us! She'll get us back at school.'

'Who cares! It was worth it!'

They sat up in bed, too keyed-up to sleep, giggling and chatting away the hour before dawn. Sally listened as Frances's breathing deepened into sleep, and awake alone she saddened. She knew the revival of intimacy would be gone when Frances woke to the new day and remembered her affections now lay elsewhere.

22

The crowd at King's Cross is chaotic, a rummage sale of coats and scarves. Tides of commuters, minds elsewhere, navigate the crush of winter bodies on autopilot. Outside, traffic grinds, indicators flash, and the evening is cold and drizzly black.

Adam drifts along the edges, where the homeless huddle on the pavement, shaking coins in styrofoam cups. He is weary enough to drop down among them, to hide in the hood of his jacket and watch the march of rain-soaked shoes, the puddle splatters on the back of nylon tights. But he goes inside the station and stands by a ticket machine, staring through the smokescreen of commuters until the dealers emerge. Deals are negotiated with a flicker of eye contact, foil packets removed from the underside of tongues and slipped into open palms; tickets to oblivion exchanged for cash. A young junkie, a necrophiliac's pin-up girl, straggles in dazed circles, a wanderer lost in the human forest. Adam is sure he'll see Julia if he hangs about for long enough; that she will turn up, *like a bad penny*, as their grandfather used to say.

But he doesn't see Julia. The person he sees is Mischa. Taller than most of the crowd, with his dark, scruffy mop of hair, the strap of his laptop case cutting across his leather jacket. Adam's heart stutters as he shouts his name, for a moment overjoyed. (What are the chances! Here in the rush-hour stampede!) Then he sees Mischa's reluctant smile and is hot with shame. Mischa swerves towards Adam, greets him with a hug. Adam asks how he is, and Mischa is an explosion of words: travels overseas, manic busyness, the strange quirks life has thrown up. He hasn't changed, his mind scattered and bright. Adam shakes at his own selfishness. Why can't he be happy that Mischa is happy? Instead his throat is clamped tight with the knowledge that he hasn't been thought of in months. Everything that is awkward about Adam rises to the surface. When it's his turn to speak he cannot think of a single thing to say. With nervous effort, he strings together maggoty sentences, as Mischa nods, politely overlooking the stammering errors of speech. He has to catch a train to Oxford and rushes away, suggesting they meet after his return. Adam leaves the station, Julia forgotten.

23

'Lemme see your finger.'
'No. Get lost.'
'C'mon . . . give us a look . . .'
'Adam, *no!* Get off me!'
The doctor had instructed that the finger be cleaned and disinfected three times a day. But after an evening of kisses and cuddles, strawberry ice cream and maternal repentance, Frances withdrew again to her room. Check-up appointment: forgotten; thrice-daily cleaning of the wound: forgotten. Julia swallowed the kidney-bean-sized painkillers morning, noon and night, but ignored the bandages, let the once sterile dressing get filthy and frayed. She developed a phobia of what lay beneath, of letting anyone touch her hand. Out of sight, out of mind, was her attitude. When Madame Tay chased her with antiseptic and a roll of lint, Julia fled downstairs to the fabric store and crawled

under the cashier desk, from where she observed the beehived manageress smiling as her decades-old enemy waddled up and down Sultan Road calling Julia's name. Frustrated, Madame Tay enlisted the help of Adam, who thoroughly enjoyed the sanctioned beating-up of his sister, toppling her to the floor in a flying tackle and sitting astride her chest as she screamed herself blue in the face. He pinned down her wrists as Madame Tay squatted and unwound the dirty bandages, *ai-ooo ai-ooo*ing as she tended to the pus-oozing stump. Julia screamed and kicked throughout the ordeal, her ribcage crushed by eight and a half stone of brother, her face, contorted by a deep irrational fear, twisted as far from the mutilated finger as her neck tendons would allow. When it was over Julia wept bitterly, stormed away from the scene of her violation, antiseptic wafting from the clean swaddling of bandages.

In the bedroom at night Adam rapped his knuckle against the bedstead.

'Julia, Julia, hear that . . . ?' he'd whisper. 'That's the ghost of your finger, come back to haunt the bleeding stump . . .'

He kneaded grains of cooked rice into pellets and scattered them on Julia's bedsheets so she yelped, disgusted, as they squidged against her thighs. *Yuck, what's this?* she exclaimed. Adam said they were flesh-eating maggots, attracted by the rotting-meat stench of her hand. Julia chucked the rice maggots at her brother as he lay sniggering into his pillow. *Sicko*, she hissed.

Had they been in England Frances would have

spanked Adam with a hairbrush for tormenting his sister. But they weren't in England, and Frances rarely saw her children, as she rarely left her room. She began sleeping in an old nightie from her adolescence, dug out of her chest of drawers, the once virginal white cotton faded to the colour of dead grass. The bodice flattened her breasts and the collar of lace ruffles choked her neck. Dark patches of sweat blossomed under the arms and the garment was irresistible to stains. But Frances was as attached to the nightie as Julia to her bandages.

One morning, a week after the accident, Adam stumbled, yawning, into the hallway bathroom and saw the sink was clogged with black stuff – as if the plughole had coughed something nasty out of its depths. The substance looked tarry, like the residue from a smoker's lung, but when Adam touched his fingers to it he felt the dry and splintery texture of chopped hair. Cut tresses wreathed the dais of the wash basin and were strewn across the tiled floor. On the toilet-seat lid was a knife – one of Madame Tay's vegetable-chopping knives, dark wisps feathering the blade. Adam grabbed the wooden handle and went in search of his mother.

Frances was at the breakfast table, drinking a glass of soya-bean milk. Her once shoulder-length hair was shorn to a spiky mutilated inch, with a few neglected strands dangling at the back and the shoulders of her decrepit nightgown sprinkled with sawn-off tufts. Madame Tay was scooping the black caviar of seeds out of a halved papaya, and Julia munched on a banana, staring at her mother's hair. Adam laid on the table the weapon Frances had used to massacre her locks, thinking it a miracle she hadn't scalped herself.

'You look really stupid,' he said. 'Why didn't you use scissors like a normal person?'

'It'll look nicer once you've trimmed the sticky-out bits,' reassured Julia. 'I'll do it for you if you like.'

Madame Tay slid the plate of papaya over to Frances. Frances lifted a slice with her fingers, sank her teeth into the succulent orange flesh and stared through her son as if he wasn't there.

'You've made a mess of the bathroom. There's hair everywhere!' he said. 'You should clean up after yourself!'

There were echoes of Frances's *Change your socks! Eat your broccoli! Don't put that chewing-gum behind your ear!* in his voice, and this depressed Adam. He was only fourteen. Whether Frances noticed that he'd inherited her nagging streak he couldn't tell. But true to the reversal of roles, she ignored him.

Later that morning, while Frances was brushing her teeth, Adam sneaked into her bedroom and stole her hand-luggage bag. He and Julia unzipped the holdall and shook out the contents on to the floor of their grandfather's study. There was a purse with no money or credit cards in it, tampons, lip salve, cherry Strepsils, money-off coupons for Daz Ultra and Weetabix, and some headphones stolen off the plane. No passports and no return tickets. They checked every compartment twice.

'I reckon we should go to the British Embassy,' said Adam, crunching a Strepsil lozenge, mouth a-swim with cherry-flavoured saliva. 'Say our mum's gone schizo and kidnapped us. They'll give us free tickets back to London.'

'She hasn't gone schizo, Adam.'

'Yeah, she has. Why d'you think she chopped off her hair? The voices told her to do it. I think we should go to the police.'

'No way. They'll arrest her.'

'She deserves to be arrested.'

'No, she doesn't!'

'Look what she did to your finger.'

'She didn't do it on purpose. Maybe she'll get better soon. Maybe Madame Tay can help us . . .'

'You must be joking! Madame Tay *likes* it that she's gone crazy. She wants Mum to stay here *for ever*. We have to tell someone what's going on.'

'Oh, please, Adam, not yet. There must be something else we can do.'

'Like what . . . ?'

Julia told Adam her idea, and Adam told Julia it was stupid and would never work. He refused to participate. At noon they played blackjack as they waited for Madame Tay to serve lunch. Frances sleepwalked into the room and sank, yawning, into a chair, her face puffy and seamed with pillow creases. Adam could see the cloudiness in her eyes, the veil suspended between her and reality. Frances was punch-drunk, her brain soupy in the tropical heat. She'd sit through the meal as if she were dreaming it. Adam wished his sister luck. Madame Tay came down from the kitchen with a tray of skewered grilled chicken and a dish of peanut sauce. Satay was Julia's favourite food. It was as if Madame Tay's telepathic powers had rumbled Julia's plan, then shown her how best to sabotage them. As her mother and brother each plucked a kebab from the tray Julia stood up.

'I'm not eating,' she announced. 'I'm on hunger strike.'

Frances dipped her chicken in the peanut sauce and twisted the skewer to coat the charred meat.

'Did you hear me? I said I'm on hunger strike,' Julia repeated. 'I'm not eating until you take us back to England.'

Frances regarded her daughter through the tired holes of her eyes. She chewed and chewed and chewed, then swallowed.

'Fine,' she said. 'Starve yourself, then.'

'I will!'

Julia stomped and slammed out of the room.

After lunch Adam found her sitting on her bed, in optimistic spirits, despite the lacklustre reception of Operation Hunger Strike.

'It won't work,' he said. 'She doesn't give a toss.'

Adam listed the reasons why the hunger strike was stupid. First, Julia lacked will-power. Second, it would take a very long time, possibly weeks of self-punishment, before the results were visible. And third, and most important, blackmail is only effective when you threaten something that matters to the victim. Back in England life had been rife with rules and prohibitions. They'd had to clear their dinner plates of every last runner bean under pain of death. But here they could do as they pleased. Jaywalk across a six-lane motorway, dance naked with the beggars in the marketplace. What did Frances care, holed up in her room?

But Julia was undeterred. Barricaded in the bedroom, she refused to open the door when Madame Tay came knocking with cakes and sugar-cane juice, rattling the doorknob and crying, *Ju-li-aah, Ju-li-aah!* A two-litre plastic bottle was Julia's companion throughout the hunger strike, filled hourly from the lukewarm bathroom tap. Lying on her bed, she drank until the bottle was empty and her bladder full, and another trip to the bathroom was necessary to reverse this state of affairs. The water-drinking regime continued until bedtime and Adam lost count of the litres that flushed through her internal plumbing. She was a human waterworks. Overflowing pipes and gushing spout.

'Give it a rest, Julia,' he said. 'You'll rupture your kidneys. People *die* from drinking too much water, you know.'

'Good,' said Julia, swigging from the bottle.

That night Julia's stomach gurgled a lullaby and Adam was strangely comforted by the belly-burbling, drifting off to sleep full of gratitude to be well fed.

Day two of the hunger strike was also spent in the bedroom, guzzling water at a rate of two litres per hour and solving crossword puzzles. The Harelip Twins called for her, but Julia wouldn't disrupt her ascetic regime to go out and play. She arranged her make-up like surgical implements on the dressing table and painted rainbows on her eyelids and a butterfly on her lips. She practised gymnastics. The splits, the crab, belly sloshing as she stood on her head then strode about on her hands. She peeled the scabs off her shins, nibbling them a little before stowing them away in a matchbox. She picked the hardened mucus out of her nostrils, ate it, and was then stricken by a purist's guilt. She zipped herself into a musty old sleeping bag and wriggled caterpillar-like across the floor. Lying on her back, with the soles of her feet she climbed the walls.

On day three of the hunger strike Julia was tearful and fractious. When Adam strutted into the bedroom after lunch, patting his belly and yum-yumming about Madame Tay's shrimp noodles, Julia shrieked at him and crawled, sobbing, under her bed. Adam wasn't the least bit surprised when he heard her sneak out of the bedroom in the dead of night. He listened for the distant creak of the kitchen door, then crept after her. He caught her red-handed on the roof, juice and seeds dribbling down her chin as she devoured a crescent moon of watermelon. When she saw Adam she threw the watermelon rind on to the roof of the jeweller's next door. Adam clicked on the light.

'Watermelon's ninety per cent water!' she said, wiping her sticky fingers on her vest. 'It doesn't count as food!'

'Yeah, it does. You wouldn't catch Mahatma Gandhi

stuffing himself with watermelon on a hunger strike.'

'It's not proper food, though – not the same as rice or potatoes . . .' Drained of conviction, her voice trailed off.

'C'mon, Julia. You're starving yourself for nothing.'

Adam lit the stove to boil water. When the kettle whistled he made cocoa sweetened with condensed milk and raided the cupboard for biscuits. Julia leant on the balustrade, staring forlornly across the armada of rooftops. The night droned with air-conditioning units as they drank the chocolate and ate until all the Jacob's cream crackers were gone. Julia put down her mug, wiping her chocolate moustache and the fine-beaded sweat off her face with her bandaged hand. She pushed some straggly hair out of her eyes and turned imploringly to Adam.

'I've had a false start,' she said stubbornly. 'I'll begin again tomorrow.'

Julia brushed the crumbs off her vest, scattering them into the alley below. They went back to the bedroom, and later, when Adam heard Julia snivelling in the dark, he really couldn't understand why she was so power-fully convinced that their fate was determined by whether or not she starved.

24

The fallout came without alarm bells or warning. They had been coming apart slowly for weeks, like icebergs in a semi-frozen sea, when Frances suddenly reversed, crashing full-speed into Sally, smashing their friendship to smithereens.

Sally was standing at a basin in the toilets, rinsing her sudsy hands under the tap. Along the row of mirrors Amethyst girls dawdled before morning registration, gossiping and fiddling with plaits and hair slides, cubicle doors opening and closing, lizards darting across the peeling paint of the walls. The toilets were dark and a strong chemical odour of bleach-mopped floors pulsed through the humidity (usurped, as the day progressed, by cigarette smoke breathed from inexperienced mouths, and other, more scatological fumes). As Sally stooped over the gushing tap, she felt a prod on her shoulder. She turned round.

'Hello, Fra—' The last syllable was knocked out of her as Frances shoved her in the chest, so her thighs bashed the basin rim. Sally's hands flew up in self-defence, fingers webbed with soap suds. 'What?' she said.

Frances was puffy and tear-soaked, tiny blood vessels raging in the whites of her eyes. Her eyelids were swollen and discoloured, as if they'd been punched.

'Why did you do it?' shouted Frances.

'Do what?'

'You know what you did!'

'I don't know what you're talking about.'

The gossiping, mirror-gazing and hair-fiddling halted as the roomful of schoolgirl eyes pivoted towards the brawl. A flush chain was yanked and a cistern surged. Even as she stared, panic-fraught, into her best friend's furious face, Sally was conscious of the visual comedy of the confrontation. Little Frances Milnar attacking her shy giantess friend like a scrappy Yorkshire terrier. As though provoked by Sally's inner mortification, Frances shoved her again with both hands.

'Liar!'

The word tore from her mouth; a bullet ripping into Sally's vulnerable flesh. Her heart beat accelerated and her breathing wheezed. To push Frances away would require hardly any effort, but her arms hung like dead things by her side. She was conscience-stricken, guilty of her unknown crime.

'I honestly don't know what you're talking about!'

'Well, congratulations. He's leaving the school.'

'Who?'

'You know who!'

'It had nothing to do with me!'

Frances slapped her. Sally was too stunned even to lift a hand to the scalded cheek. The toilet audience quivered in delight. The young ladies of the Amethyst school were unaccustomed to violence. Conflict among the girls was usually subtle, with harm inflicted via psychological means. The bell clanged for registration but no one moved.

'You're jealous,' said Frances, calmer now, as if her hysteria had been dissipated in the slap, 'so you had to ruin everything. You make me sick! Don't ever come near me. Don't you ever come near me again!'

Sally, shaking, her chin wobbling, was on the verge of tears. Frances barged through the gaggle of schoolgirls and out of the door. The girls swooped on Sally at once, cooing in sympathy and patting her arm, relishing the gossip to be spread. Sally had never been so popular.

'Are you OK? Oh dear . . . don't cry.'

'Don't worry, Sal. We all saw what happened. She was crazy! Like someone had spiked her cornflakes with acid! Don't worry about her . . . That was assault. You could get her suspended for that . . . Do you *really* not know what you've done?'

One slap and a hot blast of fury, and Sally was back in the shoes of the timid nobody she'd been on her first

370

day at Amethyst. Lessons passed in a trance, pen scribbling unthinkingly in her exercise book, the teachers' mouths making unintelligible shapes and sounds. She mentally scripted powerful emotive speeches protesting her innocence and fantasized about Frances apologizing meekly for leaping to false conclusions, though these dreams of reconciliation were shattered by a mere sideways glance at Frances, seething like a swarm of wasps. During breaks Sally hid in a toilet stall, listening to the clatter of lavatory seats, jet-streams of pee, and the whispers of teenage girls rustling like taffeta skirts. She peeled the flaking skin from her lips as she hid, so by the afternoon her mouth was raw and bludgeoned-looking. When school was finally over, she was desperate to go home after the worst day of her life. But after a surreal interception at the school gates, Sally found herself at quarter past four in the bedroom of Delilah Jones, with Delilah and the Perak palm-oil dynasty twins Lillian and Meredith.

The Jones residence was on a hill overlooking the Lake Gardens. The girls sat on rococo-style chairs by the sunny ceiling-high window as a Bob Dylan LP spun on the record player (to which Lillian gyred her head, eyes slitted in pleasure, as though there was something tantric and mystical in the tambourine shakes, guitar strumming and the singer mumbling off-key). A Chinese servant in a traditional maid's outfit entered and set down a silver tray of iced tea and sandwiches. *Thank you, Mimi*, said Delilah, and the servant departed without a word. (How professional, Sally thought admiringly, at the same time feeling an unprecedented pang of affection for the giggly Safiah and her never-combed hair.) As Delilah poured out glasses of iced tea and the heiress twins compared notes on the afternoon geography test, Sally gazed about the bedroom. Everywhere was startling evidence of the Amethyst Queen's corporeality: rose-bud-studded bra strewn across the parquet floor; the sensuous disorder of bed-sheets where she'd slept in the night; dressing table cluttered by perfume bottles, worn-down lipsticks and mascara-streaked cotton pads; hairbrush tangled with demerara-brown hair. Kandinsky posters were taped to the walls, as well as black-and-white prints of nude women (the lascivious array of buttocks and breasts confusing Sally – was Delilah a lesbian?). On the bed-side table was a well-thumbed stack of *Time* magazine and *The Economist*. Unorthodox reading matter for a teenage girl.

'Feel free to borrow anything you like,' said Delilah, waving towards the bookshelves. Sally read the cracked spines: Miller, Lawrence, Kerouac, Burroughs . . . 'I've dog-eared the pages with the dirty bits.'

When they'd descended on her at the school gates Sally had been afraid. Delilah's smile was too bright for someone drenched and humiliated by a bucket of water only three nights before, and Sally declined the in-vitation to tea. But they'd pleaded and cajoled (*Oh, you simply must!* insisted the smiling identical twins) and Sally, who'd never acquired the skill of putting her foot down, gave in. Revenge seemed the most likely motive, and as they strolled through the old Colonial District Sally wondered what punishment they had in store. Were they going to shave her eyebrows? Force-feed her with slugs? Whatever it was, Sally knew she was defenceless. Resigned to her fate, she sat in the rococo-style chair, eating a dainty cucumber and salmon paté sandwich (despite her nervousness she was peckish) and waiting for Delilah and the twins to turn nasty. But Sally's accosters remained perfectly congenial, grumbling about exams and parents and planning an outing to see *The Graduate* at the Federal Cinema. The twins ignored the sandwiches, cupid's-bow lips puckering around the cigarettes they chain-smoked. They wore their hair in pigtails with cute little fringes cut an inch above their eyebrows, dextrous, finely plucked arches that leapt about the stage of their forehead in mesmerizing performance. Whereas Delilah discoursed lengthily in her deep intelligent voice, Lillian and Meredith were pithy and quick, squeaky as speeded-up tape recordings.

'We're going to toss a coin to see who gets Sebastian this summer.'

'We took it in turns over Easter and wore the poor boy out!'

'So tired he could barely lift his ski poles!'

'Sebastian had no idea what we were up to.'

'He thought we were both Lillian!'

'We both fancied him.'

'And we were brought up to share.'

'Any other way would be selfish.'

'You should see him, Sal! He's scrumptious!'

'We swapped every other night.'

'Sometimes twice a night.'

'Sebastian had dark circles under his eyes for two weeks.'

'He used to be a real skirt-chaser, but now he wants to settle down with us.'

'Sebastian wants to marry us.'

'We can't make up our mind.'

The twins chimed with laughter and Delilah smiled and rolled her eyes. Sally didn't know what to think. Were they pulling her leg? Or were they really both sleeping with the Czechoslovakian ski instructor? Either way, they confirmed Sally's deep-seated belief that identical twins are spooky and strange.

'Do you have a boyfriend, Sal?' Delilah asked gently.

A redundant question if ever she'd heard one. Everything about her screamed: *Never been kissed!* Sally shook her head.

'So what type do you go for, then?' enquired Lillian.

Sally was flattered by the assumption she had a choice in the matter. All men seemed beyond the realms of possibility (especially Mr Milnar – her fantasy husband and the most handsome man she'd ever set eyes on). Sally told them she liked Mick Jagger, hoping he'd meet with their approval. The other three laughed.

'Well, it seems unlikely we'll run into Mick at the Selangor Club,' said Delilah, 'but don't worry, we'll find someone for you.'

Sally smiled politely, keen to move on from the

perilous subject of the opposite sex before her painful inexperience was drawn out.

A wreath of cigarette smoke around her pigtailed head, Meredith reached out and tugged a strand of Sally's hair.

'I know of a genius of a hairdresser on Bukit Bintang Road,' she said. 'He'll really tame this frizz for you . . .'

The advice stopped mid-sentence as Delilah flashed her a warning look.

'Of course,' gushed Lillian, 'your hair is lovely as it is. I'd kill for your natural curl!'

Though Sally's bust-up with Frances was the talk of the fifth form, none of them mentioned it. It wasn't long, however, before the departure of Henry Leung was discussed. Lillian and Meredith were heated in their disapproval.

'Bloody thoughtless of him to leave us in the lurch a month before exams!'

'I heard he left to concentrate on his politics.'

'If politics is so important to him, then he shouldn't have become a teacher in the first place!'

'Absolutely. He was lucky to get his job at Amethyst. International schools pay three times what the local schools pay.'

'Who's going to replace him? Not Miss McPhee, I hope.'

'I wouldn't worry too much,' said Delilah. 'We've covered the syllabus from A to Z already.'

'Not logarithms,' grumbled Lillian. 'I lost three per cent in the mock paper because I got stuck multiplying logs.'

'What's the name of the party he belongs to, again?'

'The Democratic Action Party,' said Sally: 'the DAP.'

'The DAP,' repeated Delilah. 'I can't keep track of all these acronyms. These elections are like alphabet soup.'

'I can't wait for the city to get back to normal. There's been such an unpleasant atmosphere lately,' said Lillian.

'Yes, don't these people know how to hold a civilized rally,' sniffed Meredith, 'without throwing bricks or setting fire to things?'

'It's quite exciting, though, if you think about it,' said Delilah. 'If the Opposition win enough seats in these elections there will be radical changes in Malaysian government. The non-Malay races will have power for the first time ever in Malaysian history. It's fantastic the minorities are standing up to be counted. So what if there's some upheaval along the way? Being civilized never got anyone anywhere.'

The twins nodded, though Delilah's excitement was lost on them. Minor irritations, such as traffic jams caused by marches, and their Chinese maths teacher running off to fight the good fight (without having covered logarithms in the O-level syllabus first), annoyed the twins more than the racial injustices of their host country. Sally wondered what Frances would think if she knew Delilah sympathized with her political views. She'd probably like her a bit better, she reckoned.

Before the twins left they told Sally that it had been a pleasure getting to know her and kissed her on both

cheeks (kisses suffused with loveliness, briefly transforming frog girl to princess). As Delilah saw the twins
to the front gate Sally sat in the stillness, her mind
racing with the surrealness of the past hour. What on
earth was she doing in Delilah Jones's bedroom? The
Amethyst clique had strict rules about who they social-
ized with; they were frugal with friendly gestures, even
at the level of a nod hello. Why had they lowered their
standards so drastically for a social pariah like herself?
Sally knew it had something to do with Delilah getting
that bucket of water chucked over her on Saturday
night.

'Almond and plum cakes,' Delilah announced
brightly as she returned to the bedroom with a tray,
'imported from England. I've been waiting for an
excuse to eat the rest of these!' Crossing her legs in her
chair with a yogic flair suggestive of double-joints and
a resistance to pins and needles, Delilah lit a cigarette.
Outside, the sky glowed with a burnt-orange sunset,
lighting Delilah so her hair shone russet and a few
levitating strands scintillated like gold. Between
delicate puffs on her cigarette Delilah played at being
the attentive hostess. Would Sally like some apple
juice? A fork to eat her cake? What record would she
like to listen to? Did she like Jimi Hendrix? Sally didn't
touch the cakes. Why was Delilah trying so hard?

Spurred by the sense that something was amiss Sally
said: 'Why did you invite me here? It's because of the
other night, isn't it? Because of what Frances did to you.'
The torrent of words rushed out before Sally lost her

nerve. Delilah's smile drained like colour from her face. 'You must be absolutely *raging* about what happened. Did you invite me here so you could get your own back?'

Delilah's lips parted slightly in bewilderment. 'Why ever did you come back with us if you thought I was luring you here to "get my own back"?' she asked.

'I suppose I thought if you wanted to get your own back, you'd find some way to do it eventually . . .' (God, she sounded like a complete *drip*.) 'May as well be sooner rather than later.'

'Well, you can relax,' said Delilah. 'I didn't invite you here so I could have my wicked revenge. I did it so I could apologize and explain.'

'Explain?' echoed Sally.

'I was in a very bad way the other night,' Delilah began. 'I drank too much and I was thinking non-stop about Christopher. I wanted to see him and I knew that if I knocked on the door that old Chinese housekeeper he lives with would send me away. So I threw stones at Frances's window. My memory goes blank after that. I can't remember what I was shouting . . . No, don't tell me . . . I'm sure I was perfectly charming. I was *furious* when I got drenched. But I deserved it. You both did me a favour by helping me to realize how pathetic I'd become.'

As she spoke, Sally had some difficulty reconciling the two versions of Delilah: the sophisticated warrior-queen she knew from school and the vulnerable teenager sitting in front of her, coiling her hair round her forefinger, legs hugged to her chest as if for security.

'I walked home,' said Delilah, 'and in the fifteen minutes it took me I decided that enough was enough. I've become my own worst enemy. What you and Frances did made me realize how low I have sunk. How mad I have become.'

'There's no need to be so hard on yourself,' said Sally.

'But it's true,' Delilah said. 'I miss Christopher so much, I lose control of myself. I act like a crazy person. I don't think I will ever, ever get over him.'

Delilah's eyes brightened, moistened, then were obscured by tumbling curtains of hair as she bowed her head. She pressed her fingers to her eyes, as if to damn the tear ducts. Tears leaked into the back of her throat, making her voice sound like gravel.

'Christopher and I had an affair many months ago –' (Sally bit her tongue to curb an excited cry to be privy to such scandal) 'if what happened between us can be classified as an affair. I'm not sure, it was so brief . . .' Delilah gave a bitter laugh. 'I don't blame him for any of it. I was sixteen when we first met, and for me it was love at first sight. But Christopher is different from other men. He didn't seem to notice me, no matter how aggressively I flirted, what clothes I wore or how witty and seductive I was. When I did eventually get his attention, he was irritated more than anything. But I pursued him and pursued him, and last year he finally gave in. After that I thought he'd want to see me again. But he was beside himself with guilt. He said he had made a terrible mistake and that it must never happen again. He was terrified of Frances finding out. He said she would never forgive him. I wouldn't listen. I argued with him. I was *filthy* with jealousy. I felt as though he'd chosen his daughter over me. I thought of Frances as a rival. Ridiculous, I know, but I was consumed by madness – something I'm only beginning to recover from. I'm starting to see things clearly again, to see things as they are – thank God! It's such a relief. I've behaved so disgustingly . . .'

Wow, thought Sally, a bit filthy with jealousy herself. Both she and Delilah had dreamt of Mr Milnar. But only Delilah had had the courage to go out and spin reality from the intangible stuff of daydreams. Residual madness and heartbreak aside, it was one hell of an accomplishment.

'Infatuation's a bastard.' Delilah sighed. 'Sometimes I wonder if the Christopher Milnar I'm obsessed with actually exists. If he is the same as the living, breathing man . . . If not, then who am I in love with? Where does this heartache come from? I'm trying to put it all behind me anyway,' she swallowed, as if to choke back the unpleasantness, 'but the pain won't disappear overnight. That's too much to ask. But at least I'm making a conscious effort to make myself better. To suck the poison out of the wound. That's why I'm trying to make things up with you and Frances. I tried to apologize to Frances this morning but . . . let's just say she was in a foul mood.'

'She's rather snappy today, isn't she?' agreed Sally.

'I regret everything. I regret my behaviour on

Saturday night. I regret the way I feel about Christopher. I'm trying not to be like this any more. I want to turn myself around. *We are not who we are, but the self we seek.* That's how I console myself.'

Sally nodded, not quite understanding, but liking the noble ring to the words.

'I'm not quite sure yet who I want to be. I'm figuring it out through a process of elimination. I know I don't want to be the kind of girl who makes life miserable for a man who doesn't care for her. Or throws stones at windows in the middle of the night. I don't want to hold grudges. I just want to be well again.'

Delilah phoned Mr Hargreaves's office and charmed him into letting his daughter stay for supper. Sally was jittery at first, afraid she was too dull for clever Delilah. But Delilah had a talent for coaxing Sally out of her shyness and the hours whizzed by in a blur of non-stop talking. Sally recounted the miserable boarding-school years and the chronic illnesses that had consigned her to the sick-bay. The home tutoring and reclusive bedroom years. She spoke of her adoration for Frances and the exhilarating friendship crudely interrupted by the evil Henry Leung (abusing his teaching position to brainwash a student!). And then Frances had viciously attacked her like a wildcat for God knows what, but Sally certainly had nothing to do with Mr Leung leaving the school if that was what it was about!

Delilah was full of wit and insight, transforming negatives to positives like a magician extracting ivory-winged doves from a seemingly empty top hat. From time to time Sally would be conscious of hogging the conversation, but a glance at Delilah's warm and intelligent face reassured her. Delilah was fascinated. She hooted with laughter, as though Sally was a brilliant comedian, and perched, riveted, on the edge of her seat. Sally was sorry when it was time to go home. Talking to Delilah made her feel invigorated and alive. She loved Delilah's frequent habit of introducing her name into the conversation (*What do you think, Sally? Was that before or after boarding school, Sally?*) so she flushed with pleasure, feeling special and cared for. Talking to Delilah showed Frances (who was never curious about Sally's secret yearnings and ambitions) to be childish and self-absorbed. Talking to Delilah was like an initiation into the adult world.

On the journey home Sally realized that over the course of the evening her entire life story had poured out. Jumbled and non-chronological, like misshapen jigsaw pieces for Delilah to fit together. She blushed to think how little she'd learnt of Delilah's life in return. How rude of her to have run away with the conversation like that. But Sally had been unable to help herself. To be the object of such furious attention was an addictive feeling, soothing her wounded ego and all but erasing the memory of the slap.

Sally was largely impervious to the battle for votes and the explosive violent aftermath, though thousands flocked to rallies in Petaling Jaya and manifestos loudspeakered streets near Sally's home. The booming speeches and hot-blooded cheers occasionally woke her as she drowsed on Saturday afternoons.

The day before the general elections Sally got stuck in a traffic jam as she was driven home from school. The gridlock was caused by the funeral procession for a Chinese teenager, killed by the Malay police who caught him painting anti-election slogans on a wall. Ten thousand marchers waved banners and chanted that the blood debt must be repaid, showing the city the defiance and might of the Chinese. Trapped in the sweltering car, Sally had glared at them. Her throat was parched and there was nothing to drink. Frances had been absent from school every day that week, and Sally had kept an eye out for her in the crowds. They were her people after all.

When the polls opened on Saturday 10 May, Sally hoisted the window blinds to a sky of blazing sun and cloudless blue. As she squeezed a pea-sized squirt of toothpaste on to her toothbrush, yawning in the bathroom mirror, on the other side of the city the Prime Minister prayed for election victory. As Sally spat the minty foam into the sink, the Tengku's chain of prayer beads broke, scattering across the floor in a menacing omen. Throughout the morning, as local dignitaries stalked by journalists and flashing camera bulbs made public declarations of party loyalty, Sally tackled her chemistry homework, cursing the day the periodic table was ever invented. As millions of polling cards were marked, the location of the 'X' motivated by race, ideology, illiteracy and last-minute changes of mind, Sally did her thigh-slimming exercises on the bedroom floor. In the evening, as the polls closed and the count commenced, Sally went to bed, exhausted by her day of inactivity.

Throughout Kuala Lumpur the election-night vigil began, crowds gathering in streets, gardens and private members' clubs, with beer and snacks and children up past their bedtime. The *padang* outside the Royal Selangor Club heaved with citizens waiting for results to flash up on the great illuminated signboard. As the city was wide awake, buzzing with election fever, Sally slept and dreamt. Results trickled in through the night, the Alliance losing seats, the Opposition coalition gaining them. As the Chinese and Indians celebrated the end of their political marginalization, the Malays sank into silence and gloom.

Sally woke on Sunday 11 May as the last revellers straggled home, the streets messy with streamers and celebratory confetti. She yawned and stretched, oblivious of the earthquake that had occurred, tearing apart the political landscape of Malaysia for good. She kicked the sheets off her body and contemplated the uneventful day ahead.

25

Adam lay beneath the gravity of shadows, his vertebrae pressed to the floor, the wood grain etched upon his back. The city heaved against the window shutters, and through the traffic vibrations and rattling of vendor carts he heard the skipping rope whacking concrete, the stomp of Reeboks and the chant of the playground rhyme Julia had taught the Harelip Twins:

> *Not last night but the night before,*
> *Three masked robbers came knocking at the door,*
> *And this is what they said . . . to . . . me . . .*
> *Turn around, touch the ground,*
> *Clap your hands, one, two, three . . .*

Adam imagined the twins turning the rope handles, spinning loops for Julia to jump through; the flight of pigtails as her Reeboks lifted off the ground, wounded rabbit's paw lifted to her chest as if secured in an invisible sling. Pedestrians tsk-tsked as they skirted the swinging rope, and the Good Fortune Fabric Emporium manageress came out to scold the nuisance girls, flames shooting from her dragon's mouth. Giggling, the skipping party shuffled further down the street, but they always inched their way back, as if the tinkling of the bell above the shop door lured them, like the melody of the Pied Piper's flute.

Adam thought of Frances, lying in the ruins of her nightdress, breathing her sourness in the next room. Two nights earlier Adam was woken by splashing, and followed the lapping of water to the wide-open bathroom door and his mother naked in the tub. The tap was blasting and a sheet of water spilled over the edge and pooled on the floor. Adam stepped carefully across the slippery tiles, reached across the bath and screwed the valve shut. He hadn't seen Frances naked since he was about seven, and was disturbed by her scrawny ribs and sagging breasts, the mottled goose-flesh veined with blue. *What are you doing?* he said. *The water's freezing.* The water dripped in reply. Frances didn't even look at him, arms resting on the sides of the tub as she reclined; mute queen with the faraway look of solitude in her eyes. *Bitch*, thought Adam. He wanted to slap her, shake her by her knife-hacked hair. But he went instead to bed. The silence, the absence of splashing, kept him awake for hours. Frances was dead, he knew it. Drowned. Glassy-eyed as a doll, lungs water-soaked sponges. Adam passed out, exhausted by his vigilant listening. And in the morning, when he saw Frances eating breakfast in her decrepit nightie, he was only half relieved she was alive.

The night after that they were woken by the three a.m. heart-attack shrill of the doorbell. It was the father of the Harelip Twins, with Frances in tow. He'd heard a disturbance in his furniture shop, gone down to investigate and found Frances sitting in a rocking chair. They were lucky he hadn't knocked her out cold with the badminton racket he was carrying! They were lucky he hadn't called the police! What was wrong with her anyway? Why didn't she speak? They should take her to the doctors, he advised. The Harelip Twins' father spoke crossly to the children as if Frances was a pet they'd let escape. And Adam nodded gravely, and Julia chewed saliva-wetted strands of hair. Then he spoke to Madame Tay in Malay for a very long time, while the children stared at Frances as she stood, dazed, in the parlour, indifferent to the trouble she'd caused.

She came to him as he slept, the mosquito nets rustling like dead leaves, the mattress springs barely creaking under the weight of her small body. Lifting the thin sheet and sliding beneath, she fumbled to him like a drunken lover. The ragged cord of his spine hunched against her, she buried her face in his shoulders, pushed her knees in the small of his back. The pressure of her, the heat seeping from her body into his, did not wake Adam. She burrowed deeper, trying to overcome her terrible loneliness, trying to disappear inside him like a baby marsupial burrowing into its mother's pouch. Adam jerked silently awake and flipped over, frozen for the moment it took to realize that the intruder in his bed was his sister. He shoved her and she whimpered, her hair like seaweed draped across her eyes, briny and damp, as if she'd washed up on a shore. He clicked on the lamp, saw she was wearing a dress and her Reeboks. Another shove, and he told her to get out of his bed.

'Can I sleep here, please?' she asked meekly. 'Please?'

The brackish smell coming off Julia sharpened, caustic as urine. It *was* urine. She'd wet her knickers; the mattress was soggy and stinking of wee.

'Urgh! Julia, that's disgusting. Get out!' Adam punched her chest, kicked her shin, and Julia sobbed. 'Why're you wearing your trainers? You been outside?'

Julia nodded. 'Please let me stay here.'

'Where've you been?'

'Mum,' she whispered. 'She's in the furniture shop again. I followed her there. I saw her through the window. She was taller. Her head was up by the ceiling and her feet were off the floor. She'd done it with my skipping rope.'

Adam lunged at Julia, tore her wrists apart. It was her voice that infuriated him most, the pathetic frailty of it. He shook her wrists, shook her limp bonelessness, and her head rolled from side to side, her eyes never meeting his. *Liar*, he spat, and it was the accusation rather than the shaking that made her scream.

'Go and see for yourself if you don't believe me!'

388

The doorbell rang and Julia shut her eyes. Adam let her go, left her there as he got out of bed.

Madame Tay rushed down the hall, her nightdress billowing yards of cotton. She flapped her hand impatiently at Adam, shooing him back to bed. Adam crept after her, past the emptiness of his mother's room, and squatted at the top of the stairs. Madame Tay opened the door and beneath the overhang of ceiling Adam saw the furniture-shop man's string vest and slack belly. He hadn't even finished what he was saying when Madame Tay started to howl.

26

The day after the general elections a clip of the Opposition parties' victory parade was shown on the news. Crouched before the TV, Sally had searched for Frances in the triumphant flag-waving cavalcade, imagined that she'd spotted her once or twice. When Frances's desk was empty on Monday morning, Sally guessed she'd taken the day off to recover from the celebrations. Not that she'd had much time to speculate about Frances's absence, for that same day the Amethyst clique swept Sally off her feet, beckoning to her between lessons and making room for her on their special bench in the courtyard. Rebecca shared with Sally the juicy segments of an orange and Francesca smiled encouragingly as she puffed a cigarette in the toilets (patting her shoulders when she creased up, coughing, windpipe garrotted by the smoke). The clique's vocabulary was a patois of tune-in drop-out counter-culture speak and archaic boarding-school slang. They punctuated sentences with *groovy* and *man* in clipped British accents and shrieked *Vile!* and *Horribilious!* about anything they disliked. Sally grinned, too shy to join in their banter, though they refused to let her recede into silence, consulting her opinion in their good-natured disputes (*Don't be a troglodyte, Lillian! What do you think, Sally? Doesn't she deserve a kick in the derrière?*).

Beyond the staff room the Amethyst school was a politics-free zone and Sally didn't think of the elections again until that evening, when she and Mr Hargreaves were having supper together, the radio burbling in the background. In the eight o'clock news bulletin was an item about some DAP supporters who'd broken away from the main procession on Sunday night to hurl stones and abuse at the State Chief Minister's residence in north Kuala Lumpur.

'There's no need for that kind of carry-on,' said Mr Hargreaves, pouring Bisto over his Yorkshire pudding and peas, 'no need for all that bragging and telling the Malays to go back to the countryside. It's the young riff-raff who let the Opposition down . . . Just because they've won a few seats they think they own Kuala Lumpur! The Malays are very bitter about the political stalemate in Selangor. They really shouldn't rub it in. Things are volatile enough already. I want you to come straight home from school tomorrow, Petal. I don't want you caught up in any of this . . . Aren't these spuds nice? Why don't you take a few more, Petal – go on, you're a growing girl.'

Sally chewed her roast beef and wondered if Frances was among the troublemakers outside the Mentri Besar's residence, shouting: *Melayu sekarang ta 'ada kuosa lagi!* (The Malays no longer have power), or *Melayu boleh balek kampong!* (The Malays must return to the villages) or *Kuala Lumpur sekerang China punya!* (Kuala Lumpur now belongs to the Chinese). She didn't think so. Though Frances had become very militant, she was far from being a common hooligan.

Frances's desk was empty again on Tuesday. Was she sick? Had she eloped with Henry Leung? The sting of the slap hadn't yet faded and Sally reminded herself that Frances's well-being, or lack thereof, was not her concern. But her thoughts strayed to Frances again and again. She couldn't concentrate in lessons. The day was long and the minutes limped by as if time itself was languorous and hot.

Early in the afternoon static hissed into the classroom as the tannoy system came to life, the tap, tap of the headmistress's finger on the microphone interrupting Miss Ng's account of the geological forces that transform igneous rock to metamorphic.

'Attention, students!' said Mrs Pritchett. 'Due to the United Malays National Organization procession planned for this evening, and the traffic and public transportation problems predicted, school is closing early today.'

There were shouts of *Yesss* and smatterings of

applause. Hooray for the UMNO procession! Hooray for political unrest! The headmistress's office was next door to the first-year classroom, where the cheering was loudest.

'*Girls!* Just because I cannot see you doesn't mean I don't know who you are! You will remain silent while I am speaking or I will keep you all here indefinitely . . . Never mind the UMNO procession!'

There were a few sniggers, but most took her threat seriously.

'That's better. Now, after this announcement the day pupils are to go straight home. Boarders, you shall all go to your dormitories until further notice. After-school clubs are cancelled and any pupils caught loitering will be punished. You have been warned!'

When the public address was over the fifth form was a babble of excitement.

'I saw a load of Malays coming in for the demonstration this morning on my way to school. Dozens of them, hanging off the back of a truck. They'd come all the way from the countryside and had axes and knives and stuff you use for farming.'

'They've come to teach the Chinese a lesson. They want to show them who's boss.'

'The British should never have left. That's what my father says. They wouldn't be fighting one another if the British were still here.'

Sally fetched some books from her locker and tagged on to the queue to use the telephone in the secretary's office. Anxious mothers hovered at the school gates, collecting their daughters early after heeding the ominous warnings of Malay servants, suitcases piled on luggage racks as they prepared to flee the city. Girls skipped out into the courtyard, giddy with freedom, and, as promised, Mrs Pritchett had a zero-tolerance policy towards stragglers, barking at those who'd stopped to chat or play hopscotch and driving them out of the gates.

Sally for one had no intention of hanging about. She had a headache and wanted to go home and lie quietly in a darkened room. But as she neared the front of the telephone queue, there was a tap on her shoulder. Delilah had queue-jumped behind her (eliciting no complaint from the twenty girls she'd pushed in front of). 'Fancy meeting you here,' she drawled with a flirtatious arch of the eyebrow. Sally noted with interest that Delilah wasn't as perfect as usual, but sweaty and dishevelled, an ink stain the shape of Africa on her blouse and her French plait half undone.

'Why don't you come back to mine, Sal? My parents are visiting friends in Singapore and the others are being goody-goodies and want to go home. I shall be bored out of my mind if you don't.'

'I'd better not. I'd be lousy company – I've got this splitting headache, you see . . .'

'All the more reason to come back to my house! My mother's bathroom cabinet has more drugs than a chemist. We'll magic that headache away in seconds. C'mon, Sal!'

How could she resist such a plea? Sally abandoned

the queue and, headache aside, felt very special as Delilah linked arms with her and walked her outside, jauntily saluting Mrs Pritchett as she herded them through the gates.

The atmosphere of the Colonial District was as though the city had received a severe weather warning and was bracing itself for the storm. As they strolled along Sally stared into the faces of Malay passers-by, searching for traces of violence and hostility. A few groceries were closing early, metal shutters clattering down. A Chinese butcher wobbled past on a bicycle loaded with unsold stock and Delilah joked: *Quick, the Muslims might come and steal your pig's feet!*

Back at Delilah's house the maid had left a note on the kitchen table saying that she'd been called to the countryside for a family emergency.

'Mimi hasn't got any family in the countryside,' said Delilah, tossing the note aside, 'and she won't have a job to come back to either when my parents hear of this.'

Delilah dissolved some aspirin in a glass of water for Sally to drink. Then, as Sally lay on the bed, she placed a compress of ice cubes on her forehead and practically straddled Sally to channel her weight on to the compress through the heels of her hands. Sally shut her eyes, the sensation of ice freezing her cranium and deadening the misfiring nerve-endings oddly pleasurable. Ten minutes passed and the headache was gone. Delilah asked Sally if she'd like to stay over. *Uh-huh*, said Sally. Delilah telephoned Mr Hargreaves, and Sally heard her impersonating Mrs Jones in the hall (*Hello, Clarence, Petula Jones here! . . . Don't worry . . . Sally will be perfectly safe . . .*).

When Delilah returned to the bedroom she stripped off her clothes, sliding her skirt down over her hips and pulling her shirt over her head without undoing the buttons. Sally cast her eyes away from Delilah's pink knickers and small bra-less breasts as she rummaged through the laundry basket. When she looked again Delilah was wearing denim cut-offs and a sleeveless white T-shirt.

'Monopoly?' she suggested brightly. She dug a battered box out of a cupboard of rainy-day games and set the board up on the floor. 'What colour do you want to be?'

They sat on cushions as they played. Headache vanquished, Sally was keen to recapture the mood of the other night; the conversations of life and love and past and future. But Delilah was too absorbed in the roll of the dice and acquiring a property empire (which she did with great efficiency and obvious pleasure). Conscious of the weakness of her opponent she gave Sally hefty hints, but the desire to win prevailed. Delilah's enthusiasm for the game, the handclaps and cheers, seemed affected. They were merely killing time. But why? Surely Delilah wasn't so lonely she wanted Sally there purely for company's sake? Around six-ish, after winning three games in a row, Delilah scavenged in the kitchen larder for potato chips, over-ripe bananas, chocolate biscuits, and crackers and tinned sardines.

'Isn't this delicious!' said Delilah, crumbs falling from her lips. 'I never get to eat like this when my parents are here!'

Sally smiled, underwhelmed by the makeshift picnic. On Radio Malaysia, Aretha Franklin sang 'Respect', reminding Sally of Frances (who loved to dance to the song, wiggling her bum and swinging her thumbs forwards and backwards in a move she called 'the hitchhiker'). Sally felt a sudden pang of longing for Frances and hoped wherever she was she was dancing and singing along.

The starting point of the UMNO counter-demonstration was the residence of the State Chief Minister on Princes Road. Since early that morning Malays had been arriving from outlying areas of Selangor, urged by community and religious leaders to go to Kuala Lumpur and make a stand. By six thirty p.m. five thousand men were gathered outside the Chief Minister's house, many armed with machetes and axes and home-made firebombs. There were students, clerks, servants, businessmen, farmers and the un-employed. Most were scared, excited youths, violence the furthest thing from their minds. But as false rumours of Malay women and children murdered that afternoon by Chinese perpetrators swept through the crowd, the fanatic elements rose to the surface. Two Chinese men passing by on motor scooters were knocked down and hacked to death. Further down the street a gang overturned several cars and set them ablaze. The Chief Minister rushed out of his house and climbed up on top of a bus loaded with schoolchildren. He held up both hands as the bus was shaken by the mob, begging for restraint and responsibility. The demonstrators surged out of the compound, moving off towards Batu Road. Hawker stalls were pushed over, great woks cascading oil; shouts of Malay and Cantonese echoed as people scattered in every direction. Chinese who crossed the path of the rioters were attacked. Moving vehicles were met by a volley of bottles and stones. Tear gas hazed Campbell Road as police riot squads tried to disperse the fray.

A maze of fortresses sprang up in Chinese neighbourhoods; road blocks of barbed wire and burnt-out cars. Shopkeepers and Chinese Secret Society members chased rioters away from Chow Kit Road with meat cleavers and sharpened bamboo poles. Cinemas were raided, Malays dragged out of the audience and stabbed. Malays consorting with Chinese prostitutes in massage parlours were clubbed to death before they'd even had a chance to zip up their flies. Entire streets of houses went dark as residents hid indoors, not even daring to strike a match for fear of attracting the attention of the rioters. Ambulances shrieked, rushing the maimed and dying to Kuala Lumpur General Hospital. The police radio network was choked with demands for reinforcements, background screams and shouts that the situation was out of control. Burning rags were stuffed into bottles of kerosene and hurled through windows. Across the city fires bloomed, smoke and flames spiralling upwards into the sky.

'You know what would be funny?' said Delilah.

They were downstairs in the kitchen. Sally was sitting at the table, watching Delilah rinsing dishes, the mundane chore made beautiful by her grace and economy of movement.

'No,' said Sally. 'What?'

'If we called Frances up.'

'Why would we want to do that?' asked Sally.

Delilah slotted a plate into the drying rack and wiped her hands on her cut-offs.

'For the fun of it! I love prank calls. We could sing "Happy Birthday" to her. Or put on squeaky voices and ask her if her fridge is running . . .'

'She'll know at once.'

'She'll see the funny side of it.'

'No, she won't.'

'I bet she'll be happy to hear from you, Sal.'

'I don't think so. She hates me.'

'Why does she hate you? You've done nothing wrong. She went berserk at you without even giving you the benefit of the doubt. Friends owe each other that much, don't they?'

Sally nodded in sour agreement.

'She humiliated you,' said Delilah. 'She flew at you like a wild animal in front of everyone. And now you feel guilty, don't you? You feel guilty though you've done nothing wrong. Frances has behaved disgracefully towards you.'

Sally nodded once more. How satisfying it was to nod and agree. To be cast in the role of innocent victim.

'She blames me for Mr Leung leaving. But I had nothing to do with it.'

''Course not! Let's call her up and ask her why she thinks that. She might be calm enough by now to explain.'

'I doubt it.' Sally thought of how Frances hated Mr Milnar. 'When she thinks someone's in the wrong, then that's that. She won't ever change her mind about them.'

'OK then,' said Delilah, 'if she's that stubborn, forget explanations. Forget reconciliations. Let's have some fun . . .' Delilah paced the kitchen. Then she stopped and clapped her hands. 'I know! We'll call her up and say Mr Leung wants to meet her somewhere, then we'll go and hide and watch her wait for him.'

Sally looked at Delilah in disbelief. The plan was cruel and juvenile and not unlike something Frances would contrive herself. Complications and pitfalls were many and Sally felt obliged to point them out.

'But how do we know that she's not already with Mr Leung?' she said. 'Or that she doesn't already know where he is? Or that she won't phone him afterwards to check if what we're saying is true?'

'I think we should risk it.'

'Anyway, we can't go out. There's that procession. We don't want to run into it.'

'There's no need to worry about the UMNO demonstration. That's all going on up in the north, around Kampong Bahru and the Malay areas. It won't come down this way. I tell you what, why don't you call her, ask her to meet you at the end of Sultan Road, then we'll think of what to do.'

'She won't fall for it.'

'If you say you have a message from Mr Leung she will.'

'She won't believe me.'

'Yes, she will.'

'She'll go mad!'

'Then let her go mad! Honestly, Sal! Why are you so concerned about her feelings? She never gave a second thought about yours.'

Smiling, Delilah clasped her hands and pulled her out of her chair. Swinging Sally's hands in hers Delilah pulled silly faces as she jitterbugged her reluctant dance partner out to the hall. She lifted the phone off the hook and dialled the Milnar residence (a number she evidently knew by heart).

'It's ringing!' Delilah squealed, thrusting the handset to Sally.

'Hello?' said Frances.

The voice of her estranged friend stalled Sally's breath. Sally imagined Frances plucking at the telephone cord, absentmindedly sweeping her toe back and forth in an arc on the floor (a habit of hers when she was on the phone). *For whom does the bell toll?* was how Frances usually answered the telephone. The lacklustre *hello?* was a sign of low spirits. Sally realized then that she'd been in low spirits too. She'd missed her.

'It's me,' said Sally.

There was a silence.

'Oh,' said Frances. 'What do you want?'

She didn't sound angry – only drained. Delilah nodded at Sally, eyes shining: *Go on!*

'I've a message for you.'

'Oh?'

'It's from Mr Leung.'

'That's impossible,' said Frances.

'Why?'

'Because he is in prison. He was arrested last week.'

Sally was gobsmacked. Prison?

Delilah snatched the handset. Sally thought Delilah was going to speak to Frances herself, but she clamped her hand over the mouthpiece and whispered: 'Say he's out! Say he was waiting for her at the gates after school today.'

The receiver was flung back to Sally.

'He's out now,' Sally parroted. 'He was waiting for you outside the school gates today, but you weren't there. He wants me to pass a message on to you.'

A tiny vibration passed through the network of telegraph wires. Sally detected the tremor and knew at once it was her friend's leaping heart.

'What is it?' Frances breathed.

'Meet me at the end of Sultan Road, outside the Fong and Goh Dentists. I'll tell you then.'

'No way!' shouted Frances. 'You're making this up! There's no way I'm going out on a night like this! Tell me now, Sally! Tell me now or I'll never speak to you again.'

'Hang up,' hissed Delilah. 'Quick, hang up!'

Sally slammed down the receiver, her pulse racing. 'Frances said she won't come,' she told Delilah, relieved. 'She thinks I'm making it up.'

'Don't worry,' said Delilah, 'she'll be there.'

It was not quite eight o'clock when they left Delilah's house. The air was the temperature of blood and the evening sang with distant sirens and the trill and chirr of neighbourhood insects. The smoky fragrance reminded Sally of Guy Fawkes' Night and the bonfires she and her father used to make (for the annual cremation of dead leaves, an effigy of Guy Fawkes and the odd unlucky hedgehog). But turning the corner at the end of the street, they saw that the origins of the smoke were more sinister than a humble garden bonfire. Across the horizon fires glowed as if fragments of the burning sun had fallen, setting the city ablaze. The girls were open-mouthed.

'Wow!' gasped Delilah. 'It's Armageddon!'

'Do you think those fires have something to do with that procession?' said Sally. 'It looks like rioting. I think we should go back . . .'

'But the fires are in north Kuala Lumpur,' said Delilah. 'They're absolutely bloody miles away!'

'But it looks dangerous. I don't think it's safe to be out. I think we should go home.'

'Don't be silly, Sally. The trouble's between the

Malays and the Chinese. We're British. No one'll dare touch us. Besides, it would be rude to stand Frances up. C'mon now. We don't have far to go. Just a few blocks.'

The night streets were empty and forlorn, but Delilah was perfectly calm, whistling as though they were out for a pleasant evening stroll. Sally glanced sideways at her companion; the sweep of jaw line and strong nose gliding through the dark. It was impossible to believe they were the same age. Whereas Sally had come into the world in Cricklewood Hospital, 1952, Delilah seemed to have been born several millennia ago and witnessed so many dark episodes in the history of human civilization that this little hiccup involving rampaging UMNO activists didn't faze her in the slightest. She held herself as if she owned this foreign city and, if she and the rioting masses were to meet, the masses would part for her, violence abating until she was safely out of the way.

'Did you know Mr Leung was in prison?' Sally asked.

'No! Goodness. I wonder what he's done. Plotting some Communist insurrection, I expect. I can't believe our maths teacher's a jailbird!'

They stopped on the outskirts of Chinatown, on a street where stone sheltered walkways ran along the shop fronts, coloured paper lanterns strung between the pillars. Every shop was shuttered, the doors bolted. Delilah put her hand on the back of Sally's neck and directed her gaze to the other side of the road, to a run-down building at the end of the row.

'OK,' said Delilah. 'See that teahouse over there?'

'*That's* a teahouse?' said Sally.

The façade was a crumbling mess; corrugated iron blocked the windows and the walls were pockmarked and fatally cracked, as if a bulldozer had charged into it, then changed its mind halfway through the wrecking process.

'Yes,' said Delilah. 'It's an old gambling house, now a teahouse for the poor. Listen. I want you to bring Frances over here and tell her that Mr Leung is waiting in there for her. I'm going to hide inside and give her a surprise.'

'And then what?' asked Sally.

'And then she'll be surprised!'

'I don't want to do this,' said Sally. 'I think it's a terrible idea.'

Delilah smiled. She rubbed the back of Sally's neck. 'C'mon, we're all the way here now. She'll see the funny side of it. Afterwards we'll all go back to mine. Go on now. Don't be afraid.' She winked at Sally, then darted across the road and through the teahouse door.

Sally ran in the direction of the blazing sky. The sirens wailed more urgently now, burglar alarms jangling in distress. It was the time of the evening Chinatown was usually at its liveliest, with shoppers and traders haggling and hawker-stall diners hunched over claypot chicken and Hokkien *mee*. But now there was not a soul on the streets. Even the beggars had had the good sense to seek refuge. In the upstairs windows of shuttered shophouses a few *tokays* chewed toothpicks and watched Sally's lonely progress along Petaling

405

Road. *Why's everything shut?* Sally wanted to shout. *Why're you indoors?* Three deafening bangs came from somewhere near by, and Sally screamed and crashed to her knees, head in hands, convinced the gunshots had been aimed at her back. She crouched on the ground for a minute, then got up and ran for her life.

Frances stood outside the Fong and Goh Dentists, hands deep in the pockets of her dungarees and her chin cocked like a twelve-year-old boy acting tough. Sally flashed with anger when she saw her. She looked so vulnerable standing alone. How daft of her not to have seen through the lie. Frances, who'd been squinting the other way, turned at the sound of Sally running over. Her expression hardened. Sally stopped about a yard away, not wanting to take any chances.

'Where is he?' Frances said.

'He's hiding.'

'Where?'

'I'll show you.'

Sally jerked her thumb back the way she'd come and, scowling, Frances hopped over the storm drain into the empty road, suspicious, but reeled-in. They began the journey back abreast of each other but a few feet apart. Though there was no one to be seen, male voices shouted and explosions of shattering glass echoed in the next street. Frances glanced nervously behind them.

'What's with this city tonight? Why's everything on fire? Why's everyone indoors?' Sally asked.

'Don't you know? There's a twenty-four-hour curfew!' said Frances.

'A curfew?'

'Yes. Because of the rioting. They said so on the radio and TV. The police've got permission to shoot anyone they see on sight.'

'They won't shoot us, will they? We're British after all.'

'Not me. I'm Chinese.'

Sally was stunned, but she walked on as if her legs were mechanized, carrying her deeper and deeper into her waking nightmare. She knew she'd been stupid to let Delilah twist her arm, but Frances must be absolutely brainless to have known about the curfew and come out anyway. Brainless, or madly in love. Sally had to admit the truth. The sooner the better. But part of her didn't want to. Part of her was still angry at Frances. Glad to be walking her into Delilah's trap.

'How is he?' Frances asked.

'He's OK.'

'Is he out on bail?'

'I don't know – he didn't say.'

'He can't be, if he's in hiding,' Frances decided. 'I can't believe he was waiting for me outside the school gates like that – it's so risky!'

Frances was pleased, the risk a proof of love.

'He wasn't right by the gates. He was a few streets away.'

'You said he was outside the school gates.'

The taste of tinned sardines from Delilah's picnic rose in Sally's mouth; metallic and acrid, the lick of a rusty blade.

'Oh, did I?'

Frances stopped in her tracks.

'You're lying to me! Henry isn't out of prison! You're making it up, aren't you?'

What better time to admit the truth? To get them both out of this awful mess? But as Sally stared into Frances's blazing eyes, she flared as though wrongfully accused.

'Yes, that's right. I've come out when the city's on fire, risking my neck and getting shot at, just for kicks. What do you take me for? I'm doing this so you have a chance to speak to Mr Leung. Because he wants to see you . . . though now I don't know why I bothered!'

Had Delilah been within earshot she'd have given the performance a standing ovation. Where had it come from, this outrage and indignation? This talent for lies? There was a fleeting stand-off, the girls livid and glaring hard. Then Frances backed down. She slumped as if her angry convictions had propped her up.

'Sorry,' she said. The vanished guilt returned to Sally with vehemence. 'I'm sorry I lost my temper the other day. I know now it wasn't your fault. It was my father. Someone fed him a pack of lies about Henry. Lies that linked him to political extremists and made out he'd been taking advantage of me. None of it is true. He hasn't touched me; works only for the DAP. But my father went to the police. They arrested Henry, said he was dangerous. But there's no evidence! Nothing!'

'Henry's in prison because of your father?'

Frances nodded wearily and Sally saw the weals of tiredness under her eyes.

'My father betrayed my mother, and now he's betrayed me. He hates me because I remind him of her. He wants to ruin my life. He thinks he's won, but he hasn't. Now Henry's back we'll go away and I'll never see him again.'

'Is that why you haven't been to school?'

'What's the point of school any more? I haven't left my room for days. I haven't been able to eat or sleep or think . . . I've been waiting for them to let him out. Oh, Sally, I was so afraid Henry would blame me for what my father did, that he wouldn't want to see me again. But now he's back. I'm so glad!'

Sally was going to be sick.

'You should have called me.'

The teahouse was over the road. *Tell her, tell her, tell her* – the syllables had replaced the beat of her heart. But part of her *still* didn't want to. Part of her was still jilted, writhing with rejection, and wanting to punish Frances for loving the maths teacher. She lifted her arm and pointed to the building of corrugated iron and ramshackle walls.

Tongue numb with dread, she said: 'He's in there.'

Frances hugged Sally, her thin arms encircling her neck. Then she bounded across the road to the teahouse.

Sally stared as the door slammed, disbelieving what she'd just done. She heard Delilah's blasé drawl: 'My God! She's so gullible it's embarrassing!'

409

'Delilah! I thought you were going to wait in there for her.'

Delilah was by one of the pillars supporting the stone walkway roof. She strolled over to Sally, staring at the derelict shophouse with a grimace of satisfaction.

'Wait in there for her? Are you mad! I wouldn't stay in there a moment longer than necessary.'

'Why? What's wrong with that place?'

Delilah snorted. 'I can't believe you're so naive!'

'What is that place?'

'It's where poor girls from the countryside are sold and where city girls with no job prospects end up.'

Sally grabbed Delilah's arm and squeezed with all the strength in her fingers.

'We must go and get her!'

Delilah wrinkled her nose, pulled her arm free.

'Don't get upset. I had a word with them. They're expecting her. I asked them to give her a little scare.'

'A scare?'

'Nothing less than she deserves.'

Sally lunged at Delilah and shook her with an aggression that startled them both.

'Help me get her back. Please!'

Delilah's expression was pure disgust, but instead of struggling she went slack. She tilted her head back, lips puckered as if to kiss her schoolgirl assailant. Then she spat at Sally, a leap of snake's venom in her eye. Sally let her go and stepped back, rubbing the spittle choking her vision.

'Go and rescue her yourself,' said Delilah. 'You're

certainly big enough and ugly enough. Silly Sally! Didn't take much for you to screw Frances over, did it? Makes me wonder if you're worth having as a friend.' She began to walk away.

'Don't go!'

Delilah glanced over her shoulder with a toss of chestnut hair.

'He shouldn't have treated me the way he did. He really shouldn't have. Now let's see how he likes it if someone does to his precious daughter what he did to me.'

The shophouse door swung open when Sally was halfway across the road. *Frances*, she thought and her heart swam with relief. *Let her hate me and hate me and never forgive me, but let her be OK*. But it wasn't Frances. It was a man. He leant casually against the door frame, eclipsing the light that shone some way behind him. Sally froze. She couldn't see his face. Darkness crawled over him like insects. Like a beekeeper covered from head to toe in black bees.

'Hey, English,' he called gruffly. 'Looking for your friend?'

'Yes. Can you get her for me?'

'Don't worry about her,' he said. 'We're looking after her.'

Looking after her? Sally imagined several burly men gathered round Frances, offering tea and sympathy. It wouldn't happen. She had to be in there against her will.

'Please, mister,' Sally called, 'will you let her out?'

'She's fine. Come and see for yourself.'

'Please let her out.'

'Come here, come here. You girls shouldn't be out tonight. Don't you know about the fighting? Come here . . .'

The voice seemed detached from the man in his purdah of darkness. *Come here, come here* . . . He said the words again and again, soft and lulling, as if to hush a frightened child. Sally's feet were bound to the spot. Her eyes dropped from his shadowy face to where his hands were fumbling at his waist. There was an unbuckling, an unbuttoning, a burrowing of his hand inside his trousers as it seized what it sought. The dark shifted, his arm moving in rhythmic unhurried strokes. He talked to Sally as he groped, encouraging her to go to him, sick and cloying, menacing and hypnotic. Perhaps Sally *was* hypnotized because she could only stare and stare. Then the man stepped out of the doorway and the trance was broken. Sally was off, satchel thudding her side as she tore away, the man's laughter chasing her up the street.

Sally ran through the empty streets of Chinatown. She ran counter to logic, a moth fluttering to the flickering heat of arson and the din of emergency alarms. She'd never run so far and so fast in her life, the piston surge of blood in her heart, legs pumping as she pounded the living daylights out of the pavement. She saw a gang of men carrying goods out through the smashed-up window of an electrical appliances store. A couple of the men were loading a stolen fridge on to a pick-up, and another guffawed laughter as he staggered down the road, bow-legged under the weight of an enormous TV. She didn't stop to ask them for help. She ran on and on, hands clamped over her nose and mouth as she passed a car rolled on its back, dense smoke and coppery flames pouring out of its underbelly.

China Keluar! China Keluar! A Malay in a black bandanna stood on a fire hydrant, shouting and slashing arabesques with his machete, as though the air were rife with invisible assassins. Beneath him lay a slain man in a bloody shirt, his arms spread in a V and his forehead touching the ground as if in obeisance to the fire hydrant god. The slain man didn't move and Sally cringed in terror as the black bandanna man yodelled his battle-cry at her and twirled his knife. Sally saw some more bandanna men up ahead and ducked into a cabbage-stinking alleyway, wading through heaps of rubbish bags to the haze of street light at the other end. She tripped on a crate of bottles and skinned her elbow against the wall. She got up and limped onwards, halting mid-hobble as a reverberation came up through the soles of her shoes, the ground rumbling as though in ferocious hunger. The light at the far end of the alley was obscured as a tank of the Royal Malay Regiment thundered by. The alley walls shook with artillery fire as the city came under martial law, and Sally staggered back the way she'd come. The men in the black bandannas were gone and the street was a lawn of shattered glass and broken wood, smashed bicycles and furniture looted then discarded as it was too heavy to carry. Every shophouse was in darkness, all harbouring families in whispering huddles, suitcases packed, passports in pockets, ready to escape the country at the break of day.

Sally spotted two men in police uniform straddling motorbikes, walkie-talkies held to their mouths. Broken glass crunching under her shoes, she ran over to them, wailing and waving her arms lest they vroom away. When she reached the policemen she wanted to scream about Frances, but could only pant and gasp. The Malay policemen stared at the white girl, wheezing and flapping like a pigeon in the throes of an asthma attack. Sally arched her back, hands on her knees, lungs wrestling for air. Between each lurch of breath opened narrow windows of opportunity for speech.

'Please,' she gasped. 'Frances . . .'

'There's a curfew!' one of the policemen shouted. 'Do you want to get killed? Go home!'

'Please help me,' Sally cried. 'My friend's trapped in a building near by . . .'

Sally looked around. Was she still in Chinatown? Which direction was the shophouse? She'd completely lost her bearings.

'Your friend is lucky to be indoors.'

'Please. We must help her. I think there were men in there. I think they're hurting her . . .'

'Where do you live?'

'Delilah was supposed to wait inside. But she didn't. She lied! She tricked me! If you come with me to Sultan Road I can show you the way from there. It's . . .'

'Where do you live?' The eyes of the policeman bulged in frustration.

'Jalan Perdana, Petaling Jaya.'

The policemen had a quick consultation in Malay. The policeman who'd shouted at Sally spoke into his radio transmitter, before speaking again to his colleague. Sally wanted to scream and beat her fists on the ground. They were wasting time. They had to help Frances.

'You,' said the policeman, 'stop crying and get on the back of my bike.'

'But Frances—'

'Shut up about your friend. C'mon!'

'Please!' Sally *was* screaming now. 'I can't leave her!'

'*Do you want to be left here to die?*'

The policeman's eyes bulged and a blood vessel protruded in his temple. He yelled so hard that the word *die* came out ragged and hoarse. It was no good. The policemen wouldn't help her. Sobbing, she climbed astride the back of the bike. She clung to the policeman, her eyes squeezed tight as they swerved off around the rubble in the road. She sobbed so hard that when he dropped her off in Petaling Jaya fifteen minutes later, the back of his uniform was soaking wet. Sally toppled off the bike, pulling down her hoicked-up skirt. She ignored the policeman as he warned her to stay indoors, and stumbled away from the motorbike without thanking him. The police bike revved up and sped back to the rioting city.

In the silence of the yard Sally's ears buzzed in

memory of gunfire. Trixie and Tinkerbell trotted up to her, tails wagging, sniffing furiously at the mysterious odours of civil unrest clinging to her clothes. Trixie licked her knee and the rough caress of her tongue set off a fresh wave of tears. But mid-sob Sally had a flash revelation. She'd make her father drive her back to Kuala Lumpur! Yes, that was it! Her father always did what was decent and right. He'd help her rescue Frances.

Sally dashed into the house, the door banging behind her.

'Father! Father!' she hollered.

No lights were on downstairs. Odd, thought Sally. *Why has Father given Safiah and Yok Ling the night off?* Spring-heeled, she bounded up the stairs, knocking her shin in a misstep in the dark. On the landing she held the banister, pausing to regain her breath as blood drooled to her ankle. As she stood there, Sally heard a low-pitched moaning coming from the master bedroom. She recognized the sound. Her father had made those same terrible groans of pain when he'd slipped a disc five years ago. Father had injured himself! Or worse, some men in black bandannas had broken into the house and attacked him. Damn those useless dogs! Sally flew to the bedroom and threw open the door.

'Father!' she cried.

Mr Hargreaves was not flat out on the bed as she'd expected. On the churned-up sheets was a creature of two heads, its eight limbs tangled up in a fierce, writing knot of pleasure. The room stank like a rabbit hutch, though the windows were wide open. Two dark shapes sprang apart – one of them substantially larger than the other. Sally realized the larger one was her father.

'Oh!'

She backed out of the room, trying to make sense of what she'd seen. The light clicked on and moments later Mr Hargreaves appeared in the bedroom doorway, tying the cord of his dressing gown. He was as puffed out as an out-of-practice trumpeter, a high colour in his cheeks. His sparse hair was like a halo of feathers that had drifted down upon his balding pate.

'Petal!' he exclaimed. 'I thought you were spending the night at Delilah Jones's.'

Sally frowned at her shoes.

'Oh, Petal, don't get upset! I'm sorry that you had to find out this way, but it isn't as sordid as it seems. Safiah and I are very much in love. In fact, we plan to marry. I know it must be upsetting for you, but Agnes has been dead for over sixteen years now and it's about time I moved on. I want you to know that you're still number one, Sally dearest. Do you hear me? You're still number one! Oh, don't cry, sweetie, don't cry. You'll be grown up soon and off to university. You don't want me to be lonely, do you?'

Sally stared at her father's hairy troll's feet. The toe-nails were overgrown and needed clipping. He was very neglectful about things like that.

'Petal? Are you OK? You've scraped your knee! And

your elbow is bleeding. Shall I get Safiah to fetch some antiseptic to clean it up?'

At the sound of her name the servant girl appeared. She wore a bedsheet wrapped around her like a strapless evening gown, her tresses back-combed by Mr Hargreaves's lust-crazed fingers into a wild lioness's mane. Daughter's and servant girl's eyes met over Mr Hargreaves's shoulder and Safiah smiled. If her step-mother-to-be had poked her tongue out, then Sally wouldn't have been surprised. Safiah's bedsheet slid down her breasts showing the nut-brown aureolae of her nipples. Sally glanced at her father and saw that his robe had come undone, the flabby mound of his belly mercifully overhanging the pubic thicket. Sally remembered the man in the doorway – the way he'd groped himself, eyes leering in the dark.

'She can't even speak English,' Sally muttered.

'Oh . . . darling.'

Mr Hargreaves reached out to stroke his daughter's cheek. She shut her eyes.

'I think I'm going to bed now.'

Sally went into her room and slammed the door.

During the days of rioting the city was consumed by pyromania. Hundreds of houses were fire-bombed, the streets becoming graveyards of charred chassis and exploded engines, carbonized seat springs and steering wheels. Army jeeps crashed through the defence barricades of Chinese neighbourhoods, soldiers shooting indiscriminately into the windows of shops and homes. The wounded lay in the streets, often yards from their families hiding indoors, listening to the cries of pain, too terrified to go and help. Every incarnation of blade flashed through the air, hacking human flesh and bone, the city an abattoir, the gutters flowing with blood. Men were beheaded, dismembered, and women raped, breasts crudely amputated, broken bottles thrust between their legs. In Kuala Lumpur General Hospital every basic necessity was exhausted: beds, surgical dressing, doctors, blood. The hospital morgue was so crowded that corpses dangled from ceiling hooks in plastic bags; were piled three deep on the floor – dead Malays on top of dead Sikhs, dead Chinese on dead Malays. Corpses in the street were doused in petrol and set alight. Corpses were dumped in shallow graves dug in gardens and public parks. Corpses thrown into the muddy Klang River drifted out of the city, a silent flotilla of the dead.

The phone line was engaged when Sally telephoned the Milnars, the switchboards jammed by an avalanche of calls. She crawled on to her bed in her shoes and smoky school uniform and lay shivering, her eyes wide open, for every time she closed them she saw her father and his teenage mistress, or the flames of a city plunged into hell. Later in the night she went downstairs to call Frances again, but got the engaged tone for every number she dialled. When she replaced the receiver she heard Safiah's ceiling-muffled giggling and her father's effeminate whinny of submission. She switched the television on and turned the volume up high. From the flickering dots of monochrome an apparition emerged. The Tengku. Thickly spectacled, black *songkok* on his silver hair. The Prime Minister (who was not to be Prime Minister for very much longer) was addressing the nation live on air, wiping away tears as he poured out his feelings. Democracy in Malaysia had failed. The Opposition parties were to blame. It was the fault of the Communists.

'In this hour of need I pray to Allah to secure you against all dangers. At the same time you must look after yourselves. I will do all I can without fear to maintain peace in this country. God bless you all.'

Sally understood none of it. But like many others that night she wept with him, the disgraced Prime Minister an unlikely companion in her grief.

27

The doorbell rang when he was on the brink of losing hope. She crossed the threshold of his flat, the missing days trailing like a shadow behind her.

Adam made her a mug of sugary tea, careful not to badger her with questions as she sat and drank. He saw the answers in her anyway: the nights sleeping in doorways and underpasses. She hadn't washed in weeks and her hair, clasped in a rubber band, was filthy. Her eyes were the place where her estrangement was strongest, though. She'd grown used to her anonymity. Adam wanted to tell her her name, her date of birth. To show her photos of the child she used to be. Reacquaint her with touchstones of her identity – daughter of Frances and Jack; granddaughter of Christopher Milnar; pupil of Christchurch Comprehensive School 1995–1997 – inauspicious as they were.

Julia agreed to stay the night and Adam ran her a hot

bath, pouring in Radox so the surface floated with snowy mountains of foam. She undressed in the living room, stripped to nakedness with no regard for the privacy of her body. Adam couldn't believe anyone could be so thin. The shoulder blades jutting like plates of armour, the bony pelvic saddle, her pubic hair so sparse he could see the cleft of her, as though she were a child. Water sloshed as she lowered herself into the tub. As she lay steeping, Adam gathered up her clothes; grey T-shirt, denim jacket and jeans held together by seams of dirt. He emptied the drugs and wallet from her pockets before slinging everything in the washing machine, doubting the garments would withstand the spinning of the drum.

After half an hour Julia climbed out of the bath and, wrapped in a towel, wandered, soapy and dripping, into the living room. Adam brought her Mischa's left-behind dressing gown, breathing her apple shampoo-scented hair as he helped her thread her arms through the sleeves. He heated a saucepan of tomato soup, ladled it into a bowl for her and watched her swallow a few mouthfuls to be polite. After the soup she asked for a clean tablespoon. She blackened the underside of the spoon with a disposable lighter flame, sucking her thumb that had been seared by the spark-ing mechanism. She touched a needle to the solution and slowly pulled the plunger so it drank it up. She handed the syringe to Adam. *I can't*, he said. *I don't know how*. Julia stood up and tied the cord of the dress-ing gown around her thigh. She lifted the hem of the robe above the crooks of her knees. *Just find a vein.* He knelt awkwardly, staring at the backs of her legs as she talked him through the mechanics of injecting, the syringe hovering by creases of skin, veins silted with deposits of lead. He found a passable vein lower down, tapped the barrel and squirted air from the needle tip. His hands shook as he spiked her, not sure if the needle had gone in too deep or not deep enough. He gave the plunger a slight tug, so a thin ribbon of blood shot up into the solution, then pressed down, aiming for a steady rate of depression. The needle slipped out when the barrel was three quarters empty, dribbling smack down her leg. He'd made a mess of it, but Julia said nothing. He pressed his thumb to the bauble of blood and Julia swayed slightly. She sat on the sofa and closed her eyes, content for the first time since she'd entered his flat.

Adam goes to meet Sally Hargreaves two weeks before Christmas. The city is in the midst of a cold snap, leaves stuck to the pavement by a glittering laminate of frost. Adam wants to buy a Christmas tree for the flat – a real one, that'll shed pine needles and make a mess. But he doesn't yet know if Julia will stick around for Christmas and he is afraid of tempting fate. As Adam counts the door numbers to Sally's house he regrets accepting the invite. When she'd phoned the night before, Adam's instinct was to decline, to defer meeting her to another time. But her tone was fraught and Adam sensed it had taken her courage to contact him – weeks of deliberation. He remembered the black-and-white photograph of the two schoolgirls in the Kuala Lumpur marketplace. He had not known his mother ever to have a friend.

Adam hesitates before ringing the bell. He hears a muffled voice somewhere inside the house – *Coming! Coming!* – then an avalanche of footsteps down the stairs. The door swings open to a heavyset woman nearly as tall as he is, blonde corkscrews springing around her head, bold purple dress dripping colour like feathers. When she sees him Sally Hargreaves forgets the etiquette of answering doors, the how-do-you-dos and so-good-of-you-to-comes. She forgets she is a woman of fifty-three and stares like a dumbstruck teenager. Adam clears his throat, cupped hand lifted to mouth, interrupting the beyond-the-grave reunion of teenage friends.

'Sorry!' Sally exclaims, gaze returning to the here and now, the bright spots of her cheeks brightening. 'Sorry! How rude of me! You must be Adam. Do come in . . .'

They smile shyly at each other and shake hands.

In the living room Sally is garrulous with nerves. Had he had any difficulties finding the house? Did he want to take his jacket off? Something to drink? Earl Grey or fruit tea? Rosehip or camomile? Adam reacts to her overbearing chatter with reticence, a knee-jerk shyness that cannot be overcome. This makes Sally even more nervous and forced in her earthy prattling. And so it goes, in ever decreasing circles; an awful pair, incompatible even in their social awkwardness.

After the flurry of tea-making Sally settles in an

armchair. Wind chimes tinkle outside and under the table the tortoiseshell cat, warm-blooded and muscular, rubs against Adam's denim-clad leg. Though the sky is overcast and the room quite dark, Sally makes no move to switch on a lamp. She tells Adam of the day she and Frances met, his mother rattling a stick along the railings, tormenting her dogs. How Frances got in trouble with Mr Milnar for stealing little pink cakes from the Kuan Ti shrine. Sally chuckles to recall what lazy and stubborn pupils they were. How had the teachers put up with them? Elsewhere in the house pipes clank, the radiators blasting out heat. Sally wonders if she is boring the boy as she witters on. Tears suddenly spring to her eyes. The boy notices, lays a hand on her wrist. *Are you OK?* he asks. For months Sally has been famished of human touch, but the boy's hand only makes the hunger worse. *Pathetic*, she thinks, *I am pathetic*.

'Your mother,' she tells him, ashamed of her tremulous voice, 'was such a beautiful, vivacious and forthright child . . .'

Mr Milnar went to see Sally in Jalan Perdana one evening in June after the O-level examinations. When Sally saw the Morris Minor pulling up outside the gate she nearly fled, afraid the truth had come out about the night of the thirteenth. But Mr Milnar hadn't come because of that. He'd come because Frances had run away three nights before. Packed a rucksack of clothes and left. He asked Sally if she knew where Frances was, and Sally had said she didn't. Mr Milnar stared at Sally in a very penetrating way. A little too penetrating for Mr Hargreaves's liking. He asked Mr Milnar if he'd considered the possibility that Frances had run off with the maths teacher.

'It's unlikely,' Mr Milnar had snapped, 'since the maths teacher is still locked up in jail.'

Safiah came and served them tea before squatting, impish and giggling, in the corner of the room. Meekly, Sally asked Mr Milnar if Frances had been OK on the night of the rioting.

'She stayed in her room,' he said. 'I wanted us to evacuate to Merdeka Stadium but she locked the door and refused to come out.'

Leaving his tea to cool, Mr Milnar continued to interrogate Sally, who blushed and stammered and swore her ignorance. Mr Milnar then changed tack and begged Sally to let him know if she heard from Frances – a plea he would have repeated ad infinitum if Mr Hargreaves hadn't fibbed that they were about to have supper.

They saw Mr Milnar to the door, where he broke down, babbling his regret that he'd left Frances alone to sulk. Mr Hargreaves was embarrassed. He'd only met Mr Milnar once or twice before, at the Royal Selangor Club.

'Don't worry,' Mr Hargreaves said cheerily. 'She'll turn up before long with her tail between her legs! These teenagers often get silly ideas. Don't they, Petal?'

He rumpled Sally's hair, then excused himself – said he had a long-distance phone call to make. Sally watched from the living-room window as Mr Milnar got in his car. He sat for several minutes with his head bowed over the steering wheel before starting the ignition and driving away.

Pull yourself together, Sally thinks. *The boy didn't come here to hear you weep . . . Sentimental fool.* She smiles and pours more tea in Adam's cup. She asks after his sister. What's her name again? What does she do for a living? And what does Adam do? How very interesting . . . ! Two months have passed since she sent him the letter. What had she expected? For the truth of how the friendship ended to come flooding out? For the boy to sympathize? For the boy to unlatch the cage of her guilt so she could fly out and be free? Ridiculous. Sally has lived with her guilt for so long she'd be bereft without it.

Adam stays for two hours. Three cups of tea drained, half a packet of biscuits eaten and a few anecdotes of teenage hijinks divulged – Sally nattering on to keep the silence at bay. As they stand at the door Sally tells Adam that he is welcome back any time. Any time at all. She'd be delighted to see him. And Adam nods so as not to hurt her feelings. The front door closes and Adam is glad to be walking away. She's a nice woman and it was interesting to hear some stories about his mum. But her company had grown wearying after a while. The visit a waste of his time.

The curtains are drawn when he gets home, the muted TV casting out patterns of light, bathing the sofa bed where Julia sleeps in phosphorescence. He hangs his jacket on the back of the door and eases off his shoes. He lies beside his sister on the fold-out mattress, facing the serrated curve of her spine and the pale splash of her hair on the pillow. She wears a grey cotton T-shirt, the duvet over her hips rippled as a dune of sand. Adam realizes he has never known his sister as an adult. What will she be like when she is healthy again? When her personality and desires are no longer suppressed? What will Julia look like with flesh on her bones? He wonders if he'll ever know. If he is assisting her gradual recuperation or a slow and deliberate suicide.

Whatever his role, Adam is grateful for now that she's here in his flat. The safest place for her to be. He shuts his eyes and inclines his head so his forehead touches her back, willing her recovery through the cotton of her T-shirt and across the boundary of skin.

THE END

ACKNOWLEDGEMENTS

The research for this book would have been impossible without the help of the staff of the following organizations: the British Library, the London School of Oriental and African Studies, King's College Library, Queen Mary University Library, Senate House Library, the Institute of Commonwealth Studies, Royal Malaysian Police Museum, Odyssey Trust and Milton House.

Thanks to Vivian Smith of the Axe Street Project, Barking.

Thanks to Diana Francis of the University of Hertfordshire School of Life Sciences, for introducing me to the world of lab technicians.

Many thanks to the Arts Council of England.

Thanks to Jane Lawson, whose advice has made *The Orientalist and the Ghost* a much better book. Thanks to Eleanor Bradstreet, Daniel Septimus, Carole

Semaine, Marianne Velmans and John Saddler.

Thanks to my aunts Yoke Moy, Yoke Fong, Yoke Lan, Yoke Pau and Yoke Lin, and to the rest of my family in Malaysia. Thanks to my father for his constant help and support. Thanks to my mother and Carol.

Sayonara Bar

Susan Barker

'Dry humour and crisp observation . . . Japan has not, for a long time, been made to seem so accessible, or so remote'
LITERARY REVIEW

MARY, a blonde graduate from England, has drifted into a job in a hostess lounge in Osaka. She is employed by the enigmatic Mama-san to spend her evenings with rich Japanese salarymen, playing drinking games and taking turns in the karaoke booth. Mary is in love with Yuji, Mama-san's handsome son. But Yuji's loyalty is to the petty Yakuza gangster for whom he works.

Watanabe, the introverted cook, watches Mary from the kitchen. He exists in his own manga-fuelled fantasy of the fourth dimension, and believes he can see into other people's souls. When he perceives the danger of Mary's growing obsession with Yuji, he resolves to protect her whatever the cost.

Mr Sato works for the Daiwa Trading Corporation. Obsessive overwork cannot cure the emptiness of his solitary life. Lured against his will to the Sayonara Bar by his boss, he finds himself returning there to escape his dead wife's ghost.

'Highly original . . . a major achievement by an exciting new author' INDEPENDENT

'A stunningly eclectic debut. Original, often perplexing, always intriguing, *Sayonara Bar* is a showpiece of breathtaking new talent' DAILY RECORD

'New Author Susan Barker has set her edgy, sly debut in a hostess lounge' ELLE

'A beautifully written and far reaching exploration of Japanese culture' BOOKS OF THE YEAR, INDEPENDENT ON SUNDAY

978055277240

Madwoman on the Bridge
and other stories
Su Tong

'Restrained and merciless, Su Tong is a true literary talent'
ANCHEE MIN

SET DURING THE fall-out of the Cultural Revolution, these bizarre and delicate stories capture magnificently the collision of the old China of vanished dynasties, with communism and today's tiger economy.

The mad woman on the bridge wears a historical gown which she refuses to take off. In the height of summer, to the derision of the townspeople, she stands madly on the bridge. Until a young female doctor, bewitched by the beauty of the mad woman's dress, plots to take it from her, with tragic consequences.

From the folklorist who becomes the victim of his own rural research, to the doctor whose infertility treatment brings about the birth of a monster child, to a young thief who steals a red train only to have it stolen from him, Su Tong's stories are a scorching look at humanity.

'Su Tong writes beautiful, dangerous prose'
MEG WOLITZER

'Su Tong is an imaginative and skillful storyteller'
NEW YORK TIMES

'Overwhelming and imaginative virtuosity'
RICK MOODY

9780552774529